I0573947

Facts and Feelings

A Romance Novel

Farrah Colson

Copyright © 2025 by Farrah Colson

All rights reserved.

No part of this book may be reproduced in any form or by any electronic or mechanical means, including information storage and retrieval systems, without written permission from the author, except for the use of brief quotations in a book review.

Without in any way limiting the author's exclusive rights under copyright, any use of this publication to "train" generative artificial intelligence (AI) technologies to generate text is expressly prohibited. The author reserves all rights to license uses of this work.

This book is a work of fiction, created without the use of AI technology. Names, characters, organizations, places, events, and incidents are either products of the author's imagination or used fictitiously.

Author's Note

Dear Reader,

I cannot overstate my gratitude for what you've done for me by investing in this story. I am an indie author, and whether you are the only one who reads my book (or one of more), you are absolutely changing my life.

With that said, I hope you love Danny and Gracie like I do. Their hard-earned, slow-burn, soulmate-level Happy Ever After was a dream to write.

Please see a list of content warnings next, and always remember to protect your mental health first.

Thank you for supporting indie authors!

Love,
Farrah

Content Warnings:

On-page panic attacks, on-page speech difference (*sensitivity reader reviewed*), explicit sex scenes between consenting adults, explicit language, mentions of death of mother (breast cancer), on-page depiction of alcoholism (father; *sensitivity reader reviewed*), on-page depiction of depression, on-page abuse of a main character (father to daughter; *sensitivity reader reviewed*), on-page depiction of sexual harassment, off-page death of family dog (old age). For mature readers, 18+ only.

This story is told on a dual timeline, which includes flashback chapters to childhood years, between ages ten and eighteen.

For anyone waiting for "someday" to arrive.
There's no such thing as perfect timing.
Chase your goal until your soul stirs.

And if you've already tried and failed?

Well, that's what second chances are for.

Playlist

1. **Massachusetts** - Jensen McRae
2. **Bloodstream** - Soccer Mommy
3. **Look After You** - The Fray
4. **Safe and Sound** - Taylor Swift (feat. The Civil Wars)
5. **Pancakes for Dinner** - Lizzy McAlpine
6. **Backseat Rider** - Sara Kays
7. **2002** - Anne-Marie
8. **Hands Down** - Dashboard Confessional
9. **Forget-Me-Not** - Laufey
10. **You Could Start a Cult** - Niall Horan
11. **Breakeven** - The Script
12. **i wish you cheated.** - Alexander Stewart
13. **Jackie Kennedy** - Bahari
14. **Somewhere Only We Know** - Keane
15. **Adam's Ribs** - Jensen McRae
16. **It'll Be Okay** - Rachel Grae
17. **Picked First** - Sasha Alex Sloan
18. **see you later (ten years)** - Jenna Raine (feat. JVKE)

Chapter 1

Danny

Much like developing a random food intolerance in your thirties, losing is inevitable. It doesn't bother me as much as it used to, but playoff losses hit rookies especially hard. I'm pretty sure Castillo's trying not to cry.

"We'll get 'em next year, man." I pat his helmet a few times as we head toward the tunnel, where fans dressed in black and silver jerseys crowd against the railing. They're visibly freezing in the winter cold, risking frostbite for a high five, gloves, or maybe a pair of cleats if a player is feeling particularly generous. Instead of the usual buzz of excitement, there's only lukewarm chatter. I methodically start taking off my gloves, ready to hand one to a kid near the front wearing my number.

Then, without warning, I see *her*.

My vision is blurry, but I'm pretty sure I'd recognize Gracie Sinclair by her fingertips alone.

That third quarter tackle must have hit harder than I thought. I shake my head to etch-a-sketch the apparition away, but it doesn't work. She stands out, wearing a green and white

Florida Sharks sweatshirt and faded blue jeans. The clothes puzzle me for a moment before I remember we played her ride-or-die team today.

Gracie gives me a small wave and walks down the steps to the bars lining the top of the tunnel. God, she's breathtaking. Snowflakes decorate her hair, and I want to be close enough to watch each one melt. Seeing her again sparks a flurry of memories. Us at ten, fifteen, eighteen years old. Backyard creeks and school supplies, homecoming and Friday night lights.

The corners of her peachy lips point down into a small frown of worry as she takes notice of my current state. My heart gallops at a concerning pace. I haven't had a panic attack since I started therapy five years ago, but it's suddenly becoming harder to breathe.

I break eye contact, doing my best to focus on the techniques my therapist taught me before I spiral. I manage to take a deep breath and recite the steps in my head.

Three things I can see. Her curly, red hair. Her long legs. Her left eye, which is hazel, and her right eye, a mix of blue and purple. She always was self-conscious about her heterochromia, but the mere memory of her eyes has held me captive for years. I shake my head, attempting to regain my equilibrium and focus back on the exercise.

Three things I can smell. The crisp air. Spilled beer. And I swear I can smell coconut and vanilla, her perfume of choice since she got it for her thirteenth birthday.

Three things I can hear. The fans chattering, stadium announcements, and unfortunately, the ringing in my ears.

Accepting the noise, I slowly start to feel my heart rate come down.

My reaction is to be expected, I guess. That's probably normal when you haven't seen your best friend, and love of your life, in ten years.

"Hey, are you okay, DT?" the kid wearing my number asks, antsy for attention. I quickly reach up to give him my gloves, thank him for his support, and jog over to our stadium security guard.

"Hey, Joe!"

He claps my shoulder. "Tough game, but you did good out there."

"I appreciate it," I say absentmindedly, glancing at Gracie to make sure she hasn't disappeared. She fidgets with a few curls framing her face, pushing a couple of them behind her ears only to have them pop right back out again.

"So, what can I do for you, man?"

I gesture to Gracie. "See that girl over there? With the curly hair?"

"Yeah, she yours?"

I pause for only a moment before giving an emphatic, "Yes. That's my Gracie."

I should probably take it back. But, really, it's semantics at this point. Maybe I'm delusional. *Fuck*, I might be delusional. I'm already thinking of ways to hide this particular train of thought from my therapist.

Joe looks skeptical. "The one with the green and white shirt?"

I realize he's wondering why "my girl" lacks team spirit. I could get into the weeds of how stubborn my Gracie is, but it doesn't seem like the time. My main priority is making sure she doesn't evaporate into thin air. And if she does, my next priority will be figuring out how to get her back here.

An involuntary grin takes up half my face as I happily nod at Joe. "Yep, she's mine."

I ask him to make sure she goes over to the suite outside the locker room, then make my way back toward the fans. As I pass Gracie, I hold her gaze and mouth the same words from the field that I did after every high school game senior year. *"I'll see you after, Gracie girl?"*

I hold myself back from blowing the usual double kiss.

Her eyes go a little wide, but she nods. Once Joe walks over to her, I run with a little extra energy into the tunnel.

<h1 style="text-align:center">Chapter 2</h1>

——————

<h2 style="text-align:center">Grace</h2>

A smiling man the size of a small oak tree walks toward me in the stands. "Hi there! Gracie? I'm Joe. I'm supposed to take you back to the Family and Friends Suite."

My heartbeat rockets up, and I feel its pulse in my ears. "Oh, thank you. It's Grace, actually. But an escort really won't be necessary, I don't want to waste your time. I can just go out the front and wait."

"I can't recommend that, Miss. Even if I didn't have very specific instructions from Mr. Thompson to bring you to the suite, we take security precautions pretty seriously for wives and girlfriends, so—"

Heat rushes to my cheeks, and I start tapping my foot, a coping mechanism I learned after years of stuttering throughout childhood. "I'm not his girlfriend, or wife, actually. I'm a friend...erm, well we haven't talked in a while, so.... But don't worry, I'm not a stalker or anything. We grew up in Ohio together. I knew him as a kid, pretty well, so he knows me. We used to date. But now we don't. We're fine. Everything's fine."

Joe looks at me the way I look at hardware store employees: lost and confused.

I scan the sky, hoping to find an alien who can beam me up into space so I can avoid this conversation. "Um, sorry, actually yeah, it's totally fine for you to bring me back there. I'm sure he's busy anyway, so I might just end up leaving upon my arrival."

Upon my arrival? Really, Grace? Who am I, a Founding Father? I want to sound calm and collected, like the thirty-year-old woman I am. Instead, I sound like someone from the worst local improv group anyone's ever seen playing the part of Casual Adult Woman.

Joe tilts his head, blinks a few times, then finally nods. "Alrighty then. The elevator is on the right there."

I sigh as he keeps a close eye on me. I've made a terrible first impression on Joe. As a recovering people pleaser, I'm confident this interaction will haunt me at 3:00 a.m. two weeks from now.

He leads me into a spacious suite where other girls are waiting. Actually, "girls" is an incorrect descriptor; this group of women must be models. They're beautiful. The room is all lacquered lips, short jersey dresses, and spiked heels. Honestly, I'm taking notes.

Picking awkwardly at my nails, I do the only thing one does when in a new situation where you know no one—try to look Booked and Busy. My personality becomes walking around, touching random items and gesturing at things. Those heavy black curtains over there? *Fascinating.* I must touch them and feel the velvety fabric. The reflective silver cocktail table? *So sturdy—it can even hold my elbow!*

While acting like an absolute weirdo and flailing my hands directionally like some sort of muppet, one of the filtered-but-in-real-life models waves at me. I turn to look behind me—because surely she's not waving at *me*, a mere plebeian amidst a sea of queens—but there's no one there. Swiveling my head back around so fast I nearly pull a neck muscle, I make eye contact and wave back. She beckons me closer, and I walk at what I hope is a normal pace over to this gorgeous angel.

"Hi, I'm Grace!"

"Hey! I just wanted to tell you that the WAGS suite for the opposing team is down the hall to the left," she announces.

"Oh...I'm, I'm supposed to be here. The Security Man? The big one?" I raise my right hand as high as it can go above my head in an attempt to demonstrate his size. "I guess they all might be big. Okay. He's like, six four, curly brownish-gray hair, green eyes. Honestly, kind of cute for his age. Anyway, that man brought me here because I know a player."

"A player?"

I shift nervously, rocking back on my heels. "Yeah. Danny—erm, DT."

"You know DT?"

"We're old friends." Tugging on the sleeve of my sweatshirt, I mumble, "It's kind of a long story."

Her perfectly laminated eyebrows raise. "But you're wearing Florida Sharks colors."

"Ah, I can see how that's confusing. I'm wearing these colors because I like the Sharks. My mom was originally from Florida."

What is actually wrong with me? Am I having some sort of stroke? I should've never let Officer Oak Tree bring me to this place where average-looking people go to die.

Just as I start to formulate my explanation of the complicated twenty-year history I have with the team's starting wide receiver to this stunning and bewildered WAG, I hear a voice I've only heard on televised post-game interviews I couldn't avoid over the past ten years. His voice may be deeper, huskier now, but I would recognize it anywhere.

I slowly turn around and see a tall, grown man wearing a fitted gray suit and black loafers staring at me with familiar hazel eyes. His thick, black, wavy hair is longer on top of his head, tapering into a soft fade on the sides of his face. He's smiling his Big Danny Smile behind a neatly trimmed, short beard.

Looking closer, I check for the tiny gap between his two front teeth. He always wanted to bond them together, but I told him it gave him character in an otherwise stupidly perfect face. I'm happy to confirm he's kept it, despite the money and fame.

Shifting my gaze away from his mouth, I focus on the small, white scar near his temple, which he got from falling face first into the rocky creek behind our houses. We blamed Charger for that one, saying Danny chased after him when he saw a squirrel. In actuality, I bet Danny five dollars he couldn't make it across the creek without his shoes on.

I'm so lost in him, in the memory, that it takes his voice to pull me back to the present.

"Gracie?"

Chapter 3

Danny

God, it feels good to say her name. I want to say it again. So I do.

"Gracie."

Then I say it twice more in my head (*Gracie, Gracie*) while she adorably looks anywhere but my face for a full thirty seconds.

With her eyes elsewhere, I admire Gracie up close. She's as beautiful as ever. Her hair is tied back halfway with a green ribbon, matching her Sharks sweatshirt. Her fair complexion is still dotted with a smattering of light brown freckles. I search for any new ones since I last committed them to memory, recalling how I used to count them with my lips. Her legs look just as long and lean as before, but her hips are a little curvier than I remember. It takes everything in me not to groan in appreciation.

"Hey, Dan," she says, all serious.

Oof. *Dan.* She only ever called me that when we were arguing.

For now, I take a breath and choose not to address the whole

"Dan" atrocity. I'll save that conversation for later, if I secure a later.

"Did you enjoy the game?" I ask, with a fake frown, playing into her Very Serious mood.

"I'm sorry you lost," the little liar replies, her walls firmly present.

A smile takes over my whole face. My real smile. I probably look like a lunatic. It feels so foreign, grinning like this. After Gracie and I went our separate ways, I quickly learned how to fake my way through polite pleasantries with most people out of necessity.

"We both know you're not sorry," I toss back.

Her lips part in surprise with a small smile. Finally, a glimpse of my Gracie girl and not this "Susan from Accounting" persona she has going on.

"Yeah, I'm not." She glances down at her outfit. "For obvious reasons, I guess."

She's so cute, wearing her little frown and actively rooting against my success.

Gracie taps her sneaker-clad foot on the travertine floor of this massive luxury suite filled with friends of friends of friends of someone's friends, and all I can think about is how much she still looks like *mine*.

I grin, gesturing to her sweatshirt. "Still a Sharks fan, then?"

"Ride or die," she replies, her multicolored eyes a bit brighter and playful now.

She then seems to remember she's talking to her *former* best friend and *ex*-boyfriend, and those walls go right back up again. We both awkwardly stare at each other for a few moments, waiting for someone to break the silence. I do the honors.

"So, do you want to go for milkshakes? Or to my house?"

I snap my mouth shut in horror. *My house?* My therapist is really going to have a field day with this whole interaction. Dr.

Sheila Biddle and I have actually spoken at length about how a conversation might go in the event I were lucky enough to see Gracie again. I will regret to inform her that I'm using approximately zero of those techniques right now.

"I, uh, just meant my house for privacy reasons. It can be hard for me to go out around here without being noticed." Shit, that sounded so cocky. I look at the floor—I never could control the way my words come out around Gracie.

After a few beats, I meet her eyes, and I'm surprised to find amusement on her face. I hold my breath while I wait for an answer.

"Sure, Dan."

"Danny," I mutter grumpily.

"I took the E train straight from the airport, but we can go to your house, I g—"

"Great! Let's go. Now," I interject like someone with absolutely no impulse control. I'm clearly suffering side effects from being tackled. I just never thought I'd see her here of all places. Nothing can bring me down, not even her adorable moody ass.

"DT! Hey, man." Freshly showered and dressed in his postgame suit, Kendric, our kicker, walks down the opposite end of the hallway as Gracie and I leave the suite. "Who's the—"

"Talk to you later, Ken!" I cheerily interrupt, not letting anyone or anything distract me from Gracie.

I usher her toward my red G-wagon as we walk out of the facility, gesturing at my vehicle like I'm a model on a game show and it's the grand prize. The luxury car gods are clearly smiling down upon me, because I just had it detailed this past weekend. Usually, there's at least two old protein shakes in the cupholders, coupons that probably expired when MTV still played music videos, and loose change scattered on the floor like confetti.

An unfamiliar security guard narrows his eyes at me, and I

realize what this must look like. Me, a giant man, looking maniacally happy while shepherding a frighteningly beautiful, yet hesitant-looking woman to my car. I want to say it's not what it looks like, but it's exactly what it looks like.

I give him a small, friendly wave that I hope says "I know we've never met, but I'm a nice guy and this woman is here willfully, Officer." He continues watching me like a hawk, so I don't think I was successful, but at least we've finally reached my car. I grab Gracie's clear backpack and place it in the back seat. Then, I walk around to the passenger side and open the door for her.

As she climbs in, I catch a glimpse of my face in the side mirror. Holy shit. If I went to open a bank account right now, they'd turn me away. My smile looks borderline deranged. *Is this what ten years of longing does to a man?*

I quickly glance at the security guard again. He's still watching, and now I appear even more suspicious for double-checking he's there. Dragging a hand down my face in resignation, I hurry into the car before he calls the police.

As I reverse out of the parking space and look over my shoulder, Gracie turns to face me. In this position, we are instantly, extraordinarily, wonderfully close. I give a small smile and sigh. She rears back so fast her skull almost smacks the passenger window.

Her hesitant voice echoes in the car as she faces me once more, this time from a short distance. "You're probably wondering why—"

"You cold?" I interrupt and reach for the temperature dial.

"Um, I think I'm okay. If you're looking for a reason as to why I'm—"

"This car has an advanced climate control system. It has multi-zone temperature settings and heated seats. The seats actually have six settings, rather than the usual three, so you can go from, like, a light warmth to burn-your-ass-off if you so desire. Not that anyone would want to burn their ass off, especially your ass. Ope." *What in the hell am I saying right now?* I didn't even make it one hour before I brought up Gracie's ass.

I venture a look over and see that she's avoiding eye contact and looking straight out the passenger window. *Smart.*

"Sorry about that. Safety is important, so actually, it's probably not good that the seat heat goes up that high. I should, um, bring that up the next time I go to the car dealership or something." I try to switch the subject. "Radio preferences?"

Gracie makes an unintelligible noise, seemingly pausing her attempts to tell me why she's here. Truthfully, I don't want to hear it; I'm gravely worried she'll disappear for another ten years as soon as she accomplishes whatever she came here to do.

I turn the dial to a general pop/rock radio channel with inoffensive music, the kind that plays at the dentist during a root canal. Without knowing if she's still into emo punk, this is the safest option.

She stares straight out the front window and wordlessly twirls her hair. Given everything that's occurred, I count it as a win and turn up the heat.

Chapter 4

Grace

Danny is blasting the multi-zone heat on full power. I keep turning up whatever soft rock is on the radio in an attempt to drown out the cabin air settings, and now...well, it's so loud in here. It's like I'm trapped in a hot elevator with the Red Hot Chili Peppers screaming *Californication* directly into my ears. It's not even their best work.

I'd rather have my entire patient list consist of only tiny chihuahuas than be in this car for another minute. I check the time again. Was he lying when he said he lived in New York? I'm almost positive we've been in this car for eleven billion hours.

Danny, meanwhile, is driving under the speed limit. Under. The. Speed. Limit. In New York City! Is he trying to get me murdered by a road warrior? Is this revenge? He keeps glancing over, checking on me, as if I will fall out of my seat and tumble into the East River.

Danny coughs loudly, like he's trying to get my attention, but I'm too distracted by other things. Namely, his hands, which are on ten and two like a teen driver taking the practical part of their licensing exam. He was nowhere *near* this cautious growing up. Danny was such a wild driver that pedestrians would've been better off walking in the middle of the street when he was on the road. In cars with good drivers, the stereo dash has the most wear and tear. In Danny's car, the "Oh Shit!" ceiling handle was hanging on by a thread, covered in my claw marks. I smile and think about how his mom gave him an angel figurine to keep in his car, like that would save him from himself.

"Hey, how's Janie?" I ask him.

Danny holds his hand up to his ear. "WHAT? I CAN'T HEAR YOU!"

"How is YOUR MOM?" I yell, before realizing he's messing with me. Oh, fuck him.

He smirks and ever so slightly turns down the volume knob. "She has a son in the league who pays for all of her premium movie streaming services, how do you think she's doing?"

A genuine smile spreads across my face. "Janie always did love watching the same rom-com in different fonts. Which Christmas movie was her favorite this year? Was it the one where the city boy ditched his successful fiancée to go head up his family's cookie factory in the middle of nowhere? Or was it the one where the city *girl* ditched *her* successful fiancé to go head up *her* family's cookie factory in the middle of nowhere?"

Danny's laugh booms over both the Chili Peppers and the hurricane winds from the cabin air. "I think the latter. She went back to my sister's before the final whistle to avoid traffic. I'm not typically in the mood to socialize after a losing game. But she'll be over tomorrow morning."

He sighs. "So, am I allowed to turn down the radio now, or am I suffering the rest of this trip?"

I scoff as he lowers the volume. "Oh, *you're* suffering?" Tugging on the neck of my sweatshirt, I swipe a bead of sweat trickling down from my hairline. "A chicken could lay an omelet in here."

He raises an eyebrow. "Wow. I'm sorry for being *too* considerate, Gracie. In case you aren't aware, it's snowing outside. You're not even wearing a coat. It's like you're asking for hypothermia."

"What I'm asking for is to evacuate this car," I mutter.

"Besides," he continues, "it's nice and toasty in here."

"I feel like I *am* a piece of toast right now, Danny."

Shit. We pull up to a red light and he turns to face me. Pure joy flashes across his face, eyes sparkling with delight.

"Don't be weird about it," I groan.

"What do you mean? Me, *Danny*, be weird about what?" He grins like he just won Offensive Player of the Year. "If anyone's weird, it's you, Gracie."

I let out a big breath and focus on the miniscule gap between his two front teeth that he can't stop flashing. This man is happy to see me.

If he thinks it's strange that I showed up after ten years of mutual silence without warning, he doesn't show it. In fact, he cuts me off every time I try to mention it. In a way, it's almost like he had prepared for it somehow.

Danny may want to catch up like old times, but I'm here for one reason only: to deliver the crumpled letter currently burning a hole in my pocket.

<h1 style="text-align:center">Chapter 5</h1>

<h1 style="text-align:center">Grace</h1>

Ten Years Old

The petoskey stone in my denim jumper pocket bounces up and down as I try to keep up with Danny.

"Keep up or keep out, Susannah Sinclair!"

"Stop running so fast. And d-don't call me Susannah!"

"If you want to be the greatest in the world like I do, you have to put in the work, Suze!" Danny calls as he disappears into the woods behind our houses, beelining toward our special spot.

I would follow him anywhere, and I do. My jelly sandals kick up dirt as I pick up my pace and try to hide the pain I feel in my ribs.

"Quit it with the S name! I'm keeping Charger company." I throw an affectionate smile to the chocolate labrador trailing leisurely behind me. Danny slows his pace, and I catch up to walk beside him.

"Okay, okay, Gracie. You know I like messing with you sometimes." He grins. When Danny smiles, really smiles, he does it with his whole face.

He's the only person in the whole world who calls me by my middle name, Grace. *I love it.* Mama wanted it to be my first name, but she compromised with Dad on Susannah when I was born.

"I'll kick your b-b-butt!" I puff out a frustrated breath, blowing one of my red curls away from my face. I hate my stutter.

"Gracie, slow down. It gets worse when you talk too fast."

Ever since Mama went to Heaven last year, I can't seem to control the way my words come out. My stutter bothers Dad. I think it reminds him that she's gone. But when he gets angry at my stumbles, I end up stuttering even more. Sometimes I go days without talking, just so he won't get mad.

Dad doesn't seem to notice.

Danny holds up three fingers and wiggles them near my mouth. "Take a deep breath and blow out the candles."

I smile softly and lean forward, breathing in through my nose before blowing on his hand. He puts two fingers down, but keeps wiggling his pointer finger with a mischievous look. I take another deep breath and lean closer, blowing a stronger gust of air on the remaining finger. He swiftly puts it down.

He always knows exactly what to do to make me feel better.

I can't help my grin. "You're my favorite."

He tosses the football he brought into the air and catches it. "And the New York Mustangs are the best team in the league!"

"Huh?"

"I thought we were saying obvious things. Duh, I'm your favorite. I'm kind of amazing." He gives my shoulder a gentle shove.

I try not to wince.

We finally get to our special spot, a partially shaded open space surrounded by trees. The cold water creek where we skip stones babbles behind the tall grass. Charger ambles to the shore, hunting for the perfect stick.

Danny picks up a twig and tosses it toward Charger. "Do you wanna eat at my house for lunch? Tessa's still being picky, so it'll probably just be peanut butter and—"

"Yes."

Danny laughs. "That was fast."

His mom could be serving a plate of rocks sprinkled with dirt and I'd still want to go to his house.

We sit on our log in comfortable silence for a while, playing fetch with Charger and relaxing under the hot Ohio sun. I scoot under the tree so my fair skin doesn't burn. With his light brown skin and dark features, Danny never burns.

He breaks the silence first, throwing the football in the air again. "Hey, Gracie, have you thought any more about what you wanna be when you grow up?"

I shrug. "I don't know. Probably something with animals." Animals love you no matter what, just like how Danny loves me. He doesn't care about my stutter.

Doing my best to act normal, I turn up the volume of the boombox Danny brought with him, even though I don't like the Goo Goo Dolls. Charger pays me extra attention, whining if I move too far away from him and nuzzling my leg.

"Gracie?"

My oversized T-shirt pools on the ground when I kneel down to give Charger a belly rub. Even though I'm right-handed, I pet him with my left, trying to hide my grimace of pain.

"Gracie? Are you listening to me?"

I look up through the curls curtaining my face. "Hmm? What did you say?"

"Okay, that's it. What's going on with you?"

"What d-do you mean?" Curling inward, I wrap my arms around my waist.

"Let's see. You've been quiet all morning, you didn't even care about the type of music on the boombox, you keep petting Charger with your left hand and wincing when you barely move your body. And, most of all, you're stuttering. Are you okay?"

My eyes mist over and a tear trickles out. Danny watches it roll down my face, his eyes wide. I think the last time I cried was at Mama's funeral a year ago.

"Gracie," he pleads frantically. "Tell me what's wrong so I can fix it. I hate it when you cry. Should I get my mom?"

"No. No, d-don't get your mom," I say quickly as I stand up straight. "I'm sorry, it's nothing really."

He takes a small step toward me, his eyes searching mine like he's trying to find the truth. "You're lying. I can tell. You're biting the inside of your cheek."

At this moment, I wish he didn't know me better than anyone. I hesitate before whispering, "If I t-tell you, you have t-to promise not t-to t-tell anyone."

"Okay..."

"I mean it, Danny. No one can know."

Nodding, he gives me a shaky smile. He has no idea what he's just agreed to.

"You know how my d-dad has b-been d-drinking more. Well, he came home last night really d-drunk, and...and angry. I forgot t-to t-take the wet clothes out of the washer and, well. Well, he...he..." I struggle to get the final words out.

Danny's eyes scan my body, looking for visible injuries. He won't find one—the bruises are underneath my shirt. "Did he... hurt you?"

He waits for me to tell him that he's crazy, but my correction never comes. Bile rises in my throat.

"Gracie?" he says hoarsely.

"Danny," I whisper back.

"Tell me. Tell me everything."

Chapter 6

Danny

Everything in me is buzzing with nervous energy as we finally make our way into residential Williamsburg.

Gracie sits up higher in her seat, peering out the passenger side window at the passing brownstones. "This is a pretty fancy neighborhood you've got here, Thompson."

I inwardly groan. *What will it take for this grumpy, precious woman to call me by my Gracie-given name again?*

"Oh yeah, well. Gotta spend the money on something, you know?"

I immediately cringe. What I'm not saying is that I have no one in my life to spend the money on. I try to spoil my mom, but she only wants streaming subscriptions and airline tickets to see me play. My sister, Tessa, is more agreeable to receiving gifts. Like any twenty-something who goes through frequent heartbreak, she loves to partake in therapy, both psychological and retail. She lets me buy her things when we go shopping together, but those afternoons are more about the company than the cost—which is negligible in the grand scheme of things.

To Gracie, it might seem like I have everything, but I have

little-to-nothing of what I really want. Might as well live somewhere nice.

"I know you took the train to the stadium, but do you have a rental car? Where are you staying?" A horrendous thought occurs to me, and my stomach bottoms out. In my delusional state, I never considered the possibility that she... "Are you here *with* someone?" I blurt, before glancing at her ring finger and finding it blissfully empty. My limbs feel looser as I sigh in relief.

Gracie throws me a look of pity, seeing right through my line of questioning. "No rental car. The subway was the only option that would get me there on time. I was in a hurry to leave Ohio, and booking ahead slipped my mind. I'll just grab a nearby hotel for the night before I fly back home tomorrow evening. You can drop me off at the closest subway station by your house after we're done here, and I'll wait there for the next...what?"

I narrow my eyes at her scrunched up face and turn the radio off entirely. "Gracie. I know it's been years since we last saw each other, but some things never change. Leaving you at a subway station isn't an option." I blow out a frustrated breath, barreling through. "Plus, if you don't have a hotel yet, you can stay with me for the night. Hotels in the city are expensive, especially this time of year. New York is very popular in the winter. I don't know if you've heard of them, but there's these, like, famous dancers—the Rockettes, and of course the Rockefeller tree, and tons of tourists come..."

Gracie cuts me with a doozy of a look. I sigh with fondness and familiarity. I've missed *all* her looks.

"Believe it or not, I have indeed heard of the Rockettes," she tells me dryly. "And I have enough money for a hotel, Dan."

And we're back to *Dan*. Call me the opposite of Neil Armstrong, because I'm taking neither steps nor leaps.

"Of course you do, but you'll probably have a hard time finding one that's available right now."

She worries her bottom lip. "Maybe. We haven't hung out in forever, though... You don't think it'll be weird?"

The ten years of silence sits between us like a concrete wall. I decide to bulldoze right through it. Back then, I didn't want to derail her from vet school. Now, it's different. She's here, and I can't miss my opportunity.

"No. It's definitely, totally, one hundred percent normal to hang out after ten years," I say, wishing I could call Dr. Biddle to confirm. "If that's not a good enough reason, stay with me because I want you to. I have so much space. You probably won't even see me."

It's a miracle I refrain from gagging on all these lies spewing out of my mouth. Of course Gracie will see me. She knows that. I know that. Ms. Marsha, my neighbor three houses down, knows that. But desperate times call for desperate persuasive tactics to convince her to stay.

"Plus, Mom is coming by for brunch tomorrow, and she would absolutely love to see you." My mom was in Gracie's very small "safe space" circle growing up.

"You can ask her the favorite television movie question you asked me directly. You'll get to hear it from the horse's mouth. Doesn't that sound exciting? To hear directly from the horse's mouth? You know, with the horse being my mother."

Wishing I hadn't said the word "horse" multiple times, I sigh and stare straight out the windshield. It's a low blow, using my mom as a pawn to convince her to stay, but what is a flawed man who just ran into the love of his life to do?

She slowly exhales. "Exhilarating."

I pause. "*So?*"

"I *would* love to see Janie," she muses, "and we do have a lot to catch up on. I'm also kind of hungry."

Of course she is. I'm pretty sure she invented the word *hangry*. I, on the other hand, have been so distracted by Gracie I've lost all hunger cues. But I won't risk turning around for food. I'm afraid she'll exit this car to get a sandwich and never come back. Not that I want to trap her. Except...I do want to trap her. Forever.

Inwardly, I choose to move past that concerning thought.

We don't really have time to go back out, anyway. It's getting late and traffic is worsening by the New York minute. It doesn't help that I'm driving this car like I'm bringing up the rear of a funeral procession.

When we finally pull into my heated garage, I turn off the ignition and face Gracie, who is still fiddling with her seat controls.

"Do you want me to order burgers and milkshakes for us? The delivery folks are usually pretty speedy to this neighborhood."

Gracie must be starving, because she easily agrees. "That'd honestly be great."

Finally, a win. I should've started with food in the first place. A rookie mistake I won't make twice. I unlock my phone and open the delivery app.

Gracie starts telling me her order. "I'll have a burger, hold the—"

"—pickles, add extra caramelized onions, substitute shredded lettuce for leaves of lettuce. And I got sides of BBQ sauce and mustard so you can mix them on top of the patty, like a psychopath."

She blinks slowly.

I raise an eyebrow. "Did you really think I'd forget your hyper-specific burger order?" After eating at our hometown diner with her so many times, I couldn't forget her order if I tried. It's like the *Fifty States That Rhyme* song. Useless, except in very specific situations.

Her eyes widen with surprise. "No, I'm just... Wow. You have a great memory."

"I remember everything when it comes to us, Gracie."

As her jaw ever-so-slightly drops, I realize I might've over-shared. But it's true. I remember all of it, all of us. The something, the everything, the nothing. The good and the bad.

It's nearly impossible for me to forget the bad.

Chapter 7

Danny

Fourteen Years Old

"Um, D-D-Danny? Is this a b-bad time? Over."

I'm lying in bed, staring at my ceiling, when her voice comes through on the walkie-talkie. I can tell immediately by her tone that her dad has been drinking again. Gracie only stutters when she's nervous or rushed, but she never stutters while saying my name. It takes me two seconds to fly out of bed and pull my jeans over my plaid boxers. I grab the walkie-talkie off my nightstand and press the Talk button.

"Gracie, you okay? Over."

"Yeah, I'm fine. Not t-too b-bad, b-but d-do you mind b-bringing an ice pack with you? Uh, over."

Rage bubbles up through my body. If she's asking for an ice pack, that means he left a visible mark on her. I clench my fists and then immediately unclench them. The last thing Gracie needs is another angry guy in her life. I check the clock on my dresser—10:00 p.m. It's Thursday, so her dad must've gotten home early from the bar. *Shit.*

I quietly sneak down to the kitchen and grab an ice pack out of the freezer before heading back upstairs. Carefully opening my second-floor bedroom window, I climb down the drain pipe on the side of our house. As soon as I hit my lawn, I run across the grass to Gracie's house. I push through the bushes outside her first floor window and impatiently tap on the glass.

Tap. Tap. Tap. Tap.

Four times makes up our code. Gracie appears at the window, and... *Jesus.* It's worse than I expected. The right side of her face near her temple is swollen, a small bump forming.

"Why d-do you still knock on the window? I always leave it unlocked for you."

"Force of habit, Gracie. Now let me see."

She backs up near her dresser so I have more room to get through. I take off my shoe and hand it to her before ducking my head and side-stepping into her room on one leg. Then, I bring my other leg in through the window and hover it above the floor before giving that shoe to Gracie. She sets both of my shoes on a plastic garbage bag she keeps on the floor near the window. It's a dance we've done for years.

The first incident was four years ago. After Gracie suffered bruised ribs from being dragged down the hallway to her room in a drunken rage, her dad was extremely apologetic. He blamed his behavior on the alcohol and said it wouldn't happen again.

It kept happening, but he stopped apologizing.

"It wasn't really b-bad this t-time, I promise. I'm fine." She nervously taps her foot on the shaggy pink rug beneath her window. Even in the dim light, a sheen coats her eyes, the purple-tinted iris looking especially blue.

"Don't lie to me, Gracie. Never to me." I put a finger under her chin and gently tilt her face toward the lamp for a better look. Blood pools beneath her pale skin, giving it a bluish tint. Lightly brushing my thumb just below her injury, I force myself not to dwell on the bruising. "What happened here?"

"He came home early t-today. He was upset that the b-bartender cut him off again. When he got here, I was watching t-television and eating some soup I made. He startled me b-by shouting, and I d-drop, d-dropped the soup on the carpet. So, at least I get why he was angry this t-time."

"Right, because accidentally spilling some soup warrants a backhand to your face," I bite out, waves of anger radiating off of my body.

"It wasn't a b-backhand, actually," she whispers. "He t-tried t-to pull me b-by my ponytail from the living room t-to the kitchen so I could 'clean it up faster,' and when he reached for me, his hand roughed up my face a b-bit."

I stare at her, feeling helpless and sad. "Why won't you let me protect you? I'm bigger and stronger now with all my football training."

Gracie crosses her arms across her chest in obvious frustration. "D-Don't b-be ridiculous. I'm not going t-to let my d-drunk d-dad, who's already passed out on the couch, ruin your future." She huffs. "He's not worth it."

"Then why can't we report him? You could live at our house. My mom and sister love you. We're already next door. It'd be easy."

"We b-both know that's not how the system works. I'd go into foster care and never see you again."

I blow a frustrated raspberry through my lips. "Then what about Grandma Mae?"

Gracie hasn't seen her maternal grandmother since her mother died of cancer five years ago. It's not that Mae doesn't want to see her; it's just that she lives in Florida and has a hard time flying. Gracie refuses to tell her anything negative about her home life during their weekly phone conversations, so Mae stays completely in the dark about her situation.

Her dad wasn't always like this. He was a serious guy, sure, but soft with her mom. When she passed away, it was like he purposely started sinking the ship. His drinking went from twice a week to twice a day in the blink of an eye. Gracie can say what she wants, but I know she still believes that it's *just the beer* and he *doesn't know what he's doing*. I worry she doesn't speak up because she misses who he used to be. It's difficult for her to see past the good memories, especially since it's just her and her dad now.

"I was thinking about asking Mae t-to come, but I'm worried that if she knows, she'll move me t-to Florida." Her voice wavers, quivering in her throat as her body trembles.

Gracie's words give me pause. I don't know what I would do without her. It may be selfish of me to want her close, but losing her would be like losing a part of myself.

I feel powerless as I pull her into a tight hug, rubbing her back in small circles like Mom does to me when I'm sick. I know it's not a cure, but she relaxes against me and her tears slow to a stop. Leaning back slightly, I take the small ice pack I brought from my house out of my pocket. I gently bring it to her temple and hold it there with the lightest amount of pressure.

After a few moments, Gracie pulls back. "Ah, that gets freezing fast."

I lean in and blow some hot air over her cold skin, my lips lingering close to her hairline a little longer than necessary. Things have been different between us lately. I've been… noticing her more. Gracie is smart and pretty, but she's also thoughtful and kind to everyone.

As soon as those thoughts bubble up, I shove them back down. She doesn't need me to change the dynamic between us. She needs me as a friend. A trusted best friend.

Gracie's wild curls are sticking to her cheeks, her salty tears acting as glue. She gingerly pulls her hair back into a ponytail, giving me a quick view of five raw, red scratches down her neck.

I rub my eyes and drag my hand down my face. It looks like maybe an entire curl was pulled out of her head. Taking a deep breath to temper the anger stewing inside of me, I grab a tissue on her desk and gently wipe away some blood that hasn't quite dried yet.

"Time for bed," I grit out. We both get under the covers with our clothes on and turn toward each other. I can tell she's still reeling. I wrack my mind for things I can do to make her feel even a tiny bit better.

"Fact for a feeling, Gracie girl?" I ask, initiating our favorite game.

"Oh, um, let me think."

Watching the wheels turn in that beautiful, big brain of hers might be my favorite part of playing Facts and Feelings with Gracie.

"Okay, I got one."

I rub my hands together. "I'm on the edge of my seat."

She sniffles, but a small grin tugs at her lips. "Sea otters hold hands while they sleep so they d-don't d-drift away from each other."

Gracie waits for my reaction, probably expecting me to say something playful back.

But all I say tonight is "interesting" and move to grasp her hand under the covers. Her fingers are freezing. I lace mine through hers and gently rub her thumb back and forth.

We lie there, holding hands in silence. I try to wind us down by counting each neon green plastic star on her ceiling out loud. Several minutes pass, and she snuggles closer to me for warmth. A flurry of fizzy bubbles pop in my stomach, one after another. She yawns, and my eyes feel heavy.

"Wait. What was your feeling, Danny?"

I breathe in slowly, then release a heavy sigh. "I'm feeling like I hate your dad."

She releases a soft gasp. "Oh."

I turn off the lamp on the nightstand closest to me without letting go of her hand.

"Night, Gracie Girl. Love you."

"Night, Danny Boy. Love you, too."

And when her alarm goes off early the next morning, we're still holding hands like otters. I take in my surroundings and yawn. In the morning light, things don't seem so scary. And I'm somewhere I always want to be. With Gracie.

Chapter 8

Grace

I'm somewhere I never thought I'd be: Danny's very grown up, very gigantic house.

Agreeing to come back to Danny's house after ten years of silence was an...*interesting choice* for me. Compared to previous interesting choices I've made, I put this one in between my fedora phase and saying "cool beans" unironically.

The outside boasts three stories of brown brick. It has two tall windows on either side of the double-entry door. The inside is modern, airy, and spacious with high ceilings in the foyer. Every visible wall is painted the color of oatmeal, a sharp contrast to the rich colors in his childhood home. I wander into the massive open-concept kitchen, staring at its white marble countertops, high-tech fridge, and professional oven. Danny never used to cook, but surely he uses this fancy kitchen in some capacity.

My curiosity gets the better of me. I gesture to the magazine-worthy space and cannot help but ask him, "When did you stop eating s'mores-flavored toaster pastries for breakfast every day?"

Danny has the decency to look sheepish as he walks over to

the other side of the kitchen. He slowly opens a cupboard above the fridge, revealing what can only be described as a doomsday prepper amount of s'mores flavored toaster pastries.

"Let me get this straight. You have a chef's kitchen with a robot refrigerator and *still* haven't taken the time to learn how to cook?"

He rolls his eyes. "It's not a robot fridge, Gracie."

I squint at his spaceship fridge, which I'm pretty sure NASA used as a prototype for the Mars Rover. "Danny, this fridge has a calculator. It does math."

"It's a scale and basic unit measurements!"

I think he's getting genuinely frustrated now, and I can't help but giggle. I forgot how much I enjoy teasing him. "Don't come crying to me when it kills you in the middle of the night. It's not my fault that you welcomed the second generation of AI into your home."

He blows out an exasperated breath. "If it could kill me, I'd already be dead."

The doorbell rings and Danny leaves to get the food. I pat my pocket twice to make sure the letter hasn't vanished and try to keep my nerves in check.

A few minutes later, he returns with two large brown paper bags of food and sets them on the island. I take a seat at the dining room table, which is extraordinarily long, with seven chairs on either side and then one at each end. It looks like a place where villains might gather to scheme their world domination. Scrutinizing the natural wood, I can't help but wonder if they cut down an entire tree just for this table like that one celebrity in a magazine article I read. This train of thought leads me to think about what animals were in the tree when they cut it down and if they found a new habitat.

"It's reclaimed wood." Danny's voice cuts through my thought spiral. He's been closely studying my expressions ever since I stepped foot inside his house. "Did you really think that I would ever commission custom wood from a freshly chopped forest tree when there could be a little squirrel family in there? The Oak Mural Incident of 2002 is forever burned into my brain."

"School administrations can't just cut down a tree in the woods behind the building with no regards to wildlife, Danny. You saw the bunnies in the burrow with your own eyes. *Someone* had to call the Ohio Department of Natural Resources' Division of Forestry." I lift my chin and huff. "I was the only one brave enough to do it."

"Of course, Gracie. I, too, was shocked and appalled at the thought of unhoused bunnies. And actually, if I'm not mistaken, you still hold the title of America's Youngest Whistleblower," he teases, winding me up in a way only he can.

His lopsided grin grows wider, and the mischievous glint in his eyes is the same one that bet me a milkshake he'd only moonwalk for an entire Saturday. The corners of my lips tick up, remembering how quickly he lost the bet (hard to backslide up the stairs). His logic, while playful, wasn't always sound. A dull ache, the one that formed ten years ago when we separated, pangs in my stomach. *God, I've missed this.*

I give my head a quick shake, refocusing on the topic at hand. "Regardless, I'm glad you used reclaimed wood for this excessively giant table where you...host mafia families?"

The little space between his teeth makes an appearance. "Try again."

"The Original Broadway Cast of Hamilton meets here for book club on Fridays?"

His smile reaches his ears. "Nope."

"A coven of vampires gather to talk baseball strategy?"

Danny presses his lips together, trying not to laugh. "No, that's not it."

"I'm all out of guesses."

He nods solemnly. "Sure, that *was* an exhaustive list, what with the cast of Hamilton and the vampire baseball."

"Don't forget the mafia."

"Right, the mafia," he muses, his eyes bright. "It's usually just me in here. And I sit over there." He gestures at the rectangular marble kitchen island with two stools on either side. "You good with us eating dinner there now, or should we continue to hash out how well-endowed my dining room table is?"

I ignore *that* comment, hoping the flustered feeling won't translate into a blush. Considering my stomach and the contents of this conversation, I walk over to the island. "I *am* hungry. Shockingly enough, the pint of neon orange nacho cheese I consumed at the game didn't manage to stick to my ribs."

"Dinner it is." Danny claps his hands together.

He moves around the kitchen grabbing plates, cups, and napkins before opening the bags. After Danny hands me my burger, he starts picking up fries from his plate and adding them to mine.

Shaking my head, I put a few fries back on his plate. "If I wanted fries, I would've ordered them."

"Stop kidding yourself, Gracie. Your subconscious and I both know you'll be eating my fries."

"Maybe I've changed," I protest.

He stops mid-fry and raises an eyebrow. "Okay, have you?"

"Is there ketchup?"

He nods, looking exceedingly happy with himself.

I roll my eyes and daintily pop a fry in my mouth.

Chapter 9

Danny

"So, how are you?" I ask, while she stuffs her face full of my fries she didn't want.

"*How are you?*" she echoes incredulously, a tiny piece of potato falling from her lips.

Bewitching, my Gracie girl. A fry predator, but bewitching nonetheless.

"How...are you?" I parrot.

She stops chewing. "What are you doing?"

"Sorry, I thought we were repeating each other for the bit you started." I shrug and take a sip of my pop. "I've got to be honest, it's not my favorite bit we've done."

Gracie rolls those angelic, multicolored eyes at me and takes a sip of ginger ale. Ginger ale is her favorite pop. It's also something I didn't know existed outside of airplanes until I saw her chugging a can of it freshman year of high school.

"I'm simply wondering why that's the first question you're going with," she explains, like an alternative is obvious.

"Which question *should* I be going with?"

She raises an eyebrow. "I don't know, maybe 'why are you here after ten years?'"

I roll my shoulders back to release some tension. "I'm just happy you're here. Does it matter why?"

Her eyes widen. "Excuse me?"

Exhausted from the back and forth, I rub the back of my neck. It's clear that we're at odds with our goals. Gracie, who wants to do whatever she came to do and leave again, and me, who is desperately clinging to the hope that she might stay for more than one night.

My chest rises on a deep breath. "Honestly, Gracie, I don't care *why* you're here. Just that you are."

"Well, that's not really—"

"I'm grateful for whatever force of nature or string of decisions that brought you here, more grateful than you know."

A flicker of sadness flashes in her eyes before she takes another bite of her burger.

Focusing on the steady rhythm of my heartbeat, I add, "But now that you *are* here, all I want to know is, well, everything about you. In painstaking detail. I want to know all of it."

She chews thoughtfully. "I guess it couldn't hurt, catching up. You know, while I'm here. Just for the night."

"Exactly. Now you're getting it." I nod, a little too eagerly.

I know there's plenty between us to overcome. But our friendship was always something special, something *more*. By the time we were eighteen years old, we'd faced more hardships than most do in their entire lives. And we faced them together. We can get there again—I just need time to prove that to her.

It only takes about ten minutes for Gracie to eat all the fries and most of her burger. She takes a slow sip of ginger ale, and her eyes wander. I've been cataloging her bland reactions to the interior of my house. She doesn't appear excited by my "accessible beige" walls. I haven't taken her on a house tour yet, but I know this woman has the patience of a toddler in an ice cream shop. Now that her plate is clean, she starts swinging her feet back and forth and tapping them softly against the island.

Grinning at her restlessness, I decide to put her out of her misery. "Do you want me to show you around, Gracie?"

"Obviously."

And with that, she walks out of the kitchen. To give me a tour of my house, apparently.

We make our way to the sunroom first. Next, we visit the laundry room and then the game room. I stay close to her side, shadowing her as she tests out the no-touch sink in both of the first floor bathrooms.

"I feel like I'm trying to pass a home inspection right now," I joke.

"You'll need to pass a health inspection if you keep hovering," she retorts.

I dramatically place a hand over my heart. "Oh, I'm *so sorry* to disrupt your forensic sweep of my home."

Gracie avoids eye contact with me, but her lips turn up as she continues to weave in and out of each room.

She pauses before we meander upstairs to check out the guest bedrooms. "You know, this place could do with a little personality."

"What I missed most about you, Gracie, is the way you were always so subtle with me," I tease.

The truth is, she was only bold with me. If teachers or classmates were asked to describe Gracie, I have no doubt they would have said "shy" or introverted. Neither of those terms apply to the girl I know. If she was quiet, it was out of necessity. She was constantly assessing who was safe and who would make fun of her for something out of her control. The list of people she fully trusted growing up was limited. Me, my little sister, Mae, my mom. Later, Ben. And regardless of what she said when she ended things with me, I never took that trust lightly.

"In all seriousness, you can take as much time as you'd like touring this place." I slow my pace. Gracie slows down, too, as she approaches the last guest room, the one she'll be staying in. After years of trailing each other around, I know better than to rush her. Hurrying Gracie only ever triggered her stutter. Questions I don't have the right to ask leave me wondering how she copes with rushing today.

Who reminds her to blow out the candles?

Chapter 10

Danny

Fifteen Years Old

"Stop rushing me! I'm almost d-done!" Gracie shouts through the walls of her house.

"Hurry up, we're going to miss the bus!" I yell in response.

I tilt my head in curiosity as she runs out onto the porch, where I sit and wait for her. She looks different today. Her lips are shinier and fuller. Her eyelids have glitter on them, making the purpley-blue colors in her right eye even brighter. The rest of her appearance, I recognize, with the exception of the curves she got over the summer. I'm still getting used to those. I try my best to ignore the way Gracie's body looks, but her tight blue jeans and fitted Dashboard Confessional T-shirt are making it hard not to stare.

I rub my eyes, prying them away from her for a moment. "Is it rushing when I walkie-talkied you over an hour ago to start getting ready?"

"This never would've happened if you'd just stayed over yesterday," she huffs. "You've spent the night b-before the first d-day at school every single year. It's not my fault I slept through my alarm."

"My mom has been looking for me earlier and earlier each morning. It's like she has a tracker on me or something," I lie through my teeth. Thank God Gracie isn't as good at sniffing out my lies as I am with hers. The simple truth is that it's getting harder to just "spend the night" with her.

After dreaming that we slept completely naked in her bed last night, I woke up with flushed cheeks and a hard-on. No way can that happen when I'm with her. Eventually, she'll catch on that it's not just morning wood... It's her. I have to get ahold of myself for the sake of our friendship.

We're almost to the bus stop when I notice the door closing. "Wait for us! We're coming!" I shout at the driver, who thankfully hears me over the chatter and reopens the door. Gracie catches up, and we grab a seat together.

After school today, I'll kick off my high school football career with my first varsity practice. I pull a copy of the playbook out of my backpack and start reviewing my routes. The diagrams blur a bit, and I shake my head, closing the binder. Something in my body feels different than my usual nerves, but I'm sure it's just first day jitters.

Camp went well over the summer, but now, I'll have more people to impress. Winfield High is known for their athletics, and the Boosters pour money into the football program. As the "star receiver" of the Titans, I'll be expected to perform on and off the field. My heart races when I think about it, but the end result will be worth the grind. I just need to bring my A-game, land a D1 offer, and make it to the league. I crafted this plan with Gracie when we were ten, and the most important part is bringing her along with me. She can go to vet school wherever I play football and open up her own practice wherever I get drafted. It's basically set in stone.

I turn toward Gracie, who is finally relaxed and calm in her seat.

"Hey, you're coming to my first practice later, right?"

"Like I have a choice," she teases. "Your mom is my ride home."

I pretend to be offended before mumbling, "I'm actually kind of nervous."

Gracie leans closer to me, eyes wide in surprise. "Danny. Colleges were scouting you in junior high. You're amazing at what you do, and everyone is going to love you."

Her words make me feel better, like they always do, but I still have a sinking feeling in my stomach. "Do you think you could walk with me to the field after school?"

She gives my hand a little pat. "Of course. I'll meet you at the library after my last class. Hey, fact for a feeling?"

My eyes soften. "Sure. Let me think." My facts are almost always sports trivia. "Here's a good one. When you get three strikes in a row while bowling, it's called a turkey."

Gracie laughs. "Why's that?"

"Back in the olden days, the winner of bowling tournaments won a turkey."

"Pretty straightforward, then."

I return her smile with a crooked one of my own. I'm feeling some nervousness still, but it's much better than before. "So, what's your feeling?"

Her smile grows all the way up past her cheeks, causing her eyes to squint. "I feel like you're going to crush practice today."

Chapter 11

Grace

Fifteen Years Old

I'm rushing to my final and most dreaded class of the day—English. The room is on the other side of campus from my last class, so I'm hustling to make it on time.

Hurrying inside, I survey the somewhat dated classroom, with its messy chalkboard, maroon carpet, dusty bookshelves, and rows of wooden desks. I don't see anyone I'm even remotely familiar with. I sit down at the only available seat near the back of the room and pull out my yellow notebook and favorite mechanical pencil. After writing his name on the board, our teacher, Mr. Aberdeen, quiets us.

"Hello, class!"

"Hello," everyone mumbles. I keep my mouth shut.

"You can do better than that! Hello, class!" he shouts.

"Hello," everyone groans loudly. I still keep my mouth shut. I always take any opportunity to choose silence over speech in a new situation that might trigger my stutter.

The syllabus I received on Freshman Orientation Night stated that the first unit finishes with a public speaking requirement. We have to present in front of the whole class with a partner, which couldn't be more out of my comfort zone.

"Today, we're going to start with saying our name and a fun fact about ourselves." Mr. Aberdeen scans the room, and his gaze lands on me. "You seem a little quiet today." He smiles and glances down at the class roster in his hands before looking up again. "Susannah?"

I nod.

"I remember you from orientation. Welcome, Susannah! Please share your fun fact."

Wracking my brain for a fun fact that requires me to speak the fewest words, I barely open my mouth when I mumble, "I like d-dogs."

Mr. Aberdeen leans forward and cups his ear. "I don't think anyone heard you! Say it again with some gusto!"

When he looks at me expectantly, I want to sink into the ground and become an earthworm, where I only emerge from the dirt on rainy days before slithering back into the soil.

I speak a little louder. "I like d-d-dogs."

A few heads swivel my way, and the teacher looks at me with pity. Embarrassment swallows me whole. I know what everyone's thinking. Either I'm a fifteen-year-old who's scared of her English teacher, or I'm a fifteen-year-old who stutters. It's only a matter of time before they find out which one is true.

A boy wearing an Ohio Warriors hoodie a row ahead of me snickers, loud enough for everyone to hear. "Don't be afraid, Susie. Aberdeen won't bite."

That garners a few laughs from the kids around him. I hear a "good one, Garett" from one of the boys sitting at a nearby desk.

My face heats, and I bite the inside of my cheek, gnawing off little pieces of tissue. Do they think I haven't tried everything to get rid of my pathetic stutter? Short of going to speech therapy, which Dad won't pay for, I've exhausted all of my options.

Sometimes, when people are particularly mean, I want to throw my trauma in their face to see how they react. Tell them my mother died. That I get enough mocking at home to last me a lifetime.

"I'll go next!"

I glance beside me, where an attractive boy with square glasses perched on his nose sits. His messy blond hair flops over his forehead. Sporting a dimple in his right cheek, he smiles at me before loudly announcing, "I'm Ben. My fun fact is I hate the Warriors. They haven't won in years, and their fans are real douchebags."

I'm floored. Is someone other than Danny actually standing up for me? In front of everyone? A warm feeling floods my stomach. This has never happened to me before. I tentatively smile back at him, not wanting to do anything that might ruin his opinion of me.

He leans in to whisper, "Don't let that idiot get to you. I'm pretty sure he has a total of one brain cell floating around in his head."

"Assuming he has a b-brain is giving him a lot of credit," I whisper back.

He chuckles softly. "Good one, Susannah."

I pause and take a deep breath to relax, feeling less anxious already. "Actually, you can call me Grace."

Mr. Aberdeen finishes taking attendance before reiterating the public speaking requirement in the syllabus. "Class, I'm going to give you the last half of the period to find a partner and discuss your presentations."

Ben leans closer to me. "Hey, do you want to partner up on this public speaking thing?"

My eyes widen as I stare at him with surprise. "Um, are you

sure you want to be paired with me? I tend to stutter when I'm nervous or rushing."

He stares at me, jaw dropped, with fake incredulity. "Wait. You have a stutter?"

An involuntary giggle slips out of me. It looks like I, of all people, made a friend. Ben scoots his desk closer to mine.

"Are you sure you want to be stuck with Stuttering Susie here, who can't even string two words together, man?" Garett asks Ben, snickering with a few of his buddies.

Ben sighs and looks at Garett like he's gum on the bottom of his shoe. "Here's the thing, Gare. Me and her could quite literally stand at the front of the room with our mouths closed and still get a better grade than you. Do you even *know* how to read?"

Garett sputters a "pansy ass" as he pulls his hoodie over his head.

I softly whistle. "Wow, that was..."

"I'd say he'll be thinking about my awesome insult for a while, but I'm not sure he's even comprehended it." Ben grins, and we both open the notebooks on our desks.

Instead of discussing our presentation, we talk about our interests and backgrounds. I learn that Benjamin Fischer just moved here from Indianapolis. His dad got a promotion and brought their whole family to Columbus. He has a girlfriend, Mia, back home who he's been dating for the last year. As a nature enthusiast, he wants to be a conservation biologist one day.

Once I've exhausted any other possible follow-up questions, Ben pushes his glasses back up his nose and directs his full attention to me. "Tell me about you now, Grace."

I usually get uncomfortable talking about myself, but there's something about Ben that puts me at ease. "There's not much to know about me. I've lived in Columbus my whole life. I don't have any siblings. I want to be a vet, and I plan to go to Easton State University."

"I heard Easton is a great school."

"Yeah, it is. Um, my next door neighbor, Dan Thompson? We've kind of always planned to go there. It's a D1 football school with a really good vet program."

"That's DT, right? Star receiver?"

I click my mechanical pencil up and up, before holding down the top eraser and pressing the lead against my skin—a nervous habit. "You've already heard of him? Word travels fast around here when it comes to football, huh?"

Ben pulls off his glasses and blows some dust off. "He's in my algebra class. Lots of fist bumps. He seemed like a pretty big deal."

I guess this is what Danny's life will be like for the next four years. He's always been Mr. Popular wherever he goes, but somehow also "my" Danny at the same time. It's a delicate balance we've been able to maintain as friends over the years. Now that we're at a bigger school, I wonder if that balance will shift. I let that thought flicker, then push it away. He might be busier with football, but I know we'll be "us" no matter what.

Ben and I make plans to meet up the next day at lunch and go over our presentation strategy, which gives me something to look forward to tomorrow. I feel ten pounds lighter as I walk to the South Wing library to meet Danny.

I can tell something is wrong as soon as I see him. He's furiously picking at the skin around his nails, but everything else about him is frozen. *Is he even breathing?* Danny starts frantically running his hands through his thick, dark hair, almost pulling at the ends.

I rush over to him.

"Danny? Are you okay?"

All he does is stare back at me with panic. Still frozen.

We're in a semi-public spot, in the open study area. I link my arm in his and start tugging him toward the non-fiction stacks, which is bound to be empty this time of day. It's harder than I expected. Danny's grown a lot over the past year physically, adding layers of muscle in preparation for football season.

"Come on, we've got to move."

He drags his feet, but once we get there, we sit together on the floor in between bookshelves.

"Breathe," I instruct.

Easier said than done, apparently. His shallow breaths haven't let up, and he looks paler by the second. What is happening? Where's my confident, charming, happy-go-lucky Danny? I hold his hand, and it's clammy. Pressing my hand on his chest, I check his heartbeat, and it's out of control.

"Look at me."

Danny tilts his chin up. When his eyes lock on mine, I feel his heartbeat slow. I want to keep it there, so I do what feels natural. Holding my hand in front of my face, I put up four fingers and wiggle them.

"Where did these candles come from?" I ask playfully.

The corners of his mouth tick up and his uneven breaths seem slightly deeper.

"You know what to do."

Danny leans forward, inhales, and blows on my hand.

I put down two fingers.

Danny leans his head back and forcefully exhales this time. I lower the remaining fingers, and his shoulders relax.

I pop a finger right back up again.

Grinning mischievously, I raise an eyebrow. "Trick candle. Gotcha."

He chuckles softly and puts a hand over his heart. When he blows one more time, I finally put down my finger.

"What's going on?"

"I don't know. It's the first day of school, and everyone already seems to *know* me, like... like they're all counting on me to perform or something, but I don't know *them*. The possibility of letting anyone down feels big. Then I realized that this is what it's going to be like for the rest of my life. These expectations from strangers." He squeezes my hand and draws in some air. "Anyways, I started feeling pressure in my chest and then I couldn't breathe."

"I think you had a panic attack."

"Oh."

We huddle on the floor for a few minutes in silence. Danny remains largely motionless, looking straight ahead with a vacant expression. I'm fixated on him, unblinking, searching for any signs he might relapse into panic.

He opens his mouth to speak again, and his tongue makes a dry clicking sound, unsticking itself from the roof of his mouth. "I think I'm, uh, thirsty."

Reaching into my backpack, I pull out a bottle of juice from lunch and hand it to him. He twists the top off and gulps it down, shooting me a grateful look. "Thank God you were here. I don't know what I would've done without you."

Reaching behind him with my free hand, I start to rub small circles on his back. "Do you want to play Facts and Feelings?"

Danny nods slowly, a little color returning to his face. He gives me a weak smile. "But you already know how I feel."

I think for a moment. "Well, here's my fact: Cheetahs can run up to seventy miles per hour."

"Dang, that's fast."

"I think you might be the cheetah of wide receivers," I proclaim, grinning. We hold hands in comfortable silence for a few moments.

"Speaking of football," I add gently, "if we don't leave now, you might be late for your first practice. If you don't want to go, that's fine, too. I love you no matter what you choose."

"Love you, too. You'll stay, right?"

"The whole time."

Nodding, he steels himself as he stands. Danny tugs on the bottom of his shirt to straighten it and helps me up. We walk to the field, fingers intertwined, until we get within vision of the team. He gives my hand one last squeeze before jogging over and fist bumping a few of the guys. On the outside, he's back to confident, calm, easygoing Danny. Only I know the sweat clinging to his shirt isn't from the late August sun. When his shoulders finally relax, I sit in the bleachers next to the field. Every so often, he looks over at me, and I give him a small smile of encouragement.

The guys are just starting to split up into their respective teams for drills when a group of girls start chatting behind me. Maybe they also know players on the team, and we can be friends.

If Danny can overcome his nerves, I can too.

Before I can turn around and start up a conversation, one of the girls taps me on the shoulder. I swivel my head and look at her hopefully. We went to elementary school together. Her stick-straight, light blonde hair shines under the field lights, highlighting her blue eyes. She smiles, showing off her perfect teeth and glossy lips. I love the little golden Titans stamp on her cheek.

"Hey, nice to meet you! I'm Tori."

My stomach drops. She doesn't even remember me.

"Yeah. I, um, know. We went t-to elementary school t-together."

"Oh, right. Totally!" Her sickly sweet tone sounds completely fake. One of her friends nudges her, and I swallow nervously.

"So, I saw you walking in with Dan. Are you his girlfriend?"

"No."

Her face lights up. "Great! You won't mind if I ask him out after practice then, right?"

My shoulders slump. I'm so stupid. Of course she doesn't want to be friends with me. Part of me wants to say, "Yes, I do mind if you ask him out, actually," but I don't have any stake in Danny's love life. Plus, if he wants to say no, he will.

"I d-don't mind." My voice comes out monotone.

"Perfect. He's just so hot," Tori gushes. "Someone in my history class said he's the first freshman to play varsity in, like, twenty years. Might even be bound for the league."

All I say back is "mhm" and turn back toward the field. I absorb the gut punch of being absolutely invisible, a blow I'd like to be less used to. Sucking in a deep breath, I try to focus my attention on the practice, not on the emotional bruise Tori left behind.

My mood lifts slightly when Danny looks my way again.

Tori squeals. "OMG, I think he's looking at me. *Someone's* grade school crush is still alive and well."

I never heard about Danny's crush on Tori. Did he like her? *Does* he like her?

Before I realize it, the boys are already packing up. I head down to the field and wait for Danny on the sidelines. I feel helpless as I watch Tori flounce up to him and touch his shoulder. He looks at me, then back at her. He nods slowly, and Tori practically floats. Danny says something to the student coach, who checks his watch before replying. After exchanging a fist bump, Danny jogs toward the athlete's building, and Tori follows closely behind.

I stay motionless, not sure whether I'm supposed to meet him or not.

The student coach jogs up to me. "Hey. I'm Tom. DT's

running to the locker room to shower, and he asked me to tell you to meet him there. I think some of us might be going out after practice."

"Sure, I'll head over there in a few." My gaze shifts toward where Danny disappeared. Maybe he isn't leaving with Tori after all. I'm always overanalyzing everything.

"Alright."

Tom sprints back to the locker room. I wait a few minutes before following, walking with a little more energy.

When I get to the building, two people are kissing against the wall. I roll my eyes. High schoolers are so predictable.

Wait. Blonde hair, a glint of gold on her cheek...*is that Tori?*

Oh my God. That's Danny and Tori. She pushes her chest out, arching into him, before coyly moving her lips away. Danny's hands stay at his sides, frozen in place. When he pulls back, his eyes are wide, surprised almost. She only grins in response, leans in, and kisses him once on his cheek. I avert my gaze.

My stomach roils as saliva floods my mouth. I'm going to be sick. Stumbling backward, my feet carry me toward the parking lot as unwanted tears flow out. Coming to a sudden stop, I tilt my head back, willing myself to quit crying before reaching Janie's SUV. I let the wind dry most of my tears before dragging myself the rest of the way.

Janie rolls down the window and sticks her head out. Her black hair is starting to blend in with the dusky sky, styled in a low bun with a hair claw holding it in place. Danny's tan skin and dark features are from Janie, but his dad definitely gave him his height.

She leans to the side, looking around me. "Where's Daniel?"

"I think he's going out with the football team and their girl-friends."

"Oh, did you want to go, too? I don't mind driving back solo, hon."

"Um, I, d-don't think I was invited." My eyes mist over again, and I'm mortified. I don't know why I'm emotional over this. Danny can do whatever he wants. I need to stop being so pathetically dependent on him.

The hazel eyes I'm so familiar with stare at me with empathy as her lips point down in a small frown. "Hey, kiddo, let's stop for milkshakes on the way home. What do you think?"

I turn my face away to sniffle and then look back at her with a tight smile. "Sounds good. Thanks, Janie."

I climb in the car, and she drives us to the greasy diner down the road from school. It has the best strawberry milkshake in all of Columbus. I swear Danny and I try to con her into giving us money to come here at least once a week.

Janie and I stay for a while, chatting about all sorts of things, like my first day, vet school plans, and our favorite romantic comedies. When the street lamps turn on, we figure it's best to head home so I can start on homework.

I'm calmer by the time we pull up to our houses. So what if he wants to hang out with Tori? I have to stop being selfish with his time. He's still my best friend.

That night, I don't walkie-talkie Danny, and he doesn't walkie-talkie me.

The next morning, I'm ready early enough to make myself a bowl of cereal instead of skipping breakfast. I venture a glance over to Danny's house from the kitchen window while I try to eat. He's already sitting on his porch.

He didn't do anything wrong, Grace, I tell myself. *He doesn't owe you anything.* Echoing my reminders over and over, I empty my bowl and put on my shoes.

By the time I walk over to his driveway, I almost believe myself. "Hey, ready to go?"

He looks at me, his face blank. "You're up early."

"I had a tough time sleeping."

"You never walkie-talkied me. Why did you leave without saying goodbye?"

Danny has the nerve to look hurt, when *he* was the one who ditched me so he could make out with Tori all night.

"I went t-to find you after practice, b-but you were b-busy with T-Tori. I d-didn't want t-to d-disturb you."

He flushes and rubs the back of his neck. "Oh. I, um. I wasn't expec—"

"No worries." I pause, trying to get my emotions in check so I don't stutter. "I'm happy for you t-two."

Can't I just have one moment where I can effectively pretend?

He stares at me with a look I can't quite place. "You are?"

"Mmhm."

Danny stands up and kicks a pebble onto the road. "Okay." He swings his navy blue backpack over his shoulder and walks toward the bus stop. "Let's go."

As soon as we get on the bus, a feminine voice shouts, "D! Come sit with me!"

My eyes follow the voice down the aisle and land on Tori. Tori, with her perfect, sleek blonde hair. Tori, with her short skirt and trendy fur boots. Tori, with her perfect speech and no family drama.

She must've discovered that Danny takes the bus to school during one of their conversations yesterday (when they weren't busy sucking each other's faces) and changed her transportation method.

A blush spreads across his cheekbones as Danny looks at me sheepishly. "I don't have to sit with her."

"No, you should go. I b-bet you t-two have a lot t-to catch up on."

He searches my eyes. It takes everything in me not to bite my cheek.

"Are you sure?"

I just nod and smile to avoid triggering more of my stutter.

Danny narrows his eyes, clearly hesitating, before bringing his attention back to Tori.

"Go ahead," I encourage, desperately wanting this conversation to be over.

"Alright," he says tentatively, taking another few steps down the aisle. "See you after school, then. We have a longer practice, so I'll catch you at my house later?"

"Sure, Dan."

His back stiffens before he swivels around, his eyebrows drawn together. Before he can say anything, I sit down.

For the first time in six years, I ride the bus alone. My gaze stays glued to the window the whole way to school, avoiding any potential visuals of him and *her*. With every classmate that boards the bus, the unclaimed space beside me grows wider. Loneliness oozes into my pores like an incurable rash, making my skin feel itchy.

When we arrive at school, I scramble off the bus like someone is chasing me. And deep in my heart, I kind of hope *someone* is.

* * *

Sitting at the table in the library that's become my favorite over the past few months, I wait for Ben to arrive. Even though I just saw him in P.E., we didn't have a chance to catch up. He loves running the mile, and I love running from mandatory exercise, so we don't cross paths unless he's lapping me. That said, we're in almost all of the same classes, and he's continued to be a good friend. In a time where all of the other relationships in my life are complicated, my friendship with him remains simple.

Tori's been monopolizing almost all of Danny's time spent not at football, and lately, it's been difficult not to overthink my relationship with him. We've been able to maintain our same balance as always, just *outside* of school. We still go on backyard expeditions with Charger, drink milkshakes at the diner, and watch trivia show reruns with Tess. But after the third awkward *who will Danny sit next to today at the lunch table* interaction, I started finding excuses to be anywhere other than the cafeteria at noon.

"You look sparkly," Ben tells me as he adjusts his glasses and sits down.

"...in a bad way?" This morning, I rolled cucumber melon body glitter on my cheekbones, and I'm kind of surprised it's still around.

"In a glittery way. It's cool."

His reaction does not convince me it's actually cool. "That's the last time I listen to Teen Girl magazine," I mutter.

Ben sets down his binder and yanks out a sheet of lined paper. He points to the fabric wrapping my textbook. "Nice book cover. So shiny, like the glitter on your face."

Jesus Christ. That's it. No more glitter.

"Thanks. Janie got it for me."

"Who's Janie?"

"Oh. Just my next-door neighbor—you know, Dan Thompson? Uh, his mom." Sometimes I forget Ben doesn't already *know.* I haven't let him in on my home life, including the fact that Danny and I are more than just neighbors...or maybe not. I frown, because I'm not so sure anymore. I haven't been sure of anything when it comes to Danny lately.

Ben nods. "So, what's up with you?"

"In the five minutes since we saw each other in gym class?"

"No, in general. Although, I had a good time watching you try to convince Mr. Venzel that we should play with a parachute instead of running the mile." He shakes his head.

I lift my chin. "Running doesn't prove anything. The parachute, on the other hand, requires teamwork and collaboration."

"The parachute is for *children*."

Waving my hand at him, I effectively dismiss his wrong opinion. "Whatever. You're only saying that because you're one of those freaks who exercises for fun."

"Running distracts me from missing Mia," he says wistfully, propping his head up on his hand.

I smile, loving how he gushes about her. "That's actually really sweet."

Ben spins a sheet of paper on the table. "Seriously, though. You seem down."

It's odd having my hidden emotions noticed by someone other than Danny. I anxiously tap my pen against the table.

Ben studies me for a moment. "I was thinking...hanging out in this prison has been fun, but we should take our friendship to the streets. My sister's having a sleepover tonight, but maybe we can hang out at yours?"

"No." I swiftly decline on reflex, and the playful glint in Ben's eyes dims.

"We don't have to hang out if it's a bad time, no worries." He interlaces his fingers behind his head, leaning back slightly in his chair.

I consider lying. Tell him that my dad is on a work trip and I'm not allowed to have friends over or something. But I really don't want to lie to Ben, so I decide to go with a partial truth.

"Sorry. Um, it's not that I d-don't want you t-to come over. It's just that my mom d-died when I was younger. And my d-dad and I d-don't really get along. I d-don't think it'd b-be fun."

Ben pulls off his glasses and rubs them against the cotton of his Jurassic Park shirt. "No problemo," he replies lightly, as if I didn't just stutter my way through a snippet of my tragic life. "We can do something else instead one day. Hey, can I copy your notes? I have Galloway for history, and I can't even hear him half the time. He's like the oldest teacher here. When he's teaching us about the past, sometimes I think he's just writing down a first-hand account of his memories."

I chuckle. "Stop, Mr. Galloway is the sweetest man!"

Ben slides his glasses up his nose. "I didn't say he wasn't sweet, Grace. I said that he was old. Rumors are he owns an autographed copy of the Bible."

I start laughing loudly now, earning a stern look from the librarian. I dig around in my backpack for my orange notebook (because history is orange). Handing my notebook to Ben, I think about how maybe it's Danny that needs to step up in our friendship.

"Can we go to your place tomorrow?" I ask hopefully. It would be nice to go somewhere other than home.

"Sounds good." Ben throws me an easy grin. "I can't wait to show you all of my plants in the house."

Chapter 12

Grace

"So, that's pretty much the house," Danny says as we wrap up the tour of the guest room I'll be staying in tonight. It all looks professionally staged, like no one really lives here. Danny's personality, all of his wildness, is nowhere to be found. I visualize the energetic boy who spent a whole Sunday redecorating his childhood bedroom, which he was so proud to "reveal" to me. *You're never going to believe the difference, Gracie.*

The difference was wall-to-wall, duct-taped superhero posters. I told him so, and he chased me around the room, tackling me to the bed and tickling my ribs until I cried from laughing so hard. Yet another joyful memory tinged with a sadness that doesn't belong.

God. It's so bizarre to feel like I lost someone who's standing right in front of me. I can reach out to touch him, but I'm not sure if his skin would feel the same. And I find myself yearning for when I knew the texture of him.

"I'm rarely here during football season, honestly. I'm almost always at the facility," he adds.

"Well, it's beautiful. Thanks for showing me around." I

stand in the doorway of the guest bedroom, waiting for some direction from him as to where we go from here.

He stares at me with amusement dancing in his eyes. "You're biting the inside of your cheek, Gracie. You haven't managed to suppress your tell after all these years?"

I give him a small glare, but there's no bite behind it. "I really do think it's beautiful. There's just no 'you' in this house."

His gaze softens. "Hm. And what would 'me' look like?"

I could probably come up with a list the length of a pharmacy receipt of qualities that make Danny *Danny*, but I refuse to get sucked into that right now. I'm only here for one night, and it's all because of the letter. A letter I haven't even read.

I desperately search for a subject change before realizing something. "Wait a second, you never showed me your room."

Danny sheepishly runs his hands through his black, wavy hair—*his* tell for when he's embarrassed.

"Oh. You don't *want* to show me your room." I blush. *Why did I even bring up his room? Of course he doesn't want me in his room.* I cringe to myself.

He shakes his head. "It's not that, it's just—"

"It's a sex dungeon, isn't it?"

Danny starts coughing like he swallowed a bug. "Excuse me?"

"Wait, is it actually a sex dungeon? I won't judge you. Your secret is safe with me, Danny. It's nothing to be ashamed of," I reassure innocently.

"It's not—"

"Then why are you coughing and blushing all suspiciously?" I enjoy making *him* squirm for once. "Hold up. Is *that* what you use that long kitchen table for? Some fetish thing?" I start giggling uncontrollably.

"Mercy, Grace. I beg you," he chokes out, still coughing.

I laugh so hard a tear escapes from my eye. I've missed this.

He fusses with his hair nervously. "I'm coughing because I never thought I'd hear you speak the words 'sex dungeon' in my guest bedroom."

"I didn't realize you were so chaste, Danny."

His eyes darken. "I think you remember my lack of chastity, Gracie."

It's my turn to blush while he grins triumphantly.

I put my hands on my hips. "Okay. So, if it's not a sex thing, why won't you show me your room?"

"If you would simply let me finish even *one* complete sentence, I would tell you that it's just a force of habit not to bring people to that part of the house. It's my personal space."

I wince. "Ah, you only bring *special* guests to your room. Got it."

He's still grinning for some reason. "I actually haven't ever brought anyone to this house outside of my family. When I moved here five years ago, I knew I wanted to keep my home as a place just for me."

"I understand. We don't have to go see it. I don't want to intrude," I say cautiously.

"If you want to see it, I'll show you. Anything you want, Gracie." He reaches for me, almost as a reflex, before quickly shoving his hand in his pocket. For a moment, I find myself wishing he would've followed his instinct. Would his hand be warmer now, his grip stronger than before? Would I feel the same sense of safety I did with our fingers intertwined? Instead, he leads me down a different hallway, away from the main guest bedrooms and bathrooms.

As we reach the narrow space outside his bedroom door, I count at least twenty picture frames on the wall, like a gallery. When I move closer to the frames, I slowly bring my hand to my lips. Staring in awe, I'm not sure what picture to look at first, because some of them...are of us.

Danny and me, sitting on our log by the creek on the eve of my tenth birthday. My head is resting on his shoulder, and there's a football by his feet. Grandma Mae must've captured us when we weren't looking.

Danny and me, mid-air, jumping on his bed while playing air guitar and jamming to an emo punk song. Janie took this one. She was probably laughing her ass off. We thought we were so cool.

Danny and me, giggling as we spin around in a carousel at the fairgrounds. This one appears to be an attempted selfie, as it's completely dragged out and blurred from all the lights.

Danny and me, with our arms around each other after he scored a sixty-yard touchdown during his last game at Winfield High. Definitely taken by his little sister, Tessa, because the centering is all off. I'm pretty sure that's part of her knuckle in one corner.

And then there's us, standing in front of my college dorm. A small ball forms in the pit of my stomach. It's hard to stare at that one. We were so in love, thinking that we had our whole lives in front of us.

"It's...me," I whisper incredulously. "Sorry, I just mean, there are, um, pictures of us. Not all of them, of course, but I'm there, and...and you're there," I stumble, not believing my own eyes.

I try to ignore my heart, which is beating at lightning speed. A flurry of questions race through my mind. How long have the pictures been on this wall? He said he moved here five years ago. Has this gallery been here the whole time? Was it at his last place, when he was probably seeing other women? *Did they wonder who I was?*

I can feel his gaze on my neck. "You are a big part of my life, Gracie," he says carefully. *Present tense.* I move past that and focus on each picture, zeroing in on details I haven't seen in years.

I tuck a curl behind my ear. It immediately springs back in front of my face. My eyes stay glued to the wall as I breathe out a gust of air. "These are, wow. Lots of memories."

"Yes."

I twist the bracelet on my wrist. "We look so young."

"Yes."

Lightly tapping my foot on the floor, I turn to face him. "You searched for these specific ones and printed them out?"

"It would've been harder to find pictures *without* you in them."

I blink rapidly. "Oh. Right. So, it was a convenience thing."

His hazel eyes stare directly into mine. "No."

I swallow nervously and take a moment to look at the pictures without me in them. Danny wearing a medal with Tessa after what looks like a 5K. Janie and him making cinnamon rolls together in his kitchen downstairs. Danny in a suit, standing between a beautiful couple on their wedding day. *Was he the officiant?*

In one picture, Danny's on a trail, hiking up a mountain with two pretty women and a man. In another, he's laughing with a group of friends at a bar and holding a birthday balloon with the number twenty-five on it. I stand there, closely studying the faces of people I don't recognize, like they'll tell me all about the Danny they know.

Feeling a little uneasy, I consider looking away before my eye catches on a very familiar face. I smile fondly at a picture of Charger while memories of him playing with us by the creek roll like a film reel in my mind. One of my favorite pictures of the two of them hangs in the center of the wall. Janie took the portrait, and the picture is heavily saturated to highlight Charger's rich, chocolate brown coat. You can see every whisker in detail, including droplets of drool hanging from the corner of his mouth.

As I scan the rest of the colorful Charger pictures, I spot one in black and white. Charger is sitting between us on Danny's deck, and we're all facing away from the camera. This one is a dual frame, with the picture on one side and...*Oh my God*. I take a shaky step forward. It's my eulogy for Charger. The one I nervously read aloud to an audience of one at the creek.

It's behind glass, but I reach out as if I could touch it. The amount of wrinkles in the paper rivals the letter that sits in my pocket today, both having been anxiously folded and unfolded by me while wondering when I should give it to Danny.

I turn to face him again, and his gaze pins me into place. With his eyes completely focused on me, he appears to be very interested in my expressions.

Shifting on my feet, I ask, "You kept this? For, um, fifteen years?"

"I told you I would."

I sit with that for a moment as the memory plays back. *I'll keep this forever*, he said. For a moment, I wonder why he kept this promise and not other, more important ones.

"Did you ever end up getting another dog?"

"No. My schedule makes it hard, especially if you don't have someone at home taking care of your pet. But also, I just... couldn't." He taps on the center of his downturned bottom lip with his thumb. "Not after Charger."

Chapter 13

Grace

Fifteen Years Old

Danny sobs into my shoulder, eyes red and swollen as we cling to each other, huddled up in our special spot. Shaded by the oak trees and sitting on our favorite log, a cool breeze wraps around us as silent tears stream down my face. This one hurts. Plus, his pain is my pain.

"Gracie," he sniffles, "you know how best friends always say stuff like 'promise me you'll be the best man at my wedding' or 'promise me we'll celebrate our twenty-first birthdays together?'"

Red leaves fall from the sky and land on his thigh. I take a deep breath, trying to slow my racing heart. "Yeah?"

"Well, the good times are easy. You're already happy, you know? Will you promise me something else instead?" he asks, his lip quivering.

"Anything, Danny."

He wipes the tears dripping off his chin with the back of his hand, looking hopelessly for his constant sidekick, Charger.

"Promise me, if either of us goes through something hard, we'll be there for each other. I'll need you, Gracie."

"I need you t-too, Danny."

The present tense seems to slip right past him in his grief.

I clear my throat. "Is T-Tori coming?"

"I didn't tell her."

My jaw drops on reflex. He didn't tell his *girlfriend* that his constant companion is gone? "You didn't t-tell her Charger's...?"

"We only ever hang out at her house, so she's never met him." He brushes it off like it doesn't matter. But his averted, downturned eyes tell a different story.

Trying to smooth things over, I say, "Well, I'm sure she would—"

"I don't really want to talk about her right now," he replies quietly, swiping at a tear sliding down the side of his nose.

He's right. It's Charger's day, and it's already hard enough. I muster some remaining courage to give Danny the note I brought.

"So...so, I actually b-brought something with me." I shakily pull the wrinkled piece of paper out of my pocket. "I wrote d-down some things about Charger."

"You wrote Charger a eulogy?"

I shrug. "Maybe? I guess I wanted t-to write d-down what he meant t-to me."

Danny's lips part in surprise.

"I'm sorry, is that weird? I probably shouldn't have—"

"No, Gracie. It's perfect. I just...thank you."

My face heats at how genuine he sounds. "Oh. Okay. Anyways, here you go," I whisper as I lift my hand to give him the note.

He puts his hand on mine to stop me. "Can you read it out loud? I can't read anything for shit right now. Everything's blurry."

I breathe out a small laugh. He's not wrong. Sunken shoulders, snotty noses, windblown hair...both of us have looked better.

"Actually, never mind. I know you hate reading out loud. Sorry, it was a dumb idea."

"I'll d-do it. I d-don't mind reading t-to you. Especially here." I gesture to our surroundings. Our clearing is familiar, but also entirely foreign without Charger walking alongside the cold water creek.

Wiping my hands on my jeans and unwrinkling the paper, I clear my throat a few times and start to read.

"Charger was the t-type of friend that anyone would b-be lucky t-to have...loyal, kind, and t-trustworthy. Someone who would sit in the t-trenches with you on your saddest d-days, and someone who would lift you up even higher on your happiest d-days. Charger was the third member of the most epic friendship of my life, and I will cherish every memory of him playing here, in our special spot." I take a deep breath as I finish up the note. "I hope you've found friends up there. I hope you're spending your d-days chasing after all the footballs you could ever want. I hope you're safe and warm. And, I hope the rainbow b-bridge is all it's cracked up t-to b-be, b-bud. I love you."

After I'm done reading, I look up at Danny. I expect him to still be crying over Charger, as the tears haven't stopped since we got to our special spot. What I don't expect is for him to look at me, eyes clear and wide, with...amazement? Pride? His emotional shift makes me wonder what he's thinking.

"Gracie, that was...I never want to forget this. Can I have it?"

"Sure, it's no b-big d-deal. Here you go." I place the wrinkled paper in the palm of his hand.

"Thank you. I'll keep this forever." He carefully folds the

already-wrinkled paper like it's valuable and sticks it in the pocket of his jacket.

"Fact for a Feeling?" I sniff.

"Go ahead."

"D-Dogs dream, d-did you know that? And senior d-dogs dream even more than younger d-dogs. What d-do you think Charger dreamed about?"

Danny stares at me like I'm the most precious person in the universe simply for sharing this fact.

"I bet he dreamed about the same things we do, since he spent most of his time with us anyway."

I hum. "What d-do you dream about then?"

"Us, Gracie. I dream about us."

Chapter 14

Grace

Dreams don't hold your hand on the worst day of your life, and the promises we made in the woods wouldn't hold up for either of us. He missed the happy events: my twenty-first birthday party, my vet school graduation, the grand opening of my animal clinic. But what devastated me most was his absence at the tragedies. He wasn't there when our mutual college friends ditched me. He wasn't there when we sold my childhood home. He wasn't there when Mae moved into a senior living center.

Needing someone is such a curious concept. More often than not, people view *need* as a stronger word than *want*. In actuality, it couldn't be further from the truth. It turned out that I didn't *need* Danny. I got myself through those difficult times. I came out the other side slightly more hardened to the harsh realities of life, sure, but I did it. However, the messy truth was that I *wanted* him there. I wanted him there, with me, so desperately.

Revisiting the memories is creating an invisible itch in my brain that needs to be scratched. Who is he, after all these years, since those pictures were taken? How much has he changed?

Who are those strangers in the frames? What do they mean to him?

We stand in complete silence for a few more minutes. For me, the silence is comfortable as I take my time exploring the gallery wall in more detail. For Danny, I'm not so sure. I can feel his eyes on my back, patiently waiting for me to finish looking through this visual representation of his life. I turn to face him and try to interpret his gaze. Does he wish that I had been there, at his birthday party? At the wedding he officiated? Cheering him on with a homemade poster during his race with Tessa? The desire to know is so strong that I have to be careful not to ask it out loud.

As I give the wall one last look, I realize I skipped over a frame. In the photo, Danny is wearing a fitted gray suit and a Mustangs baseball cap. Janie and Tessa are sitting on either side of him on a velvet couch dressed to the nines, and there's confetti on the floor. Janie's eyes are teary as she looks at Danny with pride. There's no question in my mind—this was his Draft Day.

I allow myself just one moment to picture myself on the couch next to Danny and his family, how we always planned.

I'll kiss you first, he'd said.

I'd pretended to be affronted on his mom's behalf. *What about Janie?*

She'll understand... It's us.

That memory feels like a microscopic bee sting, a reminder of the pain associated with the end of us. Resurfaced emotions swirl in my stomach as Danny breaks through the silence, like he knows what I'm thinking.

"Hey, did you ever watch my draft on TV?" His tone is casual, but I know the question is serious.

"Uh, no," I admit hesitantly.

How can I explain to him that it hurts to watch him play? I know it's petty. I should want to support him and watch him succeed no matter our relationship status. But the pain is over-whelming sometimes. Often, it still feels raw, like an open cut dripping blood. Other times, it's like a scarred-over wound that's barely noticeable to anyone other than me.

He allows me only a glimpse of the hurt in his eyes before he turns around and takes the few remaining steps to his bedroom door. He opens it and gestures for me to go in.

I find all the personality that's missing from Danny's house in his room. Pushed up against the middle of the back wall is his bed. The mattress sits on top of a cherrywood frame, which is the exact color of the deck outside his childhood home. Artwork on the sophisticated forest green walls includes a canvas map of Columbus, an abstract labrador made out of metal, and an oil pastel painting of Elite Stadium, where the Mustangs play. He has an old-timey record player on his nightstand next to a stack of albums, some of which are bands we listened to in high school. I swivel my head to look at the floor to ceiling windows that lead out onto a Juliet balcony.

"So... this is it," Danny says quietly.

"Mystery solved," I reply.

He cocks an eyebrow at me.

"I found the 'you' in this house, after all."

That earns me a soft smile, but I still see leftover sadness in his eyes from my earlier confession. I need to bring some light back to his eyes.

"So, um, how was it?"

The corner of his mouth ticks up. "My draft?"

"Yeah, how did it go?"

An amused smile sticks to his face. "It went okay... I was only the third overall draft pick."

"Holy shit, Danny! That's incredible. Congrats."

He laughs his genuine, loud laugh.

"Hey, why are you laughing?"

"It's just funny being congratulated for something over eight years later. I've accomplished more since then, football-wise."

I debate saying anything at all, but the truth is already pressing at my lips. "I haven't really seen *any* football over the years."

"You haven't seen any of my games?" He leans against his bedroom dresser, folding his arms in front of him.

My breathing is a bit uneven as a hollow feeling settles in my stomach. "No, at least not by choice. I avoid the sport entirely. I didn't even know who you were playing for right now. I looked you up before I came. I...I'm finding it difficult to express what the last ten years were like for me. And I'm honestly not sure you'd want to know."

He searches my eyes. "I want to know, Gracie. I told you I want to know everything."

"I know you say that, but I can see the pain in your eyes when I say certain things, like me not watching the draft," I say quietly.

He shakes his head. "The pain in my eyes isn't because of you not watching my dumb football games. That's simply an effect. It's because of us losing so much time together."

I nod, slowly, and sit down on one of the oversized chairs by his bedroom window. I want to say *you're not alone in this, I miss you,* but it's hard to be vulnerable after all of this time. It feels like writing with the wrong hand.

He gives me one last moment to respond. When I don't, he graciously changes the subject. "Okay, enough about me. Tell me something about you. You're a vet, Gracie girl. Wow."

Is that pride in his eyes?

"Erm, yeah. I actually run an animal clinic in Columbus."

"I knew you'd own a clinic one day," he says softly. "I'm confident there's no better vet than you anywhere."

The certainty is so *Danny*. Growing up, his unshakable faith in my abilities always made me melt. To be the object of his steady confidence again disarms me, and I blink hard to pull myself out of the daze he puts me in so easily.

"I'm not sure about *anywhere*, but maybe within twenty miles of Columbus," I joke.

"Who's managing your animal clinic while you're here?"

"My partner, Elle. We went to the same vet school in Indiana and knew we wanted to work together long-term. She's from Northeast Ohio, so we both had plans to move back after graduation. After much convincing, she decided to join me in Columbus at the animal clinic. You'd get along really well with her. She's very charming, but also slightly neurotic."

"I *am* extremely charming," he quips with a wink.

"Don't forget 'slightly neurotic.' That part's important," I add as he rolls his eyes. My lips curve in a gentle smile. "So how is it playing professional football after all these years? It was always your dream, and you finally achieved it. Was it everything you hoped for?"

Danny takes a few steps in my direction and sits on the edge of his bed, facing me. His gaze is unwavering and wrought with intensity. He seems to carefully choose his next words. "I wouldn't say that playing in the league was my entire dream. I actually don't think I've come close to achieving my full dream yet. There are definitely some...key parts missing."

I suck in a shallow breath, trying my best not to dwell on the missing parts.

"I do love it, though. The team is pretty great. The guys are nice and chill, and no one has an unmanageable ego. I'm lucky to be a veteran with the organization."

"So, you've played in New York this whole time, then?"

"Yeah." He shyly ducks his chin, as if that hadn't been his lifelong goal as a child.

"The biggest Mustangs fan becomes the best Mustangs player. It's wonderfully poetic. Janie must be so proud." I smile.

"She's just happy she has an excuse to visit the city. Mom's here for the art galleries more than the games, I think."

"I bet," I say fondly. Janie is an amazing freelance photographer in Columbus. Her creativity is one of the many reasons why I love her. "I'm sure being a professional football player has a lot of perks, though. I bet going out is more fun, especially with all the guys. I can't even imagine all the attention."

Danny shakes his head. "Actually, a lot of the guys on the team are either married or have serious girlfriends. There's not a ton of 'going out' anymore. Even if there was, I'm not interested."

I don't want to explore why a feeling of solace washes over me with his words. "Oh. So what do you do in your spare time then?"

He nods in the direction of a few medals hanging above his dresser. "I run. You saw on the gallery wall that I've been running 5Ks, sometimes with Tessa. My mom still lives in Columbus, but Tessa actually moved out here for fashion design school. She's also an amazing marathon runner, but I can't do those due to football restrictions."

"Hey, 5Ks are a big accomplishment. According to Mae, I have a 'weak lung capacity.' I'm inclined to believe her based on experience," I laugh.

Danny smiles affectionately. "I remember her saying that. Mae's probably the bluntest person I know, besides you."

I nod absentmindedly and yo-yo between wanting to tell him the news and waiting to tell him the news. I ultimately decide that it's not the right time.

"Other than 5Ks, I watch a ton of baseball games in the offseason with friends. I still enjoy action movies." Danny pauses for a moment, but his gaze rests on me. "And, um, I also go to therapy."

My hand flies to my mouth, covering my jaw drop. He was always a firm believer in working through his shit himself. He stopped having panic attacks entirely when we started dating, so he considered himself cured. I mostly kept my thoughts to myself at the time, but I'd always felt he'd benefit from therapy. "That's amazing, Danny."

"Yeah, well. About five years ago, I realized I was using some really bad coping strategies to deal with my anxiety. After Tessa saw some pictures of me at a nightclub, she told me my behavior was 'cringe' and I needed to 'get my ass to therapy.'"

I laugh, imagining Tessa's personality now.

"It's been really good," he adds. "After working through some stuff, I feel ready for bigger things in my life."

"You should be proud of yourself." I anxiously twirl one of my curls.

Should I share some of my truth, too? Part of me feels like being vulnerable with him might help, but the other part worries that continuing this conversation might make things worse. Yet Danny *is* being open with me, and I think it's only fair to reciprocate.

"I don't see a therapist anymore, but I did see the on-campus counselor all four years at Easton."

He looks thoughtful, no doubt wondering about the timing. In a slightly higher pitched voice, he says, "I don't remember you seeing a therapist freshman year, actually. When did you start seeing them?"

"Um, a few weeks after we separated."

He frowns. "Were you...okay, Gracie? After I left Easton?"

I consider how much I want to divulge at this point. He said he wants to know everything, but I feel like this next part will cause him to feel some misplaced guilt. Therapy taught me that Danny isn't responsible for my feelings; I'm accountable for mine, and he's accountable for his. How we cope with them is personal.

"I was fine," I say carefully. "But, um, I started stuttering regularly for a bit afterwards."

His initial confusion transforms into devastation before my eyes. "What...how?"

I anxiously brush non-existent dust off the chair. "Well, my therapist said that going through major life transitions, especially if they reopen feelings of trauma, can trigger old habits like stutters."

Danny rubs a hand down his face, looking horrified. I hear his voice becoming more hoarse as he continues. "You were traumatized?"

"I mean, yeah. It was an agonizing time for me."

He cracks his knuckles, a nervous habit for him. "You could've reached out. I would have...I would've done something."

"Short of you taking back everything you did and me taking back everything I said, I don't think there's anything you could have done that would've made a difference."

Are his eyes misty? He looks down quickly, and I can't tell. It's probably just the lighting.

"Danny, I understand now that there were things both of us could have done differently. Let's drop this for tonight, okay? I'm going to brush my teeth, but I'll be downstairs for a little while before bed."

He nods, but his expression is wrought with anguish. "Whatever you want, Gracie."

I stand up and start heading for his bedroom door, pausing mid-step when I hear his voice.

"I know you want to drop it for now, but I need you to know

that I'm sorry. I didn't fully understand the bigger picture back then."

Standing in the doorway, I turn around. He opens his mouth to speak again, but quickly closes it with a defeated look in his eyes. "Can you promise me that we'll talk about this later?"

"I promise you that we'll talk about it sometime before I leave. My flight isn't until tomorrow evening," I say softly. "I think we're both emotionally spent right now, and it's been a really long day. Okay?"

"Okay, Gracie girl."

Drawing in a long breath, I head down the hallway. While I'm craving some distance between us, I also wonder what it would be like to crawl under the covers and hold his hand until we fall asleep. Instead, I find myself standing in a perfectly staged guest room, complete with a bedside table zen garden. But I feel anything but zen. *One thing at a time*, I remind myself.

First, I decide to unpack what little I brought. I open my clear backpack and sigh. For the first time in my life, I only packed what I needed for one boring night by myself in a random hotel near the stadium. A rookie move. My usual giant suitcase, filled with everything from a thong swimsuit to a ball gown, is nowhere to be found. In its place is a small backpack containing one comfortable lounge set, a fitted white T-shirt, and approximately seven pairs of underwear. Just the essentials.

As I strip off my jeans, the letter I brought—the sole reason I'm here—sticks out of my right pocket. Obviously, I have to give it to him when the time is right. Is there ever going to be a "right" time, though? Maybe I should just leave it here, and he can read it after I'm gone.

No. I have to face this head on.

Just not tonight.

I don't want to leave the letter out in the open in the unlikely event that Danny comes in here, so I do what any other well-adjusted adult would do—hide it under the bed. Crouching down to the floor, I start to slide the envelope underneath the frame, but my hand is stopped by something. Curiosity gets the better of me, and I reach a little further, realizing it's some sort of book. *Oh no.* There is a zero percent chance I'll keep this mysterious book under the bed and forget about it. My biggest toxic trait is snooping. I'm not proud of it, but at least I'm self-aware.

Swiping the book out from below the bed, I brush the dust off. It's a large, leather-bound scrapbook. I lift the cover and slowly thumb through the pages. Everything in here is football-related: certificates from high school, ticket stubs, an auto-graphed picture of his favorite player, and a handful of articles outlining Danny's successes. I roll my eyes. *All that suspense for nothing.* Serves me right for snooping to begin with—of course it would be a snoozefest.

As I close the book, another newspaper article falls out. I flip over the article and gasp. It's not a football story.

This article, from the *Columbus Dispatch*, covers the grand opening of my animal clinic. I brush my fingers across the paper, which looks worn, like someone held it in their hands more than once. My heart is racing, and I'm in disbelief as my brain tries to process how he got this article. Has he been back to Ohio since he left? Did Janie give this to him? My stomach drops—did *Mae* send him the article?

This leaves me with many questions and no answers. I weigh my options. I can't bring this up casually, because then he'll know I snooped. But maybe I could bite the bullet and just ask him? *Shit.* Which option would a somewhat mature thirty-year-old woman choose? I pace across the room, back and forth, mulling my options over.

There's so much swirling around in my mind right now, and I need to talk this out. I whip out my phone and call the only number that makes sense for this situation.

I wait impatiently for him to answer.

"Hello?"

"Ben!" I whisper-scream into the phone.

"Grace?"

"Yes! It's me! Obviously!"

"Why do you sound like you're in an active hostage situation? Should I get Mia on the phone? Out of the two of us, she has more experience in criminal law. Unless you're in a very tense situation that requires an environmental lawyer. Are you in an area with illegal pollution, Grace?"

I roll my eyes. "Yes, Benjamin. I'm calling because not one house in the rich neighborhood I'm in has solar panels. Can you believe it?"

"Are you being serious or not? I can't tell..."

"Jesus Christ. Put your wife on the phone, I can't take this!"

"Okay, I will," he says absentmindedly. "Mia, can you come? Grace is going through another crisis of sorts, maybe a criminal law situation..."

I hear shuffling in the background. "Before I hand you over to Mia, Purrlock Holmes has been hacking up this weird type of hair lately, and—"

"Not the time, Ben. Ask me your cat questions later."

"Alright, alright. Jeez. Here's Mia."

"Grace, everything okay? Ben said something about a crime?"

"No. The only crime is your husband's inability to read a room!"

"Oh," she says fondly. "I was kind of worried, but that makes much more sense. What's up?"

"I am freaking out. I'm in Danny's guest room, and—"

"Wait. *Your* Danny's guest room? *The* Danny? I—"

"Dan Thompson?!" Ben shouts in the background. "Mia, give me my phone back. This is a Winfield High Defcon Level One Situation."

"Mia, I swear to God, if you give Ben his phone back..."

"Calm down, the both of you! I'm putting you on speaker. Go ahead."

I inhale slowly, staring at the zen garden in an attempt to absorb all the zen I can. It doesn't help. The garden mocks me, and I give it a vicious little rake in retaliation before turning my back on it. "So, long story short, you know how I came to New York to give Danny The Letter?"

"Yes," they answer in unison like a freaky married couple.

I nervously twirl a curl. "Well, when I got here, one thing led to another, and I kind of just came back to his giant house with him."

"Back all the way up," Ben loudly interjects. "What did he say when he saw you for the first time in ten years?"

"He said, 'Hi, Gracie.'"

The line goes silent for a few moments. Then, Ben's incredulous voice—"*Hi?* All he said was *hi?*"

"I mean, he asked me how I enjoyed the game."

"Like it was a regular Sunday?!" Ben exclaims.

Mia follows up with a gentle, "How was it for you?"

"I guess it was strange, but familiar. Strange that he didn't even ask what brought me here, familiar in that it's...us."

"Hmm...interesting. So, he invited you to his house?"

"Yeah, and it's actually been...pretty great catching up." I pause, pulling in a shaky breath. "I think he regrets what happened between us."

"I'm happy for you, Grace," Ben says warmly.

"You owe me twenty dollars," I hear Mia mumble to Ben.

I roll my eyes. "Anyway, he has pictures of us here from childhood on his wall, like more than a few pictures."

Ben cuts in. "Okay, I feel like we're back in a criminal law situation now..."

"Let me finish! He's been really sweet, but you know how my emotions are all over the place when it comes to Danny."

"If by 'all over the place' you mean you're deeply in love with him, then yeah, your emotions are all over the place," Ben deadpans.

"Wait, *what?*"

"Huh?"

I blink. "You think I'm in love with him?"

The pause that follows my question is long enough for me to know they are working out who is going to be the one to break the news.

Mia's voice softens as she gently explains, "We *know* you're in love with him. It's been ten years, and it's very clear that you've never gotten over him. When you see something that reminds you of him, you tear up. You haven't talked about what happened with him once. Sometimes it feels like the two of you somehow *just* broke up. You've never closed the wound, babe."

My stomach floods with that anxious feeling you only get when a friend reveals a harsh truth to you.

Ben interrupts. "We're just happy you'll finally be off the dating apps. You don't take them seriously anyway. You meet a guy and put him through an extremely strange set of impossible requirements. None of them ever pass. You're like a reverse maneater."

"Hey!" I exclaim defensively. "Henry passed."

"Henry was three years ago, and he lives in China now."

"Well, we still dated," I protest.

"I think you should stop bragging about dating Henry. He was a drug user, Grace," Ben says flatly.

Sighing in frustration, I reply, "So, he vaped here and there. It's not a crime against humanity."

"Vaping kills—"

I groan, preparing for a lecture I've heard before.

"Plants. Vaping kills plants."

Tired of our antics, Mia cuts in. "Keep going, Grace."

Ben pipes up. "Yeah. You found his creepy shrine, then what happened?"

"It wasn't creepy! It was...special. It was nostalgic."

Mia, ever the romantic, sighs dreamily. "So, why are you calling us in a panic then?"

"Well, I'm in the guest room, getting ready for bed because I'm staying here." I frown. "Did I mention that?"

Chiming in, Ben says, "This conversation is really taking a sharp 'nightly news' turn. I didn't think Dan fit the profile, but it's always the ones you least suspect."

"Anyway, I'm in this guest room, and I just happened to notice under the bed—"

"You were snooping," Ben says.

"I wasn't snoop—"

Mia interrupts. "My client is innocent on the grounds of 'she's just a girl,' Your Honor. Please continue, Grace."

"Thank you, *Mia*. So, I found a scrapbook. Obviously, I looked in it—"

"Obviously," Ben drawls.

"And a *Columbus Dispatch* article about the grand opening of my animal clinic was inside."

"Whoa," they respond in unison.

"Whoa," I agree, collapsing on the guest bed.

Ben smacks his lips. "Welp. Turns out he's just as in love with you as you are with him. Congrats!"

I shoot up into a sitting position and resume panic mode. "So, this means he kept up with me all these years? While I was actively avoiding him, avoiding all of his successes, he was following mine?" My throat feels scratchy. "It's a lot for me to process, you know? And, if he knew where I was and what I was doing, why didn't he reach out? Was it just an 'I'm happy for her' type of thing? Or was it more?"

"Grace," Ben says gently. "I think you're interpreting his feelings before he has a chance to explain them."

I bring two fingers to my temple. "What do I do? Is this just a closure thing, where we catch up and part as friends? Or do you think it could be...?" I trail off, not knowing how to finish that sentence exactly.

"After all this time, you do whatever feels right to you, Grace. What feels right to you is the best decision."

Mia's kind words quiet some of the noise in my head, and I sigh in relief. "I needed to hear that, Mia. Thank you."

"And thanks to me, too," Ben adds.

"You did nothing. In fact, you actively stalled this conversation several times," I point out.

"Sure. Alright, well, keep us posted, please! WiFi has been spotty in our neighborhood, so this nugget of information will keep us occupied for a while."

"Glad to be of service," I say dryly.

"Indiana misses you, Grace! Come visit your old vet school stomping grounds soon. We'd love to have you stay with us," Mia offers.

"Miss you, too. Love you, weirdos."

As I end the call, I take a deep breath. *You got this.*

I return the scrapbook underneath the bed, finish getting dressed, and brush my teeth. As I place my clothes in my bag, I wish I'd remembered to pack courage.

Chapter 15

Danny

Sixteen Years Old

"Don't pack up until the bell rings," Mrs. Sanders instructs as we all let out a collective groan.

It's almost lunchtime, and I'm so hungry I could eat my own leg. With my new workout plan, I'm constantly ravenous. I need the extra fuel, because the opening game of my sophomore year is tonight.

"D! Can't wait for you to rock it at the game, Handsome!" Tori whisper-shouts as she blows a kiss from the back of the room. I pretend not to hear her. I hate when she does public shit.

I never actually asked Tori to be my girlfriend. After some hang outs last year, she started calling me her boyfriend, and I never corrected her. So, here we are. She was the first girl to ever ask me out, and I guess I was flattered. Tori demands a lot of my attention, but at least she's supportive of my schedule and football aspirations.

My career hopes are about the only thing we can agree upon lately. We're not on the same page, and I don't know if we ever were. Tori's been wanting to take physical stuff further, saying it's time for us to do more than just making out and touching. Something in me balks at the idea, and my stomach feels queasy whenever she talks about it. My focus on football has kept me from analyzing if it's normal to feel that way about my girlfriend.

I drum my fingers on my desk impatiently. Ever since school started up again a few weeks ago, Gracie's been eating in the library, and we haven't had a deep conversation in forever. Whenever I offer her a seat at our table, she says she needs to study. I glance at the clock—two minutes left until lunch. I want to meet her in the food line before Tori can hold me up.

Relying on hope and chance meetings to catch a glimpse of Gracie at school has been miserable. She's been more than a little distant lately, and I'm not sure why. We were both busy over the summer, but my walkie-talkie is collecting dust. I checked in with her religiously while I was at football camps—at least twice a week. She constantly reassured me that things have been quiet at home, saying that her dad had been pretty absent between working at the car manufacturing facility and gambling at the casino. But things still feel off between us, and we need to talk about it.

The bell finally rings, and I jog to the cafeteria and get in line for food. I guess I manifested Gracie, because I spot her heading this way. She's wearing a fitted lavender T-shirt and her favorite gray-wash jeans, which hug the curve of her hips perfectly. She has one of her classic headbands on, this one with a small bow on it, which barely holds back all of her wild curls.

"Gracie, over here! We can wait together."

She weaves in and out of the navy blue and gold circular tables, grabs a lunch tray, and steps behind me.

"Thanks. I'm so hungry I could eat my arm." She props the tray on her hip and pushes her headband backwards. A lost cause, really, as the volume of her hair pushes the band forward again two seconds later.

"It would be nice if they served chocolate milkshakes here, right?"

"Yeah," she agrees as she snags a plate, "but it would be even nicer if the milkshakes were strawberry."

"The strawberry obsession again, huh?" I tease, holding out my plate to the cafeteria worker. A scoop of mashed potatoes gets plopped on my plate before a ladle of turkey gravy is poured on top. "You just say that because of your red hair. You discriminate against other flavors. It's not right, Gracie."

She laughs, and her vibrant eyes sparkle. Adding a red jello cup to her tray, she replies, "Strawberry is the only correct answer. You're ridiculous."

"D! I was looking for you everywhere." Tori walks over and kisses my cheek before cutting in front of me. "Oh. Hi, Susannah."

Tori's decked out in Titans spirit gear today, wearing a short, low-rise white skirt, a fitted Titans jersey with my number on it, navy blue knee socks and gold jewelry. Her hair is pulled into two braids, and her skin looks tanner than it did yesterday.

Gracie visibly deflates and gives Tori a look I can't quite place. Disappointment? Frustration? No, neither of those make sense. Gracie says that she really likes Tori for me. Even though I've been distracted with football, I can usually tell when she lies.

"Hi, Tori. How're things with you?" Gracie asks, adding a turkey sandwich to her plate.

"Things with us are super great! D and I had so much fun at the fairgrounds this past weekend, especially on the ferris wheel." She winks at me, like she wants everyone to know we made out at the carnival. I feel so awkward, especially in front of Gracie, who stares at her tray.

We move forward in line, and I grab a bag of pretzels.

"Anyway, I can't believe the very first Titans game is tonight. So exciting, right? It can't come soon enough. The field is basically my second home now, since I'm there so often supporting D at all of his practices. It's hard to balance everything, but I wouldn't miss watching my boyfriend do what he loves for anything."

"Wow," Gracie says flatly, picking up a bag of potato chips. "That all sounds very thrilling."

I glance at Gracie. "You're coming to the game tonight, right?"

"Yeah, I promised your mom I'd keep her company."

"I, uh, didn't know you two made plans."

Gracie shrugs in response. It seems like she talks with Mom more than me these days, and I'm not sure how I feel about that. It's another reminder that I don't know every single thing about her like before.

"Well, I'm sure Mom will love that. Do you want to sit with us today? I know you usually eat in the library, but I was thinking—"

Tori cuts in. "You know how focused Susannah is, D, always studying hard for librarian school."

"Veterinarian school, actually," I quickly correct.

Gracie sucks in a deep breath like she's gathering patience.

"Right. Maybe we should let her get to it," Tori clips before pausing for a moment. "Or, actually, now that I think about it, you're welcome to sit with us. We do have an extra spot, because I usually sit on D's lap."

I think my whole body flushes, and I aggressively rub the back of my neck like there's a mosquito bite back there.

Gracie fidgets uncomfortably as the lunch lady punches her meal card. "Um, I'll pass for now. B-But thanks."

I frown when I hear her stutter. I should pull her aside and look into—

"Grace!" A tall, blond kid with glasses comes running up to her. "Wow. I can't believe you. We decide to get out of the musty library and eat in the cafeteria for the first time in forever, and you're not even waiting for me?" He crosses his arms like he's upset. "In the wise words of Stephanie Tanner, *how rude.*"

Okay. What in the actual fuck is going on here? *I'm* the only person who calls her Grace. My *mom* doesn't even call her Grace. Who is this kid? I look at her for an explanation, but she's too busy fondly staring at four-eyed Chad Michael Murray to notice me.

His eyes stray from Gracie for two seconds. Does he notice me inching closer to her? "Hey! You must be Dan." He gives me a genuine smile. "You're Grace's neighbor, right? You play some awesome football, dude."

I look at Gracie with slightly narrowed eyes, hoping to convey something along the lines of *neighbor, really?* before responding, "Uh, thanks. Yep, we live next door. I'm her best friend."

He gives me a curious look. I need to play it cool, so I try not to look at him with too much suspicion. "And you are..."

Blondie chuckles. "Ah, sorry. This one"—he juts his thumb out at *my* Gracie—"knows that I'm always scattered. I'm Ben. Nice to meet you, man." He holds out his fist for a bump. I bump him back against my will. He then notices Tori, who is suddenly sporting a huge smile on her face, gleefully looking between Gracie and Ben.

"I'm Tori. D's *girlfriend,*" she adds pointedly.

"D. Sweet nickname. Nice to meet you, Tori." He clasps his hands together and smacks his lips. "Welp, Grace. Are we doing this thing, or—"

I cut in. "How do you all know each other?"

Ben grins at her like they have an inside joke. I try to infiltrate his brain and channel *stop looking at my Gracie* directly into his psyche, but he doesn't get the memo. Are they together?

"We actually met last year in English class. I basically begged Grace to be my partner for the verbal presentation because she has a real gift for public speaking in stressful scenarios. It's her one true passion in life, as I'm sure you know." He winks at her. He actually *winks* at her. She lights up, playfully nudging him.

What. The. Fucking. Fuck. Is. Happening.

My heart rate speeds up, and I start to spiral. How have I missed her hanging out with this guy for months now?

"Cool, um, that's cool. Super cool. You two hang out a lot, then?"

"She definitely makes up one hundred percent of my social circle within Ohio state lines, yes." He pauses and taps his chin a few times with one finger like he's reconsidering. "But, now that I'm thinking about it, I'm not so sure. Because I've been in Indiana for the last month and find her all but ditching me the second I'm back."

Gracie laughs and rolls her eyes. "I've been in this cafeteria for, like, two seconds. I haven't even exited the line."

I speak before my brain catches up. "Do you guys want to eat with us?"

Tori makes a small huffing noise, and I turn to face her. She skewers me with an icy glare and pats my chest a few times. "Susannah already said no. Plus, I'm sure they've got their own...study *date* planned." Tori wiggles her eyebrows up and down like I'm in on the least funny joke I've ever heard.

"It's up to you," Ben tells Gracie before turning his attention back to me. "I've learned through trial and error that she always makes better decisions than me. I just follow her around everywhere like an annoying shadow." He shrugs, like it's no big deal that he's stuck to her like glue. Following her everywhere, when I barely see her. I didn't even know she made a new friend, let alone a potential boyfriend. And quite possibly the friendliest guy on the planet.

Is Gracie into dating now? Has she kissed him? Does she *love* him? The thought of Gracie giving him her heart makes me more nauseous than the thought of her in his arms. I know I have no right to care, but my thoughts consume me anyway. I quickly avert my eyes, trying to focus on anything but my feelings during this nightmare. One of us has to leave. I can't keep staring at them together.

After looking so light and comfortable around Ben, Gracie's gaze finds me, no doubt seeing the very real anxiety in my eyes. She probably thinks it's related to my football game.

She glances at Ben and speaks casually, with no stutter (clearly fine now that *he's* here), "No, that's okay. I'm sure Tori and D have to review the playbook together."

Jesus. Gracie saying "D" causes a visceral reaction in me, and my whole body shudders. How did I let it get this bad? I've been a selfish dickhead.

Tori observes me closely. "That's so sweet of you, Susannah. You're absolutely right. D's just been so busy with football, and I've been swamped with homecoming plans. We haven't really had any time to connect like we've wanted," she pouts, stroking my forearm. "We'll see you at the game later, then!"

Ben is now looking around at all of us, most likely confused at the current dynamic. *Yeah, that makes two of us, buddy.* My gaze ping pongs between the two of them, still trying to untangle my messy feelings and understand their relationship.

After a beat, Gracie grabs some napkins. "Enjoy your lunch," she mutters before walking away with Ben.

I blow out a frustrated breath as they sit down together on the other side of the cafeteria.

My lunch card gets punched, and I make my way over to my usual table. I typically sit with my teammates and the cheerleaders. It started off as team bonding and then became a habit. I can't even remember the last time I sat with Gracie.

I'm lost in thought when I feel my arm get jerked to the side. Tori pulls me behind a pillar before I can sit down. "Um, what was that?" she asks, narrowing her eyes at me. "Are you jealous of Ben?"

I try to say, "of course not," but what comes out is...silence. Complete and utter silence.

"What the hell, D? I thought you said nothing's going on between you two."

"Nothing *is* going on between us."

She searches my eyes, fuming, trying to interpret my emotions. "But you *want* something to be going on, don't you?"

I try to say, "of course not," but once again, my mouth stays shut. I avert my eyes.

Tori sets down the yogurt parfait she picked up in the lunch line and lifts her fingers to her temples. "I can't believe this. I honestly cannot believe this. Un-fucking-believeable. I put in the work. I date you, support you, come to all your practices, and *this* is how you repay me? By wanting to screw your weird friend who still stutters at sixteen years old?"

I swivel my head toward her slowly, vibrating with fury. My voice lowers in disgust. "What the *fuck* did you just say about her?"

Tori glares at me, not backing down. I never thought of her as anything but attractive until now. She looks downright ugly as she sneers, "Well, it doesn't matter what I said, does it? You don't want me. You want *her*."

"This whole time, you...you what? You never liked Grace?" I wince, thinking about the dumb assumptions I made.

She huffs. "Would you like someone that *I'm* obsessed with?"

"Obsessed?" I shake my head. "What's your problem, Tori?"

Raising her chin and crossing her arms, she complains, "I told her to stay away from you, but no matter what she does, no matter how much distance she puts between you, you still choose her, huh?"

Hurt laces her tone, but I'm incapable of feeling sympathy. I'm too busy focusing on the first part of her sentence.

"Back up. You *told* her to stay away from me? What the hell does that mean?"

Tori looks only slightly ashamed. "She was taking up too much of your brain space, which should be reserved for school, football, and me—your *actual* girlfriend. She was distracting you from your goals. I stepped in to free that space up so you could focus."

I need to find Gracie. "Tori, that's so messed up. I thought you liked me. You don't do shit like that to people you like."

"Whatever. I didn't do anything to you. I did it to her."

I drop my tray down on the table next to the pillar, making a loud noise. "'Kay. In case you don't realize, this," I spit out, gesturing between us, "is over. I need to find Gracie and apologize for everything."

I've been an idiot. If I prioritized her more, maybe she would've told me about what Tori said to her.

Tori grins, but there's no warmth behind her eyes. "Well, good luck, D, because it looks like she's already moved on." She points to the table where Gracie and Ben are sitting, and he has his arm around her shoulders. My stomach plummets.

I've lost my appetite.

Chapter 16

Grace

Sixteen Years Old

"So, uh, you gonna address all of that weird-as-fuck tension back there?" Ben asks as we walk to the other side of the cafeteria.

"It's nothing that I want to get into, really," I mumble, keeping my head down.

"Come on, Grace. You listen to me go on and on about how much I miss Mia, like, every day. I show you pictures of her freaking cat. If anything, I owe you for putting up with me."

I laugh. "I'm an aspiring vet. Looking at animal pictures isn't exactly a hardship for me."

Ben raises an eyebrow. "Clue me in. DT said that you're best friends, but I have literally never seen you in the same room together before today."

I wrestle with the idea of telling Ben the truth. It would be nice to unload some of the weight I've been carrying onto someone I trust, or at least someone who won't judge me. After a few moments of hesitation, I decide to open up.

"Danny isn't just my next-door neighbor. We've been best

friends since we were ten years old. Like 'sneaking over to each other's rooms in the middle of the night, listening to our favorite songs, talking about our hopes and dreams' best friends."

He feigns hurt. "Not gonna lie, I thought I was your best friend."

"You refuse to make other friends here, so technically, I'm your only friend," I counter with a small smile.

"I already have a very full social calendar with you, Grace. Who do you want me to befriend? Good Guy Garett?"

I can't help but giggle. Ben always knows how to keep it light and breezy.

"Plus, what's the point when I'm going back to Indianapolis as soon as humanly possible?"

"I know, I know. You're just looking for reasons to leave me." I grin. We've had this conversation a million times.

His easy smile turns serious again, mouth pressed into a determined line. "So, if you're best friends, why was it so awkward back there?"

Hearing Ben use the word "awkward" to describe Danny's interaction with me causes me to break—how far we've fallen. My eyes start to mist over. *Oh my God, how embarrassing.* Ben puts his arm around me as we turn to face away from the majority of the cafeteria.

"Hey, sorry I asked. You don't have to answer if you don't want to."

"No, it's just been kind of hard. We were incredibly close, basically codependent, until he started dating Tori. Now, I hardly ever see him. The space between us is actually painful," I explain.

"What *is* Tori's deal? She seemed pretty possessive over someone who claims he's your best friend."

"Um, she actually told me to stay away from him," I whisper.

Ben drops his arm from my shoulder to fully face me. "She did *what*?"

"She said that Danny doesn't need to 'lose focus' on his dreams right now, and he was already stressed with how little time he has outside of football. She basically told me to back off and implied that's what he wants, too," I mumble.

Ben shakes his head. "I don't know, Grace. First, you're a great friend, so don't doubt that for anything. Second, Dan seems like a good dude—if not a little possessive of *my* best friend. I just don't think he'd say things like that about you."

"Maybe. Either way, he's made very little effort with me since he got with her. When we hang out, we mostly talk about classes and football." I pause, thinking about how much I'm willing to share. I don't have anyone to talk to about Danny, so it might be nice to get Ben's perspective.

"And...and I think I'm starting to see him as more than a friend. Or I was. Before Tori, I guess. I thought he...well." I weakly grin, shaking my head. "Looking back, thinking that he could like me as anything other than a friend seems silly, considering Tori is almost my exact opposite. I'm sure I was imagining it all."

Ben looks thoughtful as he asks, "Have you talked to him about how you feel?"

"No. Plus, I have you now. Who needs more than one friend?" I give him a shaky smile.

He doesn't smile back. "I think you should talk to him."

"Maybe," I say uncomfortably, wanting to brush this off. "Listen, I...I d-don't really want t-to t-talk about this anymore."

"Alright, say no more. Let's drop it for now."

I take a deep breath, feeling much calmer. "I do have a huge favor to ask you, though," I hedge, hesitation laced in my tone.

Ben's already nodding. "I'm down. What is it?"

"Would you mind coming to the game with me tonight? I

really don't want to go alone. Danny's mom will be there cheering him on, but it'd be nice to have someone there for me. I think I'll look less pathetic."

Ben frowns. "You're not pathetic, but I'll definitely come." He nudges me with his elbow. "Plus, when he becomes famous, I'll be able to say 'I saw Dan Thompson play in high school.'"

I groan. I should've eaten in the library.

Chapter 17

Danny

Sixteen Years Old

I groan as I warm up my muscles on the sideline. *You got this.*

Fans are packed like sardines on the bleachers, outfitted in full navy blue and gold Titans spirit gear. The concession line is long, with tons of people waiting for popcorn and slushies. Our pep band is playing the school fight song in the background as the cheerleaders wave golden poms in the air. I inhale the scent of grassy dirt beneath my cleats, mixed with the evening breeze. It looks, sounds, and smells like a classic Friday night under the lights. I should be raring to go, itching to get out on the field like the superstar everyone expects me to be.

But my thoughts are overwhelmed by Gracie Sinclair.

The fact that I might have missed my chance with her eats me up inside. Tori...what a mistake. I was starting to see Gracie differently, and I should've explored my feelings for her instead of dating the first girl who gave me attention.

I can't believe there are only two years left before we go off to college together. If that's even still the plan. We haven't talked about our future in so long, I'm not sure if she still sees me in hers. Maybe she'll go to a different college with *Ben*, The Nicest Boy Who Ever Lived.

Enough. I shake these thoughts out of my head and look behind the bench to see if they're here yet. Mom, Tessa, and Gracie always sit in the first row of the bleachers, reserved for families of the players. Tori usually sat with her friends a few rows behind them, because she always said she felt awkward sitting with my mom the whole game. But I don't see Tori anywhere, so maybe she decided the field wasn't her "second home" after all.

I continue scanning the area, trying to find Gracie and Mom. After a few moments, I spot Mom and Tessa taking their seats. I give them a little wave, and Mom gives me a thumbs up. She always brings a small, homemade sign with my number on it, and it's in her hands now. Tessa's nose is already buried in her sketchbook, no doubt drawing one of her designs. When Gracie comes trailing in behind her, I feel like I can finally breathe.

Everyone's here now. *Time for some football.*

I lift my hand and wave hi to Gracie when I notice someone following her. I crane my neck for a better view. Blond hair. Lanky. Glasses. Oh, *fuck my life*. It's Ben. Now I have to play a whole game of football while he sits thigh-to-thigh with my Gracie, knowing I only have myself to blame.

The whistle sounds, signaling kick-off. I can't help but glance at Gracie from the sideline while our Special Teams are out on the field. They could probably run the football all the way into the endzone, and I don't think I'd notice. I squint at the stands and watch Mom laugh at something Ben said. *Traitor.*

I jog onto the field and join the huddle, pumping myself up on the way. I need to focus.

Think about playing college football.

My mind betrays me with a vision of Gracie and me at Easton.

Think about playing in the league.

I think about Gracie and me on Draft Day instead.

Think about anything other than Gracie.

"DT! Yo! Earth to DT," our quarterback, Xander, shouts. I snap back to attention. "Alright, boys. Let's make tonight one we'll remember."

The guys nod excitedly, and I find myself robotically bobbing my head up and down in an attempt to fit in.

"ALPHA. Thirty-two, thirty-two, HUT," Xander shouts, and then throws a rocket directly into my hands. I run as fast as I can to the far outside and catch the ball for thirty yards. I don't even need blocking, because no one can keep up with me.

The crowd cheers, I guess? I'm not sure, because I'm staring at the stands. Usually, I'm laser focused during games, actively engaged in play, even on the sideline. Not today.

Today, I'm actively engaged in staring at Gracie and Ben.

* * *

We play great throughout both halves. The guys celebrate as soon as the whistle blows, clapping me on the back and bumping my helmet.

I find it difficult to breathe, let alone celebrate. This game was one of my most average in receiving yards, which doesn't surprise me. It's hard to run your best routes when your focus is elsewhere.

My eyes snag on Gracie as she walks toward the parking lot with Ben. Sweaty and tired, I make a split second decision to run off the field and catch her.

"Hey, do you mind waiting for me?" I ask when I reach her, out of breath.

I hate that she defers to Ben before she answers me.

He nudges her shoulder. "Go ahead, I've got to get going anyway. Are you okay for a ride back, Grace?"

I glance at Mom, who silently mouths *'Grace?'* WOW, at me, while waggling her eyebrows. I glare at her in response, vowing to have words later.

"She's good with me, Ben. I'll take her back."

Ben smirks at me like he knows something I don't. Why does he look so happy with his girlfriend going home with me? *Shit.* He's probably that confident in their relationship. If that's the case, I'm doomed.

"Sounds good. Thanks for coming with me, Ben." She leans in for a hug before turning back to face me. I try not to notice his fingers grazing the bottom of her curls.

Mom cheerfully faces our little trio. "Okay, kiddos. Tessa and I are going to head out. Ben, it was so lovely to meet you. I hope I see you again soon." She winks at me as she walks toward her car. I shoot daggers at my mother, hopefully conveying *whose side are you on?*

I'm still internally stewing when Gracie asks, "Where should I wait for you, Danny?"

I lift an eyebrow like it's weird she's even asking. "Where you always wait for me. Outside the locker room?"

Her forehead wrinkles, confusion written all over her face. "I wasn't sure if you wanted me there or by the parking lot."

"Why would I want you all the way by the parking lot?"

Gracie shifts on her feet. "I just figured Tori would be meeting you outside the locker room."

Rubbing the back of my neck, I say, "Um, no. We, uh, broke up."

Her jaw drops slightly. "You were together at lunch. When did you break up?"

Up close and personal with Gracie for the first time since

before summer, I'm captivated by her mesmerizing eyes and forget to filter my words.

"Right after I saw you," I blurt. "I mean, after I saw you at lunch."

She pauses before replying in a bright tone. "Ah, got it! So, that's why you need me to wait. Did she usually bring you a post-game snack or something? I don't mind grabbing it before we head out."

I allow myself to be horrified for a brief moment. If Gracie thinks I want her to wait for me outside the locker room for a fucking snack, there's some major issues we need to work through.

"No, I don't need anything. I just wanted to talk and ride home with you. We haven't hung out in a while."

The surprise on her face absolutely devastates me. "Oh. Sounds good, Danny."

"See you soon, Gracie girl." My eyes crinkle up at the ends, easily slipping into my comfortable nickname for her, but hers widen.

Absolutely disgusted with myself, I walk into the locker room and try to get ready quickly. But Kyle, our backup quarter-back, intercepts me. He's already changed into a preppy outfit and put gel in his hair. Kyle is a pretty good QB and generous with the ball during practices. We'll be in good hands with him once Xander graduates.

"Hey. Great game, man."

"Thanks. We had fun with it," I reply.

"Yeah," he nods. "Listen, I saw you talking with Susannah outside. You're her neighbor, right?"

If one more person calls me her neighbor, I swear to God I will launch myself into orbit.

"Yes..." I tread cautiously, trying to understand his intent. He can usually get anyone he wants. There's always chatter from the cheerleading squad about who's going to hook up with the future quarterback next.

"Cool. She kind of flies under the radar, but she's actually pretty hot, right? She's been in my chemistry class with Ms. Irene for two quarters now, and I feel like we have a connection. I want to ask her out. You think you can put in a good word for me?"

I know I deserve it, but I'm going to need all of this negative karma to have mercy on me. It's like, all of a sudden, every dude in Winfield High wants Gracie.

"I actually think she's with this other guy, Ben, right now."

He laughs. "No, they're just best friends."

I bristle. *I'm* her best friend.

"They seem into each other," I point out.

"Nah, he's in my history class. He has a girl back in Indianapolis he's crazy about. Susannah and Ben are definitely just best friends."

A bucket of relief is dumped on my head as I process this new information. If she's single, that means I can pursue her without feeling like a jerk. I just have to consider the timing. Tori and I broke up today. If I tell Gracie how I feel now, she might think that I'm just looking for a rebound. I need to play the long game here.

"Um, in that case, sure. I can talk to her about you."

I don't specify in what capacity I'll be talking about him. I definitely don't say I'll be talking about him cheating on his last girlfriend with a cheerleader.

He gives me a grin. "Thanks, man. I appreciate it."

I grin back, only feeling a little bad. "Anytime."

Chapter 18

Grace

Sixteen Years Old

I anxiously wait outside the locker room for Danny to finish getting ready. Standing in front of the reflective windows of the building, I take in my appearance. Worn, scuffed up white sneakers, my trusty gray-wash jeans, and Danny's old football club shirt that I threw on for this game after school. My hair is frizzy from the wind, and I look tired.

It's been a long day, and I'm ready to go home.

Why did Tori and Danny break up? It doesn't make any sense. They were fine at lunch. She was bragging about being the perfect girlfriend. He was standing there letting her pet his arm for God's sake.

I shudder uncomfortably. Maybe I should've just gone home with Ben.

Danny and I used to talk about everything, but the contrast of who we were before Tori and who we are after her is jarring. I know he's my best friend, and I have no reason to have a pit in my stomach, but I'm worried it'll be awkward. What if we struggle to find our footing and the conversation lulls? What if we've changed and can't go back?

My stomach churns thinking about what it'll be like to be alone with him again. Even though Danny got his license a while ago, I've never been in his car. Danny offered to take me to school when the semester started a couple weeks ago, but he also drove Tori, and I just...couldn't be in the same car as them every single morning.

Plus, I have a sneaking suspicion that Danny is a terrible driver.

In general, Danny's ability to follow rules appears to be limited to the sport of football. If you need to know every possible receiver route in a two hundred page playbook, he's your guy. If you need to build a small, two drawer dresser? Look elsewhere. On the scale of football playing to furniture building, I find driving to be closer to building territory.

I don't have my license yet because Dad refuses to sign me up. Even if I enroll in classes myself, without a car or willing parent, it's a lost cause. It's just another way I feel shackled in my own home.

Danny exits the locker room, freshly showered and ready to go. His thick, black hair, damp from a shower, droops slightly over his forehead, and his light brown skin glistens in the moonlight. He's changed into Titans Athletics clothes and Jordans. With a tentative smile on his face, he scratches behind his ear and appears flushed. Is he...nervous? Around *me*?

"Hey, thanks for waiting," he says.

"I really had nowhere to go. All of my potential rides have already left the premises."

Danny laughs. "Great, so you see me as a last resort. By the end of our drive, do you think I can convince you to start riding with me to school?"

"I'll let you know after I evaluate your driving skills," I say matter-of-factly as we walk toward the parking lot.

He lifts his chin. "Gracie, please. I'm an excellent driver. Flawless, really. You should see me parallel park."

"Good for you." I stop walking for a moment and look up at him. "Did you pass the test on the first try?"

He pauses and avoids eye contact with me. "I see no reason why that's relevant."

"Jeez, Danny. How many tries? Two?"

Danny resumes walking, jingling his keys in his hand.

"Holy shit. Am I going to die?" I follow after him, nearly jogging to catch up with his long strides.

"I'll have you know the driving examiner had it out for me."

I roll my eyes as we reach his car. "Please."

"He did. He was wearing a Yellowjackets shirt. You know the Yellowjackets are our rivals. He probably recognized me and graded me unfairly," he argues.

I raise an eyebrow. "Really? I find it odd that you would get the same examiner for both of the failed tests."

"Well, the other ones disliked me, too, on principle. I could tell."

"*Ones*?! Plural? Seriously, Danny, how many times did it take for you to pass the test? I deserve to know. It should be a mandatory disclosure for any riders in your vehicle."

Danny coughs to hide it, but I can still hear him say "four" under his breath.

"Should I start praying?"

"You're not religious."

"I know, but this is an emergency scenario. I feel like God would take prayers by urgency and not the order in which they're received. He just seems like that kind of guy, from what I know of him," I explain, frantically gesturing to the sky.

"You've been to church a grand total of one time, Gracie," he says flatly.

I pretend to be greatly offended. "*Wow*, Danny. Wow. Bringing up my mom's funeral before you've even started the car."

He laughs and we climb into his used blue Prius. It's pretty clean on the inside with the exception of six empty sports drink bottles on the passenger side floor. I gently kick them over so I have room for my feet.

"Speaking of moms," he says, "how come you're better friends with my mom than me lately? Not gonna lie, I'm jealous."

"I don't know, Danny, maybe that has something to do with you all but ditching me over the summer," I joke, then wince when it falls flat.

He's not smiling. "Can we talk about that?"

"About what?"

"The way I've been acting."

I fasten my seatbelt and shift nervously in my seat, fiddling with the climate controls. Going into this car ride, I kind of hoped he wouldn't address it and kind of hoped he would. "Oh. Um, okay. If you want."

"I'm sorry, Gracie. I've been a shitty friend for a while now. I let football camps and other relationships get in the way of us, and...well, I want my best friend back. I'm not just saying this because of my breakup, and"—he takes a deep breath—"I miss you."

I pause, digesting his apology. He *has* been a shitty friend. At the same time, I never told him how I was feeling and made assumptions on his behalf. Every friendship experiences ups and downs. With Danny, there were so many ups that any down was going to feel big.

I'm ready to put this behind us, but vulnerability makes me

nervous. Even though I inhale, then exhale slowly, my stutter still highlights my anxiety. "I miss you, t-too. I should've t-told you how I was feeling, b-but I guess I was scared. You were d-dating T-Tori, and I d-didn't want t-to rock the b-boat or t-take up more of your t-time," I mumble, tucking a curl behind my ear.

Danny's face hardens. "Yeah, about that bullshit. Tori told me what she said to you. Gracie, it's not true. If anything, I want you to take up *more* of my time. I hate that she put doubt in your head, but I hate myself even more for focusing on football so much I didn't notice. You're my best friend."

"You're my b-best friend, t-too," I reply quietly. "I know how important football is t-to you, b-but our friendship is just as important. I d-don't want t-to d-distract you, I want t-to support you. I forgive you this t-time, b-but I won't let you t-treat me that way again, just casting me off when it was convenient for you."

"I promise you I won't. Never again. Our friendship is more important to me than anything. I'm so sorry I didn't act like it over the past three months."

I nod, feeling better now that we've talked this out.

"Can I say it one more time?"

I smile. "Sure."

"I'm sorry, Gracie girl."

He turns the engine on and feeds the Dashboard Confessional CD into the stereo slot. We catch up on everything. He tells me about the guys on the team and asks me questions about my friendship with Ben. I swear Danny looks relieved when I bring up Ben's girlfriend, Mia, but I'm probably imagining it.

We can't stop smiling and teasing each other. It's all so easy. It's all so *us*.

Chapter 19

Danny

Sixteen Years Old

I'm kind of a terrible driver. I lured Gracie into my car under false pretenses. Her suspicions were confirmed almost immediately after I put the car in neutral instead of reverse. She sighs in relief as I pull into our neighborhood.

"I've never been more grateful for another day on earth. I think I might convert to a religion after all, or maybe hike up a mountain. There are so many things I want to do in my life that I'm just now realizing..." She trails off sarcastically, the little villain.

I roll my eyes. "You're being dramatic. It wasn't that bad, Gracie."

"Stop signs turn white when they see you coming, Danny," she deadpans.

"You would prefer I slow down a mile in front of the stop sign? The whole point is to stop *at* the stop sign. First, you have to make it there."

Gracie taps her bottom lip a few times. "You know, you're right. Accelerating before slamming on the brakes makes so much more sense." She nods as I put the car in park in her driveway.

I run my hands through my hair. "In my defense, the construction detour took us on a weird and unfamiliar route."

She stares straight out the windshield. "Agreed. For a moment there, I thought we were driving directly to Hell."

"Get out of my car, Susannah Sinclair."

"Okay, okay," she apologizes. "You know, you're not the *worst* driver in the world..."

"Thank you."

"But you better hope *they* don't die."

Against my will, I laugh. "Are you done?"

She unfastens her seatbelt, climbs out of the car, and makes a big show of kissing the grass in her front yard. My headlights spotlight her in the dark like she's an actress on a stage.

"Ah, solid ground, how I've missed thee." She picks a yellow dandelion from the ground and tosses it at me through the window. "Here, Danny. This is for you to keep in your glovebox. May it remind you that there's life worth living outside the confines of your Prius death trap."

I flip her off. God, I like her so much.

I place the dandelion in my glove box, not to remind me of my awful driving, but to remind me that I can't—I won't—take her for granted again. Then, I put the car in reverse and travel the remaining fifteen feet to my house.

While the outside of our modest house isn't anything special, the inside is a completely different story. When I open the door, my eyes snag on a new photo in the entryway. Every inch of our home is an homage to the creativity of the women in my life.

Each room is painted a rich color, and the kitchen is no exception with its deep scarlet walls. Like the rest of the house, the walls are covered in framed photos, and I can barely see the surface of our black refrigerator through all of Tessa's artwork.

Mom's washing dishes, and they're piling up on the rack. I grab a towel and start drying.

"Hello, Judas," I say, glaring at my mother.

"What's that chilly greeting for?"

"Oh, I don't know. Maybe because you replaced me with *Ben* as your son? I saw you two laughing it up with Gracie at the game."

"Please, Daniel. You need to stop playing around and get your head out of your ass."

I grab another plate to dry. "Wow, Mom. Tell me how you really feel."

"How I really feel is that you have liked your best friend as *more* than a friend since you were probably ten years old, and you've treated her like absolute garbage since you started dating that horrid girl."

"You thought she was *horrid?* Jesus." I run my hand down my face. She just stands there, unapologetically blinking at me in response. "Well," I continue, "for your information, I broke up with said 'horrid girl' at lunch today."

She turns off the water and stares at me. "You didn't."

"I did."

"Really?"

"Yep."

She wraps me up in a hug so tight I can barely breathe, and the blue dish soap on her hands soaks through my shirt. "I've never been prouder of you, Daniel."

I remove her arms from my waist. "Why didn't you tell me you hated Tori?"

"I've never been one to coddle, kiddo. You need to make your own choices and your own mistakes. You'll never be able to handle future consequences if you're not fully in control of the choices you make for yourself. Now, *she* was a particularly bad choice, but I've dated a few worse in my past."

"And yet you still judge me."

She kisses me on the head three times. "I knew you'd come around."

"Alright, alright," I complain. We're both smiling now.

"Daniel! Daniel!" Tessa comes bounding into the kitchen wearing her prized *Lion King* pajamas. Her long, dark, wavy ponytail trails behind her.

I smile and crouch down. "Shouldn't you be in bed by now, Tessie?" I fake pout. "Mom never let me stay up this late when I was nine."

Tessie giggles. "I wanted to show you my drawing! I drew you in your football uniform." She hands me a ripped out piece of lined notebook paper and beams. "I showed G my drawing at the game, and she said it was the most beautiful picture she's ever seen."

I pick Tessie up and set her on the countertop. "She did, huh? Do you think Gracie was talking about your drawing skills or how handsome I look?" I tickle her sides, and she squeals, pushing me away.

"Obviously, not you. You're a dweeb." She pokes me in the chest with her finger.

"Mom! Tessie called me a dweeb!" I whine loudly in an exaggerated tattle-tale tone.

"Tessa," Mom says in a warning voice, "you know better. That's not even a good insult."

"Hey!" I pretend to be offended. "Stop bullying me."

Tessie sighs like she's exhausted from my antics. "So, what do you think of my drawing? Are you going to hang it up in your room?"

My room is covered in her art, and so is Gracie's room. I can't remember a time when Tessie wasn't drawing. My mom definitely passed down all her creativity to her. I take a look at the paper and smile so hard my eyes squint. The sketch is pretty amazing for a kid her age. She even drew all the stickers on my helmet.

"This is *too* good, Tessie. You drew this all by yourself? I can't believe all the details you added. My jersey looks just like it does in real life."

Mom catches my eye and gives me the "wrap it up" gesture, rolling her wrist in a circle. I grab Tessie and put her back on the ground. "Do you mind hanging this up in my room for me? I'll be up in a minute to tuck you in and say goodnight."

"Yay!" Tessie sprints out of the kitchen and up the stairs.

I take my role in her life very seriously. Our dad preferred to spend his time traveling the world as a freelance journalist rather than parenting in Ohio. He filed for divorce once Tessa was born and returned to his home state of New York. Tessie never knew him, which is for the best. Over the years, my own good memories of Dad have faded into only two: watching Mustangs football together and throwing the pigskin around in the backyard.

We're doing just fine without him.

As I finish drying the last dish, Mom whispers, "So, tell me what the plan is! What are you going to do about our neighbor girl?"

"I can't tell her how I feel yet, Mom. It's too soon after the break up. I want Gracie to know I'm serious about her."

She nods thoughtfully. "That makes sense. But don't lose your chance, Daniel. You'll probably only get one."

Chapter 20

Danny

This is my chance. I scramble to take a seat on the couch as soon as I hear her footsteps. While Gracie was upstairs getting ready for bed, I was hard at work setting up a surprise in the family room: a classic Danny-Gracie movie night. It's nearly eleven, but I hope she's up for extending our time together just a bit before she turns in for the night.

I'm sitting on the couch, eagerly awaiting her reaction. I hear it before I see it.

She cackles. "*Die Hard*, Danny? Really?"

I swivel my head around and tilt my chin up. She looks cozy in an emerald cropped sweatshirt and joggers. The green brings out the red in those curls I love so much.

"It was the obvious choice, Gracie. It's been too long since our annual viewing of the best movie on planet earth."

"Did you make popcorn?"

I playfully scoff. "As if there's any other appropriate movie snack. And don't worry, I already mixed in the chocolate chips for you, you weirdo."

She peers over my shoulder into the bowl of popcorn, no doubt checking to confirm I've added enough melted butter.

Gracie was always a fiend for popcorn and a self-proclaimed "slut for melted butter." One time, during senior year of high school, she put so much butter-flavored topping on her popcorn that two movie theater employees had to replace the butter container. Any normal popcorn consumer might've been embarrassed, but not her. My little Orville Redenbacher just stood there, staring at the employees like they should've planned for a singular girl to drain them of their butter-flavored topping supply. *"How does a movie theater run out of butter?"* she had the nerve to whisper to me. I rolled my eyes and responded with, *"How does one avoid the noises of you slurping it off your little piggies during the movie?"*

"There's enough butter, I promise," I say flatly.

She doesn't look convinced. "How many sticks did you put in?"

"Sticks?! Plural? Gracie, this is one small bag of popcorn. If you want to drink the butter, I'll get you a funnel and pour it directly down your gullet. If I add any more butter to this, there's no way I can eat it. It's popcorn chowder at that point."

"I don't see how that's my problem. In fact, it sounds like a 'you' problem."

"Alright, that's enough. Sit your ass down and watch the damn movie."

She grabs the bowl of popcorn, lowers herself to the couch, and sits two feet away from me with her feet pulled up, entirely too far away for my liking. That won't do. I briefly consider pulling a Danny of Yore move, but I don't want to do anything she's uncomfortable with, so I gently place my hands on her ankles and hold them there for a minute. I wait for her reaction before doing anything else. She blushes, the corners of her lips turning up, as she wiggles her toes like she knows what's coming. As if we're seventeen again, I swing the ends of her ankles in my direction and scoot her toward me until her ass touches my thigh.

She giggles as she squeals, "Quit it! I'm going to drop the popcorn!"

I pause but don't let go of her ankles. All of sudden, I'm feeling comfortable enough to stay right here for the next seven to ten business days. "You know, you're right. I forgot to put a tarp on the couch to account for all the drippings. I know it will be nearly impossible, but please try to be careful."

"Oh, fuck you. You're making me want to get butter all over your couch even *harder*, now. And I know you can afford a new one, so don't try me."

I laugh as I start gently massaging her feet.

She softly says, "You don't have to do this, *you're* probably the sore one."

"I feel perfect," I reply. The only thing about me that aches is my heart. I'm numb to anything that isn't Gracie right now.

The title scrolls across the screen and I happily sigh. "Is this not the best? Eating popcorn, being couch potatoes, watching our favorite movie? Even though you give me shit, I've missed our conversations."

I've missed you, I want to amend. I've been miserable without you. I'm so lonely, Gracie. Have you been lonely, too?

"Well, there's always more where that came from."

There's no hope of me containing my soft smile at the thought of "always." I keep rubbing her feet to give my hands something to do so they don't travel higher and take a moment to really soak in the sight of her. God. She steals my breath.

Gracie watches the movie, and I watch her.

* * *

I order one more pack of butter through a grocery delivery app an hour into the movie.

The teen delivery driver looks at me with wide, surprised eyes when I intercept him at the door. Probably wondering what sick freak urgently needs butter at midnight. He definitely recognizes me, too. I can already picture tomorrow's headlines... *"DT And His Butter Kink!"*

It's worth it, though, because the little butter monster next to me is gobbling up her second bag, which is effectively extending our time together down here.

"This is better than I remember," Gracie quips happily through a mouthful of popcorn.

I'm not sure if she's talking about the movie, the popcorn, or spending time with me, but I'll take it as a win.

"Plus, you're definitely a better movie partner than Mae."

I chuckle. "What makes you say that?"

"You know those people that ask way too many questions during the movie, even in a movie theater?"

I nod. "Yep, my mom toes the line there. I didn't know Mae's that kind of person."

Wiping her butter-coated hands on a napkin, she says, "Oh yeah. It's always, *'Who is playing the part of this orange fish? Is it Martin Short?'*"

I bite my lower lip. "What is it with her and Martin Short?"

She giggles. "Legend has it that Mae saw him at Big Boy Restaurant once in the nineties. Ever since, any and all animated characters? Voiced by Martin Short. Doesn't matter if it's a five-year-old girl. *'It must be Martin Short!'*"

We both dissolve into laughter. God, it's been years since I've heard the sound of Gracie's real laugh. I've missed the bell-like quality to it and how unrestrained she is when something is really funny. She breathes through her nose, going completely silent in between laughs, catching her breath. Her eyes light up, sparkling with easy, childlike joy. I stare at her with wonder and disbelief that we're here again. Together.

After a few moments, we try to focus back on the movie, but I can tell Gracie's mind is elsewhere. She's biting the inside of her cheek and looking to the right of the screen. I'm about to ask her what's wrong, but she speaks before I do.

"Listen, Danny. We should probably discuss why I'm here."

My stomach drops. I want more time. More opportunities to show her how much I've changed over the last ten years. To show her that we belong together. "After the movie, Gracie. We can't interrupt John McClane like that, it's disrespectful. I'm in no rush."

In actuality, two things are warring in my head: I desperately want to know why she's here, and I desperately want her to stay. But I won't risk her leaving to satisfy my own curiosity.

She looks torn as she pops another piece of popcorn in her mouth. "I guess it *would* be pretty awful of us to not give the greatest action hero of all time his due."

Gracie yawns as she sinks deeper into the cushions. As the popcorn in the bucket dwindles, so does our stamina. Her eyes droop lower and lower until she finally drifts asleep before the ending credits scroll. I pull a cozy, plush blanket up over her body, while keeping her legs on my lap. I tell myself I'll head up as soon as the movie is finished.

Instead, I fall asleep next to Gracie.

Chapter 21

Danny

Seventeen Years Old

Gracie and I are watching *Die Hard*, again, for the fifth time this year. She's so beautiful in her short-sleeve pink shirt and matching sweatpants, curled up beside me on the sofa. A word is embroidered on the sweatpants across her ass in capital letters, and I'm trying very hard not to stare.

I don't have a game tonight, which means extra time with my best friend. We're at her house today for the first time in a long time. She has a better TV. Plus, her dad will be out late at the bars like he is every Friday night, so we have the place all to ourselves.

Her house is a similar size to mine but severely lacks personality on the inside. The main living area is closed-concept, with a white wall between the kitchen and family room. Normally, beer bottles litter the countertops, but she must've done some serious cleaning before I came over tonight. The only photos of her mother are hidden in her nightstand drawer, alongside several pictures of us. It pains me that Gracie can't proudly display them, worried sick that her dad will smash the frames in one of his drunken stupors, as he's done in the past.

Our favorite scene of the entire movie starts—the infamous Ellis negotiations. I start on my practiced impressions. I flash every tooth in my mouth.

"Hans, *bubby*," I drag out with flair, "I'm your white knight."

She can't stop giggling, her eyes rolling back.

"Come out to the coast, we'll get together, have a few laughs," she replies in the worst mafioso accent I've ever heard. She sounds like a child playing Vito in a school production of *The Godfather Junior*.

She's terrible at accents. For some reason though, when she's quoting *Die Hard*, Gracie never stutters on any of her sounds. She calls it "The Die Hard Exception," and it's something we can't explain. But if quoting the cast makes her less anxious, it's well worth the hundred views.

It's been over a year since I broke it off with Tori, and we only have a few weeks of school left as juniors. Gracie rides to school with me every day (against her better judgment), and we eat lunch together a few times a week when she's not studying in the library with Ben.

It turns out that Ben is, in fact, a very cool guy and someone I now call a friend. I'm happy he was there for her when I was being an idiot, and it's been a blast hanging out, the three of us. He'll often call his girlfriend and put her on speaker when we're all together. I love it when he does, because it almost feels like a double date.

I still haven't confessed my feelings to Gracie, but the urge to tell her the truth grows stronger every single second.

I want to tell her she's beautiful, instead of pretty.

I want to trade our hugs for kisses.

I want to ask my best friend to be my girlfriend.

But the words sit heavy on my tongue. Things are so good between us right now... I don't want to mess anything up with her ever again.

We're cuddled close on the couch, and she puts her head on my shoulder. Gracie could be in my lap, and I'd still somehow never feel close enough. Maybe if my hand was glued to her hand... I instantly shudder. My "creepy to cutesy" meter may need some recalibrating.

She nudges her toes behind my calves. I grab her feet, which are always cold, and swing them over into my lap so she's facing me. I start warming up her feet with my hands, rubbing them up and down. It's a reflexive move, one we've been doing since we were younger. My hands start to rub her ankle, and she flinches. A flicker of pain flashes in her eyes, and I immediately stop touching her.

"Shit, Gracie. Sorry. I thought I was being gentle, but I must've pressed too hard. Did I hurt you?"

She gives me a strained smile. If it's meant to be reassuring, it has the opposite effect. "No, no. Not your fault. My ankle was sore from something earlier this week."

I squint, searching her face for signs of the truth. An ankle injury doesn't make sense. Gracie didn't mention anything about hurting her ankle until now. She doesn't play any sports. Her house is a ranch, so there's no chance of twisting an ankle on a staircase.

"How did you injure it?"

"It was nothing, just a minor accident. No b-big d-deal," she says quietly, avoiding eye contact.

Something's not right.

"You're biting your cheek, Gracie. And you're stuttering." A horrible feeling soaks into my skin. "Are you...are you *lying* to me?"

Her face turns red, and my stomach bottoms out. With

shaky hands, I reach for the remote control and pause the movie.

"You told me it was better. You said he doesn't do that anymore."

"I know, and he hasn't d-done anything physically in a while. He still, um, yells at me, b-but this"—she points to her ankle—"was a one-off."

I feel like I'm going to be sick. "What happened? No lies. Please don't lie to me."

Her words come out quickly and almost all at once. "D-Don't make this a b-bigger d-deal than it is, please. He lost money at the casino this past weekend and d-drank more than usual. He's b-been, um, b-better over the past few months, so I guess I just wasn't expecting it. He was already pretty upset when he came home. B-But then, when he saw I d-didn't clean my d-dishes from d-dinner, he kind of roughly pushed me t-to my room, and I wasn't in control of my b-body...and, and I b-banged my ankle on the d-door frame."

"Is this why you didn't want to hang out with me on Sunday?" My voice trembles with every word. "You were, what? Sitting at home resting a swollen ankle?"

All she does is silently nod.

"Gracie," I whisper.

She looks down and away, eyes glued to the floor.

"Let me look at it, please. You don't need to hide from me," I say softly.

"Okay."

After placing the remote on the table, I gingerly roll up the leg of her sweatpants and pull down her sock. An angry, dark yellowish-green bruise surrounds a swollen area the size of a golf ball on her left ankle. *How is she even wearing normal shoes with this?* The sheer force he must've pushed her with to do this kind of damage... I brush my thumb in a feather-like touch against her battered ankle and suck in a shaky breath.

"You need to ice and elevate this, Gracie. It won't heal properly if you keep walking on it," I say weakly.

"Yeah, I figured. I'll d-do it after you leave, okay?" She snatches the remote off the table and turns the movie back on.

We sit in silence for two minutes before I decide I've had it. I grab the remote and completely turn off the TV.

"We need to report him. Enough is enough."

"Danny, I t-told you not t-to make this a b-big d-deal. I'll b-be eighteen soon anyway. He won't stay like this forever. I'm positive."

"You can't be serious. It's been years of the same bullshit," I reply, my voice hoarse. "I can't...*fuck*. I'm trying not to take away from how you're feeling. I don't want to make this about me. It's just...it's just so goddamn hard to sit by and watch you get hurt. Emotionally, physically, it doesn't matter. It's all hard to swallow." The blood rushes from my head, and my heart rate speeds up. "If you just let me help you, Gracie, I can fix this. I'm trying to understand."

"That's just it. You d-don't understand. He's my d-dad, and he could get b-better soon. He's still d-dealing with the loss of my mother. I'm not over her either. I'll never b-be over her." She slowly pulls her feet off my legs and scoots back on the couch.

I lean toward her, closing the distance between us. "I know, but that's no excuse for how he treats you. It's not right, Gracie. Parents shouldn't do this to their kids. I want to be there for you. Let me be there for you."

"It was a one-off thing, I'm sure of it. It had b-been a really long t-time since we had an incident b-before this one. He hasn't even b-been missing work recently. You d-don't need t-to worry."

I cover her hand with mine. "I care about you, Gracie. I care about you more than anything."

"Well, if you care about me, then you won't say anything. We've b-been through this b-before. If the police b-believe you, they'll send me t-to my only living relative, Mae, in Florida. If Mae can't t-take care of me, I'll go into the foster care system. If the police d-don't b-believe you, I'll stay with D-dad, except he'll b-be angrier than b-before. There's no positive outcome."

I snatch my hand back and nervously run it through my hair. "No positive outcome? *No positive outcome?* It would suck if you lived in Florida, Gracie, but you know what? At least you wouldn't be bruised. At least you wouldn't be hurt. At least you wouldn't be fearing for your goddamn life every single day. At least I wouldn't have to see my girlfriend beaten within an—"

She brings her hand to her mouth. "Your girl?"

Heat rises in my chest, and I can't stop barreling through my words. "Because *guess what*, Gracie? It doesn't matter if you go to Florida. It doesn't matter if you're a plane ride away. You could go to California. You could go to Amsterdam. You could live in fucking *Tokyo*! It doesn't matter. Because in any country, you'd be away from him. You'd be secure. You'd be safe. And you'd *still* be mine."

"Be, be yours? Danny, I..."

I turn my head toward her without thinking and lean in. When our foreheads gently meet, Gracie gives a small gasp. My lips are so close to hers now, hovering slightly above them. I tuck a curl behind her ear, and it immediately springs back in front of her mouth. The corners of my lips turn up, and I twirl the curl with my finger this time, gently tugging on the end. Her breath smells like buttered popcorn and vanilla chapstick.

"Gracie," I whisper, my breath warming her face. "Do you want me to—"

"Yes. Oh my gosh, *yes*."

My heart is pounding, I can feel it in my throat. This is it. I make a move to close the last bit of distance between us before the jarring sound of the front door slamming into the coat rack infiltrates our ears.

We snap apart.

Her dad is home.

Chapter 22

Grace

Seventeen Years Old

"Susannah! Where's my fuckin' food? I work all day and come home to an empty dinner table... *Susannah!* Right now, girl. Goddamn, yer sssslow as shit."

Oh my God. *No.* This can't be happening. Danny's never been with me during one of Dad's rampages. He always arrives soon after, in a rush, but usually after Dad has passed out or left. I never wanted Danny to see this side of me. I've gone through painstaking efforts to keep him separate. Shit. *Shit.*

My heartbeat quickens. I jump up and frantically smooth down my hair. "D-Danny, you have t-to go. Now."

He shakes his head, staring at me with sadness in his eyes. "I'm not leaving, Gracie."

"D-Danny. Please," I beg him. "It will make things so much worse. If you care about me, you'll leave." I start pushing on his chest, but trying to move him is a lost cause. He's a brick wall. This stubborn boy is going to get us both hurt. I can't let anything happen to him. I'd never forgive myself.

"*Because* I care about you, I'll stay," he responds.

My dad always goes straight to the refrigerator when he gets home drunk off his ass. I usually put a sandwich on the table to prevent a blow up, but I didn't think he'd be home at all tonight.

Dad's footsteps echo through the hallway. He'll be here soon if I don't meet him right away. Each step is like a blow to my heart.

Boom.

Boom.

Boom.

His heavy tread echoes from the hallway to the family room.

"I d-don't want you involved in this, D-Danny, leave!" Tears roll down my face as I frantically push on his chest, but he refuses to move. "Leave, please. *Leave*, D-Danny," I croak feebly now, losing the fight to push him away.

"No. I'm done standing on the sidelines. What we have is worth getting 'involved.' I *want* to be involved with you. Please don't push me away." His eyes mist over, pleading with mine.

"You have no idea what you're getting yourself into. He's, *God*, he's almost here…" I weakly tug at his shirt.

"Every time I see a mark on you, a piece of my heart shatters. Every fucking time, Gracie. I've had *enough*. If you want me to beg for your forgiveness after this, I will. But I'm not asking for your permission. Not anymore. You're too important to me."

My brain screams for Danny to leave, but my heart disagrees, desperately wanting him to stay. I can't deny that having him near makes me feel safer.

"*Susaaaannah!* Why aren't you answerin'? Your stutter make you go duh-duh-duh-deaf now, too?" he mocks. "Fuckin' dumbassss. Stupid as shhhhit. Your mother would be so disappointed."

The hallway bathroom door crashes against the wall, and I flinch. Danny wraps me in a hug, pressing my head against his chest and covering the other ear with his hand. That doesn't stop me from hearing the long stream of pee hitting the water in the toilet bowl. At least I won't have to clean it up this time.

My body temperature keeps throwing me for a loop, alternating between hot humiliation and frigid fear. Panicking, I pull out of Danny's embrace. "I'm... Should we—"

"*What am I lookin' at here?*" My dad stands tall and menacing, staring straight at us. His eyes are rimmed red from the alcohol, and his lips are shiny, dripping almost. He's more disheveled than I've seen him in months. The cream colored button-down work shirt he's wearing appears to be stained with beer...or God knows what. One of his pant pockets is flipped inside out, and his right shoelace is untied. He only gets this way if the bartender cuts him off, which rarely happens given how much money he spends there.

I try to take a step forward, but I'm stopped by something. I glance down. When did Danny start holding my hand? I shake my hand aggressively, trying to let go of his. He holds it tighter.

"What do you *think* you're looking at?" Danny counters. *Oh no.*

"You have about three secondsss to get outta my house, boy." My dad glares at me. "I'll deal with you after, Susannah."

"I'm not going anywhere unless she comes with me." Danny looks my father directly in his eyes.

"I shoulda known, Susannah. Having boys over like a lil' whore when your ol' man ain't home," he slurs, drool coming out of his mouth. "Such a fuckin' ssslut."

I hopelessly try to de-escalate my father. "D-Dad, you know Dan-Danny, he lives next d-door. I'm not having any b-boys over."

Danny interrupts my desperation. "Don't explain yourself to him, Gracie." His voice is dark, darker than I've ever heard.

"You don't owe him anything with the way he treats you. He won't take you at your word anyway."

My dad stumbles a drunken step closer to Danny. All six feet of Danny meets Dad's stare dead on.

"Is this how you treat your eldersss, boy?" he snarls. "I'll sssay it one more time. *Get. Out. Of. My. House.*"

Danny puffs his chest out and sniffs. "You can't do anything to me. I don't answer to you. I'll call the police."

"B-but you promised me," I whisper, frozen in fear.

My dad grins, spit gathering in the corners of his mouth. "You're right, kid. I s'pose you don't belong to me." He focuses his attention on me, now, and gives a sinister chuckle that chills me to my core. "But Susannah does, don't she? And the longer you're here, the more she'll deal with the consequences."

Chapter 23

Danny

Seventeen Years Old

I stare at her dad straight in his bloodshot eyes, unafraid of what might happen to me. I almost hope he hits me. At least then I would be able to press charges and she'd be safe. *Gracie would also move away*, my selfish subconscious cuts in. I shake my head and focus on the task at hand. Her safety is my number one priority.

Her dad burps loudly, cutting through my thoughts. "I'm not in the habit of waiting," he slurs in a high-pitched, mocking tone of voice. "And I've given you more'an enough time. I'm not usually this generrrrous." His face reddens with anger, looking almost purple now.

As he lunges forward, I get ready to go toe-to-toe, but he stumbles right past me toward Gracie. He reaches for her hair but misses and whacks her face instead. She staggers sideways toward the brick fireplace. Before she can steady herself, her forehead hits the corner of the wooden mantle and she crashes to the ground. Blood trickles from a cut at her hairline, looking like red paint against her pale skin.

"Gracie!" I quickly crouch down on the floor next to her. Holding her close as she cries in pain, I gingerly stroke her forehead, just below the cut. Blood coats my finger, and I swallow the bile rising in my throat. Drops of blood slide down her cheek, mixing with the tears streaming down her face.

Her eyes try to focus on me as a small whimper leaves her lips.

I know I will remember that sound for the rest of my life.

I don't have time to concentrate on anything else but her. I closely examine her wound and try not to cry, only vaguely noticing when her dad stumbles back out of the house. I hold Gracie tightly until I feel her breaths even out, getting drops of her blood on the shoulder of my gray T-shirt.

"It's fine, D-Danny," she whispers meekly. "He won't even really remember this t-tomorrow. He never d-does. He d-didn't even mean t-to hurt me this b-bad, b-badly. You saw for yourself. I was knocked off b-balance."

Hearing her repeatedly stutter my name cuts me to my core. "You need to come with me. Right now. I need to take care of you, of this." I gesture to her swollen head injury. "He's a lost cause, Gracie. We'll figure something out together. We can tell my mom, and—"

Her walls go up. "You need t-to let me make my own d-decisions. I'm not a child."

"I know you're not. Of course you're not. But it's okay to ask for help. Mae and my mom would only have your best interests in mind. They would never make you do anything you don't want to do. I can make sure of it. Trust me."

She crosses her arms. "I'm actually feeling much b-better. You d-don't even need t-to stay."

Huh? "Don't even need to... Be serious, Gracie. I'm not leaving when you're bleeding." My stomach plummets at the thought of walking away, and a bead of sweat slides down my temple.

"So there's a b-bit of b-blood? Nothing I can't handle. Nothing I haven't handled b-before."

I flinch. "You shouldn't have to 'handle' anything. It doesn't have to be this way. You don't deserve what's happening to you. You're worth more than—"

"I know *exactly* what I'm worth." She glares at me and pushes to her feet, but I can tell she's slightly woozy when she rises from the floor. I stand and hold her arm in case she needs the support.

Tugging her closer to me, until she's flush with my side, I gently smooth a curl back from her wound. "I didn't mean...it's just, you have to understand where I'm coming from here."

"We'll b-be eighteen soon, D-Danny. There's no point in changing anything now." She pulls away and walks over to the coffee table, picking up a tissue.

"The point is you're not safe, Grace."

With a small sniff, she presses a tissue to her wound, blocking it from my view. "I think you should go now. Please."

I rear back. "Is that really what you want?"

She crumples up the tissue in her hand, crossing her arms. "For t-tonight, yes."

I run my fingers through my hair and take a deep breath in through my teeth. The last thing I want to be is another man in her life who bends her to his will. I don't want to take away her agency, but something's got to give.

"I'm going to call you in one hour. If you don't pick up, I'm coming back over to check on you."

She doesn't even glance my way. "Sure."

Everything in me screams not to leave her right now. It's like my feet are latched to invisible sandbags as I forcibly drag myself through her house.

On the way out, my eyes snag on the open refrigerator. I walk over to close it, because the last thing she needs is spoiled food. Hanging on the refrigerator door is a magnetic notepad— with Grandma Mae's phone number on it.

Should I...

I don't overthink it. I rip a blank sheet from the pad, grab a pen from the counter, copy the number onto it, and leave.

As soon as I step into my bedroom, I shut the door and pull out the paper. Mae's a night owl, according to Gracie, so she should be awake. With shaky hands, I dial the number and wait for her voice.

"Hello?"

"Mae?"

"This is she. Who am I speaking with?"

"It's, uh, Daniel. Danny. Danny Thompson? You might remember me. I live next door to Gracie, erm, Susannah."

"Yes, I remember you," she says, a worried edge to her tone. "Is she okay?"

I stumble over my words, not even knowing where to start. "She, um. Well, she doesn't know I'm calling."

Silence greets me on the other end of the line. I steady myself and try again.

"She's, um, fine. It's just..."

Now is not the time to panic. *Just say it*, I think.

"Actually, no. She's not fine. I'm calling because I think you should come out here. I know you don't like flying, but it's important that you see what's going on with Gracie, and...and her dad. Come. Please. I'm...well, I'm begging you."

There's a long pause as I wait for her response. This was a stupid idea. Gracie's going to kill me. I never should've—

"I'm on my way," Mae replies.

Relief washes over me like warm water, replaced quickly by a cold wave of discomfort.

"She can never know I called you."

Chapter 24

Grace

Seventeen Years Old

I inspect my wound in my bedroom mirror and wince. I'm still reeling from the incident two days ago. There's no way I can go to school tomorrow. I don't know how I would cover the nasty purple-blue bruise forming around the goose egg on my forehead. Makeup wouldn't work, and the area is too swollen for a hat to fit around it. I gently reach up and touch it with two fingers, lightly pressing down, and hiss in pain. My head feels like...well, it feels like I was pushed into a brick fireplace.

While there's a little redness surrounding the wound, it doesn't look infected. I won't need stitches. If I did, it wouldn't matter anyway. I'd take the scar over going to a doctor. Grabbing some petroleum jelly and checking the expiration date, I'm grateful to find it's still okay to use. I haven't needed it in months. As I smooth some over my wound, it feels like I'm starting all over again.

Yesterday, Danny and I didn't talk at all. Granted, it was

Saturday, so it's not like I saw him at school. I asked him to leave, and he gave me my space to stew in my thoughts. The bruises on my skin will heal. They always do. It's underneath the surface I'm most worried about. Because deep down in the caverns of my heart, I know my best friend's right. I shouldn't accept my dad's abuse. But making allowances is what you do when you feel trapped. *How else would I tell myself it'll all be okay?*

Excuses aren't copouts. They're coping mechanisms.

I told him that I'm not a child, but my dad makes me feel like one. I know I need to give up my ongoing defense of him, but I don't know if I'm strong enough. When he's drunk, he's cruel. When he's sober, he's absent.

I've been running the household since I was thirteen, getting groceries with the money he sometimes remembers to leave on the kitchen counter. On the days he forgets, I manage until school or go to Danny's house if he's not at football.

Sometimes, I don't eat. But I'd rather be hungry than get hit.

At first, I thought adults might've suspected things weren't right at home, but I quickly learned that the only thing people notice about me is my stutter.

I wonder what my mother saw in him. *What am I missing?*

Tears threaten to spill over, as they always do, when I think about her. I lick the tears away and taste the salty sadness. If Mom were here, she'd know what to do. Although, if she were here, I doubt any of this would be happening in the first place.

People always talk about what it will feel like to miss a dead parent at big milestones like weddings or graduations. Yes, you experience sadness and nostalgia at those big life events.

But the ugly reality is you feel the impact of their loss much more during the small, unremarkable milestones. Instead of feeling sick with nostalgia, you're accompanied by loneliness, embarrassment, and frustration.

I think about getting my period and having no one but the school nurse to guide me. I was eleven years old and scared.

I think about staying in the classroom with the teacher during Mother-Daughter Day at school instead of going to the cafeteria with my peers. I was twelve years old and isolated.

And, I think about what happened forty-eight hours ago, and I'm so humiliated. Mortified that Danny saw me like that, embarrassed by my weakness.

But Dad wasn't always like this, and the memories of him from *before* keep me from speaking up. During my darkest moments with him, visions of the past surface in my mind and confuse me.

Look at this hair, Dad had said when I was seven, gently touching my curls with reverence. *Just like your mother's spirals*, he'd praised as my mom looked on approvingly. *My two firecrackers*, he'd added with a wink.

I need to stop obsessing over everything. All I see is self-hatred in the mirror, and I force myself to step away.

Looking longingly at the walkie-talkie on my nightstand, I wonder if Danny meant what he said the other day. Cutting through my physical pain are his words, racing through my head, dispensing microdoses of serotonin.

My girlfriend.

Did he mean them?

You'd still be mine.

Am I crazy or had he been about to kiss me?

These thoughts take up an overwhelming amount of space in my brain as I think through my next steps.

Dad hasn't been back, but that's normal for him. He goes to the casino every weekend and won't be home until later tonight, which at least gives me some time to think about what I should do. I can't just report him... It's not that simple. The longer I dwell on this, the more I think about asking Danny for help. We have a good track record of solving problems together, and we could probably brainstorm some ideas.

The doorbell interrupts my thoughts. I'm really in no state to see anyone right now. On one hand, it could be a salesperson trying to convince me to switch gas companies. On the other hand, it could be Girl Scouts. In the end, the possibility of cookies wins out. I head down the hallway and open the door.

"Surprise, surprise, Queen Bee!"

Oh. My. God.

"*Mae?!*"

"In the flesh! Bring it in. I didn't fly all the way from Florida for you to stand there like a trout with your mouth open."

"I...I can't believe it!" I squeeze her tight, and she squeezes me back just as much.

"I love you like bees love honey." Hearing her say those words in person for the first time in years fills me with a kind of warmth only grandparents can provide.

"I love you, too, Mae. Gosh, I've missed you." Tears spring to my eyes. She has no idea how I've longed to see her. I've never been so happily surprised before.

I break the hug so I can look at her from head to toe, taking stock of any changes since I saw her last. Her silvery hair—now cut into a shoulder-length bob—is held back by a bee barrette. Her bright blue eyes and red-painted lips are surrounded by more smile lines. One thing that hasn't changed are her favorite black and gold earrings with little amber jewels dangling on the end.

"Why are you here?!"

She winks at me. "Can't a grandma visit her granddaughter without an interrogation?"

"Of course, I'm thrilled you're here! It's just so unexpected and I—"

"What happened here, Bee? This looks painful," Mae interrupts, pointing toward my head injury.

Every muscle in me stills as I debate how to answer her question. I am bone-deep tired of keeping this secret. It's like I've been on a small life raft for years, in the middle of the ocean, trying to weather storm after storm. Barely staying afloat, one swell away from drowning.

My nose starts stinging, and before I can stop it, tears flood my entire face.

"Honey, what's the matter?"

Would she believe a lie? I'm so used to explaining away his abuse that it doesn't take any effort to drum up excuses. Tripping, falling, getting hit in the head with a ball...I have a menu of alibis at the ready. But as I study her, the creases near her eyes, the worried look on her face, it takes me all of two seconds to free myself from the chokehold the skeleton in my closet has had me in for years.

"I have to tell you something about Dad, Mae."

Her face falls. Ever the hobbyist beekeeper, she says, "Well, I brought fresh Florida honeycomb to snack on." She puts her arm around my shoulder and guides us both inside to the kitchen table. "Let's hear it."

Much like my tears, the words rush out of me in almost one big breath. I tell her everything. Well, as much as she needs to know without going into minor details that would only serve to hurt her.

"I'm so sorry, honey," Mae whispers, eyes glazed with tears. "I can't believe I didn't see it. I'm angry at myself for being away for so long." She sadly shakes her head. "Your mother...she'd be horrified at my lack of visits."

"For all you knew, I was with my b-boring d-dad living next d-door t-to my b-best friend. It's what I wanted you t-to think.

D-Don't b-blame yourself, Mae. Flying long d-distances t-takes a t-toll on you."

"Well, I'm here now."

I squeeze her hand, more nervous to tell her this next part than the abuse itself.

"I, um, really like it here. Obviously, things have b-been t-tough with my d-dad, b-but I love living next d-door t-to Danny and hanging out with my friend B-Ben at school. I was wondering if you would b-be open t-to me staying here. I know your life is in Florida. If you have t-to go b-back, maybe we could ask Janie next d-door if she would b-be willing t-to...to t-take me in."

A flicker of sadness flashes in Mae's eyes. "Honey, I—"

"And, if not, that's completely fine, b-but maybe you could just, um, help find my d-dad some support with his d-drinking b-before you go. Like a group or something? It's just that I really d-don't want t-to go into the system, and honestly, he really hasn't b-been this b-bad in a while..."

The sadness in Mae's eyes remains unchanged. I curve my body inward, staring into the ground. I should've known not to ask for too much. I'm so stupid.

"I'm sorry. It was a d-dumb question. I'm so thankful you're here. It's okay if we have t-to go t-to Florida. Your b-bees are there. I know how important they are t-to you."

Mae gently picks up my hand again. She ducks her chin a bit, trying to get my attention, and I cautiously look up at her.

"*You* are important to me. I was going to say that after every-thing you've been through, it's not my intention to disrupt anything good in your life. I'm giving you control. If you want to stay, you'll stay. Not with Janie. With me. He will *never* hurt you again."

Leaning forward to pull her into an embrace, I practically

sag with relief. Of course she has my best interests in mind. She'd never make me do anything I didn't want to do, especially if it doesn't impact my safety. *Danny was right*, I think, as I hold onto Mae.

We both cry.

A few hours later, Dad comes home from the casino, drunk. Mae shoos me out of the family room area in advance of his arrival.

"You've experienced enough hurt to last a lifetime, and you don't need to hear any more of that man's nonsense. Let me take care of you now." She gives me a tight hug and lightly kisses my cheek.

Even though I still feel the invisible, weighted blanket of trauma, a knot seems to loosen in my stomach. I'm not sure when or if these heavy feelings will ever go away. At the same time, while I don't feel any lighter, I do feel less afraid.

Mae has a whole life in Florida, and leaving all that behind won't be easy, but I'm calmer with her in my corner. It's only now that I can even name the emotion that's been dominating my psyche at home all these years—fear. I always thought it was anxiety or hesitation, but no. I've been drenched in pure alarm since the first time he mocked my stutter.

These thoughts set up camp in the back corner of my brain as I walk into my room and collapse on my fluffy pink bed. I grab my old CD player and magenta headphones on my night-stand and turn up the volume of my favorite Dashboard Confessional song.

While my headphones mute the noises of the outside world, they don't prevent me from seeing the red and blue lights swirling outside my window ten minutes later. I peer out the window and see my dad ushered by a police officer into their car, handcuffed. Grandma Mae is speaking with the remaining officer, her hands gesturing. When she turns around, I gasp. It's impossible to miss her swollen eye and the dried blood underneath her nose. She looks my way and gives me a small smile. I manage a weak smile back.

And I wonder if that will be the last time I ever see my father.

Chapter 25

Danny

Seventeen Years Old

I don't regret calling Mae.

Sitting in my bedroom at my desk, focusing on anything but the homework in front of me, overwhelming relief still pumps through my veins. I hadn't realized how much I feared for Gracie's safety until I saw Mae get out of that taxi yesterday. Even if there's a chance she might move to Florida, I'm convinced we'll always find our way back to each other. I'd rather she be safe and far than injured and close.

The thing is, she's lost both of her parents now. I haven't seen my dad since I was seven, and I hope it stays that way. My mom is more than enough. But losing her, too? I can't even imagine.

But I do wonder how Gracie's feeling about all of this. Would she be happy that I took the necessary steps for her safety, or blame me for her dad's arrest? I know I crossed a line, but I wouldn't take it back. He wasn't fit to breathe the same air as her, let alone live in the same house. I shove my homework to the side of my desk and stare out the window at Gracie's house.

It would've been impossible to miss the police car outside last night. I'm just thankful Mom and Tessa were at the movies. If Mom saw it go down, she'd have a lot of questions that aren't mine to answer.

Gracie and I left things in a weird spot, so I doubt I'll hear from her. No matter how much I want to run over there and wrap her in my arms, I know she needs some time with Mae. Even though she didn't show up to school today, I tried not to worry too much, reminding myself over and over again that she's safe.

Gracie's finally safe now. Gracie's safe now. Gracie's safe.

The affirmations sound like a lullaby in my head, soothing a tightness in my chest. Gracie is the best thing in my life, and I'll *always* protect what we have. I just hope I haven't already ruined it with the Almost Kiss. I bet she's already forgotten about it, and I don't want to be the one to bring it up. With everything she's going through, the last thing she needs is me acting clingy.

I'm anxiously clicking up the lead in my mechanical pencil when I hear a crackly "Danny? Are you there? Over," coming from the walkie-talkie on my nightstand. I jolt up and snatch it before accidentally dropping it on the floor.

I pick it up and fumble with the volume buttons like I hadn't already turned it all the way up. I finally find the right one to push. "Gracie? Yeah, I'm here. Over."

"Glad to see your walkie-talkie still works."

I scoff. "Everyone knows these are the real bad boys of modern communication."

"The last time I had to replace a battery, I felt like a pioneer on the Oregon Trail."

"At least the journey between our houses never results in dysentery."

Gracie giggles through the static. After everything that happened, hearing her laugh feels like a privilege.

"I'm sure you saw the police lights outside yesterday, so I wanted to let you know I'm okay, at least physically. I'm not hurt."

"I'm so glad. I was worried."

"And Danny, you'll never guess. *Mae* is here! I'm just so happy. You'll have to come and see her." She sounds elated.

"That's great, Gracie!" I wince as I feign surprise, feeling a trickle of guilt slide down my spine. "I'd love to see Mae again. Do you want me to come to your house tomorrow? I can drive us both after school."

"Um, I won't be going to school again for...obvious reasons. But you can still come over after school and hang out with us."

My body tenses as I imagine how her head looks right now. It must be really bad, because she never misses school if she can help it.

"But I was wondering if you might actually come over tonight...to hang out for a bit."

My heart starts pounding. Does she want to talk about the Almost Kiss? Or maybe what I said to her?

My girlfriend.

You'd be mine.

I meant every word.

Shit. Maybe she's freaked out. She has so much going on, and her emotions are likely running high. It was terrible timing to blurt out some of what I feel for her. Mom told me I'd only get one chance with her, and I blew it. Gracie probably just wants to move past this.

"Okay, Gracie girl. I'll be tapping on your window in a few, over."

"That sounds perfect. See you soon...over."

On the way to her window, I tell myself, *she needs her best friend* and *don't make things weird about last night* over and over again.

Tap, tap, tap, tap.

Gracie opens the window with a hesitant smile on her face and a dark bruise on her forehead. I grimace at the sight of it.

But through the surface level injuries, her expression is almost relaxed, and her colorful eyes look bright and vibrant. Even her curly hair looks shinier and springier.

"Hey, Danny."

"Hey, Gracie."

We start talking at the same time.

"Listen, I—"

"I wanted to—"

She sits on the inside windowsill, smiles, and gestures toward me. "You go first."

I lean against the window frame and gather my thoughts. "I know I can't fully understand what you're going through. I feel like I made things weird the other day, when we were watching the movie...and, well, I'm sure you want time to process what happened with your dad, and we don't need to talk about it right now. I love being your best friend, and I'll always be here for you, no matter what."

I expect to see relief on Gracie's face after hearing what I had to say. Instead, there's a flicker of disappointment in her eyes.

She pauses, then starts nodding, her curls bouncing with the movement. "Uh, thanks. I guess you're right. It *has* been a long day, and I'm getting a little tired. I appreciate you coming over, though."

My heart sinks as I watch her bite the inside of her cheek. *Is she mad at me for what happened with her dad?*

Her eyes don't reflect the comfortable smile on her lips when she adds, "I love being your best friend, too."

The word "friend" settles in my stomach and leaves behind a weight, growing heavier with every passing second. Refocusing on what she needs, my stinging disappointment fades away. I promised to support her, and I will. *Always.*

I force a smile. "Sounds good. Should I still stop by tomorrow to see Mae?"

Gracie nods. "Definitely. She remembers you from when we were kids. She's obviously heard a lot about you over the years."

I run my hands through my hair to prevent myself from hugging her. I don't want to make anything weirder. "Great. See you both tomorrow."

She gives a small wave. "Yep, see you then."

As I walk across the lawn to my house, I can't help but feel that our conversation seems incomplete. *Is this all she wanted me over for tonight?*

* * *

I rush home from school as soon as the final bell rings. I'm excited to see Mae again, and I'm anxious to check on Gracie. I stop home quickly to cut some red tulips from the flower patch in my backyard. Hopefully, the flowers will cheer her up.

Where my house is lined with begonias and tulips, Gracie's has rocks and green plants that don't require any water. When she was growing up, her mom had loved to garden. Two big, yellow rose bushes had framed their porch, with rows of red flowers blooming down the sidewalk in front of their house. After her death, her dad had landscapers remove everything, even the roses.

It feels odd walking through Gracie's front door in pure daylight instead of climbing through her bedroom window in the dark. All of the windows in her family room are open, letting in sunshine that lights up the foyer. Usually, there'd be beer stains on the carpet, but it must've been professionally cleaned.

I check the ends of the flowers I tied together to make sure they're not dripping on the floor and close the door behind me. The sound of Gracie's laughter fills my ears, seeming lighter and airier than normal, no doubt from Mae's slightly unhinged personality.

"Danny, is that you? We're in the kitchen!" Gracie shouts.

"If he can't use basic judgment to deduce we're in the kitchen, Bee, he better pray for a football scholarship to college. He ain't getting there on smarts," I overhear.

Laughing at my own expense, I walk into the kitchen with a genuine smile. Their hands are dusted with flour, messy from making bread. An open mason jar sits on the counter, and the goo inside looks like oatmeal's evil step-cousin. Mae must've brought her legendary sourdough starter all the way from Florida.

Gracie looks like spring incarnate in a pale yellow, knee-length sundress. Her curls are tied back in a low ponytail with a matching yellow ribbon. I crane my neck to examine her head and see how she's healing. The swelling is down completely, but the lingering bruise around the small cut is still dark brown in color, turning a greenish-yellow around the edges.

In contrast, the bruise circling Mae's eye is fresh and bright purple, and her lip is swollen. I only let my eyes linger briefly before the guilt overwhelms me. I know it was the right decision to call her, but I feel awful that Mae went through the same abuse as her granddaughter before that asshole was taken away in handcuffs.

Bruising aside, Mae looks nice, dressed in a classic white button down shirt and brown linen pants. A honey-colored ring sits safely on the countertop, away from the sticky dough, and it brings a smile to my face. I shake my head, giving a soft chuckle. Mae and her bees.

"Hi, Gracie. Hey, Mae, good to see you again. These tulips are for both of you from my mom's garden."

Gracie beams. "Aw, my favorite color. You didn't have to do that, Danny, but it's so sweet of you. Thank you."

I hum, giving her a soft smile. "Unfortunately, I don't have a vase though. Do you have one here that we could use?"

Gracie thinks for a moment before her face falls. "Shoot. No, not anymore. D-dad, erm, b-broke it during one of his b-benders or something."

Mae and I share a look of sadness. I know that Grace has a long road ahead in overcoming the repercussions of her dad's abuse.

"Well, we'll just have to pick up a new vase then. Tomorrow," Mae announces with resolve. I notice Gracie's shoulders relax.

"Maybe they'll have a bee-shaped vase at the flower shop," Gracie muses, smiling to herself.

"In the meantime, this will do." Mae opens a cupboard, grabbing a mason jar. She adds a few inches of water and gently places the tulips inside, fluffing them up. "See? Beautiful. Just like you," she compliments as she turns toward her granddaughter.

"Yes, she is," I say.

Gracie's eyes widen as a blush blooms up her neck.

"Queen Bee, I've been meaning to ask. Would you mind popping over to the corner pharmacy to pick up my meds? My doctor called them in before I arrived so I could pick them up right away."

"I'm happy to pick them up, Mae," I offer.

"Honey, I haven't seen you in a long time, so maybe you can stay behind." Mae leans forward and whispers like she has a secret. "Plus, I didn't want to have to say it, but I'm already getting a little sick of Bee."

Gracie laughs and rolls her eyes. "It hasn't even been a week!" She starts washing the flour off her hands. "I'll go, but don't talk about me behind my back too much, you two."

"We will, dear, but only in Pig Latin."

"Huh?" I ask in between bouts of loud laughter. Mae is something else.

"Everyone knows that if you gossip in Pig Latin, it's less toxic. It's like how if you buy a snack that says 'only five ingredients,' it's automatically healthy—even if three of those five ingredients are some form of sugar."

"Okay, okay, enough," Gracie giggles. "I'll leave."

"Bye, Dear! Now, Danny. EDDY-RAY OOO-TAY AWK-TAY BOUT-AY RACE-GAY?"

Gracie's hysterical laughter is so loud we can hear it through the closed front door.

I turn to Mae after Gracie leaves. "Um, do we really have to talk in Pig Latin?"

Mae tilts her head with a wry grin. "If I said we did, you would, wouldn't you?"

I shift on my feet. "Yeah, but I might be pretty slow."

She beams, holding out her arms for a hug. "Oh, Daniel. Honey, you have not changed a lick. Bring it in."

Mae squeezes me so hard that I feel like the last bit of toothpaste in the tube. When she pulls away, I'm surprised to see misty, emotional eyes.

"Daniel," she whispers. "You are so precious to me."

"Uh, thanks?"

"You protected my granddaughter. Better than anyone. Better than me. That makes you precious."

I put my hands in my pockets and nervously play with some

loose change, not used to all these compliments. There's so much more I could've done.

"I could live to be two hundred years old and thank you every day for what you did, and it still wouldn't be enough. I'm so happy she has you in her life, someone that loves her with all they have."

I drop the coins in my pocket. "Gracie and I are best friends... I've always loved her."

Her eyes twinkle as she takes a seat at the kitchen table. "Mhm. Anyone who has ever come remotely near you two knows what kind of love it is. Including her, by the way. She just isn't giving herself enough credit to accept that truth yet. It'll all come together in time. Like her grandpoppy and me, you're meant to *bee*. Pun intended." She gestures to the chair beside her for me to sit and winks. "It's only a matter of when."

My face heats, and my heart rate picks up pace as I lower myself into the chair. *Mae thinks that Gracie loves me, too?* Then again, we've always said we loved each other, so maybe she's confused.

Leaning forward, I place my elbows on the table. "Listen, Mae. I understand if you want to tell her I called you. I won't make you lie to—"

"No, honey," she softly interrupts as she pats my hand. "She's not quite ready to hear that from us yet."

"Oh. Okay," I mumble, sliding my hands off the table and slumping back into the chair. Looking at the floor, I consider my options, but nothing feels right. I trust Mae's judgment.

My head snaps up. "I've been meaning to ask—are things, um, worked out with Gracie's dad?"

Mae's face hardens as she looks straight ahead. "He went to jail but got out on bail a few hours later."

My mouth hangs open. "How? So, this isn't over then? He's coming back?"

She turns to face me, and it's hard for me to avoid staring at the bruises surrounding her puffy eye. "It's over, Daniel. I made a deal with her father not to testify at his trial in exchange for him eventually signing over custody to me. He agreed in under two minutes." She leans forward, lowering her voice. "It's not really above board, but I doubt the DA will hold me in contempt given the situation."

"How did Gracie take that news?" No matter how terrible her dad was, having a parent give you up without a second thought must be a tough pill to swallow.

"She'll have plenty to work through due to her father's abuse. I'll give her anything she needs—therapy, time, space. But you'll be there to support her, too, right?"

"Of course. I'd do anything for her." Clearing my throat, I ask nervously, "So, you're staying, then? In Ohio?"

"Yes. Your Gracie," she winks at me, knowing that's what I'm really asking, "is staying. Given that *he* doesn't want to live here anymore, I hope to purchase the house. For lack of a better phrase, once the consequences of the state's trial are over, he can 'take the money and run.' Walk away without a glance back. From my end, I hope he does." Mae frowns before relaxing her face again. "It'll be a long process, but my lawyers assured me we'd be safe."

The calm that settles over me is maybe the best thing I've ever felt in my life. I'm almost woozy hearing that Gracie is staying, high on the fact that we won't be separated. It's dizzying, but with Mae right in front of me, I also think about what she's giving up.

"And what about your bees?"

"*Precious*," she mutters under her breath. "Not many people are interested in saving the bees. I miss them dearly, but they'll be well cared for by a friend with a farm in Florida. I'm getting older now, so it wouldn't have been long before I had to hang up my beekeeper hat anyway. Thank you for asking."

"Sure, I know how important they are to you."

She smiles. "In a lot of ways, Daniel, you remind me of a bee. You're a hard worker, a complex problem solver, and fiercely protective of your queen."

Knowing how much Mae loves her bees, the comparison lands like sweet, syrupy honey on my tongue.

She lets her compliment sink in before clapping her hands. "Now. I heard you're on the football team. Do you throw the ball or catch it?"

Chapter 26

Grace

The first thing I see when I wake up is an award plaque with a picture of Danny catching a football. Still drowsy, my eyes flutter close again. I breathe in through my nose, picking up on the familiar scent of clean laundry and oranges. Sighing happily, I tilt my head toward it until my cheek settles on something warm. I yawn against soft fabric, relishing the comforting heat against my skin.

Slowly opening my eyes again, I quickly realize I'm nuzzled against Danny's chest, resting sideways on his lap. His hands grip my thighs protectively, as if he's afraid I'll vanish while he sleeps. He's completely passed out, softly snoring in a sitting position, his head bobbed against the back of the couch.

I'm warm and wrapped up in a blanket I didn't put on myself, which means I must have fallen asleep first. The thought of Danny tucking me in causes an ache in my chest I'd prefer not to explore. I soak in this visual of us for a few minutes and think about the fact that this might be the last time I'll see him like this, all soft and sleepy.

Then I feel his morning hard-on underneath my ass and rapidly discern it's *definitely* time for us to get up. Right now, actually, or else I'll be compelled to wake him up for *other* reasons.

I'm confident that when I shift off his lap, he'll wake up.

I'm more confident that when I say "Danny" at a reasonable volume, he'll wake up.

I am even more confident that when I get up and turn on the overhead lights, he'll wake up.

And yet, he's still fast asleep.

I walk back to the couch and sit beside him. Turning my body toward his, I bend my knees up, feet on the couch, and lean in toward his face. "Danny, wake up."

He rustles, hands feeling for me with his eyes closed. Finding my legs, he grouchily yanks them back onto his lap.

"Gracie baby, why're you up so early? Go back to bed," he slurs sleepily.

My heart simultaneously swells and shatters when I hear "Gracie baby" for the first time in over a decade. I inhale sharply. "Dan. You need to wake up."

Eyes still half closed, he frowns. "Stop calling me Dan all the time. It hurts my feelings, baby," he grumbles in his dream state.

Blowing out a frustrated breath, I close the remaining gap between us. "Danny, hello, please awaken before I die of starvation," I announce directly into his ear canal.

His back straightens as his eyes dart all around before landing on my face. It takes him only a moment to deduce he has glued my thighs to his hard-on, and he immediately drops my legs and pulls the discarded blanket over himself. "Sorry, I, uh, sometimes have a tough time waking up in the morning."

"Yes, the eight alarms you set every morning freshman year of college were a dead giveaway."

He laughs awkwardly as he rubs the back of his neck. "What're you talking about? I thought you *liked* hearing 'Viva

La Vida' every fifteen minutes between the hours of five a.m. and seven a.m., Monday through Friday. I did it for you."

I giggle. "You've ruined it so much for me that I can't even listen to that song anymore. And some days, I find myself thinking, 'How am I supposed to viva la vida without 'Viva La Vida,' you know?"

Danny's shoulders shake with silent laughter. He looks brighter and more awake now. "We should probably get ready. Mom'll be here any minute."

I launch myself off the couch with a huge smile on my face. "That's right! I forgot Janie is coming over. I can't wait to see her. I need to find something to wear."

Danny stretches his long arms above his head, showing off just a sliver of his bare torso, where my eyes linger. My gaze follows the trail of dark hair to the top of his sweatpants, remembering what his lower V used to feel like under my hands. He looks...so hot. It's honestly not right. His eyelashes are longer than mine, and his lips are fuller in a way that's an insult to women everywhere. Danny grins when he catches me obviously gawking, but graciously doesn't call me out on it. Instead, he lifts his arms even higher above his head, giving me a whole show on purpose.

"You always look great, Gracie. No need to impress Mom. She loves you just as you are, and frankly?" He looks at me, assessing something. "She's seen you in worse condition."

"*Excuse you?*" I glare at him.

"Don't look so surprised. Remember the white eyeliner phase you went through?" He raises an eyebrow at me and bites his lower lip to keep from laughing.

"How *dare* you, Danny. Everyone knows white eyeliner makes your eyes pop. It's an extremely flattering choice. Teen Girl Magazine said so."

"Did Teen Girl Magazine also tell you to cover yourself

head to toe in hemp jewelry with little shells on it? Because that was another...choice."

I tilt my chin up and sniff. "For your information, the puka shells gave me a beachy allure."

"We lived in a landlocked state. You'd never seen the ocean."

"Whatever," I huff. "I could go on and on about your 'choices,' but you don't hear me talking about your three month skater boi phase."

"The business professional tie with the ripped t-shirt underneath was pure class and you know that, Gracie," he says, wagging his finger at me like I'm in trouble.

"Enough of this. I'm getting changed into something cuter for Janie. End of story," I announce with determination. "Does she always come over the morning after a big game for brunch?"

"Only if we lose. If we lose, she comes over and makes her cinnamon rolls."

"Ah, so these are sympathy cinnamon rolls."

"Typically, yes. But today, they're happy cinnamon rolls. Because you're here."

Chapter 27

Danny

Gracie is upstairs changing when the doorbell rings. I nearly jog to the door, praying I get a few moments alone with my mother before Gracie comes down the stairs. I throw open the door and see Mom standing with a kitchen mixer in her arms.

"Mom, I told you last time that I bought a mixer for my house. You don't have to pack your own in a checked bag when you come to games now. Honestly, it feels like you're manifesting our loss at this point."

Her hazel eyes twinkle as the mixer all but engulfs her petite frame. "Please, Daniel. My mixer is better than yours; that's why I have to bring it."

"I bought the same model, just the newer version."

"Exactly."

I run my hands through my hair. "Okay, whatever. I—"

She narrows her eyes at me, paintbrush earrings dangling in the cold breeze. "Why do you look stressed? Are you sweating?"

"Give me one second to explain." I nudge her back outside onto the porch and close the front door behind us.

"What's going on? My fingers will freeze before I make your loser cinnamon rolls." She winks.

"Loser? Is that what you...? You know what, never mind. I don't have time for this."

Her teasing expression is replaced with one of concern as she asks, "What is it, Daniel?"

"Grace is here."

Mom's jaw drops so much it almost hits her kitchen mixer. "Grace as in...the person?"

"What else would I be talking about?"

Mom starts gesturing so wildly that I grab the mixer before she drops it. "I don't know! Maybe you started up yoga or something, and 'grace is here' is more of a spiritual thing!"

"Well, she's here, and she's not a metaphor, and I need you to chill out."

Suddenly, her floundering halts. Mom relaxes her arms and stares directly into the sun. "What do you mean? I'm perfectly natural."

"That's the opposite of perfectly natural. I don't need you scaring Grace away. She's hesitant as is, and I don't want her to feel uncomfortable. I have to leave for my end-of-season wellness appointment with the team physical therapist soon, so it would be great if you could keep her company while I'm gone." Taking a deep breath, I think of the ticking timeline I have with Gracie. "She's technically only here until her evening flight. I'm trying. I'm trying to..." My face falls, thinking of how little time we have together.

"Okay, sweetheart." She rubs my arm reassuringly. "I'm more excited than anything. This is good. I'm happy for both of you."

"Well, nothing's happened yet, but I want to apologize. I want to fill in the years we spent apart. I just...want *her*." And I don't want to wait any longer. Now that Gracie's finished vet school and runs her own clinic, I'm no longer standing in the way of her achieving her dreams.

Mom gives my cheek a pat. "I know, Daniel. All in due time." She slaps her hands together. "What a thrilling morning. Let's get back in there before we turn to ice."

My whole body shivers in agreement. I'm freezing my ass off out here. "Amen to that."

I turn the knob, push the door open, and yelp in surprise when I find Gracie standing just on the other side.

She releases an exasperated sigh. "No need to be scared of me, Danny. What were you doing outside?"

"Well, I was helping Mom bring in—"

"Janie?!" Gracie shouts, peering around me.

Mom squeezes past me to greet her. "Kiddo? Gosh, it's great to see you!"

Both women shove me aside in a surprisingly rough fashion, hugging each other.

"Look at how beautiful you are! Wow, it's been so long."

Gracie blushes. "Thank you, Janie." They pull back from their embrace but still stand only inches apart.

"Are you in the mood for some cinnamon rolls?" Mom waggles her eyebrows hopefully.

"The sympathy ones Danny told me about? For when he loses?" Gracie flashes a toothy smile, a little bit too happy for my liking.

"I'm not a loser," I mutter under my breath.

"Yep, those are the ones," Mom says cheerily.

Glaring at my mother, I whisper, "Et tu, Brute?"

"Do you need help making them?" Gracie asks.

Mom lovingly pats Gracie's shoulder. "I'll take any chance to spend some extra time with you." She turns to face me with a smile on her face. "Daniel, are you off to your appointment?"

"Yep. Are you okay to stay here, Gracie? I'll be back as soon as they're done."

If Gracie's disappointed to lose time with me this morning, she doesn't show it. "I'm more than okay with Janie time. I can't wait to catch up."

"The feeling is mutual, kiddo. Alright then. We'll see you after, Daniel. Have a great appointment!"

"Yeah, Daniel, bye!"

Gracie's mimicking attempt draws an eye roll out of me. "I'll be back soon."

I feel lucky I have these two women in my life...at least, for now. The alternative makes me sick to my stomach.

Chapter 28

Grace

Seventeen Years Old

"It's too late for me now, the sickness will take me soon. I am plagued. Leave me and save yourself, Gracie."

I pull the thermometer out of his mouth. 103.5 degrees. "You have a fever, Danny."

He looks perplexed. "I don't understand, I'm always in peak physical condition. It's the end of summer. How does a little virus take me down?"

I shake my head, knowing all too well where this is going.

"Unless...it's not a little virus. Maybe I was bitten by a radioactive insect and I'm turning into Wolverine."

One thing about Danny is that he turns into a bit of a conspiracy theorist when he gets even mildly sick. Add in a high fever, and he loses his ability to keep his hero origins straight.

If Janie were here, she'd be caring for this delusional boy, but she's taking pictures of the new music wing at the children's museum. She even has to stick around for the evening banquet. Since Danny's in no state to babysit, Tessa's at her friend's house for a sleepover, and I enthusiastically agreed to check on him.

This past summer with Danny was perfect. While it's been filled with football camps for him and volunteer work at the shelter for me, we're intentional about spending most of our free time together. Our friendship has never been stronger.

And Mae continues to be my rock. She trusts me to manage my own life. She's started spending some time at our local garden center, where she tends to the flowers and hangs out with her beloved bees every day.

I turn off the overhead light in his room, leaving only his desk lamp on, and tug him up from his chair. "Okay, Tobey Maguire. Time for bed, big guy."

We start senior year in just a couple of weeks, and I wonder how things might change. I can't stop thinking about him. The emotions I feel when I'm with Danny are so much bigger than a teenage crush. I'm just scared to bring up my feelings. After he emphasized our "friendship" following our ill-fated movie night, I figured he wasn't interested.

"Think about it, Gracie. It doesn't check out that I'd get sick. I drink a ton of water. You know how many Flintstones vitamins I take," he adds, like he's proving a point.

I roll my eyes. "You're ridiculous. It actually doesn't make medical sense how messed up you get when you're ill. You should be studied for science."

Danny sighs and lies down in his bed, snuggling under the covers. When he reaches his hand out for mine, I let him lace our fingers together. He shakes our joined hands up and down like we're acquaintances meeting for the first time.

"Gracie, my Gracie girl. The Graciest Grace Who Ever Was. The peanut butter to my jelly. The shredded cheese to my tortilla chips. The MJ to my Spider-Man."

Tucking him in with my free hand, I pull the covers tight

around his shoulders. He probably won't remember this in the morning. I smile and seriously consider taking a video to tease him with later. He would absolutely document me for posterity if our roles were reversed.

"Can you get into bed with me? I want you in my bed so bad, Gracie. It's almost all I think about," he pouts.

Oh. Okay. I guess I won't be taking a video after all.

"You really don't know what you're saying, Danny Thompson. You're in a fever dream," I chide.

He shakes his head, brows furrowed. Looking particularly determined, he announces, "I do know. I know it in my bones. I know that you're my best friend. And I know I want us to be more. I've always known."

"Always my ass," I scoff playfully. "Does the name Tori ring a bell, *D*?"

"I couldn't love her, Gracie baby. Not like you."

Ope. I choke on my own spit and start to cough. What is going on? I've never heard him call me anything other than Gracie or Gracie girl, and certainly nothing remotely close to "baby." Did he take some kind of hallucinogenic earlier? I scan his room for odd pill bottles. Nothing.

"And please don't call me D again." He shivers, and I don't think it's from the fever. "It made me throw up in my mouth a lil bit."

I giggle and try to pull myself together. "I think you need to sleep off whatever this is. Immediately."

"You are in denial, my friend. My best friend. My best girl friend. My girlfriend." He pauses and stares at me solemnly. "Hey, Gracie girl? Do you want to be my *real* girlfriend? The kind of girlfriend where I kiss you?"

How honest should I be? I thought he didn't want to be more than friends, but now...maybe he's changed his mind.

Or maybe he's deep in delirium.

Either way, I know my answer. He won't remember this anyway.

"Yes. I want to be your girlfriend, Danny."

The utter joy in his eyes is palpable, and a huge grin spreads across his face, bringing a touch of color back to his cheeks. "*I knew it*, Gracie. I knew it all along. I wanted to be right, and I am. I should've known. I'm always right...about everything. All the time." He boops my nose.

"Now, now. That's a little too far," I tease and pat the top of his head.

Sometimes my heart feels like it might burst when I'm around him. Like it's itching to climb out of my chest. Danny's presence constantly hums in me, even when we're not physically together. He brightens every good experience and softens the bad. I wonder what he would think, knowing how desperately I want him to be mine in all the ways that matter.

Instead of revealing too much of myself, I whisper, "Go to sleep, Danny," near his ear.

"I'll sleep," he agrees happily. Then he narrows his eyes at me. "But no takesies backsies, Gracie. You're my girlfriend now, so quit messing around."

"Mhm, whatever you say."

"Night night, beautiful girl. My otter." He smiles and closes his eyes.

I lie next to Danny on top of the covers, still holding his hand. My eyelids get heavier. I close them and fall into a deep sleep, peacefully dreaming of us as something *more*.

The next morning, I wake up slowly. Yawning, I turn on my side to check on Danny and startle, surprised to find him completely awake. He's staring at me with an unreadable expression, so I reach up to touch his forehead with the back of my hand. It feels cool. And when I lean forward to examine his eyes, they appear clear. He looks healthy and calm.

My heart, on the other hand, is anything but calm. It's still racing from last night, and waking up next to him definitely doesn't help matters. I don't have a fever, but I wouldn't be surprised if a thermometer said otherwise. The way my body reacts around Danny is getting harder to suppress.

He looks serious as he sits up in bed. "Grace."

"Morning! Let me take your temperature really fast." I'll see if his fever is gone and then head downstairs. Janie should be home by now, and if we're lucky, she's making her famous cinnamon rolls. I grab the thermometer and stick it under his tongue before he can say anything else.

After a minute, it beeps, and I check it—97 degrees. "Hey, so great news," I tease. "It appears you've survived the plague. Or a radioactive spider bite."

He doesn't return my smile. Instead, he leans closer to my face.

"What are you doing?" I whisper.

He gently nuzzles his forehead against my cheek. "I said no takesies backsies, and I meant it, Gracie baby."

A barely audible gasp leaves my mouth. *He remembers?*

Danny stares at me with rapt attention, like I'm the most interesting thing he's ever seen. His gaze lingers briefly on my right eye before returning to my mouth again. "Do you want this?"

"Yes."

Then he kisses me. He kisses me like he's been waiting his whole life for this.

I've been waiting, too.

Danny's lips are warm and soft as they press against mine, and our kiss is comfortable and ingrained, like we were always meant to be doing this. Finally kissing him sends a fizzy rush through me, and my eyelids ever-so-slightly flutter open as I steal a glance at his face. He pulls back to look at me, too, and my breath hitches when I see pure contentment settled across his features.

"I'm yours, now." Danny presses a tender kiss under my chin. "And you're mine," he whispers, before kissing me on the side of my nose. "I've always been yours," he murmurs, as he kisses me on my temple near my hairline. "And you've always been mine." He kisses me on the corner of my mouth. "So quit messing around, Gracie," he teases.

I touch my fingers to my lips, trying to imprint the sensation deep into my memory. *Is this really, finally happening?*

"Hey, Gracie?" he asks softly. "Do you want to be my girlfriend? The kind where I kiss you?"

"Yeah," I breathe.

Danny finds my hand on the bed and laces our pinkies like a promise. Then he leans forward and lightly presses his mouth to mine.

"Okay, then." A quiet smile plays at his lips.

"I've never kissed anyone before," I whisper.

"Well, now you have," he replies, reaching up and lightly caressing my cheek. I tilt my face into his palm, relishing the warmth of his hand. A curl falls over my eye, and Danny nudges it off my face with his nose.

Our pinkies stay locked as we silently process becoming different, becoming *more*.

It doesn't feel sudden. It feels like an evolution.

* * *

"I feel like the luckiest guy in the world right now." Danny wraps his arm around my shoulder as we walk from his car to Kyle's large suburban home.

About two weeks after Danny first called me Gracie baby, we're on our way to Kyle's house for our first time out together as an official couple...and my first high school party, period. I've always been too terrified to go anywhere except right next door, out of fear my dad would get home early. The closest I've been to a party with friends was me handing Ben a piece of cafeteria cake in the hallway on his birthday. It was peanut butter flavored. He promptly informed me that he was allergic to peanuts, and I ate the cake myself. It was a very mild time.

"I had an amazing game tonight with my amazing girlfriend there cheering me on, and now we get to go party together, which will be—"

"Amazing, I'm guessing?"

Danny stops walking and playfully squeezes my cheeks together with one of his hands. "Hey! Your sarcasm has no home here. It *is* going to be amazing." He slides his hand to the back of my neck and presses his lips to mine before gently coaxing my mouth open with his tongue.

For a self-proclaimed "anti-PDA" type of guy, Danny is very pro-PDA with me. I soak up every second, because it's almost unbelievable that we're finally together, in a real relationship.

I grin against his lips before leaning back. "I agree, boyfriend. So, what happens at these so-called parties, considering I've never been to one before?"

Danny generously rolls his eyes like that's a lie, even though we both know it's true.

"I don't come to them much, but they're pretty chill. I'll introduce you to some of my friends on the team, and there'll be food and drinks. It's fun."

He opens the front door and guides me through the foyer area to the open-concept kitchen and living space, where most of the team is hanging out. The kitchen is Tuscan-style, with warm beige walls covered in painted grapes and wine chalices. It's packed in here, wall-to-wall with athletes, cheerleaders, and other people I only recognize from watching Danny's practices. There's no way Kyle's parents approved of this party.

"It's loud in here!" I shout over the music, but I don't think Danny hears me.

A linebacker mans the stereo, blasting a rap song at a volume so loud a glass filled with booze rattles on the side table next to him.

The liquor bottles scattered on top of the counters give me a few small heart palpitations. I've never drunk alcohol before, or, more accurately, I've never been presented with the opportunity, I guess. But I want to be open-minded. I want Danny's teammates to like me. Our relationship is solid but also incredibly fragile. It's hard to explain. I'm new to parties, new to being a girlfriend, new to *all* of this.

Danny says that I don't have to change myself to fit any sort of expectation, but it's easy to tell other people "don't change" when you're the one everybody wants to be.

"Hey, DT! DT is here, everyone! Hell yeah, the party can start!"

Some of the guys cheer, and Danny receives pat after pat on the back. He gets a "good game, dude" from an athlete with huge muscles and dirty blond hair. "You're the man!" a guy wearing a varsity jacket shouts.

Danny's popularity is not limited to the male contingent of partygoers. A group of girls dressed in short denim skirts, tank tops lined with lace, and branded jackets saunters our way.

"D, it's so good to see you! I feel like we haven't hung out in forever." I recognize the girl speaking as one of Tori's friends—one of the nicer ones. She's wearing the top of her cheerleader uniform with a frayed jean skirt. Her straight brown hair hangs down her back, and her caramel-colored highlights match the shade of her fleece zip-up almost perfectly.

I'm happy to be with Danny, but I can already tell he'll be

pulled in a million different directions all night long. I wish I'd forced Ben to come to this party with me, but he'd rejected my offer as soon as it came out of my mouth. He works at our local arboretum and has an early morning shift tomorrow.

"Hey, Alicia. Yeah, I've been kind of busy with football... and with my girlfriend. Have you two met?"

"Susannah, right?" she asks, her tone overly bright.

I wince and give her a quick nod. I hate my given name, but it feels too awkward to change it senior year of high school.

"D! You don't even have a drink in your hand yet. Do you need me to get you something? You're a beer guy if I remember, right?" she asks, at his beck and call.

Danny rubs the back of his neck, clearly uncomfortable by her offer. "Uh, I'll get myself a drink after we settle in for a sec."

"If you're sure," Alicia hedges.

"Yep. Nice seeing you, we're just gonna go say hi to some of the guys."

Danny tugs on my hand and leads me to a guy with reddish-brown curly hair who fist bumps him.

"DT, 'sup dude?"

"'Sup, man. This is my girlfriend. Baby, this is Sean, he plays cornerback."

"Hey, nice to meet you..." His eyes dart to the ceiling as if he'll magically find my name there.

"Susannah. You too."

Danny turns to face me. "You want anything? Pop? Gatorade? If you want something stronger to drink, he usually has hard lemonade or something."

"Just water, I think. Thanks."

"Cool. I'm going to grab us drinks from the cooler outside before it gets crazier."

Craning my neck, I try to find the deck. "Oh, where is that?"

"It's just off the kitchen. I'll be right back."

"Sounds good."

I really don't want Danny to leave, but I also refuse to be clingy. The last thing he needs is to babysit me. Hell, when he's in the league, I'll be by myself all the time. Better get used to it.

"Hey, Susannah?"

I swivel my head and see Kyle, the quarterback, approaching. He's wearing a long sleeve, striped rugby shirt in Titans colors. Holding a red solo cup in one hand, he uses the other to turn his baseball cap backward.

"Yeah, that's me."

"Danny's friend?"

"Um, his gir—"

"It's been really great having *chemistry* with you," he interrupts suggestively, "if you know what I mean."

Is he hitting on me? Does he know I'm with Danny?

"It's good having class with you, too, but—"

"Maybe we should see if we have chemistry outside of class tonight." Kyle takes another step toward me.

I instinctively step back, but I'm almost completely backed up against the kitchen island.

"I don't think Danny would like this," I blurt out.

Kyle's face scrunches, confusion flickering across his face. "DT was the one who said he'd put in a good word for me."

"Danny said *what*?"

"Don't worry about a thing, babe. Listen, I'd love to show you my room." He inches toward me until the cold countertop digs into my back. I start vigorously shaking my head as he leans in. Smelling the alcohol on his breath, nausea coils low in my stomach. It reminds me of my—

Stop stuttering or I'll give you something to stutter about.

Kyle lifts his free hand and strokes my hair.

Your hair looks like a goddamn mop.

"Hold still, babe." Kyle's voice sounds predatory as it crawls into my ears. When his hand creeps down to my neck, I freeze.

Stop right there, you stuttering, stupid shit.

"No," I protest quietly, curling inward, not wanting to cause a scene. The room feels smaller and smaller as my chest tightens uncomfortably.

He either doesn't hear me or doesn't care. I lift my hands to protect my face. *Where is Danny?*

Kyle reaches for my wrists and starts to pry them from my face. "No!" I say louder, and every head turns toward us, including—*oh thank God.*

"What the *fuck* is going on here?"

I've never heard Danny use such a dark, low tone of voice as he shoves Kyle away from me.

"Whoa. Chill out, man. Susannah and I were just getting to know each other. She's playing a little hard to get, but—"

"Step the *fuck* away from her. Can't you see she's uncomfortable? She said *no*, you drunk dickhead!"

I'm mortified. Heat creeps up my neck, and I drop my gaze to the floor as my vision blurs with tears. I can feel every eye in the room stare at me.

A girl loudly whispers, "What's wrong with her? What a weirdo..."

"*Caitlin*," Alicia reprimands.

And suddenly I'm not at this party. I'm back in my living room, and the smell of my dad's favorite beer is making me sick.

I can't be here anymore. Bolting out of the house, I run across the lawn. When I reach the curb, tears of frustration roll down my face, and I sink down to the street. Why would Danny still want to be with me? I can't even handle one stupid party without embarrassing him.

"Why are you like this?" I mutter, taking shallow breaths.

"Gracie!" Danny sprints my way, wrapping me in a hug from behind. "I turned around and you were gone."

He gently strokes my head as he holds me, whispering, "I'm sorry, baby. I'm so sorry for leaving you," into the back of my hair.

"It was his breath," I whisper.

"What?"

My throat tightens, and fresh tears threaten to spill over. "I could smell the alcohol on his breath when he reached for my hair, and I...I..."

"It's okay. Let's blow out the candles together, okay?" He moves to crouch in front of me, holding up his hand and wiggling his fingers.

I wipe a tear from my eye. "Okay."

"You go first, Gracie."

I blow hard on his hand and he puts down all of his fingers and smiles. "Good job, baby."

"Your turn." I give him a weak smile, feeling a little calmer. Wiggling my fingers in front of my chin, I nod my head.

Danny leans forward, right in front of my face. He blows softly, and I recoil.

Get out of here before I do something that'll get me in real trouble.

Danny's face is one of horror as he immediately covers his mouth. "Gracie, I only took one sip before I came back to find you, I swear. *Fuck.* I wasn't thinking..."

My hands fly up on either side of my face and cover my ears. *Why can't I be normal?*

Danny stands up and takes a step back. "I'm so sorry, baby. God. I would *never* hurt you."

"I know," I sniff. My limbs feel too heavy to stand, gluing me to the street.

Danny briefly looks at the house and his gaze hardens. *Oh*

no, what if people are watching? I tell myself to get up and move, but I'm frozen.

"Let's go home, Gracie, away from all this."

"Yes," I whisper, though there's no way I'm getting out of here by myself. My legs betray me as I try to move them.

"Can I pick you up and carry you to the car?"

I nod, and Danny pulls me into his arms, lifting me. As he cradles me against his chest, he makes sure to face his mouth away from me, breathing off to the side. He gently sets me down outside the passenger side before opening the door, and I gingerly climb in, my adrenaline fizzling out.

We sit in the car in silence as Danny reaches around me to buckle my seatbelt. For a few minutes, we both stare out the front window.

I face him, embarrassment twisting through my expression. "I'm sorry. You must b-be so humiliated. God."

Danny turns to me slowly, his eyes locking onto mine.

"I will *never* drink again," he vows.

His promise might as well be a marriage oath, the word *never* digging itself into the center of my heart.

Danny reaches out and carefully takes my hand, brushing his thumb back and forth across all of my knuckles in a soothing rhythm. "And I'm the one who should be sorry. I am so fucking sorry, Gracie," he says hoarsely.

"It's okay," I breathe out. "You d-don't have t-to—"

He gives my hand a firm squeeze. "I do have to. You're the most important thing in the world to me, you know that right? You're safe with me."

I meet his eyes and find nothing but devotion. "I know."

"Fact for a feeling, Gracie?"

Without thinking, I open my mouth to say something but surprise myself when nothing comes out. My mind revolts against me focusing on anything other than the events of tonight. I cement my lips back together, balking at our game for the first time in my life.

"Um, no thank you," I whisper. "I d-don't want t-to play t-tonight."

Danny looks devastated, but he doesn't let go of my hand.

"Okay, Gracie girl, maybe later. I love you."

For years, Danny has told me he loves me. And gazing into his eyes, I wonder if it's finally starting to mean something different for him, like it does for me.

"I love you, too."

Chapter 29

Grace

"So, that's how I fell in love with Roger," Janie finishes telling me about her long-term boyfriend. We're on the loveseat in the family room, enjoying the pear vanilla tea she brewed. The cinnamon rolls, which are baking away in the oven, perfume the entire area with a sweet and spicy aroma. I wish I could bottle the scent.

"Wow, that's amazing, Janie. I'm really happy for you. Finding love again, a son in the league, and a budding fashion designer daughter. You really crushed it at the whole parenting thing, huh?"

Janie laughs warmly. "I don't know about all that, sweetie. My amazing kiddos, including you, kind of came out that way all on their own."

I sigh. Janie is serotonin for the soul; life is just richer with her around. "Thank you for saying that, it means a lot to me."

"It's the truth. Even though we haven't seen each other in forever, you've always been one of mine. I look forward to our phone call on your birthday every single year. Now that you're back from Indiana, I'd love to see you more. I know your animal clinic is downtown, but maybe you can swing by the suburbs sometime to meet Roger. He's heard a lot about you."

I start nodding before I realize I never told Janie that I opened my clinic in Columbus. "Have you been keeping in touch with Mae? I thought when we moved out of the neighborhood you two lost touch."

Janie's eyes twinkle. "Was it the mention of the animal clinic that gave me away? Sweetie, she was my next door neighbor for over five years! I couldn't keep away once she moved."

"Well, I'm glad to know you kept her company when I moved out of state. I always felt guilty that I didn't go somewhere closer."

She puts her hand on my lower arm and gives a comforting squeeze. "Oh, she was thrilled when you got into that vet school in Indiana. She was pushing so hard for you to live a little bit of life outside of Ohio."

"I wonder why she never mentioned you," I say absentmindedly, then realize how rude that sounds. Before I can explain, Janie cuts in.

"She never mentioned it to you for the same reason I never mentioned it to my son. You two weren't ready to hear that we remained friends. We laughed over how stressed both of you would be if you found out that we saw each other every Tuesday night."

"Tuesday nights! What the hell? She told me not to call Tuesdays because she had water aerobics class!"

Janie cocks an eyebrow and takes a sip of tea. "And you believed her?"

I giggle, and Janie does, too. Yeah, that one's on me.

"After Mae moved to Ohio, she became one of my closest friends and confidants. We used to sit in the kitchen and gossip about you and Daniel. The two of you sneaking out at night was one of our favorites. Neither of you were as slick as you thought."

My face heats. "But you, um, never said anything."

"Of course we never said anything! We knew there was no stopping the two of you, even when you were ten years old. Might as well lean into the swerve, right?" Janie chuckles.

"Right." I awkwardly clear my throat, tapping my fingers on the side of my mug. "And does Danny know that you, um, knew about us sneaking around?"

Janie smiles. "We've never spoken about it, but he must have suspected it. There's only so many times you can climb down a drainpipe without ripping your pants. I had to patch up his favorites from time to time."

I laugh, imagining Danny's state when he reached my lawn. "Point taken."

Janie sets her teacup down on the dark wood coffee table. I do the same as she turns to face me. She gently takes my hands in hers and says, "I know about the letter, kiddo."

A combination of panic and sadness courses through me. I blink away tears and respond with a simple, "Oh."

Janie's expression echoes my own sadness, her eyes downcast. She heaves a sigh. "I'm assuming you haven't given it to him yet. I'm not here to tell you what to do, but I want to encourage you to give it to him sooner rather than later."

I shift nervously, clasping her hands a little tighter. "I know. It's just so hard. And...I'm still processing."

Janie nods thoughtfully. "Yes, it's entirely your decision. All Mae and I ever wanted was for the two of you to find your way back to each other, in whatever capacity. If it's friendship, perfect. If it's more than friendship, that's perfect, too."

"Really?"

She gently pushes a loose curl back from my forehead. With

a knowing gleam in her eye and a loving smile on her lips, she says, "Yes."

Dropping my hand, she picks up her cup and drains her tea. "Now, two things. First, I want to see and talk to you more often now—not just once a year. I don't care what your relationship status is with my son. I want *our* relationship to be strong. Second, I need to get out of here and give you two some space, huh?"

A soft grin ghosts my lips and I exhale, easing some tension. I honestly don't know if space for Danny and me is good or bad.

"As Mae always says, 'Know when it's your time to exit stage left. It's usually sooner than you think.'"

We both dissolve into laughter.

* * *

"Away–ee-ay-ee-ay!" I loudly sing "Ocean Avenue," my voice echoing off of Danny's stock furniture, brought to you by the Cullen's interior decorator. Yellowcard is blasting on full volume as I stir my homemade soup.

I'm an experienced chef. My father obviously wasn't going to make me dinner, so I taught myself from kids' cookbooks at the library. I eagerly inhale, smelling notes of chicken broth, onion, and toasted bread. Chicken and wild rice soup is my favorite. One time, in high school, I made a huge batch, froze it, and ate it for an entire month.

"What do we have going on in here?"

I jump, almost dropping the spoon in my hand. "Don't startle me like that; I thought you were an intruder!"

"You do know there's a sophisticated house alarm system here, correct?" Danny says dryly.

"I don't care how many robots run your house, Danny. I'm a

thirty-year-old woman who watches serial killer documentaries."

He chuckles and walks closer to the stove, peering into the pot.

"Are you making chicken and wild rice soup?"

"Well, I had nothing to do after Janie left your giant manor, so I ordered groceries and decided to make us something to eat."

"Not tomato?" he asks innocently. Tomato is *his* favorite soup, but I wouldn't be caught dead eating it. He smirks, probably knowing exactly what I'm going to say next.

Setting down the spoon, I put my hands on my hips. "Tomato soup is just marinara sauce propaganda, Danny. It's not real. The people behind tomato soup are the best marketers in the world."

"Uh huh." He turns on the oven light and crouches down to look inside. "Do I smell grilled cheese?"

"Yep, they're keeping warm in there. I added bacon, too."

He stands up and leans against the island. "Thanks for doing this. I rarely get home-cooked meals. It's really nice of you."

I nod and resume stirring, adding pepper to the simmering pot. This line of conversation is feeling a little too domestic for me now, so I introduce a subject change. "How was your physical?"

"Passed with flying colors. No injuries to work on during the offseason," he confirms, setting two bowls next to the stove.

I ladle the soup into the bowls. "That's great. I'm sure that can be nerve wracking."

Danny hands me an oven mitt, and I grab the grilled cheeses out of the oven. He brings the bowls to the island, and I join him with the sandwiches.

"Thankfully, it was a pretty light year for me. I didn't have as many tough tackles or hits as previous years, and no concussions."

My heart stumbles at the thought of serious injuries in his previous seasons—*years* I know absolutely nothing about. I want to ask, but all I can manage is a weak, "Concussions are so scary."

He takes a bite of the grilled cheese, licking at a thin string of melted cheese stuck on his bottom lip. "Yep. Hey, this is so good."

My cheeks warm with the compliment, and I mentally count the carrots in my soup to avoid sinking into his hazel eyes. "Thanks. I have a lot of practice. I eat this once a week at home."

"I can see why." He grins.

Soup is not a food that allows for much conversation, so we eat in silence for a few minutes. The clock on his kitchen wall mocks me. Instead of the usual numbers, all I see is a countdown to my flight tonight—and a conversation about the letter.

As if he's in my head, Danny asks, "Hey, Gracie? Would you, uh, want to go somewhere with me tonight?"

My head tilts in soft surprise. "My flight leaves at six."

"Yep."

I blink a few times. "I'd miss my flight."

"True."

Leaning back in my seat, I study him with a healthy dose of suspicion. My throat feels sticky, like I've swallowed a handful of the pricing stickers they use at TJ Maxx. "Is this, like, a date or something?"

"It doesn't have to be," he replies casually, seemingly unbothered by my question.

I search his eyes, trying to determine his true intentions. "I don't want to give off the wrong impression by being seen out with you when it's—*we're*—not like that."

Danny shrugs. "I don't care about what other people think."

"I think I...do."

He swallows and averts his eyes, hiding from me. *What isn't he saying?*

"If you're concerned about being seen with me in public, we can stay here. It's not a big deal or anything. Just...I'm hoping you'll stay a little longer."

I blink a few times and determine that maybe I should stop overthinking his offer. I haven't seen much of New York, and there's probably no harm in staying one extra night. "I'll need to reschedule my flight and call Elle to make sure she can hold down the fort tomorrow. And I won't be able to stay past tomorrow evening because I have a team meeting at the clinic on Friday that I can't miss. Where did you have in mind?"

My heartbeat spikes, and I wonder what it'd be like to leave this bubble with him, beyond the confines of his home. When I refocus, Danny still hasn't responded. Is he nervous, or...*oh God.* What *is* his idea of a 'date'?

"I swear, Danny. If your idea of a good time is an escape room, the only thing escaping will be me, out this door, directly to the airport."

"You think I'd take you to an escape room? On a da—erm, friendship hangout?"

Jesus Christ. *Friendship hangout?*

"I don't know. Escape rooms are very popular. I just read an article about them that said there's over fifty thousand of them across the world."

Danny raises an eyebrow. "Wow. Sounds like you're really into escape rooms. You sure you don't want to go to one?"

I start rubbing my temples. "Tell me where we're actually going."

"Well, assuming you're still into animal facts," he says, breezily, "I thought we'd go to this place nearby. They have trivia Monday nights, and tonight is supposed to be animal themed."

I try not to show too much interest off the bat. The thing is, I absolutely love a scenario where I am a shoo-in to win. Snooping and the burning desire to crush strangers in a battle of wits are my two most fatal flaws. No one can beat me at animal trivia. It's almost unfair, but it should make for a satisfying night.

"That does sound *kind of* fun," I admit.

Kind of, my ass. This is my idea of heaven, and Danny knows it.

"Great, I'm glad it sounds 'kind of' fun. Maybe we'll upgrade to 'fun' by the end of the night," he tells me, his tone dripping with sarcasm.

"I'll go call Elle. If she's okay with it, and there's a reasonable flight out tomorrow, we can go."

I feel more pressure going into this non-date-friendship-hang than I did before my vet school exams, and I don't want to analyze why that is. Instead, I take a deep breath and blow it out into the void, daydreaming about candles.

Chapter 30

Grace

Eighteen Years Old

"Blow out the candles," Mae says, hovering over me at the kitchen table. I glance at Danny, and he throws me a wink. It's weird to hear those words from someone other than him.

Every year on my birthday, I extinguish fake candles in our special spot. When we were younger, he'd bring me a red flower in lieu of a gift. *A strawberry flower for the strawberry girl,* he'd always say. Even though Danny's tacked on actual presents in years since, the flower ritual is still my favorite.

"Bee...before I turn seventy, please," Mae sighs.

"You're older than seven—"

"That's it. Take away the gifts, Janie." Mae waves to the gift boxes on the coffee table I hadn't noticed until now.

I can't hold myself back from asking, "You guys got me presents?"

Eight eyes snap toward me, six with sympathy and two with devotion, as I swallow the truth of what I've implied through my question.

Outside of Danny, the last birthday gift I received was perfume from Mae for my thirteenth birthday. From that point on, she mailed money. I needed that fifty dollars more than she knew, but there's something different about tearing wrapping paper off a box someone dressed up just for you.

Danny interrupts the awkwardness, clearing his throat.

"Make a wish, Gracie."

I smile gratefully and lean forward to blow out all eighteen candles. I'm an old pro, so they go down in one swoosh.

Danny bends down and whispers in my ear, "What'd you wish for, Gracie girl?"

I shiver. "I'll tell you tonight."

"Okay, love you," Danny whispers.

We say 'I love you' all the time...but we've said that for years, as friends. Every time he tells me that he loves me, I wait for the 'in'. I am hopelessly *in* love with him, but I haven't had the courage to say it first. With graduation right around the corner, I want to tell him how I feel. If I've learned anything through the therapy sessions I've been going to twice weekly, it's that being open and honest with your emotions is key to healing.

Two slices of strawberry cake later, I've opened all my gifts. Homemade braided string bracelets from Tessa, a book from Janie, and enough trendy clothes from Mae to outfit me for a whole month.

It's nearly sunset when Mae leaves for her Friday night gardening club meeting. As soon as the door clicks shut, Danny and I lock eyes.

Less than three minutes after that, we're upstairs making out on my fluffy, pink double bed. His hands travel up and down my sides, sneaking under my shirt to rub my back. I don't think I'll ever get over this feeling, what it's like to kiss him. His lips are so soft, and he smells like clean laundry and oranges. I love how his thick hair is long enough for me to run my fingers through the strands.

He pulls back slightly and gives me a crooked, teasing smile. "So, what's your wish?"

I don't say anything in response. Instead, I stare into his hazel eyes. I admire the little gap between his two front teeth. And I decide that this is it.

"I'm in love with you, Danny."

He lifts an eyebrow in what appears to be confusion. Oh my God, is he that thrown off by my confession? I flush and avert my eyes.

"Yeah, baby. I love you, too?"

Steadying myself, I take a deep breath and decide to confess my feelings one more time. If he doesn't feel the same way, that's fine, but at least I'll know.

"But I'm *in* love with you, Danny. I love you. As more than a friend."

"I should hope so?" He narrows his eyes, searching mine. "Why're you acting weird?"

"I...what? I'm not acting weird."

"I say 'I love you' all the time," he says defensively, then pauses. "And you say it back."

I take two moments to join his confusion before I start giggling. I am way overthinking this. Danny is nothing if not a straightforward guy. Of course he thinks "I love you" means, well... I love you. How did I have such a wrong read on this?

He isn't laughing. "I don't understand. Do you love me or not?"

Poor, poor, simple boy. I grab his cheeks with both hands. "I love you, Danny. I love you so much."

He sniffs and tilts his chin up. "Oh. Okay then."

Grabbing his neck and tugging his face toward mine, I smile into our kiss as we start making out again. His fingers brush up against my bra strap underneath my shirt. We've only done over-the-bra-and-underwear-stuff since we started dating, and I'm ready to move this whole shebang forward. *Too* ready. Danny's always saying there's no rush, because we're "in it for the long game." But I might die from his chivalry.

After a few minutes, I pull back and decide I want more tonight. Breathing heavily, I announce, "I'm ready."

It takes him a few beats before he understands. "Gracie," he whispers. "Are you sure?"

"Yeah. But if you don't want—"

His voice lowers. "I want. You have *no idea* how much I want."

"Oh." My cheeks warm. "Good...that's good. Um, do you have a...?" I trail off.

Danny knows I take birth control every night. We can thank Mae for that prescription. I'm religious about the timing. He blushes every time my reminder alarm goes off. But I still want to be extra safe.

"Yeah. Um, you said I could keep whatever I wanted in the desk drawer, so I, uh, put a condom and a small bottle of lube in your pencil pouch last month." My eyes widen in surprise. "I wasn't expecting anything from you," he hastily clarifies, "but I wanted to be prepared."

I give him a small smile. "I'm glad you did."

He nods and moves toward my desk to collect the condom and lube. As he does that, I stand up and start taking off my clothes. I think that's next in this whole order of events, but what do I know? It's the first time for both of us. We'll just have to make sense of it together.

First, my sweater, then my shirt, then my pants, then my socks, then my—

"*What are you wearing?* Oh my God. I...what. You? *Jesus Christ.*"

I glance down at my body to make sure everything's in place. Looks good to me, so I'm not sure what's going on here. I frown. "Do you not like it? Ben said..."

"BEN? Did you go *lingerie shopping* with Ben?" Danny screeches in confusion, looking like he's trying really hard not to be mad.

I wince. Bringing up another man while propositioning this one probably isn't in good form. Standing in the emerald green lace lingerie I bought at Victoria's Secret, I quickly correct myself.

"No, oh my God. Sorry. Ben mentioned that he loves when Mia surprises him in different ways since they've been together so long. So I thought I'd...are you surprised?" I gesture toward my body like it's the latest computer model.

"I can't remember a time in my life when I was *more* surprised," Danny squeaks out in a high-pitched voice I'd only ever heard him use with Charger.

"Not even at the end of *The Sixth Sense?*"

"Not even then," he says solemnly.

We both stand, in silence, for another thirty seconds. Now that Danny's come down from The Ben Lingerie Fiasco, he's openly gawking at me. A minute passes, and I wonder if I should blow on him like I do his Nintendo 64 game cartridge when it doesn't work, just to see if that does something.

When I start to lean in, he says, "Gracie, I don't want to assume. You have to be specific. You want to..."

"Go all the way. Have sex."

He takes a deep breath and blows it out through his teeth, looking a little out of control.

"So I can..."

"Do everything. Take my clothes off, touch me anywhere, talk me through it."

"Fuck." Then he starts muttering a flurry of words under his breath. "*Slowdownkeepittogether.*"

I wonder if he knows I can hear his inner thoughts and patiently wait for him to either acknowledge me or come back to reality. It doesn't appear that he will be doing either anytime soon, so I reach behind my back to unhook my bra.

He stops me with his hands. "Wait, Gracie. We haven't even done the other bases yet. I can make you feel good doing something else, if you don't want to go all the way." He clears his throat. "Just touching underneath our clothes, or I've, um, never done anything with my mouth before. So, that would be new for both of us, too."

My body temperature continues to rise with every word he says. "While that sounds good, I'm feeling very ready to have sex. Let's do it."

"Hold on. I don't want to hurt you. We can do other things first to warm you up. It'll hurt less that way, I think."

"But we'll do it after that stuff, right?"

He smiles his Big Danny Smile. "Yeah, if you want. I love you."

"I love you, too. Touch me, please."

He groans. "You can't say things like that to me right now."

"Why not?"

"Because I feel like I'm already two seconds away from coming and I haven't even taken off your bra yet."

"Okay," I say thoughtfully, "then let's take off my bra. Before you do that."

"*Jesus.*" A bead of sweat forms on his hairline. "Can you come closer?"

I step right in front of him. He swiftly takes off his shirt before easily unhooking my bra with one hand. He nervously wipes his hands on the side of his pants and breathes out, "Gracie, you're so beautiful."

I soak up the compliment as Danny leans closer to me and lifts his hands. My breasts have grown fuller over the past year due to having regular meals, and they fit perfectly in his palms. He lightly squeezes them before circling my pink nipples with two of his fingers. I shiver, and my nipples seem to get harder.

"I love these," he murmurs as he places one in between his thumb and index finger and lightly pinches. I gasp and a tiny whimper slips out of my mouth.

"God, Gracie. I'm obsessed with the noises you make. Does this feel good?"

"Yes," I breathe. "It feels *so* good."

"Are you getting wet?"

"Yeah." I'm definitely wet. I feel tingly all over.

"You're doing great."

My breasts drop slightly when he removes his hands.

"Leave your underwear on for now."

I nod and run my hands down his chest.

"You're perfect, Gracie baby. No one has ever or will ever compare to you."

I love when he calls me Gracie baby. It reminds me that we're different now, more than friends. I feel so wanted and warm all over. I knew it would be like this with Danny.

"Lay down on the bed, okay?"

I do as he says, not really feeling self-conscious with my panties still on. I open my thighs a little.

"Wider," he coaxes, pushing gently on my knees to spread my legs. "Like that."

He looks at me hungrily, laid out like this for him. "I'm going to start with my mouth on you here," he taps my nipples with the flat of his hands, "so you can get even wetter here," he explains as he taps the wet spot on my underwear. "Then, I'll touch you through your, um, panties until you come for me. Hopefully."

I give him a little moan. "Yes, Danny."

He gulps, looking pained. "Fuck. You saying my name when you're naked like this... It's better than I imagined."

I have no time to respond as he kneels between my legs and leans forward to put his mouth on my breast. He starts by kissing all around them. Short, sweet kisses. But then, he swirls his tongue around my nipple, causing me to squirm and arch beneath him. "More, please."

Danny grins. "I knew you'd be polite, but I didn't know you'd be greedy."

His words light a fire in me as he continues licking my nipples. The sensations I'm feeling are so, so welcome. I whimper and moan, chanting "yes, more, please." I don't even know what I'm asking for, but I can tell I need something.

Danny groans in response. "Having you beneath me, begging like that, is making me even harder."

Propping myself up on my elbows, I glance down and nod. Sure enough, the outline of him is completely erect underneath his gray sweatpants. "You are really hard down there."

"Do you think you can, um...can you say 'cock' when you talk about it, Gracie? 'Your cock is really hard.' I've always wanted to hear you say things like that. About me, I mean. If you want."

A drop of sweat slides down my temple. "Yeah, I want to."

"Okay, go ahead," he says hoarsely.

"Your cock is really hard, Danny."

He stares at the ceiling and holds his breath for a minute. "I —that's good, Gracie," he praises.

Danny moves up and starts kissing me, his tongue swirling around mine. In between long, languid kisses, he murmurs love confessions, like "you're everything I dreamed you would be," and "this is everything I wanted, for years."

I feel so grateful our first time is together.

"I'm going to take care of you now." He leans back and studies the wet spot on my underwear. With my legs open, cold air hits the wetness and causes me to shiver.

Danny plants a kiss on either side of my neck, and I melt. I can't believe we're here. I thought I might be scared or anxious, but I've never felt more certain. Certain about him, about this, about *us*.

"I'll be so gentle, Gracie. You're safe with me. Say stop if it's too much." His low voice brushes against my skin, painting me with affection.

I don't see any possibility of wanting to stop given how good everything feels right now.

He scoots down the bed. Danny starts rubbing me back and forth with two fingers, over and over again, through my underwear. The material shifts, brushing against the wetness. He changes direction, moving his fingers up and down. With every touch, I get more and more out of my head. While rubbing the outside, he pushes on the harder spot near the top and a warm, tingly sensation floods my lower stomach.

Danny groans, "Oh my God," under his breath.

I start crunching up slightly, my muscles tightening and releasing of their own accord. The feeling is so intensely pleasurable, and my thighs start to shake. "I can't stop—"

"Keep coming, Gracie, for as long as you want. You're so beautiful, it's insane."

"I'm hot all over. I feel so, so—"

"It's good, huh, baby?"

"Yes," I hiss out, my spasms slowing. I squeeze my eyes shut, feeling overwhelmed in the best way.

"Okay. Okay," he mutters, pulling himself together. "I'm going to take these off now."

Any remaining shyness leaves my body after that orgasm. I lift my hips, and Danny slides off my panties. He stares with adoration. "Gracie, you're so pretty everywhere. I'm so lucky." Leaning down, he kisses the top of my trimmed, reddish hair. "I am obsessed with this."

Danny starts touching me bare, rubbing my wetness all around. He grabs the bottle of lube, puts some on his finger, and gently slides it inside me. My hips all but jump off the bed.

"Fuck. You're so tight," he chokes out. His wide eyes meet mine as he slowly curls his finger inside of me. "Does this hurt? I can stop."

"No, don't stop," I breathe. It feels foreign, yet familiar in a way I can't explain. It's like my heart already knows Danny so intimately that my body does, too.

He nods. "Do you feel ready?"

"I'm ready." I just can't believe it's finally happening.

Danny pulls back and strips off his sweatpants and boxers. He reaches for his cock and holds it, stroking once. My breath catches, watching him touch himself because of me.

"Is this okay?" he asks, giving himself another rough stroke.

"Yeah." I'm mesmerized by how firmly he squeezes it, loving how hard he is just from watching me.

Danny grabs the condom and rolls it down his cock, which is now hitting his stomach. "I'm going to make this so good for you."

"I know, I trust you."

He crawls back on top of me and props himself up on his hands. Lowering himself slightly, I savor the feeling of his body pressed against mine.

"I love you, Gracie. More than anything."

"I love you too, Danny."

And with those affirmations, he starts slowly sliding in. We both gasp. It's a stretch. Pausing, he waits until I'm used to the feeling of him. Danny's face is flushed, his eyes bright with intention. He reaches down and rubs me again with his thumb above where we're connected, and I start to feel sparks like before. After a few moments, he thrusts deeper, and I wince when I feel a pinch and a sting. Our eyes lock, and the air shifts between us. As I lose myself in his gaze, the soft stretch of pain melts away into something warmer.

"Sorry, Gracie, I don't think I could've totally avoided the pinch."

"I'm okay. I love being this close to you. I feel so...full."

Danny freezes and lets out a groan. "Shit. I might come before you have the chance to again."

"I already came," I remind him, slightly confused.

He slowly thrusts in and out. "When we're more used to doing this, I think you might be able to come again when I'm inside you."

Danny puts his right thumb in his mouth to get it wet and brings it to one of my nipples. He rubs it back and forth, and it feels incredible.

"Doesn't this feel so right, Gracie? Me inside you like this? Doesn't it make sense?"

It makes perfect sense.

"You're doing so good for me. Do you think you can come again?" he asks in a strained voice, intent on making me feel pleasure the whole time. I can tell it's taking everything in him not to finish.

I shake my head. I feel good, but also oversensitized in a way that's different from when he touches me with his fingers.

His thrusts get faster until he can't hold back anymore. "I can't hold off—I'm going to come. I'm coming."

I feel a rush of warmth inside me as Danny moans on a twitch. "You were perfect, Gracie. You *are* perfect," he praises, as his chest curves in over me. Completely spent, he angles himself so some of his body weight falls on me. I sigh happily, relishing the heat of his skin.

We both pause and stare at each other as we process what just happened. He pulls out slowly and collapses next to me. Danny takes off the condom, then ties it off, wraps it in a tissue, and tosses it in the trash can underneath my nightstand. He covers us with a blanket, and we both turn on our sides to face each other.

"I can't believe—"

"That was—"

We dissolve into laughter, because clearly, we're too high on each other to speak. Danny snakes his arm behind my head and rolls me over so I'm resting on his chest. I hear his heart beating fast, then slower, as I gently stroke his side. My body is a little sore, but in a blissful way. I wouldn't trade a single ache for anything.

"How are you feeling, Gracie girl?" His voice encompasses me, the tone of it feeling like home.

There are so many ways I could describe how I feel, but right now, one word comes to mind.

"For the first time in my life, I feel kind of *glowy*."

"Well, then you finally feel how I've always seen you." Danny's words are muffled by my hair, but I swear I hear his voice crack.

We relax into each other, happier than we've ever been.

"There's no one else for me but you, Gracie."

Grinning, I tilt my head up for a forehead kiss and echo his words. "And there's no one else for me but you."

Since age ten, we've belonged to each other in so many ways. But with an ear over his heartbeat, I feel closer to him now more than ever before.

"So, what was your wish?" he asks, twirling my hair.

"I wished that we would be together forever. Kinda cheesy, I know."

"Nah," Danny replies with a toothy smile so big it rivals mine. "Not cheesy at all."

* * *

"Say cheese, kiddos!"

My black polyester gown might as well be an oven in the scorching Ohio sun as Janie snaps the two hundredth picture of the day. After posing for photos in front of their house, in front of my house, on their deck, on my porch, and in front of the rose bushes in her garden, my entire body feels like a Hot Pocket fresh out of the microwave.

"How do you play football in this kind of weather?" I mutter to Danny, who looks completely unbothered. "It's not fair. I probably look as red as the stop sign you consistently blow by in our neighborhood."

"You look gorgeous, as always." He dots my heat-stroked cheek with a kiss.

"Aw, Daniel. Kiss her cheek again for the camera this time! I wasn't ready."

"Janie, enough. Poor Bee is about to collapse." Mae grins, standing cool in the shade.

"*Wait!*" Tessa comes running out of the house, holding two graduation caps. "Mom, you have to get a picture of them wearing the caps I designed." Almost tripping over her bare feet, she does a little jump off of the front porch and dashes toward us.

I crouch down slightly and reach out for a hug, like I always do for Tess. Even though she's twelve now, she still squeezes me just as tightly as she did when she was five years old.

I gave her complete control over designing the tops of our mortarboards. Standing next to me, Danny releases a barely audible groan. He was not pleased with the decision to let her run wild with them, assuming she'd write "dweeb" on his cap in pink glitter glue.

"Close your eyes!" Tessa claps her hands together excitedly, and I comply before she carefully places a cap in my hands.

"Okay, open them!" she squeals. Even though my cheeks ache, I paste on a smile in advance of even seeing it.

My forced smile becomes genuine as I inspect the cap. It's lined with painted paw prints in different shades of brown. Winding in between the paws is a long green stethoscope made with glitter. The words "Round of A-Paws for the Future Dr. Sinclair" are printed in small rainbow letters in the cap's center.

I brush my fingers against the words *Dr. Sinclair*. "Tess. This is so thoughtful. I'm going to have the best designed cap there."

"Not sure about that," Danny interjects, his voice low with emotion. "Mine is pretty great."

Glancing down at his cap, I take in the white block letters "MVP" written over a green painted background, meant to represent turf. Mini footballs line his cap with golden glitter dusting them.

Danny turns the cap in his hands, admiring it from every angle. "Thank you, Tessie."

"I'll keep this forever," I add.

Tessa nods before throwing her arms around Danny's torso. "I'm going to miss you. I wish you didn't have to go to college!"

It breaks my heart to see her already dreading the absence of her big brother. He crouches down to her level and wraps her in a hug. As he whispers reassurances into her ear, Janie looks on with tears in her eyes. After a few sniffles, Tessa giggles at something he said.

Danny clears his throat as they separate. "Let's do this thing. We gotta head over for the rehearsal. We'll see you all there!"

"Wish me luck!" I chime in.

"Good luck with graduation! See you there!" Tessa yells after us.

"I meant with his driving," I mumble.

Danny playfully shoves me. Picking up my purse off the ground, I open it and make sure the essentials are packed.

"Bee, can I grab you for a second?" Mae calls.

"Sure!" I join her underneath the tree in Danny's front yard.

She looks me up and down and beams. "Before you leave, there's something I want you to have. I know your father tossed some of your mother's things after she passed. I'm still pissed about that." Mae's jaw clenches.

My own memories have faded over the years, partially due to my age when she passed and partially due to the trauma I experienced at the hands of my father. Mae has shared so many stories about my mother this past year, and I've soaked each one into my soul.

"Well, I wanted to give you this." She opens a necklace box to show me a delicate golden chain with a dangling letter M. "It's hers, and I think it should be yours. I gifted it to her on her high school graduation day. The 'M' was for Melanie, of course. But I thought...well, I thought that it could stand for 'Mom' now, if you want to wear it."

I wrap Mae in a huge hug as tears well in my eyes. She carefully clasps the necklace around my neck.

Running my fingers over the necklace, I kiss her on the cheek. "Thank you, Mae. This means the world to me."

She pats me on my arm. "Now, now. Get going, or else you're going to be late for your graduation."

Danny is waiting for me across the yard, and as I meet him, he gently asks, "Everything okay?"

"Yes, everything is perfect." My lips curve into a wide smile.

As we walk toward his car, I slip off my gown to get some

air. I smooth out the wrinkles in the new dress Mae surprised me with this morning. It's short and white with a v-neck halter top and a flared skirt. Delicate lace that looks like petals lines the hem and frames the neckline.

I reach Danny's car on the street in front of our houses, only to realize he's stopped walking. When I turn around, he looks like he swallowed his tongue, and I remember that he's only seen me in my graduation gown today.

"Gracie, you're stunning."

Just as I was cooling down, my cheeks heat all over again. "Um, thanks. You look great, too."

"You're always beautiful. But wow," he breathes, "I've never seen you in a dress like that before."

"Yeah, Mae bought it for me as a surprise. Janie actually helped pick it out."

The corners of his lips turn up as he opens the passenger door for me. "Remind me to thank them later."

I climb in, and he starts the car. Before shifting into gear, he glances at the graduation cap in my lap.

"You know, if you do end up keeping your graduation cap forever, it's going to need some editing."

"What do you mean? It's perfect!" I exclaim, affronted on Tessa's behalf.

"The last name looks a little off," he says with a wink.

I, along with my witty retorts, melt into my seat.

A few hours later, we're standing outside the convocation center watching everyone throw their hats in the air for a class picture. Danny and I leave ours alone, of course, protecting the keepsakes at all costs. Instead, we hold each other tightly in celebration.

After hugging Danny, I turn to Ben, who's currently waving at his family.

"We did it!" I squeal, giving Ben a friendly squeeze.

"Hell yeah, we did!" He beams, holding his cap underneath his arm.

"Are you and Mia still up for going to the diner with us after this?"

"Absolutely. No way do I want to share Mia with my family; she's only here for a few days."

I grin. "You do realize you'll see her every day starting next week, right?"

"Yeah, yeah. Like you wouldn't want to spend as much time as possible with Lover Boy," he teases, tugging on my cap's tassel.

I nudge his shoulder. "We've come a long way from public speaking and library lunches, huh?"

He lifts his hand up like a visor over his forehead and pretends to scan the crowd. "I don't see our good friend Garett here... Do you think he even graduated?"

Laughing and linking my arm with Ben's, we happily stroll out of the student area. Danny follows closely behind, chatting with a teammate.

I recognize the girl with the high cheekbones and stick straight, inky black hair as soon as I spot the lone pink streak framing her face. "Mia!" I shout with excitement.

"Grace?! Is it really you?" She jogs my way, all but shoving Ben to the side and wrapping me in an embrace.

"Hey!" Ben shouts, fixing his glasses.

Mia pulls back with a smile. "I feel like I already know you."

"Same. The pictures don't do you justice. I love your hair," I gush.

"Of course the pictures don't do her justice," Ben announces, stepping in between us and putting his arm around Mia's shoulders. "No picture could ever capture her essence."

"Oh please," Mia snorts, but gives him a peck on the cheek.

Danny holds out his hand for a fist bump. "Hey, Mia. It's really nice to finally meet you."

"And you must be Dan," Mia replies, giving him a bump back.

"Ceremony, check. Class picture, check. Introductions, check." Ben starts listing off items, making an invisible check mark gesture with each one. "Can we please leave now? I'm starving."

"Let's get out of here," I agree. "We'll meet you at the diner."

We arrive at the same time, grab a booth together, and order burgers. Milkshakes are a must for dessert: chocolate for Danny, mint for Mia, cookies and cream for Ben, and strawberry, of course, for me. In between sips, we make small talk about college. Ben and Mia are going to Indianapolis Tech University and have plans to go to law school in the area post-grad.

"You know, Grace," Ben says, wiggling his eyebrows. "When I was researching colleges in Indiana, I just so happened to notice that Indianapolis–Metro has an amazing veterinarian school."

Mia jumps in. "Yes, I read that too, actually. You should definitely apply there as one of your post-grad options. How fun would it be if you followed us to Indiana one day?"

"Hey, who's gonna follow me?" Danny playfully interjects, looping his arm around my shoulders.

My gaze traces over the planes of his face, the texture of his skin, and the lips that have captured mine countless times. Every feature is one I know by heart, and I can't wait to keep memorizing him over the course of our life together.

"I'll follow you anywhere, Danny."

Chapter 31

Danny

Eighteen Years Old

A swarm of buzzing, busy bees invades my stomach as we follow the printed directions to Gracie's dormitory. Mom's driving—at Gracie's request. The rental truck is filled to the brim with dorm room staples. Mini trash cans, ramen noodles, shower caddies, and sheet sets.

"We're going to Gracie's dorm first, right, Mom?"

"Right. She has more things, so we're going to stop there first to unload and make sure she's all settled for her internship orientation. Then, you and I will head over to the athletic side of campus."

"I think it's bullshit we can't just room together."

Mom plugs one of her ears with her free hand. "La, la, la. I do not need to hear anything regarding that, Daniel."

"I didn't say anything bad! I just meant to hang out together more. We'll be further apart in distance at college than we are at home."

She gives me a flat look in the rearview mirror, eyes rolling. "Sure... I'm *sure* that's exactly what you meant. Just make sure to use condoms, please. I'm too much of a free spirit to be a grandmother right now. In fact, I'm about to date as soon as you munchkins leave the house. Tomorrow, maybe."

I try not to gag. "Mom, please. Can you not? You're making Gracie blush!"

Gracie sinks down into her seat with slight embarrassment. "It's fine, Janie."

We stop at a red light, and Mom holds her hands up in protest. "Sorry, sorry! As a mom dropping you both at college for the first time, I'm legally obligated to say that. It's in the Mom Code of Conduct. Take it up with the president's mom if you don't like it."

"Yeah, you can stop with all that now. We're well versed in 'the talk,' thanks to Mae." I shudder, remembering Mae's very literal approach to the birds and the bees. "I miss the person I was before I watched that video."

Gracie nods in agreement. "Same. If a bee flies up to me, I just close my eyes and hope it stings me now. I can't bear to look at its little bee face after what I've seen."

"Enough with the bee sex, children," Mom says in exasperation.

"You brought it up!" I shout.

"And I sincerely regret it!" she yells back.

Gracie snickers in her seat.

"Thank God Tessie's with friends today," I mutter.

Tessa, the family pre-teen, will always be five years old to me. I'll miss her at college, but with Easton being only about ninety minutes away from our houses, we'll see family often.

"Moving on. Sweetie, do you think you have everything you need?"

"I don't think there was anything left in the whole store when we were done with it. I'm good, Janie. Thank you again for everything," Gracie replies.

"My pleasure, kiddo. Daniel, you're all set for practices? You have your gear?"

"They actually provide it now that I'm in college. I can't wait to wear the uniform while I compete in a sold out stadium. It feels like forever since I've been in a *real* game. I miss it."

"Tessa's already been telling everyone that her brother's going to be on TV," Janie laughs. "It'll be a blast watching you. You two have your scholarship stuff figured out?"

We answer in unison. "Yep!"

I face Gracie and grin. "This is really going to be our year, huh?"

"I hope so. I've already connected with some other students in the pre-vet program and they seem amazing. I'm just excited for a fresh start."

I grab her hand and lean closer so I can whisper in her ear. "And we'll have more opportunities for alone time."

She shivers. I honestly can't get enough of her. Ever since we started having sex this summer, my protectiveness has increased tenfold.

Rolling down the window as we pull up to her dorm, I breathe in the fresh air and admire the campus. Lush green grass, trees for miles, and little squirrels scurrying around every corner.

"I think this is it!" I call, pointing at the building.

"Drackett Dormitory, kiddo?"

"That's the one," Gracie answers as Mom puts the car in park.

I hop out. "I'll start unloading some of the heavier stuff on the curb to bring in. It's going to take a while to get all these boxes out."

"Sounds good!" Gracie holds up her phone. "I might give Mae a call—you want me to put it on speaker?"

I smile. "Always. Can't wait to hear what wisdom she has for us today."

Gracie dials her home phone, and it rings three times as we wait to hear Mae's voice.

"Queen Bee?"

"Yes, hi!" Gracie grins at me. "Danny's here, too."

"Aren't you two at college now?"

"Yes..."

"So, why are you calling me? Don't you need to go sing the school fight song or something?" Mae asks with a dose of her classic sarcasm.

"Singing the fight song is on the agenda later tonight, actually," I tease.

Mae laughs. "Alright then. How's move-in going?"

"It's going great." Gracie pushes a few stray curls out of her face. "Danny's doing all the heavy lifting. Janie decided to drop me off first so I could spend some time getting settled. I'm here a little bit earlier than most students because of my animal sciences internship, so I haven't met my roommate yet."

"I hope you'll claim the better bed, Bee."

"Uh, probably not." Gracie blushes.

After years of minimizing herself for her father's convenience, taking the "better" furniture is something Gracie would never do. She's still learning how to curb her habit of making herself small.

Mae chuckles, her voice raspy over the phone. "Make sure you stick up for yourself over there. You're the strongest kid I know. Don't let anyone walk all over you. Never again."

"Or, if things get tough, maybe I'll just come hide at home with you. You're close enough," Gracie teases.

"Girl, don't make me put a barricade around this house. If I see your face in the next ninety business days, we'll be having words."

I stifle a laugh. "Business days? Sounds serious. Shall we prepare a presentation for our next reunion?"

"I'm not kidding. Bee needs to live it up! Pull all nighters, go to parties, dye her hair. Hell, join one of those groups where you pay people to be your friends for all I care."

Gracie giggles. "A sorority?"

"Yes, join a sorority!"

We both chuckle, and Gracie leans her head against my shoulder.

"Thanks for your input, I'll definitely consider it." Gracie playfully rolls her eyes. "We already miss you, Mae."

"Miss you, too. Well, I've got a hot date with a puzzle, here. I'm going to let you go. I love you like bees love honey."

"Love you, too," we say in unison.

* * *

"Nice set, Gracie baby. Keep it up," I encourage as she pulls on the rowing machine handle and pushes off the foot rest with her legs.

"Thanks," Gracie replies, out of breath. "I think that was the most resistance I've done. I'm going to be so sore tomorrow."

"I'll help work over your muscles tonight," I promise, drawing a blush from her.

God, things are so good with us. We've fallen into a solid routine after just two weeks at Easton. On the weekends, we explore campus and hang out with mutual friends. Gracie's already close with the girlfriends of the guys on the team, jokingly telling me I've been demoted from "best friend" to "male best friend." On the weekdays, she joins me at the campus gym for my personal workouts, even though she hates intentional exercise. For me, all of my exercise is intentional.

Gracie may call it a "torture dungeon with air conditioning," but I call it Monday through Sunday. Football isn't just a sport to me—it's a part of me. Every workout, every meal, just serves to ingrain it further into my DNA. Nearly every choice I've made has led me here, playing as a Division 1 starter.

I increase the resistance on my machine as my girlfriend eyes me up and down, unashamedly checking me out.

"Wow, Danny. I'm pretty sure you could lift all my emotional baggage with one hand," she jokes.

"Ha ha. Very funny, Gracie," I deadpan.

It's my turn to stare at her now, and my eyes linger on the curve of her ass. The pale blue of her fitted tank top and leggings brings out the vibrant blue color in her right eye, making it appear brighter. Her cheeks are pink, and the light sheen of sweat on her face only makes her glisten. I could spend all day admiring this girl, but I tear my gaze from her to focus back on my workout.

"I'm going to get some free weights over there. Be right back." I jog to the other side of the gym.

As I wait for someone to finish their rep, I glance back and watch a jacked guy wearing a ripped tank top walk over in her direction. He sports the type of over-the-top muscles that make you wonder if it's *just* protein powder.

Muscle Guy holds out his hand, and Gracie tightens her grip on the machine in response. She still has a difficult time trusting men after her asshole father. I know Gracie can handle herself, but I'm not sure if *I* can handle watching the Hulk chat her up. It takes me all of two seconds to abandon the weights and run back to her.

"I like your outfit, by the way. The light blue looks great on you. Do you come here often?" I overhear him ask.

"I usually only come with—"

"Me. Hey, dude. I'm DT." My breath comes in short puffs, and it's not from the workout.

"DT! Whoa. Nice to meet you, man. Can't wait to see you on the field this year. I was just talking to..." He looks at her expectantly.

"Grace. My girlfriend." I bend down, hooking my arm around her back and practically hoisting her up to my side. "Your outfit does look nice, baby," I murmur softly in her ear.

"Ah, shit. I didn't know she was your girlfriend. Sorry about that, man."

I roll my eyes. "You don't have to apologize to me. I'm not her keeper."

Gracie bites her bottom lip, trying not to laugh.

"Nice meeting you though," I say, politely dismissing him.

After he walks away, I squeeze Gracie's hip. "Let's get outta here. We can't have you too exhausted before I get my hands on you."

She flushes. "Can we repeat last night? I really loved when you—"

I cut her off with a groan. "Please stop talking."

Tugging her behind me, I hurry us out of the facility. She playfully swats my ass, and I swoop her up in the air, tickling her sides and soaking in the sound of her laughter.

Time has been kind to us, and we fall for each other a little harder every day. I may not know what every tomorrow holds, but I know she'll be in it. And that's more than enough. Because even after years of belonging to Gracie Sinclair, I still can't believe she's mine.

Chapter 32

Danny

Gracie looks like mine.

The lack of weather-appropriate clothing in her backpack led to her reluctantly accepting my eager offer to wear my Mustangs hoodie, which completely swallows the top of her blue jeans. She's pulled her red curls into a loose braid, but a few stubborn strands peek out. I clench my hand, stopping myself from brushing them back.

I spent too much time upstairs, debating what to wear, until I frantically texted Tessa some options and received an excited "which one matches her energy?" With that in mind, I threw on a light blue half-zip athletic shirt and jeans.

I don't usually take advantage of the team's car service, but I did tonight. Gracie joked that I must not have wanted her to suffer through more of my driving. In actuality, I'm hoping to hold her hand while cuddled up in the backseat on the way home.

The driver takes the scenic route to a little bar in Windsor Terrace called Anemone. The front half of the building is an active flower shop with an abundance of all different types of unique flowers. As we walk in, a variety of reeds, greenery, baby's breath, and ferns line the walls. Acoustic guitar music is playing softly over the speakers, and there's a warm glow from mismatched lamps throughout the shop. In the center of the space are several round tables with cut, colorful flowers displayed in glass jars of varying heights.

I turn to face Gracie. Her head tilts to the side in surprise, eyes wide, as she takes it all in. "I've never seen anything like this." She walks further into the shop and gently touches a few of the garden figurines. "I thought we were going to trivia."

"We are. This is actually a combination flower shop and bar. We'll head back to the bar area soon. You always enjoyed flowers, although I don't know if that's changed, I guess."

"It hasn't," she says softly. "I love it here."

After all this time, hearing Gracie say the word "love" feels like a luxury. I almost say it back with a different meaning attached.

"Ah, DT. You called about the red tulips!" an older woman, who must be the shop owner, shouts from behind the cashier's desk. She's wearing khakis, a shirt that says *Daffodil With It*, and a nametag reading "Betty" as she putters over to us.

"Red tulips?" Gracie asks.

If she's wondering whether her favorite flowers are currently available in the dead of winter...they're not.

"I'm so sorry our tulips aren't in season yet, but like I mentioned, I hope this makes up for it." Betty hands Gracie a white porcelain vase with hand-painted red tulips crawling up the sides.

Gracie gives a small gasp as she turns the vase in her hands. "I...wow. This is beautiful."

"We're known for our hand-painted vases, but we keep them all in the back. Too many accidents over the years," Betty explains.

Gracie lifts her chin, staring into my eyes with warmth and

affection. "Danny, thank you so much. This is incredibly thoughtful. I'll treasure it."

I smile, happy and relieved she loves it. "When Betty sent me a picture, it reminded me of you. Now you can have red tulips all year long."

Gracie returns my smile with a blinding one of her own as she hugs the vase to her body.

Now I wish I *was* the vase.

"Okay, well. We don't want to be late for trivia. Thanks for everything, Betty."

"Anytime, dear. Go Mustangs!"

With my hand on the small of her back, I guide Gracie through the hallway that connects the flower shop and the bar, wrapped in the scent of her coconut and vanilla perfume. It all feels so surreal.

As we approach the end of the hallway, she abruptly turns around. "Before we get back there, there's something you should know about me."

"Okay..."

She cringes. "I've only gotten more competitive over the past ten years."

"Jesus, Gracie. How can you get *more* competitive?"

She drums her nails against the vase. "I wasn't *that* competitive before."

"You made Tessie cry when we watched *Kids Jeopardy!* together. She was ten."

"I'm sorry!" She gestures wildly. "It's hard for me to pretend not to know things!"

I try to find the door at the end of the hallway very interesting, so as to not laugh in her face.

"Anyway, I hate to say it, but just let me do the talking." She takes a small step forward, having said her piece.

"You don't want me to answer any questions?" I ask, my voice dripping with exaggerated innocence.

"I want to win." She throws the statement over her shoulder.

I give a long, low whistle. "Wow. I thought this would be a roman—um, *friendship* hang, but you're leaving me in the dust."

She raises an eyebrow. "*Roman Friendship Hang*, huh? Sounds very Italian."

"Fine, Gracie. Silence me."

She pats me on the arm a few times. "Great. It's *animal trivia*, Danny," she explains, like her reasoning is obvious. "You understand."

It's hard not to grin. Her casual touch, her offbeat logic, her comfortability to be her full, authentic self around me...*this* is what I missed.

She pushes the automatic door button as I respond in a warning tone, "But let me say this: If I know an answer, I *will* be buzzing in."

"Sure, sure," she brushes me off with a wave of her hand. "*If* you know one."

We take a seat at the last remaining table in the bar. I receive a few curious looks from patrons, which is an everyday occurrence for me in New York. Strangers either try to place where they know me from or ask for a picture. There are a few families here, which is even more dangerous. A boy who looks to be about nine years old bounces in his seat and points to me. His mom tries to gently push down his arm, but it's no use. The boy gets more animated, eagerly waving to me now.

"I forgot you were famous for a second," Gracie says.

"Yeah, um, around these parts at least." I shift uncomfortably in my seat.

She smiles at the boy. "You should go say hi to him."

I shake my head, entirely focused on her. "I don't have to; I'm here with you."

She nods. "It would make his whole night."

"Are you sure?"

"It'll be fun for me to watch. I always thought this would be a cool part of your job. Being a hero to kids."

"Hero is too big of a word, but I'll venture over there and say hi to the little guy." Giving Gracie one last look, I get up and make my way over to the table.

I always wondered what it would've been like to have Gracie by my side for the last ten years. I'd try to convince myself it was for the best. *Maybe she'd have been frustrated by all the interruptions, the picture requests, the downsides of fame. She deserves a life of privacy. It's probably good that she's out of the public eye. Not with me.*

I should've known my Gracie girl would only see the silver linings, the happy kids, the grateful families.

"DT!" The kid jumps up and hugs me around my waist.

"I'm so sorry about this," his mom apologizes. "You're his favorite player."

I give his head a couple of pats, mussing his hair a little. "Really? That's awesome, dude! Are you an athlete yourself?"

The kid nods shyly now, winding down from his initial overexcitement.

"I could tell, on account of all the muscles you have. What's your name, big dog?"

Shaking his head, the kid blushes and keeps his mouth closed.

"It's Charlie," his mom interjects. "Your poster is on his wall. He plays the wide receiver position at his school."

"Oh, man. I'm lucky I'll be out of the league by the time you get there. You're probably gonna break all my records, huh?"

That pulls a smile out of Charlie as he throws his mom an *are you seeing this right now* look (my favorite kind).

"Listen, I have to get back to my...my girlfriend over there, but I'd love to get a picture with you, if you wouldn't mind? Just so I can say I knew you before you were famous?"

"That's very kind of you." His mom smiles and pulls out her phone, snapping a photo of us.

I fist bump Charlie and walk back to a beaming Gracie. "That was so cool. You've always been good with kids. With Tessa."

"Yeah. She's all grown up now, though. I'd love to, um, have kids of my own one day. If that was something that my partner was into."

It's barely audible, but I hear a soft, "Me too," from her.

The air is thick between us, but before anything else can be said, a loudspeaker voice cuts through.

"Welcome to Trivia Night!" An MC, dressed in all black, with a septum ring and dark lipstick, walks up to the front of the room.

"Tonight is all about animals! The questions will cover all different types of animal-related topics. There's a buzzer on each table. If you know it, press the button to answer. Whoever buzzes in first will get the first shot at answering. Each question is worth one point, except the final question, which is worth five. We'll tally the points up here." She points to the dry erase board on the wall. "Everyone ready to get started?"

A few half-hearted "woos" join the sound of tepid applause in response.

"Okay! First question: What is the largest living species of lizard?"

Gracie buzzes in immediately. The MC points to us. "Table two?"

"What is the Komodo Dragon!" Gracie unnecessarily shouts across the small space.

"Ding ding! First points on the board go to table two. But, um, you don't have to say 'what is' before your answers."

I snicker as Gracie mutters, "I was trying to be official," under her breath.

"Question two: How many eyes does a honeybee have?"

I buzz in with the correct answer, shocked Gracie doesn't push the button before me. "Five." I turn toward her and smile. "Do you think Mae planted that question from Ohio?"

She gives an awkward smile and shrugs.

The MC asks two more questions, both of which Gracie gets correct. It's starting to get uncomfortable in here, like when you're watching a college basketball game and one team is getting completely demolished. With only a few questions left in this round, some patrons give us sideways glances. I inherently know that we should not stay for a second round.

"Question seven: How high can penguins jump?"

I buzz in with confidence. "Trick question—penguins can't jump."

Gracie swivels her head slowly, and it's at this moment I know I've made a grave error.

"Penguins can't jump?" she hisses. "Seriously, Danny? You've never seen a penguin jump from an iceberg to another iceberg? Or into the water?"

Another table buzzes in correctly with "nine feet!"

I face her. "*Nine feet?*" I ask incredulously. "That's not possible. Are these penguins stacked on top of Lebron James's shoulders in a trenchcoat or something?"

Bickering about penguins, we completely miss the next two questions. My partner is not pleased.

The MC brings us back, announcing, "Final question. This one is worth five points, everybody!"

"Let me buzz in. We need to get it right if we want to win. Don't ruin this for me, Danny," she warns.

I hold my hands up in mock surrender. "Harsh, but I'll allow it."

"Question ten: what animal holds hands while sleeping so they don't drift away in the water?"

Gracie and I whip our heads to face each other so fast we almost collide. Her breath warms my face, and I wordlessly reach out and place my hand on top of hers.

Serenity seeps into my skin as I feel an overwhelming sense of contentment. Sitting with Gracie like this, my hand covering hers, feels like finding my favorite sweater I thought I'd lost.

I'm warm. I'm comfortable.

And everything is as it should be.

We're so busy looking into each other's eyes that a different table buzzes in and wins the whole shebang.

Gracie doesn't care.

We hold hands in the backseat the whole way home.

* * *

"One strawberry milkshake for the girl with the strawberry hair," I tease, adding a striped straw from the kitchen drawer before handing the tall glass to Gracie.

She takes it, throwing me a huge smile. "Who needs a robot refrigerator when you can make me the best dessert ever invented?"

I laugh as I rinse the blender and start making myself a chocolate one.

Gracie sips her milkshake. "Mmm, this is actually so good."

She plays with the straw, picking it up and licking some of the frothy liquid off the bottom. I remember her at eighteen, doing exactly this, her curls nearly spilling into the rim of the cup. It takes my breath away, the intersection of then and now; who we were before, and who we are today.

After adding a scoop of protein powder, blending, and pouring my milkshake into a cup, I lead her to the kitchen island, and we each sit on a stool. My eyes dart to the clock on the wall, and I sigh. We're on borrowed time. Gracie goes home tomorrow, and we haven't even talked about what happened between us. I know she came here for a reason—a reason I've been too scared to seek out. So, I've done what I can to delay the inevitable, and I can only hope it's enough. I need to apologize for everything, so we can finally move forward—together.

"You know, Mae's favorite milkshake flavor was strawberry. It might not be as much of a hot take as you think," Gracie ribs.

"How *is* Mae, by the way? You know we still keep in touch from time to time, right?"

Gracie stiffens and blinks a few times, almost like she's snapping herself out of something.

"Yeah," she says absentmindedly. "Mae mentioned that on a few different occasions over the years, but I wasn't quite ready to hear any details about your conversations. I'm glad you kept up your relationship with her, though. I know it meant a lot to Mae."

Something isn't right. I know that look. That look is her *I'm about to tell you something that you're not going to like* look. I saw it after I asked about her injured ankle when we were young. And I saw it right before she ended things with me.

"Gracie, you're worrying me. Is Mae okay?"

"She's actually, um, why I came. To New York, I mean. To see you and deliver a letter. It's from her. She told me to come here. Basically forced my hand. You know how persuasive Mae is. Not that I didn't want to come. I mean, I did want to come too, in a way, so that's not what I meant," she babbles, pulling a crumpled envelope from her pocket. "Sorry, this is coming out all wrong."

"Slow down, Gracie girl. You can always take your time with me." I hold up just three fingers, wiggling them near her face. "You remember what to do, hmm?"

Memories hit me like a live wire as she takes a shallow breath and blows warm air toward my hand. I smile softly and put down one finger.

"You can do better than that," I coax softly. "Look, there's two candles left."

Gracie takes a deeper breath, leans toward me, and lets it out. Both of my other fingers go down. Before she can pull back, I reach out and tenderly caress her cheek. Moving my fingers slowly, slowly down her neck, I gently tug on the end of one curl, preventing myself from running my whole hand through it.

"Do you want me to read it now?" I ask gently.

"Sure. I mean, if you want." She hands me the letter. "I'll step into the other room to give you privacy."

I nod and feel a cool breeze when she walks away. Sliding my finger underneath the envelope flap, I pull the letter out and start to read.

My Dearest Daniel,
I want to start by saying I love you like a son. You are and always have been my most precious boy.
If you're reading this letter, it means two things:
1. My Honeybee made it to New York.
2. I'm with my husband and daughter now, enjoying life somewhere else.

Confused, I reread the beginning of the letter. Then, I read it again, looking for hidden meaning that'll change my initial interpretation of her message. One more time, but it still says the same thing.

Mae is *dead?* My throat closes up as I swallow once, twice. Based on the emotional current running through my body, I assume that I'm crying, but I can't feel a thing. I'm completely numb from the bottom of my heart up.

> *Before you wonder what happened, let me say that it was my final wish that I be the one to tell you. It was all very sudden, and at the same time not sudden at all. Your Gracie was instructed to bring this letter to you in the event I passed, and I'm proud of her for doing so after so much time apart.*

I didn't even get the chance to say goodbye. I ball my hands up, crinkling the edges of the letter slightly as I grapple with my emotions.

> *This next part is for you and you alone, so pay close attention (and don't let her read this letter).*

Mae is absolutely kidding herself if she thinks I have any sort of self-control around Gracie. If she wants to read the letter, she will.

Bee is a prisoner of her own mind when it comes to you, Daniel. She's scared, not knowing for certain how you feel.

When I contacted Mae five years ago, feeling better after starting therapy, I wanted to reach out to Gracie, too. Once I realized she was at vet school in Indiana, I knew it wasn't the right time. She wanted to succeed on her own, and I didn't want to hold her back.

Knowing Gracie's trapped by anxiety too...changes things for me. After we separated, I spent years reflecting on how she might be feeling without me. Angry, hurt, apathetic, maybe, but anxiety never crossed my mind. Could it be that the same thing has been holding both of us back all these years?

I'm proud of what you've accomplished professionally and what we've accomplished together.

You've said I've given you more purpose over the past five years of working closely together, but you've enriched the last years of my life, too.

When I look back on my life, I am extraordinarily grateful for two phone calls: the one you made when you were a teen, scared and confused for Bee, and the one you made five years ago as an adult, ready to take on more responsibility in your life.

I'll keep my last request to you as simple as possible: Can you keep your courage close? Can you

*be brave one last time? Your steadiness will bring
out her strength.*

 *I love you forever, to the smallest hive and
back. Be careful with her, Honey.*

 Ee-bay rave-bay,
Mae
 *P.S. I can't believe I literally have to die to
nudge you and my granddaughter back together.
Hell, you two and your walkie-talkie silence prob-
ably killed me faster than the cancer.*

I choke out a laugh as fresh tears well in my eyes. God, it's
so Mae.

 *P.P.S. I know you'll break immediately and
offer her the opportunity to read this, you coward.
Both of you need to work on your self-control. It's
a real problem.*

Her voice is so strong, it's as if I can almost hear the gravel in
her tone as she reads the words to me. This letter feels like a
farewell and a caress at the same time. It's unexplainable how
quickly a piece of paper can transform into something sacred.
After one last brush of my fingers against the handwriting of a
woman who always seemed unbreakable, I call out to Gracie,
who is not so subtly observing me from a close distance. She said
she'd give me privacy, but I know this woman too well.

"I know you're spying."

Gracie sheepishly steps out of her hiding spot behind the

kitchen wall, shrugging as she meets me by the kitchen island. "You got me."

"When did she…"

She straightens. "Two weeks ago."

My stomach roils. I feel like I'm going to be sick. "How?"

"Breast cancer. Same as my mom. Mae and I found out last month, and by then it was, um, very aggressive, and too late for treatment."

Confusion floods my mind as I try to sort out the timeline. I stand from my stool and start to pace around the kitchen. "Mae said she was fine when I talked with her a month ago. 'Feeling her age,' but doing fine. Why didn't you tell me as soon as you got here?"

"Tell you as soon as I… You didn't want to hear anything I had to say, Danny. I didn't know what Mae wrote in the letter. And honestly? I just went through the loss of the only living relative I had left. I'm still processing everything, too."

My chest caves in, saturated with sorrow. I loved Mae, but so did she.

"Shit. Sorry, Gracie. I hate that you're hurting." I stop pacing and direct my full attention to her. "You know how much I loved her, right?"

"I know."

And just like all those years ago in our secret spot, I plead, "Tell me. Tell me everything."

She leans against the kitchen island, facing me. "We received the news together, sitting across from the oncologist we'd met a grand total of one time. God, Danny. The conversation was so…*polite*."

"Jesus. I'm so sorry. That must've been… I wish I was…"

Gracie forges on like she prepared for this exact conversation. "She was projected to live only days, but it ended up being longer."

It doesn't surprise me that Mae's stubborn personality held out longer than expected.

Gracie's tone becomes harsher, more biting. "Getting a front-row seat to Mae's fight with cancer has given me some brutal insight into what she experienced with my mother. Cancer is insidious, but swift. It's inspirational... yet cruel."

I reach for her, trying to find comfort for both of us. But she pulls back.

"She was all I had left, and losing her devastated me. But you know what hurt the most over the last ten years? Until I lost Mae?" she asks, hands gripping the edge of the kitchen island.

My brain immediately runs wild with scenarios of what could've happened while I wasn't in her life. A horrible thought occurs to me as I squeeze my eyes shut.

"With Mae and your mom, are you...*sick*, too?" Panic creeps up my back and infiltrates my mind.

"No. When Mae was diagnosed, I was tested for BRCA1 and BRCA2. The results came back negative for both genes."

My shoulders sag in relief. The short-term adrenaline I built up in my body comes crashing down, and I stumble a few steps back to sit on a stool by the kitchen island.

"Thank God, Gracie. I can't even imagine..."

"Losing you. Until Mae, *you* were my biggest tragedy."

I go still, blinking at her. "Me?"

She scoffs and waves her hand in the air, angrily brushing me off. "The fact that you can't fathom it as a possibility tells me everything I need to know about how much I valued you and how little you valued me."

Can someone have a head injury without being hit? I'm dizzy, like I've been sucker punched and shaken up a few times. Am I *bleeding*? I jolt up with renewed, furious energy. "How *little* I valued you?" I bark. "You can't be serious." I look around for an audience to agree with me, to see if anyone else is hearing this blatant lie.

"You moved to a different state, Danny. What was I supposed to think when—"

"You were my whole *world*, Gracie." My voice comes out broken and hoarse. "You were, are...I, *God*." I flounder, not knowing which deep truth to confess first. There's so much to untangle.

"I never even *considered* that my decision would cause us to break up. It didn't even cross my mind. If I'd known that you were going to end things, I never would've done it. I would've quit football entirely if it meant staying together. Make no mistake, it was *you* who left me. I've been selfish with you, in so many ways, but the most selfless act of my life was letting you go. Even if it killed me." My pulse kicks up and my breaths become shallow.

"Selfless? *Selfless?*" Her gaze is sharp and unblinking. She looks as furious as the day she broke up with me. "You think I *wanted* to end things? You think it was *easy* for me to go back to my dorm, alone? Hang with the friends I only made through you? Try to bond with the girlfriends of boys on a team *you left* in the dust?" She shakes her head and rubs her eyes with the palms of her hands. "It was *selfish* of you to take the meetings without telling me. It was *selfish* of you to not involve me in your decisions. Decisions you made on your own. Decisions I thought we would make together. It was like I wasn't even a consideration—"

"A *consideration?*" I'm astonished that's even a word she would use to describe what she meant to me. I search for words powerful enough to describe how I felt—feel—about her. "You were my *life source*. It was like I could only breathe normally when you were with me. When everything was ripped away from me, the panic attacks would've consumed me if you hadn't been there supporting me those first few months. You were the only thing sustaining me at the time." I wipe a bead of sweat trickling down my hairline. "After you ended things, it took me...fuck, it took me *years* before I was even comfortable going out, meeting new people."

I'm looking everywhere but her face, as I'm not sure what I'll see. After a few moments of silence, I risk a glance. Her eyes are tightly closed. A few tears leak out anyway.

"Gracie, I'm sorry." I lift my hands for a hug, then swiftly retreat.

She opens her eyes, their colors looking particularly muted. "Then why did you do what you did?"

I walk around the kitchen island, needing some physical distance between us. "If you were my life source, I was your parasite. My anxiety, the insomnia, the attacks...they would've consumed you, too. I didn't want to drag you down with me."

Gracie turns toward me and sits back down on a stool. I can hear her foot tapping against the bottom of the island. "That's the whole point of being in a relationship, Danny. I was helping you."

"I wasn't *able* to be helped, Gracie. I walked around, unfeeling, like a bag of skin and bones. My soul felt detached from my body. When I heard myself speak, it sounded like...like an echo."

Her brows furrow in confusion, concern etched across her face as I continue.

"If I had stayed, it would've only gotten worse. The depressive episodes... I would've only been a burden to you."

She desperately searches me for clarification. "Depression?"

"Therapy helped me identify it for what it was."

Sharply tapping her fingers on the countertop now, she asks, "Did you ever consider that I *wanted* you to burden me? To lean on me for support? God, so often, people see the word 'burden' as something negative. Giving someone permission to burden you with their baggage is probably one of the most intimate things anyone can do."

I shake my head. "After everything you went through, you didn't deserve another unstable man in your life anyway. You—"

"*You* abandoned me."

Gracie throws me a searing glare. I've only seen it once, years ago.

Chapter 33

Grace

Eighteen Years Old

I glare at my phone...no new text messages. Something's off with Danny. There's three days left before his first game, so I figured he was just tired from long practices. But when I texted him to come over after their weekly team meeting a few days ago, he said he was still at the facility with the guys. His explanation didn't make sense, though. I was with Jessica and her boyfriend, Cooper, who told me the meeting was long over.

Now it's been two days since I last heard from him, and it feels like he's avoiding me. I tried to call him last night, but he didn't pick up. We've seen each other every day for the past two months we've been at Easton, so the lack of contact has me really worried.

I won't wait any longer for him to come to me. Taking the shuttle to his dorm on the other side of campus, I get off at Lane Tower. When another resident opens the door, I slip through behind them and walk up the stairs. I knock four times when I reach Danny's room.

227

His gruff voice is so loud it carries through the heavy door. "Dude! I told you and everyone else on the team. I'm fine. I just want to be alone, Coop. Go hang with Jess."

My heart drops. He didn't recognize our knocking code.

"Danny? It's me."

I'm met with silence. It's like he completely disappeared. Is he *pretending* not to be home? I knock on the door again. "Danny. I know you're in there."

"Oh! Gracie, is that you out there?" His voice sounds unnaturally high.

I tap my foot impatiently outside his door. "Uh, yeah. Can I come in?"

"Hm? Come in? Sure." I hear scrambling on the inside of the door, like things are being shifted around and put away. After what feels like an eternity, the door finally cracks open. It's dark inside his room, and he squints from the contrast of the hallway light.

My lips part in surprise when he opens the door all the way. Danny's sporting deep, dark bags under his eyes. His thick hair is matted and greasy, and he's wearing a stained white shirt and boxers. It looks like he hasn't slept or left this room in days. A video game is paused in the background, and a bunch of dining hall carryout containers are overflowing in the trash can.

"What's going on? Why haven't you called or texted me back?"

His eyes scan our surroundings, as if the answers to my questions are written on a slip of paper he's somehow misplaced. I can tell the minute he decides lying is a lost cause. "I...I'm sorry, Gracie. I'm so fucking sorry." He rubs his eyes aggressively with the palms of his hands, covering the top half of his face.

I lean closer to him. "I want to be here for you, but I have no idea what's going on. Talk to me. Open and honest, remember?"

I try to softly pry his hands away from his eyes, but they won't budge. "Danny. *Danny*. Look at me."

He slowly lifts his face and starts sobbing. My stomach twists. The last time he cried like this was Charger's funeral. Worst case scenarios run through my mind. *Did he cheat on...?* No, Danny would never.

With renewed panic, I urgently ask, "What's wrong?"

I push into his room, closing the door behind him, then lead him to the bed, urging him to sit. I settle behind him, positioning him between my legs and wrapping my arms around him so I can talk into his ear. Even in his fragile state, my body applies firm pressure to his, like I'm physically reinforcing our bond.

"It's so fucked up, Gracie. *I'm* so fucked up."

"What? Why?"

Lacing his hands through mine, I hug him tighter in hopes he'll calm down. He just shakes his head, either unable or unwilling to talk through his sobs.

I try changing the subject. "Remember when we were eleven and couldn't agree on Halloween costumes? You were adamant about going as something 'mighty,' which may have been your word of the year. My initial suggestion, Gordo and Lizzie McGuire, did not go over well."

His reaction to that was visceral at the time, pretending to gag over the mere thought of going as Disney Channel characters.

"After two weeks of arguing, do you remember the costume you ended up wearing?"

"A...a lion," he breathes.

"A lion. I went as a witch. And what did I force Tessa to wear to complete our theme? Can you tell me?"

He slumps, shaking his head like he can't answer.

"That's okay, don't worry about it."

He heaves an exhausted sigh. There's a long pause before I hear him whisper, "A closet. Tessa went as a closet."

I laugh. "Yep. The Lion, the Witch and the Wardrobe. Absolutely no one got it. Not one person. It was the flop of the century."

"I didn't care. You loved it," he says softly, sounding miserable.

"I love *you*," I reply, nuzzling the side of his neck from behind him. "I love you," I repeat over and over again, punctuated by soft kisses behind his ear.

He leans his head back against my shoulder. "Sorry. I just didn't—"

"Why don't we just listen to a song or two before we get into whatever it is?"

He turns his head and nods gratefully. We sit like this, me wrapped around him, and listen to music.

After listening to Yellowcard's entire album, it's dark outside, and we've missed the dinner window at the dining hall. Danny squeezes my hands once before he turns around, grabs me by the waist, and hoists me up onto his lap so I'm straddling him.

"Tell me," I say. "Tell me everything."

And he does.

He tells me Coach redshirted him for the whole season, essentially benching him for the year.

He tells me they don't want him to get injured. That they want to give him time to develop, even though the team's current starters aren't performing well. Even though he's worked *so hard* for this. Even though they *promised* him that he'd play this year, only to change their mind at the last second.

He tells me about the team's lukewarm reaction to the news. He tells me about the delayed timing. How the lack of exposure may lead to a decline in eventual draft placement. How he might not be able to enter the draft in four years or graduate with me as we planned.

What he doesn't tell me is how he's feeling about any of it.

I respond with what I can, based on how little I know. "That sucks." I push his thick, dark hair away from his face so I can see his expressions better, but he's giving nothing away. "But it does sound like you should be flattered, from what you're telling me Coach said. Staying injury free for as long as possible is always a good thing. Plus, redshirting means you may be at Easton an extra year. Maybe I can do one year of vet school in Columbus and extend my time on campus, too. I've been really liking it here. We can figure this out, as long as we're together. Open and honest, right?"

He looks down and to the side. "Right."

"Hey." I grin, knowing just how to brighten his mood. "I have an animal fact for you. Did you know that octopuses have three—"

"I'm not really in the mood," he interrupts.

My whole body deflates. I know he's hurting, but the swift rejection stings.

Danny yawns and stretches his arms above his head. "Listen, I'm getting tired. It's been a long couple of days."

"I'm happy to stay. I don't want you to be alone."

"And I love you for that, but look at me." He gives me a surface-level smile, but I can tell it's completely fake. "I'm overdue for a shower, and I should clean this place up before Cooper gets back. I also have some homework to finish if I want to get the assignments in on time. It wouldn't be fun for you to stay, believe me."

I let him get away with this obviously fabricated excuse for now. Soon, he'll be ready to talk to me about his feelings. Soon, he'll let me share the burden with him, as we've always done. I'll let him have tonight, and then we'll talk tomorrow.

"Okay. I love you," I whisper, then I'm out the door.

Chapter 34

Danny

Eighteen Years Old

"You need to get it together, DT. The guys are starting to notice."

Cooper Shields, the team's best tight end, has been on me to shape up ever since my redshirt status was announced to the players a month ago. He hangs his headphones around his neck and crouches down to tie his shoes, about to leave for a gym session with some of our teammates.

"The guys should be focused on playing. Some of us don't get that privilege," I reply in monotone.

Coop rolls his eyes and throws a pillow at me from the couch. "This is what I'm talking about. Cut that 'woe is me' shit out. Being a crappy teammate and friend won't magically get you playing time, believe it or not. Might as well *not* be a douchebag."

Two games have passed now, and I don't even know if we won. I black out every time my spotless cleats hit the sidelines. I built my life around football—high school to college to pro—and

I feel paralyzed thinking about a reality in which that dream crumbles.

"You've been ditching team hangouts, team workouts—"

"*Voluntary* team workouts."

"You've been hiding in our dorm room and playing video games whenever you're not at a mandatory meeting. You're even avoiding Grace," he points out.

I glare at him, hating the way my name for her sounds coming out of his mouth. I understood her decision to go by Grace in college, but selfishly, I miss it being mine. "You don't need to talk to me about Gracie."

"Well, if you're not going to talk to her, talk to me."

"There's nothing to talk about. I'm benched. I have to suck it up and wait until I can play next year. How I spend my time until then will be up to me. End of story."

Coop shakes his head. "Listen. Meet with Coach and see what he's willing to do as a compromise."

I pick up a bag of gummy worms and tear it open, popping one in my mouth. "They seemed set on me not playing at all this season."

Coop grabs a purple Easton Eagles baseball cap and puts it on. "Then just aim for making this season as painless as possible. I'll do extra workouts with you to stay fresh, practice one on one, whatever you want."

I sigh, a deep exhaustion weighing on my bones, even though I've done nothing but play video games for the last twelve hours. I've never felt this fog before, this sadness. It's different from my anxiety...*something else.*

I shrug. "What's the point? It feels like I'm working toward nothing."

"Toward nothing? How about being a good teammate and showing the guys how to act when they go through something difficult?"

"*Teammate?* I dress in uniform for the hell of it at this point. I'm nothing but a glorified cheerleader every Saturday."

I don't feel like myself.

I don't feel like me.

I don't *feel*, period.

"I'm going to give you one more week of this shit, DT, because I know it hurts like hell. I can't imagine not playing every week, but football isn't everything. So what if you're picked a little later in the draft? Keep up this attitude much longer and it'll bring down the whole team dynamic."

Cooper grabs his water bottle and opens our door. Before it closes entirely, he says, "I know you don't want to hear it, but you need to reassure Grace. Jess told me she's worried about you."

I know she's worried about me, but it's a sucker punch to hear it from someone else. I overhear her talking to Mom on the phone sometimes after she thinks I'm asleep, whispering things like, "I can tell he's hurting, Janie."

But they're wrong. I'm not hurting, I'm numb.

I feign sleep when Gracie spends the night, watching her closely and waiting until her breaths even out. Then I alternate between staring at Gracie and blinking at the ceiling, blanketed by the darkness in the room and the darkness in my mind. In the mornings, when she points out the bags under my swollen, over-sensitized eyes, I excuse them away with new allergies.

Hiding a significant amount of my misery from her takes almost all of my energy. She's experienced enough mentally unstable men to last her a lifetime. I won't be another one.

But some of the secret panic attacks I've been having aren't normal. I can't seem to dig myself out of my own emotional graveyard. It feels like I'm buried six feet underground, but it's concrete above me instead of dirt.

I sigh, running my hand down my face, and open my laptop

to check my personal email before I spend the rest of the night switching off between studying and gaming by myself. I start clicking through my messages and stop when I come across one from the head coach...of our rival school?

From: Gary Patrick <gary.patrick@wvu.edu>
Subject: WVU Football

DT,

It's been a while since we last connected during scouting season. Hope you and your mom are well. I saw the Easton coaching staff is redshirting you for the year. I'd like to speak with you about it. Call me.

-GP

Westchester Valley University

I read the email five times. Then, I read it a sixth time for good measure. I double click his email contact and start typing the number into my phone. Before I can second guess myself, I press the call button. It rings only once.

"This is GP."

"Uh, hi. Coach Patrick? It's DT."

"Ah, DT! So thrilled you called, kid. I assume you read my email. Listen. I didn't want to put it in writing—you know the rules about poaching—but if you want to transfer, we'd have a spot for you here. We could use your talent."

A mixture of excitement and anxiety buzzes under my skin. "Yeah, I read it. It's obviously a lot to think about. I have some questions, and, well, there's someone I'm here with, and we're a package deal."

"You got a girl, huh?"

"Yeah, my girlfriend. But she's more than that, I've known her my whole life. It's serious. I won't go anywhere without her.

And she's thriving here. She has a full scholarship and a competitive internship in animal sciences. She won't be able to leave without a comparable situation somewhere else."

"Hey, why don't you email me a list of your conditions? We're very motivated to bring you to WVU, kid. I imagine we'll be able to make it happen."

"Oh." I thought for sure my requests for Gracie would be a dealbreaker. "Uh, okay. I'll send it over today."

"Great. I'll get it to my people over here and then get back to you tomorrow with more information. Sounds good?"

My chest loosens a little, and some of the tension slips from my shoulders. "Yeah, that sounds...great, actually."

"Let's set up another time to talk after that and discuss some other details. You won't have to fight for playing time here. We see your talent and want to help you achieve your goals."

"Wow. Um, thanks. That's really good to hear."

"It's the truth. Alright, kid. I'm on my way to a team workout, but I'm happy you called. I'm sure we'll be able to work something out that sets you up for the future you want. I'll be in touch."

"Okay, bye, Coach."

New energy fills me, sparking feelings I haven't felt in some time.

First, I feel a little guilty.

But then, the guilt is replaced with an emotion far more dangerous.

Hope.

* * *

"Thanks, Dr. Smith. I can tell your program will be a great fit." I end my call with Westchester Valley University's Dean of Zoology. Leaning back in my dorm room desk chair, I feel relaxed and at peace.

It's been two weeks of constant WVU research. I've had conversations with teachers and students and read countless reviews of the department and staff. At this point, I know more about Animal Sciences at Westchester than I do about their football program.

I needed to be sure WVU would be a perfect fit for Gracie, and it is. If I want to achieve the life I promised her, transferring is the only way.

In addition to the prestige of their vet school, there are other bonuses. Gracie's always wanted to live in a city. Granted, when we've spoken, she's primarily talked about the city of Columbus, but you cannot beat New York's cityscape. Also, WVU is near three different animal hospitals, which provide a lot of potential job opportunities and connections for students post-grad.

I know she'll be hesitant to move so far from Mae, but Mae is constantly encouraging her to get out of Ohio, take risks, and live life. I can't think of a better place to live life to the fullest than the Big Apple. I know Mae'll be on my side when she finds out.

Coach Patrick promised me that news of the move wouldn't be officially communicated until one week from now. That gives me ample time to tell everyone before it's announced. I intended to tell Gracie sooner, but my research bumped me up right against the decision deadline. While I know she'll be a little surprised, she's always been supportive of our shared goals.

My phone jolts me from my thoughts of Gracie. I grab it off the desk and spin around in my chair as I answer the call.

"Hey, Mom!"

"Hiya, sweetie. How're we feeling today?"

With how busy I've been researching, it's been too long since I've heard her voice.

"Great. Better than great. Fantastic. I was actually just going to call you."

Her tone perks up. "Really?"

"Yeah. I kind of have news. About football."

Mom gasps. "Kiddo, are they playing you? You know Tessa and I have the poster ready to go."

I laugh. "No, Easton is still benching me."

"Oh." She sounds confused. "What's this football news then?"

I open my mouth to speak, but pause when I realize I haven't actually said it out loud yet, not to anyone. This whole week has been a blur. "Well, I was contacted with an offer to transfer."

"You were what?"

"Coach Patrick from Westchester Valley University contacted me with a transfer offer. You remember him? He came during scouting season."

"I remember Coach Patrick," Mom says cautiously.

"Right. You called him a 'good guy' at the time."

"I think I also said 'New York is pretty far.'"

"Yes, but circumstances change. If I knew then that I wouldn't get any playing time at Easton, I never would've signed here on Decision Day."

"Is transferring even allowed, Daniel?"

"Coach P told me that stuff like this happens more often than anyone thinks and to let him worry about any approvals. So, yeah."

"So, you...you're moving? To New York?"

"Yes. And I know what you're thinking."

"What am I thinking?"

"You're probably thinking it's reckless, and I've already devoted time to the team here. You're probably thinking I'm letting them down, or I should stick to my word and wait it out.

But, Mom, *they* didn't stick to *their* word. They said I would play, and they took that away from me at the last possible second. It's taken me a few weeks to wrap my head around it, but I'm happy with my decision to transfer and think it's best for my future."

"Okay, it sounds like you've given this a lot of thought. You know I'll always support your decisions when it comes to football, no matter where you play. If you want to quit tomorrow, I'll have your back. Football is a sport at the end of the day, and what you choose to do with it is all your own decision."

I breathe a sigh of relief. "Thank you."

"Mhm. So, what did Grace think about it?"

"I'm telling her tonight, actually, but I know she'll be—"

"You're telling her tonight," Mom interrupts in a flat tone. "You're *telling* her...*tonight?*" Her voice is more animated now, panic lacing her words.

"That's what I said. Why are you saying it like that?"

"I...I thought you two were still together. Do you need to tell me something?"

"What? No. We *are* together. We're better than ever now."

"Daniel," she chokes out, sounding strained all of a sudden. "It's a big deal that you signed without telling her first. How did that happen?"

My heart rate increases at her tight and uneven tone, and I stand up. "I wanted to tell her in advance, but I spent so much time researching the animal science program at WVU, speaking with teachers, and ensuring her scholarship would transfer over. The deadline just ended up getting ahead of me."

"Oh, sweetie. I don't think Grace is going to take this news the way you think she's going to take it." Sympathy leeches into her voice, and it bothers me.

"I'm not stupid. I know she'll be hesitant. Gracie is always timid when confronted with new situations, but I'll be there for her every step of the way like always. It was a narrow decision deadline, but I made sure she'll be set up for success there. I did the research."

"I know, but the most important research would've been asking for her opinion," she gently responds.

My stomach sinks as I consider Mom's words. "I should've slowed down. But I still know her better than anyone, and she'll come around sooner than you think. She understands how much playing means to me, and she's seen what *not* playing does to me. Gracie is the most supportive person I know."

Mom exhales, and a few moments of silence pass while I wait for her to agree with me.

"Sweetie, have you thought about what you might do in the event she doesn't want to go?"

That's not even a remote possibility. This is a forever thing for us. Even if Gracie needs time to process, not being together is a reality I know neither of us will accept.

"I already signed," I whisper, my breaths short and ragged. "So there's no option for me to back out at this point."

Another minute of silence. When Mom speaks, she doesn't address my response at all. "I love you. And hey, kiddo?"

"Yeah?"

"Congratulations."

"Thanks."

The congratulatory sentiment fades away as I sink down onto my futon. *Did I completely miscalculate this?* I shake my head. No, Gracie knows me through and through. Plus, she's always told me she'll follow me anywhere.

I have it all planned out. In every future, it's us. We're going to be fine.

Chapter 35

Grace

Eighteen Years Old

I pound on the door four times before leaning over to catch my breath. Running from the campus shuttle to his dorm wasn't my brightest idea, but I couldn't wait a second longer to see him. Danny yanks the door open, his hair still wet from a shower.

I don't even know where to start. My brain is so messy, and a buzzing noise fills my ears. "How could you... *Why* would you..."

Danny stumbles back into his dorm room as I shove him through his own doorway. He looks behind me, seemingly searching for someone else responsible for the hurt expression on my face, not knowing it was him who caused it.

"Wha...?"

I shove a copy of the school newspaper into his chest. When Danny told me yesterday that he wanted to "talk about something important" tonight, I never pictured *this*.

He glances at the article in clear surprise, his eyes wide.

"Gracie. Don't freak out. I'm sorry you found out about it

like this. Nothing was supposed to be formally announced for another week."

The heavy door slams behind me, and I stop in my tracks. "Formally announced? When did you know?"

Danny runs his hands through his hair, tugging slightly at the ends like he's trying to physically pull the words I want to hear out of his head. "When did I know transferring was a possibility? Or when did I make my decision? I'm going to tell you everything, just—"

I lean against the door in shock. "Are you breaking up with me?"

Danny takes a step toward me and grasps my hands, mine limp in his. "What the fuck? Gracie, no. Jesus. I'd *never* break up with you."

"So, you're not going to New York?" Confusion muddles my mind, like I'm trying to place missing pieces in a puzzle with my eyes closed.

He squeezes my hands tighter, like he's afraid I'll slip through his fingers. "It's an amazing opportunity for both of us, I promise. There's so much I need to tell you. That's why I wanted to get dinner tonight, so I could explain everything and we can talk about our future. There are so many things I want to say."

I shake off his hands and poke a finger in the center of his chest. "Is this why you've been happier lately?"

"What do you mean?"

"When your mood improved a few days ago... Did you know about the transfer then?"

Danny has the self-awareness to look sheepish. "Well, yes, the decision deadline was three days ago."

My hands fly to my temples as I mutter, "The decision deadline." Louder now, I say, "The decision...*you made a decision already?*" My knees buckle, and I stagger to the futon.

"I had to make one before the deadline or else I wouldn't be eligible to play." Danny's all stoicism as he joins me on the couch.

Avoiding eye contact now, I desperately try to sort out how this happened. "How...how did you make a decision like that so quickly?"

"I'd been thinking about it for a few weeks. I did a ton of research, for both me and you, and—"

I shoot up from the couch. "*Weeks?* You did a ton of research over *weeks*. You were thinking about transferring for... weeks. And then you didn't tell me for three days." Squeezing my eyes tightly shut, I wish this was just a nightmare.

"I wanted all the information before I brought you into it, Gracie. I wanted to do the bulk of the work so you wouldn't have to stress. I did so much research, baby. I talked to all of the animal science professors, and they're going to match your scholarship terms over to Westchester. They have an open internship spot under their dean ready for you. It really is a perfect scenario, where we can both live out our dreams, and—"

"I'm not going to New York, Danny."

"You're not...what?"

Opening my eyes and staring directly into his, I repeat, "I'm not going to New York."

He leans forward as if he wants to move but can't. "This was always the plan for us, me playing for the Mustangs one day."

I raise an eyebrow. "Yeah. One day after college. Or did you forget that we made plans for Easton in the here and now?"

"I...I got your scholarship figured out. The vet school there is great."

"You just *got* me a scholarship? I didn't earn that, Danny. I didn't even apply. I don't want it."

"They looked at your credentials. It was based on merit."

I roll my eyes. "It was based on your ability to catch a ball."

He stands to meet me, ducking his chin in an attempt to catch my gaze.

"They know we're a pair. It's like we're both a part of the team. They're even going to give us a stipend to fly back and visit home a few times per semester."

Overcome with nervous energy, I start to pace back and forth. The room is so small that I can only take four steps in each direction.

"Mae is here. My friends are here."

He backs up toward the door, giving me space to walk. "Mae wants you to live life, Gracie. Imagine how much life there is to live in New York. And I've spoken with some of the current WVU players. There's a really tight group of girlfriends there, like there is here at Easton. You'll fit right in. We're only a couple months into college, so there's still time to build social circles." Danny pauses. "And...and you'll have me."

I scoff. "Like I have you now? With all of your secret keeping, all of your silent planning, and how could I forget? All of the *transferring to another state without telling me?*"

Danny tilts his head in shock at my harsh tone. The icy edge is new to me, too.

I want to cry, but I'm surprised to find that anger is my leading emotion. I'm not sad, and I'm not anxious. I don't feel rushed... I feel *furious.* I can't remember ever being this angry. Not when Danny was dating Tori, not when I was bullied at school for my stutter, not even when my mom died.

"I know you're upset, Gracie, and I blame myself for not telling you sooner. I just was so deep in the thick of it. I didn't want to bother you."

I'm nearly shaking with rage as I abruptly stop pacing to face him. "You didn't want to *bother* me, so you made decisions on my behalf and assumed I would...what? Just tag along? Like some sort of puppy?" I gesture wildly, feeling out of control.

He pauses a second too long.

"Oh. I see," I seethe. I lower my voice as I pretend to be Danny. "'Poor Gracie, she doesn't have any roots. Mae is getting older. I'm her world. My future is her future.'" I turn away from him and catch my breath. "Am I right?"

"Of course not. I don't think that at all. I...I honestly thought you'd be happy for me."

Swiveling my head around so quickly I get dizzy, I ask, "Are *you* happy for you, Danny? Giving up on your team during the first sign of adversity? Is that who you are now?"

He crosses his arms. "That's not fair. They broke their promise to me first."

I silently nod. "They did. And that was shitty, Danny, it was. But *you* broke your promise to me."

"What? I didn't—"

"Open and honest, right? Or was that just a rule for *me* to follow?" I shake my head, placing my hands on my hips and planting my feet. "This is like freshman year of high school all over again. Football was your number one, no matter the cost. Here you are again, taking me for granted. I told you that our friendship had to be important, too. That I wouldn't let you treat me like that again. And I meant it." I look up at the ceiling and run a hand over my curls. "God, I've been so stupid."

"Hey. Don't say that about yourself," Danny reprimands in a stern tone. "You're everything to me."

I physically hurt all over my body. "Please don't waste my time trying to convince me that I'm your priority, because you can't. I'm not, and that's okay." Shrugging, my gaze shifts downward, pinning the floor into place. "I actually understand."

"No, you don't understand. You *are* my priority, Gracie. I just... This isn't coming out right and—"

"If I was your priority, Dan," I say, my voice hoarse, "we would be having this conversation *before* the transfer deadline."

I gesture between us and shake my head. "It's not your decision that shocked me. It's the fact that you made it without me."

"Gracie, I—"

Taking a small step forward, I'm inches away from his face now. I tilt my chin up, my next words tinged with betrayal. "No secrets. That was the agreement."

"I never meant to keep anything from you. I was just getting everything prepared so I could show you what we could build together in New York. Easton benching me was a wake-up call for me. It proved they never cared about my goals."

"You transferring without telling me is a wake-up call for *me*."

His chin dips to his chest as he frantically tries to explain his actions. "I...I promise I was thinking of us, of our future. My intentions were pure on this, Gracie."

"I'm not saying this is just your fault. It's not. If anything, I'm equally to blame here. Maybe I did follow you around too much over the years, mistakenly thinking you'd choose me first."

"You didn't."

"Maybe I was foolish to think you'd include me in all of your decisions regarding football." When I search his eyes, I look for some sort of sign that will reassure me and come up empty.

"You weren't, Gracie."

"You *lied*, Danny."

His breaths are ragged. The anxiety radiating off of his body is nearly palpable. "I didn't... It wasn't like that for me. I was just trying so hard to prove to you that this would work, and time got away from me."

A few tears roll down his cheeks, and my heart aches.

"I know," I whisper, my tone dipped in empathy.

I can feel what's coming. *Can he feel it, too?*

"You know?"

"Yes, I know you would never intentionally hurt me," I agree softly. "I know you gave this a lot of thought. I know you love me."

He wipes a tear away with the back of his hand and inhales. "I do love you, more than anything."

"I know you see our future together. I know you're good. I know you're genuine."

Danny gives me a small, unsure smile.

My next words will irrevocably change us, downgrading our unconditional love to one smothered by unforeseen conditions. Before I break the bones that form the frame of our relationship, I take a beat to indulge myself...to close my eyes and breathe in one more moment of what it's like to be his.

It feels like a last breath, and I guess, in a way, it is.

"And I know I can't be with you anymore."

"Gracie," he whispers. "You don't mean it."

I touch his face, my hand cool against his hot, agitated skin. "I'm happy for you, Danny. Being the starting wide receiver as a freshman is everything you dreamed, and you deserve it. You've worked so incredibly hard for this."

"No. Not without you," he pleads, more tears welling in his eyes.

"Our love is something that I will carry with me always. Our relationship was everything to me."

He reaches for me and cradles my face in his hands like it's glass that's about to shatter.

"I'm so sorry. I'm trying to get my thoughts straight...please don't do this to us," he begs.

"I've been put third, fourth, fifth, *last*, from other people my entire life. If I don't put myself first, you'll continue to put me second—whether you mean to or not."

I love him enough to settle for the same cycle of treatment. It's time for me to take care of myself.

"That won't happen. I'll make sure it won't. I promise." His voice comes out hoarse, drenched in agony. I remove a hand from his face to wipe away the tears dripping off his chin.

My eyes are glassy, my own tears refusing to fall. I shake my head. "I have no doubt in my mind that you'll become the best player the league has ever seen. Go be great. You were destined for this."

"I'm destined to be with *you*, Gracie. I'm destined to be yours. I can't do this without you. I can't do *anything* without you." Desperation laces his tone.

"If you ever find yourself trapped in anxiety, don't forget to focus on your feelings, not just the facts. You'll get through it. I know you will." My hands fall to my sides, and his drop, too.

"I don't want this, Grace."

I give him a sad smile and wrap him in a hug. Tired of standing, we slowly drop to the floor and sit together, holding each other on the cold tile.

"*I will always love you. I will always love you. I will always love you,*" he whispers into my hair, over and over again.

"Shhh. It'll be okay," I murmur into his neck.

"I'll never get over you."

I say nothing back.

Chapter 36

Grace

He says nothing back. My declaration that he abandoned me seems to have stunned him into silence.

"Let me ask you something. How do you think I found out about your transfer, Danny?"

He shifts on his feet, visibly uncomfortable. "I know it was the newspaper article, Gracie."

"Yes...and no. I was in class with a teammate of yours. He walked in, slammed the paper on the desk, and shouted, in front of everyone, 'your boyfriend is a sellout.'"

He winces.

Shivering, I recall how it felt. "The aggression...it reminded me of *him* all over again."

He bows his head, maybe realizing that not everything went the way he thought it had.

"I was a kid." His voice cracks on the last word. "We planned for you to come with me when I got drafted anyway. To me, it was simply moving our timeline up by a few years."

"You were thinking about timelines while I was thinking about us. I was so...fragile at eighteen." My voice comes out soft, and I instinctively make myself smaller, grabbing my elbow.

After Danny dropped Easton, my group of friends dropped me. It was a slow burn dismissal, one that I didn't know was happening at first. I thought I was still in the group chat, but I didn't know they'd created a new one without me. I thought they weren't having a ton of parties due to the season starting, but I just wasn't invited. The elation I felt at gaining a group of girlfriends quickly fizzled into a devastating reminder that most friendships aren't actually forever.

"You knew what I was going through. I was at a new college where I only felt truly comfortable with you. Mae was getting older, and I still had so much of my past haunting me," I whisper, like it's still a secret I have to keep. "If I was so important to you..."

Danny starts pacing again, back and forth in the kitchen, running his hands through his hair. "Did I want it to come out the way it did? Obviously not. Am I sorry it did? Absolutely. I am unbelievably sorry, Gracie. I hate that it hurt you, and I wish I could take everything that happened back, even if it meant I never got drafted."

I raise my eyebrows and tilt my head in annoyance. "It's not even the fact that I was the last to know, Danny. It's that you didn't communicate that you were considering leaving at all." I obsessively tap my foot, and my voice falters. "And when we broke up, I thought that I was ending things with my boyfriend of two years, not my best friend of ten."

His jaw slackens. "You...you didn't want to lose touch with me?"

"When I said *best friends always*, I meant it. The abandonment I felt when you left without looking back absolutely wrecked me. But the silence for *ten years*, Danny? It shattered me."

He stops moving entirely, and I avert my eyes.

"Your status made you impossible to ignore entirely, randomly pulling me into your orbit against my will. It was a special form of torture to see you in magazines at the grocery store."

When I look up again, he's standing right in front of me, nearly chest to chest.

"It was like I couldn't escape you, no matter how hard I tried," I whisper.

"I didn't want to escape you, Gracie. I *never* did. When you ended things, I was convinced you knew you'd be better off without me."

I shake my head in disbelief, blinking away tears. My brain is hazy, thoughts scattered, confusing me with all the noise in my head. Overwhelmed, I try to sync up my heart and head but fail miserably.

"Fact for a feeling, Gracie." His voice comes out soft.

Memories flood my mind and wash away the here and now. He knows exactly what to do to get me out of my head. I grasp for an animal fact—any animal fact—struggling until I land on the perfect one.

"Fact: French angelfish perform a special dance when they reunite with their mate after spending time apart."

"Feeling: I've never stopped loving you."

My eyes widen. "Danny, you can't just say things—"

"I was in love with you when we were something, and I was in love with you when we were nothing."

His lips are moving, but all I hear is ten-year-old Danny, saying *I love you* for the first time. I hold my breath.

Intense and unwavering, his eyes stay locked on mine. "It would be a fool's errand to try and fall in love with anyone but you, Gracie."

Exhaling slowly, I bring a hand to my mouth. "I—"

"You want to know how I spent the last ten years we were apart? I spent every single one of them loving you."

Danny's confession steals the air from the room, leaving ten years of unspoken feelings behind.

I've never stopped loving you.

His words hit a spot in my chest that's been sore for so long, it's painful to hear them. The biggest lie I've ever told myself is that I don't care if the boy next door loves me or not. God, I was pretending. I've *been* pretending. And the response in my body proves it. My traitorous heart flutters in the aftermath of his truth, but there's also a tightness in my throat.

There are so many thoughts swirling in my head that it's hard to know what to focus on first. I feel a sense of peace in having delivered the letter, like there was a loose thread in a tapestry that's been sewn up. But it's almost like it was stitched with a different color; although fixed, I can tell what happened. I can tell it was ripped.

Danny stays quiet, head tilted. He rubs my shoulders up and down a few times, warming me up, before leaning away.

I meet his gaze. "Before, when I missed you, I thought I must have imagined it all. Like some kind of fever dream I had for over half my life. Part of me used to wish I made it up, because then maybe the ten years of memories I carried with me wouldn't be so painful. Each memory served as a hurtful reminder of what we lost," I confess as tears slide down my cheeks. "But love wasn't enough. When everything happened, I needed to find who I was without you."

I pause, carefully choosing my next words. I don't want to lose him, not when I've just gotten him back, but I can't—I won't—force this.

"I'm not ready, Danny. And I don't know when, or if, I ever will be."

After what I've been through lately, my tolerance for risk is at an all-time low. And Danny is the ultimate risk. I know what it's like to be loved by him, and I know what it's like to lose him.

He hunches over slightly, like my words have tackled him. His mouth turns down in a frown of hurt before slowly shifting into a thin line of resolve.

"I haven't even processed Mae's death," I continue. "I can't feel her anymore. Did you know that when you told me you loved me just now, it was the first time I've heard those words in two weeks? I'm struggling with all of this. It's only been a couple days, and I'm already feeling... I just can't be consumed by you, like before."

"*Consumed* by me? That's what you think our relationship would be like now? After what I've shared with you? After the work I've put in to be worthy of you?" he chokes out.

"Honestly, I don't know. I...I wasn't expecting any of this, and it feels overwhelming."

"So we go back to how we were before? We don't talk at all? I'll respect your choice, Gracie, but *God*. It's..."

"No, I don't want to lose you as a friend."

He ducks his chin, trying to look directly in my eyes like he's searching for any indication I didn't mean what I said. "That's what you need? For us to be friends?"

"Yes. For now, or... I don't know how long. That's what I need."

Danny nods, resigned.

As he walks to the fridge to refill our water glasses, I barely catch him saying, "We'll get there again."

Chapter 37

Grace

March

One Month Later

I glance down at my scrubs again, which are coated in slobber, fur, and a little bit of dog vomit. I sigh and repeat my mantra, as I do every time I find myself covered in animal fluids:

At least my patients aren't human.

At least my patients aren't human.

At least my patients aren't human.

Breathing in and out through my mouth, I feel better already. The mantra works every time. I try to remember how many clean pairs of scrubs I have on hand as I walk down the hallway to my office. My day is almost over, but I'd rather not see my last patient in splattered scrubs. I peek in the closet right outside my office door and pull out my personal favorite—a bright pink set.

As I strip out of my blues and put on my pinks in my office, my cell vibrates on my desk. I eagerly snatch up my phone, knowing right away who messaged me.

How's the Best Vet Within Twenty Miles Of Columbus doing today?

Currently covered in dog vomit and slobber.

That good?

Yep, and I already got three "can you trim his nails today, too?" requests.

The Curse of the Overgrown Nails strikes again.

The vomit and the nail trimming I can handle, but I also had a frustrating case. One of my patients wasn't responding to the medicine as well as I'd like.

Why don't you try prescribing bacon? That always made Charger feel better…

If you suggest "bacon" or "a little treat" one more time for a sick patient, I will block you.

You wouldn't.

After our intense talk, digging up old feelings and addressing new ones, we took some time for ourselves before my flight back home. We'd both needed to process what happened. Danny reached out after a few days and sent me a text requesting a picture of my Unofficial Patient of the Week. From there, we've talked regularly for almost a month now, tentatively building a friendship again.

Through our conversations, I've learned small things about Danny, like he can't handle caffeine after 2:00 p.m. He's fully into all things Marvel, which is unsurprising for Mr. Spider-Bite Conspiracy Theorist. I am dismayed to learn he golfs now, too.

I also learned big things, like how he kept his vow not to drink alcohol again. I cried when I learned he's been sober for thirteen years. Danny also told me that his dad reached out to him six years ago, notably after his most successful pro-football season. He's firmly no-contact with his dad, so his response was crickets. But it stings I wasn't able to support him during the hard times, like we'd promised each other years ago in the woods.

My goal is to get to know *this* Danny so well that I can fully understand all the places and faces on the expansive gallery wall in his home. I want to know about his friends, trips, accomplishments, and failures. I want to know it all, clinging to each of his facts and trading some of mine in return.

> I gotta run, seeing a patient in five. Talk later?

> Yes.

I pull on my fleece zip-up and tie a new bandana in my hair. As I grab my phone to put it back in my desk, I see one last message from Danny.

> Remember to eat something, please.

I grab a protein bar from my desk drawer and take a bite, washing it down with a swig of water.

Being the only two vets in our high-demand practice, Elle and I are stretched thin around here. Once he found out I was accidentally skipping meals, Danny started catering lunches for the office and having my favorite snack delivered to my desk. *I've been wanting to spoil you for the last ten years, please let me,* he said when I protested his generosity.

After I finish up my last—and thankfully, easiest—patient of the day, I hurry to my office and pack up. I hustle to my gray SUV and call Danny. The phone rings only twice before he answers.

"Best names so far today?"

It's always the first question that flies out of his mouth when we get on the phone after I've worked a full day at the clinic.

"Freddie Meowcury wins for CATegory. Two sibling dogs—one named Cheesy and one named Tots—win for DOGegory. Bringing up the rear in the catchall 'Other' category is Hamlet, the guinea pig."

Danny's laugh sends shockwaves through the speakers. "Damn, people are so creative. Any funny animal pics for me today?"

"Yep. One coming your way now." I send him a picture of the rattiest little dog I saw today.

Danny snorts. "Oh my God. He kind of looks like... I hate to say it."

"Who?"

"Martin Short."

I dissolve into laughter. "*Mae?* Is that you? You sound different. Alive, primarily."

He laughs. "She'd love that joke. Look at him again, Gracie, and tell me you don't see it."

Glancing at the picture, I see... damn it.

"You think he looks like Martin, don't you?"

"Whatever, Daniel."

"Hey, that's Danny to you. I haven't heard it nearly enough over the past ten years."

My eyes squint from the smile taking up half my face. He's almost done with his postseason duties in New York, and I'd be lying if I said I wasn't eager to see him.

"I can't believe I see you in two days." I shift in my seat, unable to contain my excited energy.

"Me either. It'll be good to be in Ohio for the offseason, and I can't wait to see your clinic, Gracie."

My body warms at the thought of him walking through the

door and seeing all my hard work in action. I don't *need* him to be proud of me, because I'm proud of myself. But I *want* him to be.

"Tell me more about it. What should I expect?"

"Well, it's always chaos here. Barking and meowing overpowers the waiting area music. Our receptionist, Hannah, is our Resident Young Person. She runs our social media handles and works the front desk, scheduling patients and handling walk-ins."

"I love some chaos. I'm excited to meet Elle, too, and get all the dirt on your twenties."

I shudder, thinking of the things Elle knows. Crying into a box of donut holes at five in the morning after an all-nighter during vet school, I told her all about Danny. She comforted me at all the right moments and agreed with me throughout the entire conversation like I did nothing wrong (the best sort of friend).

Avoiding the subject of my cringey twenties at all costs, I pivot our conversation. "Enough about me. How was your day?"

"I met with the board of my charitable foundation. I don't think I've mentioned it to you yet, but I started a foundation with some teammates a few years ago."

"Danny, that's amazing!" I'm not surprised his generous heart led him to foundation work.

"Yeah, and it's even better having some of the guys' support. Speaking of my foundation, I actually wanted to ask you something."

"What is it?"

"Our inaugural gala is in two months in New York City. I know it's kind of far out, but, um, I was wondering if you'd like to come with me as my plus one. It will be nice to have a... friend there."

The word "friend" sounds like it's being yanked out of his

mouth by a dentist. Yes, we've been rebuilding our friendship, but using that word to describe us is starting to feel wrong. We're in motion, fluctuating between friends and *more*. Lately, my heart is leaning toward more. I just need my courage to catch up.

"Sure, it sounds like fun." Even though I've been out of the football world for a while, getting back into it through a sports charity will be a great start.

"Perfect, Gracie. Thank you." Danny sounds almost relieved, like he wasn't sure if I would say yes.

"I've never been to a gala, and it would be really cool to meet some of your teammates."

"I'm excited to introduce you to them. A couple of the guys already know a little bit about you," he admits. "Oh, I almost forgot to mention. I have to give a speech."

"You *are* kind of a big deal."

He chuckles. "I don't know about all of that, but I'm going to *feel* like a big deal, being your date for the night."

I light up, glowing so bright he might be able to see the glare from his window in New York. "Well, I'm looking forward to it. I'll need to pick out a dress."

"You could wear your green and white Sharks sweatshirt and still be the most gorgeous one there."

My face heats, and I'm suddenly grateful he can't hear my loud blush.

"But I actually wanted to talk to you about the dress. It's totally up to you, but, um, Tessa offered to design one for you if you don't already have something. You'd just have to send her your measurements. She'll be at the gala and can bring it to the house beforehand. No pressure at all, though."

A pang hits my heart as I ache for another person I haven't seen in years. "Tessa wants to design a dress for me?"

"Yes?"

"Of course I would love for her to design me a dress! I'm honored. I'll email you my measurements so you can send them. I'm actually dying to see her."

"She'll be so excited, Gracie. Thank you."

"Thank me? Thank her. I hate dress shopping. She just made my life so much easier."

Danny clears his throat. "And, since I asked you to come, I'd like to foot the bill for your plane ticket. The team has a travel agent, and I can give you their information, if you'll let me. Also, if you want hair or makeup done, I'm happy to send someone to the house."

"That's all really thoughtful. I'd love my makeup done. I doubt I'll do anything different with my hair."

"You're perfect. I mean, your hair is perfect," he praises.

I smooth a flyaway back from my forehead.

"Listen, I'm so sorry, but I have to run. I promised I'd grab dinner with Tessa tonight. We haven't caught up in a while."

"Tell her I said hi. I miss that girl."

"She misses you, too. And...I've been missing you."

I hesitate for a moment, then decide to be honest. "I've been missing you, too."

Chapter 38

Danny

When I land in Columbus one day earlier than expected, the first thing I do is buy a big container of fries and a ginger ale from Gracie's favorite diner. After a month apart, I'm eager to see her in her element. I know it's difficult for her to grab snacks or even drink water during a day filled with patients, so I didn't want to come empty-handed.

After getting the goods, the rideshare drops me off in front of the clinic. From the outside, her practice is unassuming. A modestly sized, red brick one-story building with the words "Columbus Metro Animal Clinic" on the front. The names *Dr. Grace Sinclair* and *Dr. Elle Todak* are etched into the glass on the main door, alongside their business hours. They close in about an hour.

As soon as I open the door, I see all the love Gracie injected into this place. The waiting room has vibrant, deep pink walls decorated with photographs of happy animals. The space is filled with an eclectic assortment of small couches and colorful chairs.

"Hi there!" A smiling woman who looks to be about twenty

greets me from the reception desk. I realize by the social media handles sign sitting on the desk next to her that this must be Hannah, the clinic's "Resident Young Person." She pushes her purple hair behind her shoulders. "What can I do for you?"

"Are you Hannah?"

"Yes," she replies slowly. "And you are?"

"Sorry. I'm Danny, Gracie's boy... Grace's friend. Dr. Sinclair's friend."

Yuck. "Dr. Sinclair's friend" tastes disgusting coming out of my mouth.

Hannah gives me a curious smile. "Did you want me to page Dr. Sinclair?"

"I know the clinic closes soon, so if you're okay with it, I'm happy to wait in her office. I don't want to bother her if she's in the middle of something with a patient."

She quirks an eyebrow, looking skeptical. "Yeah, I'm going to page Dr. Sinclair."

Fair.

Hannah presses some buttons before I hear a responding beeping sound. "Okay then. She's with a patient but says you can wait in her office. It's the last room on the left once you get through the door."

I nod and wait as she buzzes me through. Gracie's voice travels through the wall in the babyish tone she reserves for animals.

I find her office and settle in the squeaky chair behind her small, high-gloss white desk. Sitting on her desk is a pink laptop and a few pens with flowers on the end. I set down the food I brought and spin in the chair while I wait.

Not even five minutes later, I perk up when I hear her voice traveling down the hall. "You have a good day, Mrs. Baer! Jett is such a cutie. See you at his next check-up!"

I stand as soon as Gracie walks in.

Her eyes widen and a huge smile spreads across her face. She crosses the small distance between us to wrap me in a tight hug. Her body pressed against mine, familiar and warm, just feels right. We make so much sense together. I hope she feels it, too.

"You're here a day early!"

"I was able to grab an earlier flight as soon as my team meeting ended."

She pulls back and notices the new items on her desk. "Did you bring me fries? And a pop?"

"I figured you didn't prioritize eating today. I ate on the way here."

Gracie groans as she takes a long sip of the ginger ale. "You were correct. Oh my gosh, this is so good."

I clear my throat and move around the desk so she can sit in her chair. "*You* look so good."

"I'm in slobber-covered scrubs, please." Gracie cringes and sits down, but not before I notice the quiet blush blooming across her cheeks.

"So, how often have you, uh, been back since we broke up?" she asks, swirling her straw.

"I fly home to visit my mom once a year for the Fourth of July weekend. She still loves the firework display at the park. Roger makes these delicious shishkabobs on the grill—you'll have to eat one this year. It's a good time, but once a year is about all I've been able to handle."

"Handle?"

I frown. "It wasn't exactly fun to go back home after we broke up. It felt like your old house was glaring at me through my bedroom window."

Gracie turns her body to fully face me. "Can I ask you something?"

"Anything."

"I found something in your guest room. Under the bed. I was just looking around and—"

"Snooping." I grin, knowing this woman through and through. "You were snooping."

"I wasn't snooping! Jesus." She wipes her hands on a napkin, muttering, "You and Ben are so annoying."

"Ben? Like Ben Fischer? From high school?"

"Yeah, we're still really close. Me, Ben, and Mia—his wife, now. You remember her from graduation, right? After college, I went to vet school in Indiana to be closer to them. We all did post-grad at the same time, with me doing the vet thing and Mia and Ben going to law school."

My posture relaxes, relieved that Gracie had a support system when we weren't speaking. "It's cool you both stayed friends all these years. What's he up to now?"

"He's an environmental lawyer, which means that I've been forced to drink out of soggy paper straws in the dark—against my will—whenever I visit them."

Curiosity gets the better of me as I quirk an eyebrow. "The dark?"

"Yeah, he has solar-powered everything. Anything that can be solar-powered is solar-powered. But, like, Indiana doesn't get *that* much sun. You know?"

Loud laughter bursts out of me. So much uncontrollable laughter that I start to wheeze.

"Ha, ha. Go ahead. Laugh it up at my misery."

I calm down enough to narrow my eyes at her and ask, "So, tell me, Gracie. What *does* Ben have to do with my guest bed?"

She flushes. "I, um, kind of called him in a panic when I found the scrapbook, and—okay. Fine, I was snooping. It's in my nature; you know that." Then she throws me an accusatory look.

"Actually, *you* should have hidden it better if you didn't want me to find it, so you really only have yourself to blame."

All I can do is smile at this ridiculous, lovable woman. "I don't care, Gracie. It's okay that you went through my stuff. What's your question?"

"Well, I saw an article in there. A *Columbus Dispatch* story on my practice. Did you...?" She trails off, all flustered and adorable.

"Ask me what you want to ask me, Gracie girl."

"Did you look me up while we were apart? How did you find out about the opening?"

"Well, you know I kept in touch with Mae over the years. We had a firm 'No Talking About Grace' rule, but one day, I had to know. If you were doing okay. If you'd moved on. If you were still chasing your dreams. I asked Mae during one of our conversations, and do you know what she said?"

"What?" she asks anxiously.

"Mae said, and I quote, 'look it up yourself.'"

That bell-like laughter I love tumbles out of Gracie as she bends forward and cracks up.

"So," I go on, "I looked you up. And I saw that you were thriving, Gracie. And for the first time, it felt like we were on parallel paths. Both of us, succeeding professionally, but without each other. I made a decision that day to do whatever I could to become a better version of me, one that you would be proud of. That's when I started working on myself."

She nods shyly, satisfied with my answer, and pops another fry into her mouth.

"So, are you done for the day?" I steal a fry.

"Yep! Elle is closing up today, but she's with back-to-back patients right now." She pauses. "Did you want to come check out my apartment?"

"Of course I want to see your place, but there's no rush. I'm happy to wait for as long as you need. I'm not trying to get in the way of baby turtles returning to the sea."

"Do you... *know* what a veterinarian in Ohio does?"

I wink, and she throws a fry at me.

I catch it in my mouth.

"Get your bags, Thompson."

Chapter 39

Grace

I tap my foot nervously as I hold open the creaky, heavy metal door. Stepping inside the stairwell, which smells faintly of wet laundry and lemon-scented cleaner, we walk up two flights of stairs to my apartment. I'd be lying if I said I wasn't a little anxious about bringing Danny, CEO of Robot Appliances, to my modest, one-bedroom Columbus apartment.

"Walking up these stairs is my exercise every day. Probably good for me since it's the only workout I get."

I turn back with a smile, but Danny isn't smiling. "There wasn't a doorman at the desk down there."

"Oh, yeah," I say sheepishly. "Craig is the only doorman. He takes breaks throughout the day, so sometimes it's unmanned. But this area is really safe, so we don't even really need him."

A muscle ticks in his jaw. "The main lobby was unlocked, though. Anyone could get in."

I try to lighten the mood. "Sure, but it comes in handy when I get food deliveries. They can just walk right up to my door, so I don't have to go down in my pajamas. A perk, if you will."

It doesn't take us long to reach my place. I take my keys out as we pass the shared laundry space. With slightly shaking hands, I open the door and gesture him inside with an exaggerated flair. "Welcome."

He steps into my apartment and takes his shoes off before picking them up and setting them neatly on the mat by the front door. Watching him transports me back into my childhood bedroom, waiting in anticipation for him to remove his sneakers before climbing through my window.

When he straightens to his full height, I realize just how big he looks in my space.

"I know it'll be hard, but try to refrain from jumping for joy during this tour or else I'll be treating you for an offseason concussion," I joke.

He softly chuckles. "I think I'll manage."

As soon as the "tour" starts, I realize how ridiculous that word is to describe what we're doing. Everything in the living area of my place is within several steps of the next place we're "touring." I've never felt that my apartment was abnormally tiny until now.

Forging ahead, I gesture to the entire living area, an open-concept space with laminate wood flooring. Big, bright paintings decorate the tenant-white walls along with a large, colorful tapestry. A small magenta loveseat, a vintage wooden coffee table, and two conversational chairs upholstered in mismatched jacquard patterns complete the space.

He walks closer to my really-nothing-special flatscreen, sitting on a black and silver stand. I laugh when I notice him looking at the stack of old DVDs underneath the TV.

"Yeah, I don't even know why I keep those. I don't have the equipment to watch them," I snort.

Danny only hums in response as I guide him down the short hallway to my one full bathroom.

"A self-explanatory room, one might say," I playfully introduce. "There's just a regular sink in here, no touchless faucet to be found."

Stepping inside the bathroom, Danny picks up my coconut vanilla perfume on the counter. "Is this the same one that—"

"Yeah, it's the one that Mae got me for my thirteenth birthday. I've been wearing it forever."

"It suits you," he says simply, setting the perfume back down.

"Thanks. So, uh, if we're done in here, the last stop is my room right across from us."

I take approximately two steps to my bedroom door, which is already cracked, and gently push it open. "Go ahead," I tell him, curious to see what interests him first.

Heading over to my dresser, it's the pictures on top that catch his eye. He picks up a frame with a photo of me and Ben and studies it for a moment.

"This was your graduation from vet school?"

"Yep! Mia actually took that picture."

His eyebrows raise. "She didn't want to be in it?"

"Well, it was just easier to have Mia take pictures." Averting my eyes, I add, "It was, um, only Ben and Mia there."

He gently sets the frame down. "Only Ben and Mia came to your graduation?"

"Yeah. I mean, obviously I didn't have parents there. And Mae was too old to be on her feet walking across campus the entire day." My voice comes out quieter than normal.

Danny's whole posture stiffens. "I wish I was—"

Coming up behind him, I touch his shoulder. "We can't go back and change it."

Nodding, he turns around and sits on the rose-colored quilt on top of my queen bed.

The corners of his lips twitch as he touches the fabric. "Pink flowers, pink scrubs, pink bedspread."

I join him, sitting on the corner of the bed frame. "I'm a pink girl. All girls decide what their color is at age five, Danny, and that color follows us around our entire lives."

"A strawberry girl, through and through," he says softly, tucking a curl behind my ear.

I clear my throat. "Well, um, shall we check out my fully functional, but robotless kitchen?"

Danny laughs, and we head back into the main living area together.

"This is the kitchen." My kitchen is tiny and U-shaped, like every other apartment kitchen in the Midwest, with laminate countertops and a dated, white refrigerator that hasn't been updated in years. I'm pretty sure the serial number is in Roman Numerals.

"I know a whole family of *mafiosos* wouldn't fit here." I gesture to my small circular wooden table. "But Mae actually bought it for me. You can see a tiny bee she had custom-carved into each leg." Made with warm-toned reclaimed oak, darker knots create thick streaks throughout the wood grain, adding interest and personality.

Danny reaches out and runs his fingers across the table before crouching down and carefully touching one of the carved bees, gently pressing his fingers into the grooves.

"It's beautiful," he admires.

"Yeah. It's probably my favorite thing in this place."

We're quiet for a moment while Danny takes his time appreciating the craftsmanship. Once he's completed his inspection, we each take a seat in one of the four matching oak chairs. In the center of the table sits a pair of salt and pepper shakers in the shape of a dog and a cat and a large bowl of avocados.

Danny raises his eyebrows and gestures toward the bowl. "Big avocado girl now, huh?"

I swivel my head toward him. "*That's* what you're focusing on after this whole tour?"

"You know, I don't think anyone really likes avocados." He scratches the stubble on his chin.

"I like avocados."

He shakes his head. "No, you just like the flavors that go on avocados."

"That's not true!"

Leaning forward in his seat, Danny places his elbows on the table. "It *is* true. If you put garlic, salt, and lemon juice on your face cream, you'd eat that, too."

My jaw drops slightly. "Well, this *is* America. You're entitled to all the wrong opinions you want, I guess."

"It's like how no one likes plain chicken," he continues. "They're just keto or kidding themselves."

I blush and look away.

Danny narrows his eyes, immediately clocking my embarrassment. "Uh oh. What's that look for?"

"Nothing, I just... I dated a guy that was on the keto diet."

"Tell me it was a special diet for his health."

I absentmindedly twirl my hair, trying my best to look *Cool* and *Casual*. "It wasn't. He, um, had a podcast...about 'Living the Keto Lifestyle.'"

"You dated a man with a podcast? A man with a podcast was your boyfriend?" A huge grin spreads across his face as I glare at the gap between his teeth.

I huff and cross my arms. "Why are you smiling? Shouldn't you be jealous or something?"

"Jealous? Of the Keto King?" Danny's shoulders shake with silent laughter. "I'm thrilled, Gracie. This is the best news I've had all week. The bar for me is much, much lower than I thought."

"Hey!"

"Can we call Ben about this? I really want his take, and I haven't talked to him in forever." Danny pulls his phone out of his pocket. "Is his number the same as it was in high school?"

"Ben liked him!" I protest.

"He didn't, Gracie. He didn't," Danny says matter-of-factly.

I shoot up from my chair. "Fine! He didn't like him! He told me to burn my phone, so I wasn't tempted to go on dating apps anymore! Is that what you want to hear? Stop laughing!"

"No, I just—" He breathes between wheezes. "I just can't stop thinking about him looking down upon your precious strawberry milkshakes. I bet you were secretly enraged."

"I just drank them by myself when he wasn't around," I admit quietly.

Danny stands up and holds out his arms to me in mock sympathy. "Aw, come here. I would never deprive you of your milkshakes. Your milkshakes are safe with me."

I begrudgingly walk into his arms. "Okay, now I feel like you're making it a sex thing," I mumble into his shoulder.

"Just say when," he murmurs in my ear.

My body buzzes with electricity at the implication. Even though I'm not ready to return his "I'm in love with you," my body feels extremely ready to see his body naked.

"Let's forget about the Keto King," he announces as I try not to grin.

Danny pulls back from our hug and takes a few steps toward the main sitting area. I follow him and sit down on my loveseat. Looking lost in thought, he surveys the space in one glance.

"Can I ask you a question?"

"Go ahead."

"Why do you live here?" His voice comes out gentle, almost

careful, as he lowers himself next to me on the small couch. "It's nice, but I know you can afford a bigger place."

"I never wanted a whole house."

"Why not?"

"I just knew I would never be able to maintain the upkeep, like shoveling the snow, mowing the lawn, doing repairs by myself. I don't have anyone that can help me with any of that, and I couldn't pay someone to do it when I first moved back to Ohio. I was saving every penny I could for the launch of my clinic, and we're still paying back the start-up loans."

Danny frowns and scratches his facial hair. "I hate that you didn't have anyone here to help with that kind of stuff, Gracie."

"It's not like I need a ton of space for one person, anyway. Living so close to Mae, but not with her, was actually the hardest part."

"Mae must have been so proud of your clinic."

"Yes, she was." I smile fondly. "Actually, I still have her sourdough starter in the fridge. I bake a homemade loaf of Mae's sourdough every Sunday. It helps me feel close to her."

"I'd love to make it with you sometime." His large hand blankets mine, warming it up.

My eyes roam his face. The walls I put up ten years ago with Danny are still there, guarding my most vulnerable feelings. I wonder what would happen if I let just one wall down.

"Do you want to spend the night with me here?"

Nodding, Danny's throat bobs. "But I can sleep on the couch."

"If that makes you more comfortable, you're, um, welcome to do that; although, it's small. My bed isn't a California King, but it's more comfortable than the couch."

"Are you sure?"

I nod slowly. "Platonically, of course."

He clears his throat, before squeezing my hand. "Anything you want, Gracie girl."

"Good. I think I have an extra toothbrush."

"That reminds me. My bags are still in your car." He stands up.

I really don't want him to go anywhere. Now that he's finally here, the idea of him leaving slightly unsettles me. My face heats, thinking about what I could offer him, not knowing whether or not I'm brave enough to mention it.

"You don't need to leave, I have something you can—"

"Grace, I'm sorry if this sounds like toxic masculinity, but I am *not* wearing another man's clothes." His lips press into a thin line.

"No, it's not that. I, um, actually have something of yours. One of your football T-shirts, from high school. I can grab it. I usually wear it to sleep, it's just so comfortable..."

"You wear my old shirt to sleep?" His eyes darken with heat as he steps toward me.

"It's not a big deal. Like I said, it's very comfortable, and—"

Looking smug, he throws me a toothy smile. "Great. I'll take it."

The pure joy on his face is contagious. My eyes crinkle at the corners as I walk to my room and pull his shirt out of my top dresser drawer. I peek out of the doorway and throw it to him, trying to catch him off guard, but—of course—he catches it, no problem.

Rolling my eyes and grinning, I head to the bathroom. "I'm going to wash up, okay?"

When I come back from the bathroom, Danny is sitting on the bed, wearing his Winfield High Football shirt and boxers. In his hand is my old walkie-talkie I keep in the nightstand. A ghost of a smile graces his lips as he brushes his thumb over the well-used buttons.

"I snooped."

He stands up, still grasping the walkie-talkie, and comes around to meet me by my bedroom door. His arms envelop my shoulders, pressing my body to his. This hug isn't romantic. It's a hug best friends give, one that I have years of experience with but haven't felt in awhile. My face is scrunched up against his chest as he murmurs into my hair, "I don't think this will reach Brooklyn."

My cheeks lift and my eyes well with happy tears, though none fall.

After a few moments, we climb into my bed, which barely fits both of us. His breath warms my face when we turn to face each other. He scoots down so his forehead is level with my collarbone. When he turns his head to the side, his ear is gently pressed to my chest, right over my heart. Wrapping his arms around my waist and curling his legs up, he listens to the beat of me. I run my fingers through his thick, wavy hair and dip my chin to rest it on his head.

Without moving his head, he releases one arm around my waist and reaches for one of my hands in his hair. He brings it down with his, laces his fingers through mine, and for the first time in a long time, we fall asleep as otters do.

Chapter 40

Grace

May

"Thank you so much! I love it, Morgan," I shout compliment after compliment as the makeup artist waves goodbye. "I feel so fancy. You're very skilled at your job! You should win a major award for this!"

"You are too sweet, Grace!" She giggles as she walks out the front door of Danny's Brooklyn home.

I catch my reflection in the hallway mirror. My eyes look bigger than normal, framed with brown mascara and a softened wing of smudged, dark brown eyeliner. Morgan put a shimmery opal gel shadow on my lids, and I have a slight glow from a pearlescent highlighter on my cheekbones. My curls, swept up in a half ponytail, look shinier with some hair spray to tame the frizz. As I apply a coat of clear lip gloss, I feel absolutely perfect.

I meander into the kitchen and my mouth waters at the spread Danny had delivered this morning. It smells amazing in here, like a bakery. My dirty chai is as delicious as the donuts he ordered.

I'm thinking about taking *just one more bite* of a glazed twist when the doorbell rings. I rush for it, knowing who awaits me on the other side.

"Tessa!"

"G! Oh my God!"

I go in hard for a hug before she stops me. "Makeup, hair!"

"Thanks for the reminder. I'm not used to all of this." I pull back, gesturing to my face.

"After a few years in the fashion industry, it's all I'm used to," she replies with a genuine smile.

Tessa stands tall and regal, looking statuesque. Her thick, black hair is waved into an Old Hollywood style. The golden shadow on her eyelids highlights her dark features, and big gold hoops decorate her ears. Her deep red, trumpet-style dress fits her like a glove, and her skin glows in a way where I can't tell if it's just her beauty or shimmer.

"Wow. You look gorgeous, Tess. Did you design that dress?"

She flushes. "Um, yeah. This is one of mine."

"It's breathtaking. Your talent is unbelievable."

"Thanks, that means a lot coming from you," she says fondly. "Just wait until you see your dress, it's my favorite piece I've designed so far."

I squeal. "I can't wait! Should we try it on now?"

"Yeah, we have to leave for the gala in about thirty minutes. Daniel is giving an opening speech, and he'll murder me if we miss it." She laughs. "He's been practicing for days."

"I definitely don't want to miss it. I asked him if I could listen to him practice, and he all but hung up on me, acting like it's classified information. Who am I going to tell? I'm not even connected in the sports world."

Tessa looks at me with questioning eyes before her lips turn up in a smile. "Um, yeah, he takes anything to do with his... sports foundation super seriously."

"Do you ever help with the foundation?"

"He's kind of a control freak, so not really. But the creative director I work for donated couture dresses to auction off, so I brought them with me."

"That's so nice! I bet they go for a hefty price."

She brushes a stray eyelash off my nose. "Yep. He's a *Vogue* darling. They definitely sell."

Tessa hands me the black garment bag she's holding. "Here's your dress. I brought my sewing kit if needed, though I'm not great at alterations. I really hope you like it. I smiled the whole way through designing this one."

I hold the garment bag lightly, not wanting to wrinkle the gown. "I've always loved your designs."

Tessa rolls her eyes and scoffs. "I'm sure the garbage bag dress I made you in the fourth grade was a real highlight."

"Hey! Don't talk about my first Tessa Couture gown like that. *Grocery Chic* was super in that year."

We both burst out laughing.

"I think my mom still has a picture of you wearing that somewhere."

"Good, I hope Janie keeps it for posterity. When you blow up and a streaming service makes a documentary about you, we can point to it as an early design."

Tessa's smile holds steady, but her eyes begin to mist over. "You haven't changed a bit. I'm...I'm so happy that you and my brother are friends again." Shaking her head, she blows out a frustrated breath. "Ugh! I need to pull myself together, or the glam will be ruined. It took me hours to get ready."

"Tessa," I breathe, "I wanted to say...it was incredibly hard to lose contact with you over all of these years. It was immature of me, but any reminders of him—including you—left me in agony. I'm sorry. I never stopped thinking about you." I reach out and hold her hand in lieu of a hug.

She laces her fingers through mine. "Same. I've always loved you like a sister. I hope you know that, G."

I let go of her hand and bring mine back to the bottom of the garment bag, holding it up off the floor. "Okay, I'm going to go try this life-changing dress on."

She waves her hand, brushing me off. "Oh, stop. Let's see if you even like it first."

I skip off to the bathroom down the hallway. I unzip the garment bag and my breath catches in my throat. It's a gorgeous floor-length periwinkle gown made entirely of satin.

I carefully step into the dress and pull up the hidden zipper on the back of the corset top. The delicate spaghetti straps slide easily over my shoulders and frame the elegant sweetheart neckline. Gently swaying my hips, I watch as the gown flows seamlessly to the floor in a softened mermaid-style. The design almost looks like a cascade of water, angelic and fresh. It fits perfectly.

When I walk back into the kitchen, Tessa is looking out the window. I give the donuts a longing stare before clearing my throat to announce my presence.

She turns around and gives a small gasp. "Not to brag, but this might just be my Magnum Opus. You're stunning. I have to take a picture for Mom."

Tessa grabs her phone from her purse, and I smile for at least five minutes while she takes multiple pictures from different angles for Janie, who is home sick with the flu.

"I knew it would be perfect because you designed it, but Tessa...it's on another level. This is art. Hang it in the Louvre."

She flushes. "Thanks, G."

"I mean, how did you even pick this color? It goes so well with my—"

"Eyes," Tessa interjects with a grin. "My brother picked the color."

It's my turn to blush. "Oh. Well, that's..."

"Romantic, right? It's kind of gross, as his sister, but definitely romantic. He is so gone for you."

My throat constricts. My heart races. A wonderful, heavy, warm fog blankets my mind.

"Yeah," I breathe. "The feeling's mutual."

And the feeling *is* mutual. It always has been. It hasn't taken me a long time to realize it; it's taken me a long time to *believe* it.

Tess nods, giving me a knowing look. "When he came with me to the fabric store a few weeks ago, he spent, like, two hours trying to find the perfect color to complement your eyes and—"

"He went to a *fabric store?*"

"Yeah," she replies shyly.

"Wow." I hum, trying to tame my emotions for this man before I ruin my makeup.

"Anyway, he said he was specifically looking for a bluish purple tone, and this was the closest match."

"I don't even know what to say."

Tessa glances at her phone. "Well, whatever you want to say, you can tell him at the gala. The car should be here now."

"I'll grab my clutch. And thank you so much, again. I can't believe how perfect it is, and the fact that you designed it makes it even better."

"You're welcome. It was fun designing it for you."

I slip on strappy nude heels and get in the car, which turns out to be a limo, because *of course* Danny sent a limo.

After a surprisingly fast car ride, we pull up outside the event. A flurry of butterflies begin to flutter in my stomach. It's more excitement than nerves, because I'm itching to see Danny. I'm ready to wrap my arms around him and tell him that I'm in love with him. I still can't believe that he went through so much effort, on top of being busy with football meetings and gala planning, to shop with Tessa for my dress.

I'm walking on air as we carefully wiggle out of the limo.

Glamorous gala-goers exit their private cars and walk the green carpet. I expected to feel out of place at an event like this, but tonight, my confidence is at an all-time high as we head toward the Step-and-Repeat for pictures. I pose next to Tessa until we reach the large front door to the event.

Instead of knobs, the front door has two golden bee-shaped handles to grab. I smile up at the sky at the reminder of Mae. *She would've loved these*, I think to myself as the attendants open the doors for us.

When I walk into the event space, I drop my clutch in shock. As if she prepared for my whole-body reaction, Tessa bends down to pick it up and pats my hand a few times.

"*What?* I thought... what is this?"

Tessa gives me a reassuring look. "Like I said, he's far gone for you."

"Danny did this? When did he do this?"

She pauses. "He started working on the charity about five years ago."

"And it's..."

She gives me a small smile. "I think you know what it is."

I stare at the big sign written in golden calligraphy hanging above us: The Honeybee Charitable Foundation. My gaze lingers for a few moments, waiting for the words to make sense. To our right, there's a giant vinyl poster with Danny and two teammates on it, wearing shirts that feature the charity's logo: the letters HCF forming a hive.

There are bees everywhere—golden bee tablecloths, arching indoor trees decorated with frosted glass hives and twinkle lights, and floor-to-ceiling curtains embroidered with miniscule bees. Little bees swirling around the hives on clear wire. A lounge area resembling a forest, with couches that look like logs and an electric campfire.

A jazz trio plays in the corner, and behind the stage is a

massive drop-down screen displaying a slideshow of images. Right now, it's showing a picture of Danny standing with what I assume are some foundation employees in a grassy area. Another picture rolls by, this one of a smiling crew in beekeeper gear with their arms around each other.

A tech crew manages various computer screens in the back corner of the room, not far from where we're standing. With them, and looking devastatingly gorgeous in a classic black tux with golden bee cufflinks, is Danny. His dark, wavy hair looks lightly tamed with gel, and he's cleaned up his facial hair. He seems to be doing a mic check for his speech. They finish up, and he shakes one of the crew's hands before turning back to the party area.

When he spots me, his mouth parts, like he's awestruck. Or maybe he's wondering what's wrong, because I'm gawking at him. His eyes twinkle, and he shrugs. He gives me a sheepish smile, almost conveying *this is no big deal.*

This is a very big deal.

My feet move before my mind gives the order. I walk faster and faster toward my Danny boy. I thought I would hug him, but all I want to do is touch his face. I slowly reach up and gently stroke his cheek with my thumb.

"Danny," I whisper.

"You're captivating, Gracie," he praises quietly, marveling at me. "Look at you."

"This is…"

"Do you like it?" His voice sounds unsure, which baffles me.

"Do I like it?" I breathe. "Do I *like* it?"

I bring my other hand up to his face, and now I'm cradling his head in the palms of my hands. I want to say *I love it.* I want to say *this is the best thing you've ever done for me.* I want to say *it's perfect.*

What comes out is an astonished, "Thank you."

He gives me a beaming smile.

"Thank *you* for coming. I want to talk more, but I have to give my speech, okay? The guest seating chart is over there by the entrance, but I have you and Tessa at the table in the front. Grab an appetizer, relax, and I'll come find you afterwards."

I absentmindedly nod as he gives me a kiss on the cheek.

In a daze, I somehow find our table. Tessa sits there, smiling from ear to ear. There's no doubt she saw the interaction between Danny and me.

"So, it turns out this isn't a charity for sports."

"Um, no," she laughs.

"Thanks for the heads up," I tease.

She playfully elbows me. "Hey! I wasn't sure how much he told you, and I didn't want to ruin a potential surprise."

"I get it. It's just... *wow*."

Tessa starts to respond but is cut off by the MC announcing Danny to the stage. My eyes lock onto him, mesmerized by the pure stature and heart of this man. He walks to the center of the stage and pulls out a small piece of paper from his inner pocket. I'm suddenly anxious to hear the speech he's been practicing over the past month, now understanding why he wouldn't let me hear it.

Danny clears his throat. "Hi, everyone. You all look great tonight."

Remaining guests take their seats as he unfolds the piece of paper.

"First and foremost, I want to thank you all for being here. This cause is near and dear to my heart."

He scans the crowd and squints a bit at the spotlight. His eyes find mine, and he takes a deep breath, bringing his attention back to his paper.

"I started the HCF about five years ago, at a low point in my life. I wasn't, um, doing well at the time. While football has led to some of my greatest triumphs, it's also led to some of my greatest regrets. My therapist encouraged me to start by doing something small for others, like volunteering at a local soup kitchen. I did that, and it was humbling, but, as many of you know, I'm kind of a 'go big or go home' type of guy." The crowd laughs politely, and Danny gives a small smile.

"So, I decided to start a charitable foundation. I knew the cause had to be something that was meaningful to me. I was looking for guidance, which got me thinking about the last time I received advice from a trusted friend. That friend was Mae Clancy."

A whirlwind of emotions engulfs me as he says her name. When Mae died, I scrambled for scraps of her...checks she had signed, doodles she'd drawn in the margins of the Sunday crossword, the broken chain from her reading glasses. To hear her name in a room full of people, to know that she's *remembered* by someone other than me, it's like a hit of dopamine. My eyes water, and Tessa hands me a tissue from her purse. I shoot her a grateful look as I dab underneath my waterline.

"Mae was like a grandmother to me in so many ways. She was an expert at maintaining the delicate balance of reassuring me *and* roasting me regularly enough to keep me humble. Mae was also the first to clue me in to how I felt about her granddaughter back in high school. She told me it was obvious I was in love with the girl next door, and that she loved me back but was too scared to tell me. Her advice that day changed my life. *'You can't rush her heart, you can only busy yours,'* she told me."

When was this? How did she know?

"So, while I was busy loving her granddaughter, Mae kept busy loving her bees."

I was busy loving you, too, I think as a tear escapes my eye. Danny nervously straightens his already-straight tie and takes a sip of the water bottle on the podium before continuing.

"Her greatest passion was bee conservation. I used to sit and talk with Mae about two things the summer before college. Bees and the girl next door. God, I learned so much about bees and the perils of losing more and more of them every year. I learned about their importance to our planet. Most importantly, I learned how you can get a stomach ache if you eat too much fresh honeycomb at one time—that one was from personal experience." The audience laughs, completely enthralled by Danny's story.

I knew Mae and Danny talked, but they were closer than I realized. My stomach twists as I think about the goodbye he didn't get to say because I was too scared to reach out to him.

"We talked about her granddaughter and the bees...until we didn't. And years later, I thought about how much I fucking missed talking about my best friend and bees. Excuse my language."

"One morning, I was drinking a cup of coffee on my balcony and a bee landed on the rim. It was at that moment that everything fell into place. Even if I couldn't have everything—*everyone*—I wanted, I could save the bees." He clears his throat. "But I didn't want to move forward blinded by my own ambition, thinking this was the right decision without consulting the people it would affect. I did that once before, and it didn't end well for me." He swallows tightly, and a flicker of sadness flashes in his eyes.

"I called Mae that same day. She was all in. And that's the origin of The HCF."

The crowd starts clapping. My heart rate quickens as I think about the implications of his words. I knew they kept in touch, but she *knew* about this foundation. She cosigned its creation. I remember all the times she tried to talk to me about him, and all the times I refused to listen.

Danny shifts on his feet, swaying a little from side to side before taking another deep breath.

"After scolding me for not talking to her for years, we talked about what this could become. She said she was honored, but it was *me* who was honored. Mae was one of the most selfless people I've ever known. She was a great, um, woman. Fierce, and uh..." Danny's voice strains as he tries not to cry.

For me, not crying is a lost cause. Tears, and most likely my mascara, slide down my cheeks.

"Fierce and loving. Funny and kind. Loyal and honest." He takes out a handkerchief and dabs his brow. "I always wanted to bring her out to see the foundation. She planned on being here today. Unfortunately, she—" He chokes, cutting himself off, before swallowing and carrying on. "She passed away this year. I'm devastated she can't see this, but I know she's watching from somewhere else."

His eyes mist over. After a brief pause, he folds the paper up and returns it to his pants pocket. Danny fixes me with his gaze, and I can tell that whatever he's about to say is unrehearsed.

"During my last conversation with Mae, I shared my intentions to invite her granddaughter to this very gala. And, while I did end up asking her a little later than I expected, I'm grateful that she decided to attend."

Danny was going to invite me here, all along? The crowd starts buzzing, searching the room for me, but I'm still hung up on the meaning behind his words. The knowledge that we might've reconnected, even without the letter bringing us together, sends goosebumps down my arms.

"Finding my way back to you has been the greatest privilege of my life." His voice, low and throaty, cracks.

He angles his body slightly away from the audience for a moment, before taking another sip of water and facing front again.

"Gosh. I need to get a grip, huh?" The audience laughs, but I see some teary-eyed guests, too, including Tess beside me.

"Well, with that, a big thank you to my teammates for joining me on the journey to build this foundation. I don't think anyone anticipated three professional football players being so passionate about saving the bees, but here we are." He laughs into the microphone, and I think the tenor warms the room by a degree or two. "Eat and be merry! We're alcohol-free tonight, but I hope you enjoy our custom bee themed mocktails. And please spend all of your money. It's for a good cause."

Pure awe flows through my veins as he jogs down from the stage to our table. Tessa stands up. "Yeah, so I'm going to check out the mocktails."

Danny doesn't take his eyes off me as he responds, "Probably for the best, Tess."

I stand to meet him. "Danny, I..."

"Do you mind if I say something first?" he asks softly.

"Go ahead." I need a few minutes to gather my thoughts.

"We don't have much time right now, because I need to mingle with the donors. And I want to talk about everything later. But I don't know when we'll get cut off." He straightens, suddenly all business. "So, I want to talk about your dress."

Confused, my eyes search his for clarity. "My dress?"

"Mhm. You look perfect."

"Tessa told me you picked out the color. Danny, that's so thoughtful. It's lovely."

"It's beautiful because it's you." He gently strokes his thumb underneath my blue eye, and my pulse races.

"It's so sweet, thank you."

"That's not what I wanted to talk about, though. I mean, it is and isn't. It's not the first time I've picked out something for you in that color," he says carefully.

I wrack my brain trying to think of all the presents Danny

has gifted me throughout the years. Nothing in this color comes to mind. Most of my birthday presents revolved around experiences, like concert tickets.

"I'm so sorry, I don't remember..."

"I actually never gave it to you. I wanted to give it to you the day that I told you about the transfer."

"The day we broke up?"

He nods with a heartbroken expression, as if he's remembering that day.

"I picked something out for you in this same color. I spent some of the money I'd saved up from mowing lawns over the summer to buy it. But, um, obviously the conversation didn't go the way I thought it might, and then we didn't talk anymore."

He pulls out a small, wooden box that looks weathered around the edges. It's the size of a... *Holy shit*. It's a ring box.

My heart starts pounding, almost leaping out of my chest. "Were you going to...*propose* to me?"

Danny grins. "If I thought you would've said yes, maybe." He shakes his head a few times. "But, no. It wasn't for a marriage proposal."

I feel a little relief and...disappointment, maybe? But we definitely weren't ready for marriage then.

"I want to give it to you now so you can wear it tonight. It matches your dress perfectly. And, if you're open to it, I'd like for it to mean the same thing now that it was supposed to mean then. That I'm committed to you. That you're it for me, Gracie. If I have your permission."

He hands me the box, and I gently pry it open so as to not disturb what's inside. A small tanzanite gemstone sparkles up at me. It's sitting in the middle of a dainty, silver band. Danny picked this out for me ten years ago. *He's held onto it all this time?*

"You were going to give me a promise ring?"

"Yeah." His words are quiet, threaded with emotion. "Even Mom knew."

"Janie knew about this?"

He rubs his hand down his face. "She was happy. She said that you were already like a daughter to her."

"I'm...I'm angry at us for going this long without speaking. We wasted so much time," I say between sniffles.

Danny scratches his chin. "Looking back, you were right to do what you did for both of us. We both had growing up to do. We found our way back to each other, and that's what I choose to focus on."

"You're right." I stare into the floor. "It's just hard, thinking about what could have been."

He places a finger underneath my chin, tilting it up, and our eyes meet. "You know what's better than 'what could have been,' Gracie girl?"

"Hm?"

"What's happening right now."

A sob wracks me, and Danny hands me his handkerchief.

I take a deep breath. "I've always loved you, Danny. Then... and now."

Even with that simple confession, a tear rolls down his cheek. He chuckles and wipes it with the back of his hand.

"I loved you when you were just a memory," I whisper. "I loved you when I didn't know if we would ever be 'us' again."

"God. Me too, Gracie."

We lean in at the same time for a hug. He showers me with soft praises, murmuring, "you're my best friend" and "love of my life" over and over again in my ear, like a refrain to a hymn only we know.

After a few minutes, we pull back and chuckle at each other's puffy eyes and splotchy faces. Danny hums softly. "We're a mess, aren't we?"

I gesture to my face, feeling my cheeks tighten from crying. "What are you going to do with me?"

"Marry you one day, if you'll let me."

I tilt my head and stare at him in wonder. He gently cups my face and hovers his lips over my mouth. He pauses, searches my eyes, and asks, "Do you want this?" Just like he did when we were young. It feels like our first kiss all over again, but with different promises attached to our lips now. The nerves are there, but so is the muscle memory.

"Yes." My tone is soft, fervent, like a prayer.

He kisses me, and my heart whispers *finally*. He kisses me with so much longing it makes my eyes water and my toes curl. It feels like the Danny-shaped cracks in my chest are slowly being repaired, like we're making commitments we can keep this time. His lips nudge mine open, and then his tongue is tangled in mine, before he seems to realize where we are and pulls away.

He stares at me like I'm rare, then picks up my right hand and gently kisses the inside of my wrist. He does the same with my left wrist, my pulse point beating beneath his lips. I bloom under his gaze for a few more minutes before he reluctantly leaves to mingle with potential donors.

The rest of the gala goes off without a hitch. According to Danny, it's their most successful event yet, with donations almost doubling the goal. I spend the evening watching him in his element—shaking hands and mingling with guests, confidently chatting up potential donors, and making everyone feel welcome. Meanwhile, he frequently checks on Tessa and me, often requesting servers stop by with refreshments and platters of food at our table.

And when dinner is over, Danny makes sure to deliver the dessert himself: a strawberry milkshake, garnished with chocolate-covered honeycomb.

Chapter 41

Grace

Fresh honeycomb still lingers on his tongue as he deepens our kiss in the back of the town car. Our languid, leisurely strokes turn into something more urgent and desperate.

When we finally arrive at his Brooklyn home, he quickly tips the driver and guides me into the house. As soon as we step over the threshold, he draws me to the entryway wall and leans in, one arm on either side of me. I tilt my chin up, and he nudges my mouth open.

As his tongue circles mine, his fingers graze the exposed skin on my back, leaving a trail of goosebumps behind. God, I'm so wrapped up in him. I'm *surrounded* by Danny's touch. Each caress down the top of my spine feels saturated with gentle but firm intention.

Our mouths still fused together, he kicks the front door closed. The thud reminds me of my window shutting whenever he snuck into my bedroom at night.

Different house, same us.

"Are we finally, actually doing this?" I ask breathlessly in between needy kisses.

"You want it tonight, Gracie baby?" Danny exhales the words against my skin.

Without a beat of hesitation, I nod. His fingers lazily unzip my dress until it falls to the floor, leaving me in my white lace bra and matching thong. The precision of his touch is a contrast to the nostalgic messiness of the two teenagers we once were, figuring it all out together. Taking off his suit jacket and unbuttoning his shirt far too slowly for my liking, Danny grabs my hand and guides me toward the couch in his living room. He sits down and gently pulls me onto his lap. I can feel his breath skate over my lips.

He tilts his chin toward my chest, meeting my eyes. "Show me."

I unhook my bra, and it drops to the floor. He swallows hard at the sight of my bare breasts. A few moments of charged silence pass between us, and a nervous flutter stirs low in my stomach. His expression softens into something tender as he carefully grabs my hand and presses it to his chest. The rhythm of him is a familiar lullaby for me, like my favorite song on a soundtrack only found inside Danny's body. I've been homesick for his heartbeat for years.

"It's going to feel so good, Gracie girl," he murmurs.

His voice is so soft but firm, and I know it turns both of us on when he talks to me like this. Danny was always so sweet and playful when he had me naked, but he was also so *in charge*. I love that I can really let go with him, that I feel safe enough.

He brushes his thumbs over my nipples, and they harden at his touch.

I squirm on his lap. "Finally."

"I almost forgot how eager you get," he grins in response.

I've always been *eager* for Danny, for his touch. The way he soothes the quiet ache in me, the one that only he can find.

"Your nipples are so hard for me, I bet I could hold onto

each one while you ride me. Do you think you can come like that?"

I nod ferociously.

"Words, Gracie."

"Yes, Danny," I breathe.

He caresses my cheek. "My good girl."

I'm so wet that I can see a spot starting to form on his suit pants.

He bends his head and licks each nipple before lightly blowing on them. Danny is so damn good at taking his time with each part of my body. Intimacy with him feels like an absolute luxury.

"I'm just going to grab each one here," he lightly pinches my left nipple, "and here." He does the same to my right. "If I tug, slow down, okay? I'll get you there."

"I know. I know you will," I say in between shallow breaths.

"Okay, go ahead." He gives my nipples a little extra pinch. "Get after it, Gracie."

I grind on him, slowly for a few moments, but then faster. Much faster. I can feel the seam of his pants rub against my clit, and the friction of my thong against the material heightens the sensations. *I'm so close.*

"God," I moan. I needed this. I needed *him*.

I pick up my pace and add in swirling motions. *I really might come like this*, I think as I push down harder and move even quicker, and—

Danny shakes his head and gives my nipples two gentle tugs, moving them up and down when he does it this time. "Slow down so we can savor this."

I blow out a frustrated breath. "Danny, I was close."

He never used to deny me, but just like when we were younger, he's introducing me to things I didn't even know I liked.

Danny drops my nipples. They point down from all of the attention as he hungrily watches. "Be good, baby. Take off your thong," he orders, his gaze sweeping down my body.

I stand and slide it off in one fell swoop.

"Can you sit on the chair for me over there?" He points to the leather chair facing the couch. I throw him a *look*, and he grins, his eyes glinting with warmth. "Please."

"Are you coming, too?"

"Oh, I'll be coming," he says with a wink.

Danny proceeds to take the rest of his clothes off, and I proceed to unabashedly stare at his body. His muscles stand out, but they're not outrageously big. They look like they belong on his frame, like he didn't have to do countless workouts to achieve them. As a wide receiver, his shoulders are broad, but his torso is streamlined. The smattering of hair on his chest dusts across his light brown skin. He's still soft around his ass, which I love.

He catches me looking and a boyish smile spreads across his face. "Are you trying to make me ask again, Gracie? Because you know I will."

Shaking my head at his antics, I grin and head over to the chair, where I lower myself and wait for him.

He follows and crouches in front of me, tapping his hard cock twice against the side of my thigh. "Lean back in the chair and spread your thighs for me, yeah?"

I slowly open my legs, exposing myself to him.

Danny lifts my thighs to rest on the arms of the chair and groans. "I've missed this view so much. These wisps of red hair right here, especially. Nothing and no one compares to you."

The affirmations are everything I need and want to hear, and the feelings are more than mutual.

He leans closer before pausing. "Before we do anything more, I want you to know we get tested regularly for football. And...I've always been clear."

"I've always been clear, too," I reply slowly. "And I'm still on birth control."

Danny holds his cock in his hand and runs the length of himself through my center a few times, coating himself in my arousal.

I might be dying, but he just lazily smiles. "You look so sexy right now. I can't wait to get inside you soon."

"Now," I demand.

His gaze holds affection as a faint smile dusts his lips. "Not tonight, Gracie girl. Let me worship you, hm? Let me memorize you like this."

I'm simultaneously disappointed and excited by his promise, but I know that coming with him, in any capacity, will be extraordinarily overwhelming.

Danny slowly slides two fingers inside me. The fit is perfect and snug. He brings his other hand to my clit and starts rubbing in small, firm circles.

He glances down to watch where his fingers disappear. "Look down, Gracie. See how good my fingers look inside you? They're going so deep. I pull them out of you, and you suck them right back in again."

Holding onto his forearms, I lean forward to watch us. Danny splays one hand on my lower stomach as he licks a strip up my core before moving his tongue to my clit, where I crave him most. Then he sucks it into his mouth and hums.

My soft ache gives way to a rush of relief traveling up from my toes, and it's all I need to come. I close my eyes as the moment stretches into something timeless. Danny lavishes me with his tongue until my legs stop shaking. My eyelids flutter open, and he pulls up on his knees.

The quiet happiness in his gaze takes my breath away.

He peppers my lower stomach with kisses. "Gracie, you are so insanely beautiful when you come."

I feel a shy warmth bloom in my chest. "Danny, I want you to come, too."

A grin tugs at his lips. "Okay. Where?"

God. After a moment of thought, I decide to be bold in an attempt to surprise him for once. "My chest."

Danny bows his head on a moan. "All of this feels so right between us, doesn't it?"

I lose focus as his words take me back to our first time. *Doesn't this feel so right, Gracie? Doesn't this make sense?*

He grabs a pillow from the couch, picks me up, and carefully lays me down on the thick rug in front of the fireplace. It's plush and smooth against my back. Danny kneels, puts the pillow underneath my hips, and runs his hand down his face as he stares at me.

"It's been too long since I've had you, and I can't... It's going to be fast," he says hoarsely, pumping his hand up and down his cock, which seems to get harder and harder. Neither of us are fully in control now as he places his slick cock in between my breasts, squeezes them together with his hands, and slides up and down. I reach for my clit, steadily massaging it with my fingers as he rocks against me.

Danny's breaths pick up, and so do his thrusts. I feel his touch everywhere. He groans loudly as he comes, his release warming my chest. Combined with the pressure on my clit, it feels so good that I come again, gently swept up in his wake.

His gaze settles on me, eyes wide with awe, like he can't believe what just happened between us. For a few minutes, we stay caught in this moment, completely content.

"I've always been yours, Gracie," he murmurs, pulling back on his knees. He lowers himself next to me on the floor and wraps me in his arms. "Can we always be together?"

A peaceful hum escapes my lips as I snuggle into his chest. Soaking in the timbre of his voice, I close my eyes and relax.

* * *

"Gracie." *Kiss.* "Gracie girl." *Kiss.* "Baby." *Kiss.*

I squint and slowly realize I'm no longer lying on the rug. I'm in Danny's bed. He must have carried me upstairs after I closed my eyes.

"Did I nap?"

"No, Gracie girl, it's only been ten minutes, but we need to wash up. You did so good for me. Let's shower and then get back in bed."

I glare at him playfully. "I'm so relaxed my limbs feel like jelly; there's absolutely no way I'm showering."

A smile skims his lips as he strokes my hair. "Okay, bath then."

Danny leaves to grab towels in the hallway closet, and I get up to look myself over in the bathroom mirror. Stretching my arms above my head, I smooth down my messy hair, completely satiated. He returns with towels and a bottle of bubble bath, setting them aside before turning on the hot water and adding Epsom salt.

"Are you coming in with me?" I ask him hopefully.

"This is just for you to relax. I brought your book and put it on the side of the tub. Take your time."

"Okay. If that's, um, what you want." I avert my eyes to hide my disappointment.

He throws me a lopsided smile. "Do you want me to sit on the bench near the tub so we can hang out while you soak?"

"Yes!" I rush out. "I mean, yeah, if that works for you. I'd like that."

"Anything you want. Always."

I throw my hair up in a messy bun, pulling out some of the smaller curls near my face. We sit and talk while I enjoy my bath. Every so often, I lift my feet up out of the water and comment on my pruney toes. He adds more hot water, and I hold bubbles in my hands, sometimes blowing them in his face. I tease him about the unhinged amount of salt he added to the bathwater (*I could make taffy with the amount of salt water in here, Danny*).

It's all so domestic and normal that my chest aches.

I thought I'd never feel it again. But now I do.

The simple, ordinary moments of living life with him.

Chapter 42

Danny

I wake up the morning after quite possibly the best night of my entire life to music playing in the kitchen. Based on the empty bed beside me and the punk music blaring downstairs, Gracie is the only possible culprit. My mouth quirks into a grin, and I throw some boxers on, heading downstairs with a burst of energy. I feel like I'm eighteen all over again.

When I round the corner, Gracie's snipping up canned biscuits and dropping them in a bundt pan. She hasn't seen me yet and is currently shaking her ass to the music, frizzy curls falling out of her messy bun. She's wearing her pale blue polka dot bra and a pair of my white and blue plaid boxers. The waistband is rolled up a few times, so they rest comfortably on her hips. She sets down the scissors to stir something on the stove.

"Are you making monkey bread, Gracie girl?" I walk closer to her.

She drops the spoon on the floor. "Shit, Danny! Why would you scare me like that?"

I pick up the spoon and place it in the sink. "Sorry, baby. I thought you could hear me coming down the stairs, but I guess not through the loud music and all the...dancing," I lie, my shoulders shaking with silent laughter.

"Oh, fuck off. You know you love it." She backs her ass up, hopping toward me.

I give her ass a gentle spank and peer around her over the stove, where a brown caramel sauce is bubbling away. "I knew it. Monkey bread! Thanks for making it for me."

"Who said it was for you? Maybe this entire concoction is for me."

"Please. Monkey bread is *my* favorite. It's definitely for me." I waggle my eyebrows.

"It's for you," she admits with a smile.

Gently lifting a loose curl resting on the back of her neck, I press a kiss to the top of her spine. "I love it." I pause. "And I love *you*."

A rosy flush blooms across her chest. "I love you, too."

I open the drawer and hand her a new spoon. "Do you need help with anything?"

"Nope! I'm all set. What are your plans today?" She returns her attention to the sauce.

I hesitate, feeling a little nervous about sharing. "I actually have a video call with my agent that I want to talk to you about."

"Of course. One sec." Gracie pours the sauce over the dough in the bundt pan and slides it in the oven before giving me her complete attention. "Okay, what's up? Your tone sounds big."

I grab her hands in mine. "It *is* big, I guess. And, well, I didn't incorporate you in decisions I made regarding football before, and it was the biggest mistake of my life. I won't do it again."

She nods and gives my hands a reassuring squeeze.

Taking a deep breath in through my nose, I blow it out

slowly through my mouth. I haven't uttered these next words to a single soul. It feels right that Gracie is the first.

"I think I want to retire." I shut my eyes tightly, not knowing how she'll react. *Shocked? Disappointed?* "I just want to focus on the foundation and start really living my life. Of course, if you want me to play longer, I can do that, too. It's a family decision." I wait anxiously for her response.

"I'm so proud of you, Danny."

I snap my head up and find a beaming Gracie.

Raising an eyebrow, I ask, "You don't think I'm giving up too soon?"

She shakes her head. "You've accomplished big things. Football, the foundation...you've inspired so many people. Take the win." Gracie punctuates her words with a soft kiss on my cheek. "Thanks for involving me."

I hug her to my chest, resting my chin on her head. It feels so good to think of this as a mutual decision. But discussing our future together makes me wonder about our past, and I know I need to bring up Mae's visit. It's haunted me for years, not knowing if Mae ever told Gracie the truth. I can't risk leaving her in the dark, not when I just got her back.

"I don't want there to be any secrets between us." My voice comes out quiet.

She tilts her head, and I hear a tapping sound. My eyes travel to the floor, where I find her bare foot pattering against the wood. "Is there something I don't know?"

I swallow. "It's just that, I'm not sure if Mae ever told you over the years. We never spoke of it past that day."

Gracie takes a shaky step back when I reach for her again, so I keep my hands busy by picking at the skin around my nails.

"The timing of Mae's visit to Ohio when we were teenagers after the last confrontation with your dad wasn't just lucky. I, um, called her."

A small gasp escapes her lips. "*What?*"

My words come out in one big rush. "I know it was wrong for me to do that without asking you. But I was seventeen, and I was scared, Gracie. I had all these huge feelings for you. Your dad, Florida...it all felt like an impossible scenario."

"So *you* called Mae that night. That's why she came to Ohio."

"Yes. And I'm sorry. I never should've reached out on your behalf. And I should've told you sooner."

Her eyebrows knit together. "Why didn't you?"

I shrug. "Mae said she'd tell you when you were ready to hear it. But I called her, so it's on me. And I was wrong to make that decision for you."

She nods slowly. "I'm trying to imagine what seventeen-year-old me would've thought about this, but—God, it's impossible to get back in her head, and I don't want to. It was terrifying there. All I can do is react to this now, and...I'm grateful. I'm frustrated that neither of you told me. But for calling Mae and bringing her to me when I wouldn't do it myself? Today, I'm thankful you did that, Danny. I forgive you."

My shoulders slump, and I wrap my body around hers, bowing my head in relief. "Thank you, Gracie."

* * *

"DT! Good to see you, man." Jeff sits at his huge, mahogany desk on my screen. "I've gotta say, I'm surprised. Usually, you want nothing to do with me during the off-season. You wanna do a commercial all of a sudden?"

Jeff Kranz has been my agent since I started in the league. He barely had a clientele back when I signed with him, which appealed to me. For years after Gracie and I broke up, I didn't have much confidence in my own decisions. If I was blinded by my ambition that badly, what else would I miss? When it came time to declare, I sought out a smaller agent in hopes of securing someone who could really focus on me. As my star power grew, so did Jeff's client list. He's now one of the most successful sports agents out there, but that hasn't changed his good guy status.

I laugh and shake my head. He knows me too well. "You can fuck right off with that nonsense. I'd rather record a shout-out video with a stranger who accosts me on the street than film a commercial."

He slumps in his brown leather chair, pretending to be offended. "You know, your lack of interest in sponsors and media opportunities is leaving money on the table for me."

"Somehow, I think you'll survive," I joke. "But if you don't like my continued disinterest in commercials, you're really not going to like what I have to say next."

That gets him to put his serious face on. He leans forward and puts both elbows on his desk, giving me his full attention. "Whaddaya got for me, D?"

"I want to retire."

His jaw drops. "What? *Now?* Two months before the season starts?"

"No, no. I want to announce my retirement next year."

At my reassurance, he takes a deep breath, no doubt relieved this won't be a breach of my contract. "Can I ask what's driving this decision?"

"I'm starting to feel my age," I lie.

"You're thirty," he counters.

I grin. "And I feel it."

He clasps his hands behind his head. "You're not performing any worse."

"I'm slower, though."

"Still just as many receptions." Jeff picks up one of his fancy pens.

"You're not going to convince me."

"Eh, worth a shot." He gives a good-natured wink.

We both look at each other for a moment with matching smiles. He starts writing on his notepad. "I'm going to have to make some calls."

"Same," I sigh.

He stops writing and looks up for a moment, meeting my eyes. "Does this have anything to do with Grace, by chance?"

Jeff knows all about her. We've talked about the mistakes I made on my journey to the league. I can't help but think about how far I've come since our first conversation.

"The desire to 'call it good' is my own, but the decision is supported by her. We're back together." I can't help but grin.

"No shit. I was at the gala. Pretty sure everyone in the tri-city knows you're together. Thank God I didn't bring my kid. I would've had to cover her eyes for that kiss."

I chuckle and relax in my chair. "So, you're okay with this?"

"Of course. We'll give it one last hurrah this year. With your girl cheering you on this time, yeah?"

The visual of Gracie cheering me on from the stands has me grinning from ear to ear. "Yeah. Gonna have to hide her Sharks sweatshirt, though."

Chapter 43

Grace

June

"This is Dr. Sinclair."

"Well, hi, Dr. Sinclair. This is DT, Mustangs Wide Receiver."

I beam at my empty office, wondering if he can feel my smile. It's been one month since Danny moved to Ohio for the offseason, and we've spent almost all of our free time together. But I never tire of hearing his voice.

"Well, hello, DT. What a pleasant surprise! Do you have a pet that needs an appointment?"

"I didn't tell you about the turtle I bought?" he jokes. "Nah, I knew you had a full day today and wouldn't be on your cell."

"Yeah, it's been a doozy. Thank God it's over now."

"I figured. So, I know we usually hang out at your place, but I was wondering if you wanted to come by the ol' neighborhood today. Mom is on location this week for a shoot, so we'd have the whole place to ourselves."

I spin back and forth in my desk chair, swinging my legs a little with each movement. "I, uh, haven't been back since Mae moved to the care facility."

"Really, it's been that long?"

I stop spinning and pause to think about it. "Yeah, it has. I guess I never had a reason to go back."

"If you feel like it would be uncomfortable, I'll come straight to you once you're done for the day."

"No, no. I just haven't really considered it before. It's not like I'm walking into my old house. Your place was a safe haven for me."

Danny hums softly, but doesn't push.

I make up my mind. "Let's do it. I'd love to see your house again. Is your walkie-talkie still in your room?"

He laughs. "I don't see why it wouldn't be. Mom left that space exactly as it was when I left. It's basically a museum at this point."

"So many memories, I bet," I muse, thinking back on a few of my favorites. Tessa's drawings of us, the football lamp on his bedside table...the hopes and dreams we shared under his covers.

"Yeah...and I was thinking maybe we could make new memories, too."

My ears perk up. "New memories?"

"Mhm, new memories on my couch, new memories on the floor, new memories on my bed..."

My body lights up with his words. *Finally*. We've been taking things slowly, not wanting to rush sex, but enough is enough.

I glare into the phone like he can see me. "Are you being serious? You better not be joking."

"Oh, I'm being extremely serious." His voice comes out low and gruff.

I breathe a sigh of relief, feeling his words in every fiber of my being. "Thank God. Don't move. I'm leaving right now."

His laugh booms so loudly over the line that I have to pull the phone away from my ear.

"Be mindful of traffic laws, please," he warns through shallow breaths.

"I could literally break every single traffic law and still be a better driver than you."

"Hey," Danny pouts. "That's not nice."

"Then let's just say that one of us passed our driver's test the first time, and the other one of us took a quartet of tries."

I hear Danny wheezing over the phone as I hang up and hustle to change into anything clean that I have on hand. I throw on a white, ribbed cotton top with bell sleeves and decide to forgo underwear—*what's the point*—before pulling up my fitted gray jeans and booking it to his house.

As soon as he opens the door, I jump on him. He chuckles and catches me with an "oof!"

Leaning back, I rake my gaze over the Mustangs baseball cap, gray henley, and worn, faded light wash jeans he's wearing. I'm still amazed at how much he's grown from the last time we had sex. His eyes gleam with amusement at my obvious appraisal of his body.

The pull of longing for Danny, of longing for this *moment*, tugs at my chest. I'm past the point of holding back. "Take my clothes off, please. Right now."

He dips his head to my neck and laughs into my skin. "Slow down, Gracie girl. We have time."

"There's been lots of 'time' over the last several weeks. Enough with all the time. Any longer and we'll be in the year 3000. Take your pants off."

Snickering, he mutters, "You're something else."

I squirm, antsy to be with him. But he pauses, bringing his eyes to mine. His gaze lingers for a moment on my right eye, and every edge of his face seems to soften.

"Fuck, Gracie," he murmurs quietly. "The way I've wanted this so badly. The way I've wanted *you* for years..." He trails off, shaking his head. "I planned something special for our second 'first time.' Will you follow me somewhere?"

I nod and echo my youngest self. "I'd follow you anywhere, Danny."

And just like when we were kids, I do. The sunset casts a burnt orange glow over us as he leads me into the woods behind his house. When we arrive at our special spot, there's a thick blanket covering the middle of our log and a red tent set up next to it. Twinkle lights decorate the inside of the tent, which has a mattress and pillows inside.

The scene presses against my ribs, the rush of nostalgia so strong it nearly hurts. My heart stutters as tears prick my eyes. *First love, last love.* "You set this all up for me?"

"I'd do anything for you, Gracie." Danny presses a soft kiss to my cheek. "But don't think for one second it's not for me, too. Fucking you in our secret spot is maybe my longest-running fantasy."

My jaw drops slightly, his words knocking the air right out of me. When I look up at him, his lips are curved in a boyish smirk. He knows just how to unravel me. Our surroundings melt away as he strips my top and bra off.

"First, I want to eat you out while you lay back on our log. Then I'm going to bring you in there," he points to the tent, "and love on you the way I've wanted to for the past ten years."

With that promise, I hastily peel off my jeans, and he groans at the missing underwear.

Danny nods toward the covered log. "Go ahead, Gracie."

He trails me as I walk over to our log completely naked. The padded blanket is soft beneath me when I sit down. Danny strips off his shirt, leaving him in only his jeans.

He swallows. "Lean back a little so I can see your tits better."

My breathing picks up as I plant my hands behind me.

"There you go, just like that. You're making such good choices today, Gracie. You deserve a reward." He kneels down, eye level with my center. "Soaking wet for me, dripping all over our log. Want some attention, hm?"

I nod eagerly. "Yes. I need it."

Danny grins. "So sweet to let me lick your pussy again, when I just ate you out yesterday."

His words drive me absolutely crazy as I wait for him to devour me. I was already hot from the sun, but now I feel a bead of sweat dripping down my brow.

After a few moments, my impatience gets the better of me. "Do you want me to beg?"

The corners of his mouth tick up as a glimmer of mischief flickers in his eyes. "Great idea. Beg."

As freeing as it is for me to give him control during sex, it's his playfulness that I love most.

"I'll do anything," I plead.

"You'll do anything for what, Gracie?" His eyes flicker to my breasts before traveling back down between my legs.

"For your tongue on me."

Danny lifts my legs over his shoulders with a wide smile. "After all these years, hearing you beg for my tongue might just be my favorite sound. Think you'll get louder when I do this?"

He licks a long strip straight up my core.

"Yes, just like that. *More*," I demand, louder now.

Danny chuckles against my center, his hot breath raising my body temperature even more. "Let me cool you down a little first." He softly blows on me, and I shiver, already close to the edge.

He starts giving my clit small, short flicks of his tongue over and over again. I moan, grabbing his hair and pushing his face closer to me.

"Keep going, please," I whimper.

Danny lightly rubs the wisps of reddish hair on top of my pussy that he still can't seem to get enough of as he continues to lick me. He pulls back only for a moment. "Are you going to be good for me when we get in the tent?"

"Yes, yes. I'll be so good for you," I breathe.

Satisfied with my response, he fucks me with his tongue and brings up two of his fingers to massage my clit. I can't hold off any longer. The tingling sensation is tactile, entirely overwhelming me. It resembles the sparks I used to feel when I was with him years ago, but it's so much more intense now, like a wildfire.

"Danny," I moan loudly.

"I love it when you say my name. I want more of that when I'm inside you," he replies hoarsely, licking me through my orgasm.

Both of us breathing heavily, he carefully picks me up and brings me inside the tent. Danny gently lowers me on my back and places a pillow between my hips and the air mattress. After swiftly removing his jeans and boxers, he kneels in between my legs.

"You're so pretty, Gracie. I have such a good view of you like this." Danny rubs me up and down my sides, from my hips all the way to the sides of my breasts. "Perfect hips. Perfect stomach. Perfect thighs." He continues to praise nearly every part of my body.

"Danny, I want you now. Bare."

His eyes go wide with desire, but I catch a glimmer of wonder in them. Years of longing and love have led us here. We both seem to realize it at the same time, because the urgent pace we've set settles for a moment.

Gratitude is too inconsequential of a word to describe the feeling of being here with him. There are so many feelings fighting for my attention right now, but most of all, I just want him to know...

"I've missed you, Danny."

Even though I'm naked, his gentle stare somehow undresses me even more.

"I've counted every breath since you've been gone, Gracie. Every single one. And after ten years, I can't wait any longer."

Danny pins me with his gaze as he guides his cock inside me. Rolling my hips, I adjust to him for a moment. "I'm so full," I murmur, still disbelieving that we're finally *us* again. I rock my hips against him slowly, fighting the urge to let go out of fear it'll be over too soon.

Pumping in and out now, he angles his pelvis, and the friction feels incredible. His thrusts get deeper as he loses some control.

"Can I put my hand around your throat? Light pressure?"

"Yes, *please*," I moan as he gently circles my neck. I imagine how I look to him, with his hand wrapped around me like a necklace. I wish I had a mirror to watch us.

A small groan escapes him. "You look so beautiful like this. One hand around your throat while my cock stays warm inside of you. How'd I get so lucky?"

His gaze travels down my body, and I can tell from his heavy swallow exactly what he wants from me next. Danny has always loved watching me touch myself. He'd beg me to show him what felt good to me as I learned more about what I liked when we were younger.

Before he can ask, I move two fingers to my clit and start rubbing myself. Danny takes a labored breath and a pink flush blooms across his neck. A gentle moan escapes me, but I need more.

"Give it a pinch," Danny instructs.

When I do, pleasure unfurls low in my stomach. My eyes roll back as a reflex, unable to maintain focus.

"Fuck, Grace," he says hoarsely. "You're doing so well."

His praise runs over my body like a warm current, and I feel his cock twitch inside me.

"Another pinch, now. Yes, like that," he encourages, his voice strained. "I'm so proud of you."

Impatience sits heavy in my chest. "I can't wait any longer."

"I know, I know," he soothes, pulling up on his knees. "There's just so much I want to do with you before I leave for camp."

"Let me have you," I demand in between shallow breaths.

He stares at me for a moment, his gaze tracing the slope of my neck. "You do have me. You've *always* had me."

A soft smile brushes my lips. "You've had me, too. I love you."

"I love you, too. Now, put your hands in your hair and keep them there while I fuck you."

"*God.*" I run my hands through my curls, which are splayed out on the mattress behind me.

His eyes move over me, like he doesn't know which part of me to appreciate first. "I love your hair, Gracie. I've waited forever to see you like this. This is everything to me."

Danny reaches for my hips and starts thrusting again, maintaining a steady pace. I surrender myself to him, arching my body to meet his movements.

"There is no one." *Thrust.* "Else." *Thrust.* "For me." *Thrust.* "But you." He gives a final thrust and then comes deep inside me. I can't hold off any longer either, and lose myself to the irrepressible orgasm coursing through my body.

Danny looks down and stares like he wants to commit the visual to memory. For a few moments, all we do is grin at each other, just like our first time. When he pulls back, I feel some of his release leaking out of me.

He groans. "It's so much better than my fantasies."

"What is?" I ask breathlessly.

"Watching my cum run down your thighs."

Well, that's *not like our first time.*

Danny starts pushing it back in with his softening cock. "Soon enough," he mutters under his breath, and somehow *that* is what finally gets a blush out of me.

Collapsing next to me on the mattress, Danny catches his breath. I love that I wore him out. I turn onto my side and prop my head up with my hand. "Let's do that again."

He chuckles. "We need to get cleaned up. And I think I need an electrolyte drink, a shower, and maybe a nap before we go again."

Danny gets up and pulls his boxers back on. Then, eyeing me like I'm made of porcelain, he gently wraps me in a blanket before carrying me into the house bridal-style, where he deposits me on the bathroom countertop. When he walks to the other side of the large bathroom and starts running a bath, I cross my fingers that he'll get in with me.

This time, he does. Danny helps me into the water first so I don't slip, and then lowers himself in behind me. I lean back against him. We soak in comfortable silence while he washes my hair and trails kisses down my neck.

Staring in wonder and a little disbelief as we get out of the bath, we dry off and climb into bed.

He turns toward me and strokes the crown of my head. "Hey, Gracie?"

Yawning sleepily, I roll on my side to face him. "Yeah?"

His forehead touches mine as he leans in closer. "Do you want to be my girlfriend? Like the kind where I kiss you?"

I reach up to cup his cheek with my right hand. "Are we not already together?"

"I didn't want to assume anything," he says solemnly.

I grin. "Yes, Danny. I want to be your girlfriend."

"*I knew it.*"

He turns off the lights and grabs my hand. Danny lightly rubs my ring finger in a circular motion with his thumb. Feeling safe, warm, and happy, I blissfully fall asleep.

Chapter 44

Danny

July

After ten years apart, a few months together hasn't been nearly enough. I know I'm making the right choice in retiring, because I'm dreading the end of this offseason.

Gracie and I are just trying to savor every last moment before I leave for training camp tomorrow. We start by spending our morning outside, lounging on Mom's cherrywood stained deck. Before she left to shoot a wedding today, she waggled her eyebrows in a not-so-subtle way and said, "*I figured I need the practice, if ya' know what I mean.*" Gracie beamed, and I couldn't help but smile, too.

I feel like I'm discovering new things about her every day, like she's someone I just met. Yet, sometimes, it's like no time has passed at all.

We sit in padded wicker chairs. Given the heat, I'm not wearing a shirt, and Gracie's in a sports bra and cotton shorts. I open up the bags of food we ordered, ready to devour the Greek salads and salty fries.

She squints at the bag and then at me. "Why are there two orders of fries in here?"

I roll my eyes. "Gracie. Not this again. You get your own because you eat all of mine."

She huffs. "When? That doesn't sound like me."

"I'd prove it, but the evidence is gone," I say flatly.

She eats a couple of her fries and frowns. "These don't taste as good as when I steal them from you."

"Jesus Christ, here. Take my fries, you maniac." I aggressively shove them over to the side table next to my chair, and she happily starts devouring them.

I take a long sip of the iced tea we made yesterday. It's the lemony powdered kind that you have to stir in, and we're drinking it out of cups covered in watermelon print. Everyone knows that you must drink the tea out of a thick plastic cup filled with ice. It's practically codified in the Ohio state constitution.

"Look inside this cup, Gracie. You can still see a red-stained rim from all the Kool-Aid we drank in our youth."

She giggles, craning her neck for a better look. "Ah, yes. Fruit punch is to plastic cups as spaghetti sauce is to Tupperware. It's just never going to come out."

I bark out a laugh. "You're the funniest person I know."

She blushes in response, her face turning the same shade of pink as her painted toenails.

God, I'm going to miss her.

Both of us support each other's dreams wholeheartedly. Unlike last time, we've been creating concrete plans to make it work. Long distance during the upcoming season with visits sprinkled in, and me in Ohio full-time after retirement next year. Every day and every night.

"When do you have to leave for work?" Her clinic is open one Sunday per month, and Gracie pushed her patients to later this afternoon to allow for extra time together.

She groans and climbs out of her deck chair and onto mine,

straddling my lap and burrowing her face in my neck. I love the feel of her body against mine.

"Far too soon." Her lips move against my skin as she speaks.

I chuckle and trail my fingers down her back, rubbing gently back and forth across her spine. "It isn't goodbye. We'll talk every day, and we already have the next six months' worth of visits planned. Think about it this way: when I officially retire next year, I'll be here permanently."

"Are you still coming to the clinic to say goodbye?"

"I wouldn't miss it. I won't have a ton of time, but I should be there after I finish packing."

She pulls back and squeezes her eyes shut. "I love you."

I lean forward and stroke her chin. "Hey." I give each eyelid a light kiss. "I love you, too."

With that, we head into the house and get ready for the day. Gracie pulls on her scrubs, and I start packing my belongings. Whatever I can't fit in my suitcase will be shipped to Brooklyn.

I open the dresser drawers in my bedroom, pulling out clothes I brought with me that I'll need at home. I grab my hairbrush and wallet from on top of the dresser before wandering over to my nightstand and pulling it open. I grin when I see my old walkie-talkie sitting on top of a tin of expired mango sour Altoids.

Here, Gracie. I asked my mom for walkie-talkies for my birthday.

I call the red one!

Of course you'd say that. You always want anything red, like your hair.

I toss it in my bag. It's coming with me.

* * *

"I'll be back in about ten minutes, give or take," I tell the rideshare driver through the car window. Opening the door to her clinic, I'm greeted by Hannah's smiling face. Now that the staff knows me, the conversation flows easily.

"Dan! Hi, how's it going?" Hannah waves from behind the front desk.

Sauntering over to say hello, I rest my hands on the desk and drum my fingers. "It's going alright. How are you?"

"Terrible! Thanks for asking," Hannah replies.

Laughing, I ask, "Why are you terrible?"

"Ugh, don't even get me started." Hannah leans closer like she wants to tell me a secret. "This lady, Mrs. Hale, brings an animal psychic to every appointment so that her cat's 'needs are vocalized.' But the 'needs' are always just billing complaints. She's back there now," she warns, shuddering.

"Yikes. You want me to talk some sense into her? Anything I can do?" I ask jokingly.

Hannah laughs. "No, you'll only make it worse."

"That is absolutely accurate. And, unfortunately, I don't have a lot of time. Do you mind paging my girlfriend to let her know I'm here?"

"Sure thing. It shouldn't be too long." She presses a few buttons on the intercom system.

"Great, thanks." I plop down on the nearest waiting room couch and pull out my phone from my pocket. I'm scrolling through sports news headlines when Hannah says, "Daisy, right?"

A golden retriever barks as an older woman with graying brown hair walks out from the back area to the front desk. "Oh, I see here you're a member of the Charger Program, so you're all set!" Hannah says cheerfully.

I lock my phone and sit up straighter. *Did she just say what I think she said?*

"Thank you so much; have a great day." Hannah waves goodbye as the woman and her golden leave the clinic.

I take a moment to gather my thoughts before heading back up to reception. Hannah glances up from her computer. "I think Dr. Sinclair is on her last patient before lunch. Do you need something?"

"No, no. I just had a question for you."

"For me? Sure."

I drum my fingers on the desk. "I might've misheard something while I was camped out over there. Did you mention a program named 'Charger?'"

Hannah nods and pulls out a brochure from the wall rack. Handing me the pamphlet, she explains, "It's been around since we first opened. Pet owners who need financial assistance can apply for the program. If they're accepted, Dr. Sinclair does preventative care and in-office procedures pro bono. Honestly, she never declines an applicant."

She continues talking, but all I can focus on is the brochure in my hands, or more specifically, the logo on the front—an outline of a chocolate labrador. The lab has a collar that says "Charger Program" on it.

I interrupt Hannah as gently as possible. "You've been incredibly helpful. I'm actually going to wait in her office to read this, if that's okay."

She gives me a questioning look but buzzes me through. I glance out the window to make sure the rideshare driver is still waiting before hustling down the hallway for some privacy. Gracie's office smells like her, but not even that can distract me from this news. I sit on the squeaky office chair behind her desk to process everything. If she created this program when her clinic opened, it's been a few years now.

All this time, she was thinking of me, just like I was thinking of her, both of us weaving little pieces of each other into the fabric of our lives. I gently unfold the brochure Hannah gave me. Happy, drooly dogs are on every page, alongside the chocolate lab logo.

"Fucking Mrs. Hale," Gracie mutters, walking into her office. "Agh! What are you doing in here?"

"I'm sorry for startling you."

Gracie studies me as a tiny pinch forms between her brows, visibly confused. "What's wrong?"

I slowly lift my hand, facing the brochure out.

Her eyes widen. "Where did you...?"

"Hannah." I shrug, ducking my chin to better view her expression. "Is it... It's for *our* Charger, right?"

Gracie slowly nods, taking the brochure from me and setting it on her desk. We both move to hug each other at the same time and collide in a hard embrace. We softly sway together for a few moments.

Holding her tightly, I admit, "Sometimes, when I used to dream about us getting back together, just like this, I'd think, *maybe she's thinking of me, too.* But I'd dismiss it, Gracie. I never thought you..."

"I was *always* thinking of you," she whispers.

Breathing in her coconut and vanilla scent, I find myself transported back to high school. I lean away slightly to kiss the side of her nose. I knew that Gracie cared for me, but to have proof that she loved me—as more than just a memory—even when I wasn't with her nearly brings me to my knees.

Our fingers intertwine as we walk to the car waiting in front of her clinic. Stopping just outside the door, we turn to face each other. She tilts her chin up in question, and I answer with my lips, pressing mine to hers in a quick kiss.

"Hey, Danny?"

"Yeah, Gracie?"

"I'd say 'be safe,' but you're not driving, so you should be fine." She winks.

I flip her off before giving her a final hug, one that best friends and lovers give. There are only four parting words left to say, and I murmur them into her hair.

"First love, last love."

Epilogue

Grace

One Year Later

I stretch in bed and check the clock—8:00 a.m. Today is Mae's birthday. Danny and I have plans to celebrate in ways that would definitely win her approval.

First, we'll grab brunch in the Short North, where we'll people-watch and gossip...but only in Pig Latin. Next, we plan to visit her favorite spa and get facials because she would absolutely tell me that my skin currently looks "drier than a saltine." Then, we're going to end the day by bringing two honey sticks to her grave and sharing our favorite Mae memories.

We've had the most amazing time in Ohio since Danny retired earlier this year. It's been filled with charity work, lunches at the animal clinic, and nights at our new house just outside of Columbus.

We're house-sitting Danny's childhood home this week while Janie and Roger are on vacation. Danny's finally conquered Janie's famous cinnamon roll recipe, which was a surprise for all of us. He even hung up the recipe on our new robot fridge, like a C student who finally aced a test.

Danny's picked me a fresh flower from Janie's garden every single day this week, and I can't wait to see what he put in the painted vase today. My guess is one of the deep pink roses that just bloomed. I hustle downstairs, expecting to hear his voice or music playing, but the house is completely empty.

Peering around the corner into the main family room, I shout, "Danny?"

I walk into Janie's office next and call out his name again. Nothing. When I meander back to the kitchen, I find a note with my name on it taped to the refrigerator. My mouth falls open. *Why does this look like...* It can't be though, right? Because it looks like Mae's handwriting. And the name on the front is a dead (pun intended) giveaway—*Queen Bee*. But *how*?

No time to ponder as my ferocious curiosity takes over. I rip open the envelope and start sobbing the minute I read the title at the top.

To be Opened on the Day of Your Engagement

Bee,

To answer your top two questions:

1. Yes, you're getting engaged today. Surprise!

2. Janie is the one who held onto this letter in the event you would be in Ohio for your proposal. It was all very "Mission Impossible" of us.

I'm writing to you, on the day of your proposal, for one reason: to tell you that your mother would be staggeringly thrilled with the person you are today. You are more than she ever hoped or dreamed. "Proud" wouldn't even come close to a word big enough to describe how she would feel about you and all you've accomplished.

And she would feel the same way about that neighbor boy. You have no idea the amount of gratitude I have in my heart for Daniel. While I wish, with all my heart, that I could've gotten to you sooner, I'm resting peacefully knowing he's getting you forever.

When your mom was nearing her end, she didn't expend a lot of energy talking, but I do remember her saying this: "I can't believe I'm going to miss all of the big, brave things she does."

Keep doing those big, brave things. We'll be watching from wherever we are.

Love you like bees love honey.

Mae

P.S. He's bound to mess up the proposal somehow, dear. Knowing him, he'll force you to hike up a mountain to get the ring. We both know you barely have the lung capacity to walk ten laps around a department store without getting winded. Whatever he has planned, please do take an inhaler. I'd hate to see you soon.

I reread the letter.

A proposal...it doesn't feel real. I wipe my face with the kitchen dish towel that lives on the oven handle. I just want to see Danny. Am I supposed to wait here for a smoke signal that will lead me to where I might be getting engaged? Is this the part where I meticulously apply contour so I look beautiful for a secret photographer like some kind of celebrity?

Shit. I just remembered my soon-to-be fiancé *is* a celebrity. This probably *will* end up in a magazine, and I just expelled all of the water in my body through my eyeballs. First order of business will be finding clothes, then eye masks. I walk upstairs in a daze to Danny's room and hope I packed something presentable for a magazine. I'm sifting through my suitcase for a pair of shoes without holes when I find another note taped to my makeup bag—this one in Danny's handwriting.

Gracie Girl,

Stop panicking. You don't need to be anyone but yourself, on this day and every day. You're all I want, just as you are. But can you hurry? The sun is merciless, and I'm probably sweating out here.

There's no one else for me but you,

Danny

P.S. Do you happen to know where your graduation cap is? Tessa will need to make some alterations.

It's not a smoke signal, but I know exactly where he's hiding. My boy is by the creek. I abandon the notion of looking more presentable and throw on an old pair of flip-flops. A whirlwind of memories hit me as I walk out the back door and through the woods. I feel like I'm following in the footsteps of little Gracie and Danny.

My flip-flops kick up dirt like they're my old jelly sandals.

My curls bounce in front of my face, sticking to my forehead.

Our favorite emo punk song plays on repeat in my head.
I *swear* I can almost hear Charger barking.
I arrive at our clearing.
The creek babbles.
And Danny's on one knee in our secret spot.

Grace
Ten Years Old

"Gracie, when the robots take over earth, they better not mess with our secret spot." He sounds so serious, gesturing to our woodsy surroundings.

I roll my eyes. "Danny, if robots are taking over our planet, then they were created by humans. So we'll have figured out force fields to keep them out of certain places. Duh."

"Well, when you learn how to create force fields, you better stop here first and put it around our log."

"Our log will rot before then," I say grimly.

He gasps dramatically and sits down on the peeling log, accidentally breaking off one of the small branches poking out of the bark. "Susannah Sinclair. You take that back. Apologize to our log."

I look at the log and hold my hands together like I'm praying. "Dear Log, I am sorry for saying that the rules of nature apply to you."

He places his hand on the log and leans down, pretending to have a secret conversation with it. "The log accepts your apology as long as you promise to come back to our spot, with me, when we're, like, thirty years old or something. Just so the log can prove you wrong."

I crouch down and give Charger a kiss on his head. He happily wags his tail and licks my chin.

"I'd follow you anywhere, you know that." I throw the branch he snapped, and Charger takes off running.

I brush the dirt off my hands. "Hey, Danny? You wanna play our game?"

"Sure!"

"Fact?"

He thinks, scrunching his eyes shut briefly before opening them and holding a finger up like he has an idea. "Got one!"

Hands clasped together, I eagerly reply, "Tell me."

He smiles, showing off the space between his teeth. "I love you."

It's the first time he's said he loves me, and my heart swells up like a balloon. I bounce on my heels a few times, careful not to float away from happiness.

"Loving me is a feeling, though," I reply.

"No, Gracie. It's a fact."

THE END

Freebies

Bonus Scene

Subscribe to my free newsletter on Substack to read Danny's proposal speech and Gracie's reaction!

Announcing Book 2 of the Love and Longing Series

Ready for Tessa's story?

Read on for an excerpt from Book 2 (a summer romance) in the *Love and Longing* Series, following a bespoke Italian tailor with feelings more complicated than couture corsetry, and a junior designer who would rather wear lycra than be alone in a room with him.

Book 2 Bonus Excerpt

Chapter One Sneak Peek

TESSA

Should I cut my hair into a bob after this?

I study my emotional support mannequin across the floor, but the hollow expression on her plastic face is impossible to read. It's probably too early in the day for inanimate telepathy, anyway.

Sucking in a deep breath, I will my frazzled nerves to settle. I'm one intrusive thought away from tossing my design in the shredder and fleeing the fashion haus for the salon. At least I have a backup plan.

Fail in fashion.

Cut all my hair off.

Start a new life.

A puff of air at my back tousles my soon-to-be-chopped hair, and I turn to find another junior designer standing behind me, breathing heavily. "Subway was down. But I made it!"

I glance at my watch and give her a tight smile. "With nearly a minute to spare."

The designer chuckles, but the rest of the group hovering around the table remains silent. It appears I'm not the only one marinating in anxiety. The familiar scent of crippling fear wafts off the others as we all wait for our renderings to be assessed.

Just as I start to reach for the lip gloss in my pocket to keep my hands busy, the haus's namesake arrives, and a collective gulp echoes among us. Even the mannequins seem to be disassociating.

Lamont's red tinted glasses cast a scarlet glow across his rich brown skin as he joins us. His composed, brisk movements are a stark contrast to the frenzied, nervous shuffling of the design team. He begins lazily leafing through the submissions in front of him, pausing on a sketch of a mid-length asymmetrical dress with a toile pattern. "If you plan to present patterns this loud in the future, do me the kindness of providing ear plugs. *Undesirable*, Austin."

Our textile design apprentice visibly droops like the plants I haven't watered in my shoebox apartment. I didn't even know succulents *could* wilt.

"Are your legs tired, Brooke?" Lamont's voice is a hushed whisper, so Brooke leans in to hear him, her purple curls grazing the table.

"Um, from what?"

"Running away from good taste. *Undesirable*."

Next to me, Peyton shifts nervously, flipping her blonde hair over her shoulders. My muscles tighten as she launches into an explanation before Lamont can say anything. "Okay, so, as you can see, I'm referencing culottes *à la* Miu Miu '02—the Fall/Winter couture? That seventies flair, but preppier and without the patch pockets, which I know you've been hating recently, so—"

"Streaming services were really onto something with the 'Skip Intro' button, don't you think?" he muses, not bothering to look up from the sketch holding hours of work—and probably a few of Peyton's tears. "*Undesirable*."

A secondhand pang of disappointment aches in my chest as Peyton's face falls. As much as I want to be selected, I'd be thrilled if it was one of my friend's designs. I rise on my tiptoes to check on the number of sketches left, and panic courses through me. Only four remain. Feeling very much like a piece of rotary sushi on a conveyer belt from Hell, I continue waiting in purgatory to meet my condemnation.

When Lamont holds up a design of a sleeveless yoke dress with a removable cape, I breathe a sigh of relief.

Not mine... *yet.*

Lamont sighs. "Shondra, is this your final sketch?"

I cringe at his most vicious critique yet. No designer would dare present something unfinished to Lamont. Shondra wordlessly nods, and I send up a silent prayer for her design, which will never see the light of day again.

"Undesirable."

He always serves his critiques straight up with a shame chaser, but I've never heard Lamont quite this cutting. It's been sixteen hours since an insider informed him that *Popova* showed a similar gown to our planned finale look at their private salon show. And with Milan Fashion Week looming, we have three weeks to come up with something better.

Lamont doesn't even bother to comment on the next two renderings, shuffling them to the side as if they're cable bills.

Then, he pauses. Every single designer leans forward in anticipation. *Whose is it?*

A *pause* means you're only a mild inconvenience, not a complete catastrophe. A *pause* means you're somewhat competent, not totally inept. A *pause* means you're going to Milan Fashion Week.

Or maybe Lamont is just buffering.

"Tolerable, Tessa." Lamont nods toward the design in front of him.

My design.

He lifts his chin and makes direct eye contact with me. Or, at least I *think* he does. Hard to tell behind the glasses. "The aquatic influence isn't an insufferable direction. Inspired by Gianni's Spring/Summer '92, no?"

More like Valentino Spring/Summer '15.

I vigorously nod, biting back the correction.

"It's a bit *wearable*, though, don't you think?" Tilting his head to the side, Lamont draws invisible circles with his finger on my rendering, a sign he's considering something. I hold my breath, wondering if he's already regretting his choice.

He flattens his hand on the sketch. "Embroidery."

My stomach drops. *God. No.* Anything but embroidery. Anyone but *him*.

"I, um, specifically designed it with a pattern, given the time constraints, so embroidery wouldn't be necessary," I hedge.

"And that's why it looks prêt-à-porter."

Silence. Then...unwrapping? I turn toward the sound and find Peyton slowly lifting a piece of gum into her mouth, wide eyes darting between me and Lamont. I give her a quick "put the popcorn away" look before swiveling my attention back to my judge, jury, and executioner.

Lamont picks up my rendering and taps it on the surface of the desk. "Embroidery will elevate the look."

As much as I want to disagree with him, I can't deny that couture beading would look beautiful on the gown. Fortunately for the haus, our tailor is an incredibly gifted embroidery specialist. Unfortunately for me, I'd rather be buried in a *Juicy Couture* tracksuit than spend time with him.

The weight of Lamont's words sinks like a stone in my stomach. Shifting on my feet, I make one last stitch effort to save myself from The Tailor of Terror. "I'm happy to send your assistant a PDF of the rendering. She can share it with him, and

I can gather periodic status updates as he executes the embroidery."

He levels me with a look. "Three weeks, under normal circumstances, is a rush job. And you know how he hates to rush."

I don't think the word "rush" is even in our tailor's vocabulary.

"If you want to go to Milan, you'll be his shadow until we show. See to his every whim."

And there it is. *Milan Fashion Week.* The whisper of a promise I can't ignore.

Lamont hands me my design and slides the rest of the renderings across the table. "These would all get me mocked. Next time, less *Sound of Music* with the moods. This is New York, not the Abbey. Tessa, stay."

He gives the group an indifferent wave of dismissal. The other designers and apprentices file back to their workstations, a few of them glaring at me. Peyton gives my arm a friendly squeeze, and Brooke mouths *congrats*. The textile apprentice sulks past me with a haunted look on his face, heading straight for The Supply Closet of Broken Dreams, where he'll probably stare into the abyss of paper reams until the abyss stares back at him.

Once Lamont and I are alone, I don my most optimistic voice and brightest smile. "Thank you for the opportunity."

The corners of Lamont's lips point downward. "Your designs have potential, but they need elevation. Working with Giovanni will be quite educational for you."

I nod, but my blood starts to boil.

Giovanni Cattaneo would rather embroider an image of pineapple pizza on a tarp than *educate* me.

Lamont must be desperate, because he rarely makes big decisions without input from his prized tailor, and there's no way Giovanni would readily agree to this plan. I'm confident that Giovanni's unenthusiastic response to working with me remains unchanged.

I consider making one last appeal, but Lamont's disinterested body language—checking his watch like *I'm* the one holding him hostage—tells me he's done with this conversation. A moment later, he nods and walks back to his office. A classic Lamont exit: no goodbye included.

Despite the blow of having to work closely with Giovanni, I'm still floating on a high from being chosen when I slip into my usual spot next to Peyton at the large table in our open office area.

"Congrats, Tess. The envy that's consuming my body right now is extremely toxic. Girls supporting girls is bullshit. Keep one eye open." She huffs, but her smile betrays her real feelings, fake silver freckles crinkling on her cheeks.

I snicker. "It's okay to be jealous. As long as you don't stab me with a fork in the break room like Steve did to Alyssa two years ago."

"Well she did steal his almond milk creamer twice. I'm pretty sure he milked those almonds himself. Definitely worth a stabbing in my opinion. At least a lil' poke," she deadpans.

My eyes squint from the smile stretching across my face. These last five years would've been painful without her.

"I might prefer a light stabbing over working with Giovanni, to be honest," I joke.

Peyton chews her piece of cinnamon gum. "I'm sorry, but I don't get it. He's such a sweetheart. When you were off for your brother's wedding last year, I ran errands for Lamont. Giovanni was so appreciative, saying that junior designers are the 'backbone' of the fashion industry. Not to mention his Italian accent is so freaking hot. And one time, I *literally* saw him walk an old lady across the street."

I lean back in my chair. "Did you stay to see her reach the other side? Maybe he was slowly pushing her into moving traffic."

Peyton grins, shaking her head. While her sunny take on Giovanni is almost certainly incorrect, all of my publicly aired grievances about him are annoyances at best, which is why she's never understood my lack of reverence for Lamont's beloved tailor. The real reason I dislike Giovanni is like an oil stain on silk... It will *never* come out.

My stomach rumbles, and I glance at my phone. "I'm starving. Do you want to grab lunch before I head to *Cattaneo's Bespoke*?"

Peyton folds her arms. "I'm not ready to eat yet. Lamont's 'skip intro' comment is making me nauseous."

"Please." Shondra slumps down in a chair across from me. Lowering her voice just above a whisper, she mimics Lamont. "*Is this your final sketch?*" She hunches over, putting her head on top of the table, and speaks directly into the particle board. "I think I'm entitled to worker's compensation for that emotional slap in the face."

Peyton pats her back. "Do you want me to call HR on his ass, Shon?"

"Do we even have that here?" Shondra asks.

"I think we did, once, but the HR lady left due to this being a hostile work environment."

We laugh, relatively immune to the harsh culture. Crying is for first-year apprentices. Tenured designers understand that gallows humor and dairy-free lattes keep this place running.

I squeeze Shondra's shoulder. "I'm sorry, girl. It was a good cape."

She nods miserably, much like she did in front of Lamont.

"I loved the yoke style, too, Shon," Peyton adds.

Peyton and Shondra start chatting about the merits of their

designs, hyping each other up, as I begrudgingly collect my things to go to *Cattaneo's*.

As I drag my feet out of the space, my shoulders are so tense they nearly reach my ears. Before the door closes behind me, Peyton calls after me.

"Love him or hate him, he's your ticket to Milan, Tess!"

Acknowledgments

First, thank *you*. I am incredibly humbled you chose to read this book. As an indie author, it feels like magic to have even one reader enjoy your book. I'm so grateful for you and the time you spent with Danny and Gracie. If you want to leave a review, it would mean the world to me!

Apologies on the laundry list below, which reads very much like the "About the Cast" section of a high school musical playbill. But as someone with no team, these amazing people really made the book what it is, and I must scream about them.

To my husband. There is no reality in which this book would get completed without you. You've encouraged me, taken the kids to the park so I can get some writing in, and just overall been the best person I've ever met. My first love, my last love.

To Devin. The first person to read a completed version of F&F. The person who told me, "yeah, having Danny say 'horses' two times is funny, but you know what would be even funnier? Having him say horses a third time." I cannot begin to describe what your mentorship has meant to me. Thank you for telling me that this novel should actually be published. I would've never done it without you.

To Julia. The person who stuck with Danny and Gracie the absolute longest. Your calm and steady support throughout this process was everything to me; not to mention your sharp and truly brilliant mind. I am so lucky to have met you, and even luckier to work with you!

To my sister. You were the first person I told about this idea, and you didn't kill my hopes. Thank you.

To Izzy. My British author soulmate (I know you hate that word, but I'm sorry, it describes us). I'll keep this short. I would absolutely lose my ever-loving mind without you.

To Caroline. Thank you for always being a listening ear and lifting me up no matter what. You are the definition of a girls' girl, and the person I turn to when I need uplifting. Plus, you're a phenomenal writer, and I can't wait for your book!

To B. I cannot believe I somehow manipulated you into reading this for me in such an incomplete state. The amount of real-life karma points you have obtained from this is infinite.

To the Tortured Romance Authors Department. My found family of writers, our hype squad, truly we keep each other sane.

To the Queens of Early Reading: Brandy, Amy, Bri, Juls, Sara Elise, Tyanna, Kat, Yara, K, Danielle, Sarah, Lauren, Gayla, and Charlotte (plus anyone else I missed!). I must've done something right in life to get y'all as readers. Each one of you is so incredibly special to me.

To Ashley. Those early trenches would've been absolute hell without you! Thanks for commiserating with me.

To Coco from BRS. Thank you for reading this book when it was objectively chaotic. I'm so grateful.

To the best Anonymous readers a girl on the internet could ask for: Dr. A., Little Witch, A Princess, Zen, Yoon, B Snail, E, Nicole, MH, and R Anxiety. Your comments had me cry-laughing, throwing up, and absolutely preening.

To babydragonart. Thank you for designing such an amazing book cover and character art.

To Naughty Nook. Thank you for running my ARC campaign!

Finally, to aspiring authors. You are not defined by who is—or isn't—in your corner. You've got this!

And thank *you*, once again, Reader. I wish you love, happiness, and all the melted butter on your popcorn in the world. I hope you stay tuned for Tessa's Book (a summer romance) and TBA Book 3 (a fall romance) in the Love & Longing series. And if you want to say hello, please don't be shy—I'd love to hear from you on socials!

Xoxo,
Farrah

About the Author

Farrah Colson writes stories full of emotion, yearning, and witty banter. She lives outside of Chicago with her two young children and husband. When she's not writing indie romance, you can find her reading indie romance, decorating early for any holiday, and spending time with her family.

www.ingramcontent.com/pod-product-compliance
Lightning Source LLC
Chambersburg PA
CBHW050512110726
47899CB00005B/1429